LOST AND FOUND I

Lost and found in

blue

Iron Dogz MC #2

René van Dalen

LOST AND FOUND IN BLUE

LOST AND FOUND IN BLUE

Iron Dogz MC Book Two

Copyright © 2019 René Van Dalen

ISBN 9798306777580

Cover Design Danielle Burrows Art

Cover Copyright 2019 Danielle Burrows

Cover Photograph Unsplash.com/Justin Clark

All rights reserved. In accordance with the U S Copyright Act of 1976, the scanning, uploading and electronic sharing of any part of this book without permission of the publisher is unlawful piracy and theft of the author's intellectual property. Thank you for your support of the author's rights.

This book is a work of fiction. Names, characters, places and incidents are a product of the author's imagination or used fictitiously. Any resemblance to actual events, locales or persons living or dead is coincidental.

Warning: This book contains graphic language and sexual content. Intended for mature audiences, 18 years and older.

LOST AND FOUND IN BLUE

DEDICATION

13 1 13

For the ones who hold my heart

†††

Only the road and the dawn, the sun, the wind,
and the rain,
And the watch fire under the stars, and sleep, and the
road again.

We travel the dusty road till the light of the day
is dim,
And sunset shows us the spires away on the world's
rim.

The Seekers By John Masefield

LOST AND FOUND IN BLUE

AUTHOR'S NOTE

It has been an amazing experience sharing the men and women who make up the Iron Dogz MC with you.

Thank you for enjoying and loving them as much as I do.

Trigger warnings: This book contains graphic language, sex, violence, abuse and violent situations.

Important note: My books are set in South Africa and written in **South African English.**

I use Afrikaans and Zulu words in my writing. I've translated those as the story unfolds. Please check the glossary at the back of the book if you find one that slipped through the cracks.

As with all my books I take walks on the dark side.

Come and walk along with me.

LOST AND FOUND IN BLUE

PROLOGUE

Hawk

Hawk parked at the curb and sat looking up at the big-as-fuck house before he kicked the stand down, threw his leg over the saddle and stood next to his bike. He took his time taking off his helmet and gloves before he walked up the fancy path to the front door. Emmie Coetzee had come a long way from the tiny two bedroomed flat in the rundown building where she had lived with her mother. The houses in the secure estate where she now lived went for between three and seven mil. He estimated her mac-mansion to be priced somewhere in the middle.

Fucking pretentious bitch.

He swallowed down his anger as he rang the bell and waited. She knew he was here. He had gone through a whole damned song and dance before he was able to gain access to the estate. Access she gave him.

The door opened and there she was, the bitch who had come close to breaking his cousin.

Emmie had matured while she had been away and the woman who stood in front of him exuded class and money. A fairly low cut blue dress hugged her curves and fell to just above her knees and she wore sky high heels on her small feet. The heels were probably her idea of adding some height, to make it seem she was taller. Her light brown hair which had been down to her ass in a curly mass when he had last seen her was now chin length, dark blonde and stick straight. Not a curl in sight. Her face was carefully made up accentuating her brown eyes, so different from the young girl he used to know who never wore any make up and hadn't needed it either. She had been a pretty girl now she was a pretty woman.

He watched as she scanned the road behind him and Hawk held back an angry growl. The bitch had dressed up expecting Ice to be with him.

"Hawk." She said softly.

"Emmie, we need to talk." He said as he pushed past her.

"Why don't you come in? And I'm Emma now." She said sarcastically as she closed the door and followed him into the large lounge.

"Don't fuck with me, Emmie. I don't like you, have never fucking liked you, but my cousin was into you so I dealt with it. Sit your fucking ass down and listen."

Hawk didn't wait for her to sit down on one of her fancy couches before he started laying it out.

"You ran out on Ice after Jane confronted you with her fucking lies. Everyone knew she was lying. Ice never hooked up with another bitch, not since the day he claimed you. And you knew it. What I want to know is what Jane had said that changed your mind? What did she say to make you believe her lies?"

Emmie, or Emma as she now wanted to be called, sank down on the couch with a sigh as Hawk stood over her.

"It's going to make me sound like a total bitch but I'm really not. Back then I was so damned young and scared." She played with the hem of her dress before she looked up at him and Hawk knew something totally fucked up was going to come out of her red painted mouth.

"You're right. I knew, I knew she was lying. Gray would never have cheated on me, never. He never knew how much I hated your club, hated the drinking, the fighting and the whores." She gave a deep sigh and shook her head. "I had these idealised dreams back then. Dreams of how we would settle down, me a doctor and Gray a lawyer. He would give up the club and we would live happily ever after. We had a fight about the club the night before Jane confronted me. Gray told me he would never leave the club and was never going to be a practising lawyer. As far as I was concerned he had shattered our dreams, but it had never been his dream, it had been mine."

Again she sighed and Hawk wanted to shake her so bad his fingers tightened around the strap of his helmet.

"Jane told me all those lies and I used it as an excuse to get out. And I ran. I was angry about my broken dreams and I just wanted to get away from him for a little while. He was always so forceful and he knew exactly what he wanted. Unlike me, I really didn't know what I wanted. I called him ten months after I had left to do my residency in Durban. Gray told me to never call him again, we were done. He cut me off before I could explain. I tried to call back but he blocked me. I tried to call Genna but she wouldn't accept my calls." She looked up at Hawk and gave a small shrug.

"So I did the next best thing, on my first weekend off I drove up from Durban and came to the clubhouse. A prospect let me in and the first thing I saw as I drove up was Gray leaning against the outside wall of the clubhouse with a club slut on her knees in front of him giving him a blowjob. When he saw me he didn't react and there was nothing in his eyes, they were cold and empty. That's when I knew I had lost him. I turned my car around and went back to Durban. At the end of my residency I was offered the opportunity to continue my studies in Boston and I took it." She looked up at him with a strange look on her face and Hawk braced for more fucked up shit.

"I've tried to call Gray since I've been back but he no longer has the same number and there's no way I can call anyone in his family. Will you please tell him I need to speak to him? I want to explain why I did what I did. I owe it to him. I know you don't like me but please ask him to call me. I still love him, Hawk, and I always will. I know I can make him happy."

Hawk couldn't believe what the bitch had just laid out for him. She had fucked up his brother's life because she had been pissed at him. And all because she couldn't have her pathetic little dream life.

Ice had loved her for fucking years. He supported her in every way while she was at University. All she had to do was open her mouth and tell him of her fears. His cousin would have moved heaven and earth to give her anything she wanted. And the bitch knew it. Now she was sitting here in her fancy fucking house thinking she was going to fuck with his brother again.

Not if he had anything to say about it.

"I see what this is all about. You've got half of your fucked up dream and now you're looking for the other half. Wake the fuck up, bitch. He knows you're back. And do you see him around? No, you don't, because he doesn't want to see you. Stay away and move the fuck on. I've heard you've got a new man so why don't you focus on him and not my brother. Don't ever come to my clubhouse, Emma Coetzee, you won't like what happens if you do. You wore out your welcome a fucking long time ago."

Hawk was done and without saying another word he walked out of the house, thankful to breathe air untainted by her overwhelmingly heavy perfume. As he rode away he saw the bitch in his rear view mirror, standing outside her front door watching him leave. At first he had come here to tell his cousin's woman she had fucked up and she should use this chance to fix it. Now, after seeing who and what she really was, he would do everything in his power to keep the bitch away from Ice.

His cousin didn't need a grasping, lying bitch in his life.

RENÉ VAN DALEN

CHAPTER ONE

Ice

Ice sat next to Hawk and listened as his cousin and president brought the rest of the brothers up to speed on the meeting with Dominick Maingarde. It had been an extremely tense meeting but at the end they all got what they wanted.

"The meeting went as well as can be expected with all the shit flying around. Dom assured me he wasn't involved in the move against the club. As far as he's concerned it's business as usual, and he's committed to finding out what the old bitch is up to. We will honour our contract with Dom but we are going to be very, very careful. He now knows we will no longer accept cargo without a complete manifest of the contents. I don't care what the fuck he puts on the transport documents, it's not my problem. We transport his crates from point A to point B, if the documents say it's car parts then that's what it is."

Those sharp eyes of his cousin missed nothing and he zeroed in on a few of the brothers who weren't looking happy.

"If you have anything to say let's hear it. Don't keep quiet and mumble about shit later." His president snarled.

Rider stepped forward and Ice had to admire the kid's courage to talk when the rest of the brotherhood stayed silent. The boy had potential and he would be keeping an eye on him.

"Would we be covered if what's in the documents isn't what's in the crates, Prez?"

Hawk pointed at Rider with a sharp nod. "Very good question, Rider. According to our lawyers and our VP, our very own non-practising lawyer, we will be because we took the cargo on in good faith. It's not our jobs to open the crates and check the contents against the documentation. So we're clear on that one."

Ice shook his head at Hawk who just smirked at him. Fucking bastard.

"Any more questions?" Hawk continued.

"No, Prez, I'm good." Rider said and sat down.

"Anyone else?"

Wolf raised a hand and Hawk nodded. "Can we trust Maingarde, boss?"

Tapping his fingers on the table in front of him Hawk stayed silent as he looked around the table and then the room.

"If I thought Dominick Maingarde was going to serve us up to his fucked up grandmother our meeting would not have taken place. I trust him as much as we can trust an ally with questionable ties to an enemy of the club. We need him because he's on the inside of the Maingarde organisation and can provide us with advance warning when she comes for us once again. Note I said 'when' not 'if', because believe me, she isn't done with us. She'll be back."

Nods and mumbles circulated around the room.

"If there's nothing else then let's get back to work. Keep your eyes open and the order against riding alone is still in force. If you need to take personal time make sure you have a brother at your back, no one is exempt from the order."

The loud clunck of the hammer against the block of steel rang through the room.

"Ice, Kid, Beast, Spider, Ziggy and Bulldog stay behind."

Ice watched his Prez with narrowed eyes. Hawk was up to something. He had known him all his life and there wasn't much he could hide from him. And right now he was hiding something. As the door closed Hawk looked at Gabriel "Bulldog" Walker, his uncle, and Ice's dad, where he sat at the other end of the table. Bulldog nodded and his Prez sighed before he turned and looked Ice right in the eyes.

"You're going to be pissed at me so I'm going to tell you up front everything I did come from a good place. I'm worried about you, brother. No, fuck that, we're all worried about you. You are one of the best men in this club and it pisses me off knowing you aren't happy. You're my family, one of my best friends and I love you brother, but this shit has to end."

Ice could feel anger slowly starting to churn in his gut. "What the fuck are you talking about? I'm happy. I have my club, my brothers, uncomplicated pussy whenever I want it. What more could I want?"

"I went and saw Emmie or Emma as she now likes to be called." Hawk dropped the bomb.

Every single muscle in his body froze. "You did what?" Ice whispered.

"Brother, you know as well as what I do it is long past time to put her behind you. And if I can help it along you know I'm not going to fucking wait. So I went and saw her and heard the fucked up story of why she left, how she came back and saw you with a club whore and left again. She's no longer the girl you knew, Ice. She's a woman with an agenda. So this is me, your brother, giving you a heads up. You need to brace, brother."

Shaking his head Ice looked at his dad. Bulldog didn't wait to answer his unasked question.

"Your mother and I loved her like she was one of our own, Ice. But over time she started changing, little by little. You didn't see it because you loved her but your mother and I, we were worried. She told Genna of her plans for the two of you, her as a doctor and you a lawyer. When Genna disagreed with her they had a huge fight. After the fight they were still friends but Genna no longer trusted her. Emmie never really saw you, didn't see the man beneath the kutte, didn't realise how deep the club ran in your blood. I'm not saying she didn't love you, she did, she just loved her fucked up dream of you more." Bulldog met his eyes and Ice felt his heart contract. "She's not the one for you, son. I know you loved her, most probably still do, but she's not who you think she is. People change, Ice. We all change as the years progress. Sometimes not for the better."

He couldn't believe the shit going down at the table right now. Why were they bringing this shit up now? What about Kid and Beast, both of those men had major female skeletons in their cupboards? Why concentrate on his? Fuck.

Scrubbing his hands over his face he sighed then tried to explain where he stood with this shit.

"I'm well aware that she's been back for a while now and that she has a man in her life. I don't want her, haven't for a long damn time. So stop going over old and forgotten shit and let's have a beer." He started to get up but when Ziggy spoke he sat back down.

"She hasn't got a man anymore." Ziggy said as he tapped on the laptop on the table in front of him. "Her facebook status changed to single three weeks ago." He swung the laptop around so Ice could see her facebook page and there she was. The woman who had fucked up his life and broken his heart. She looked different but still damned good.

Ice's gut clenched and he fought hard to keep his face impassive. He didn't know how he felt about her being available again. He didn't know how he felt about her. And that alone was dangerous for his peace of mind. Something he had fought long and hard to obtain.

"So what if she's single? She fucked me over once and I'm not setting myself up for it to happen again. It's all in the past, done. And now I'm done. I don't want to fucking talk about this shit."

Hawk sighed then nodded. "Okay brother, but if you need us we'll be there, no questions asked. Okay?"

Dragging his hands through his hair Ice looked at his cousin and had to smile. The bastard was all touchy feely now he had an old lady in his bed.

"I hear you, brother, and I appreciate it. Are we going to sit here like a bunch of bitches and natter about our feelings or are we going to have a beer?"

Laughter followed his comment but he hadn't fooled his dad or his brothers, they knew him too well.

Leaning on the bar sipping his beer everything he had been told ran through his head. Emmie was back and she was single and apparently looking for him. Why? They lived in two completely different worlds and it would never converge. Not fucking ever.

The way she had left him seven years ago had hardened him. It kept him from making the same mistake ever again. His brothers were right, it was time to close that chapter in his life and put it all behind him.

He wasn't getting any younger and his mum was constantly on his case about finding a woman and giving her the grandbabies she craved. She carried on as if she didn't have any when the contrary was in fact true. His sister Gail and her husband Johan had given her two perfect little girls and they had another baby on the way. Everyone was hoping for a boy this time. Although Johan claimed he wouldn't mind another little princess. Ice grinned when he remembered how pissed off his sister had been. She was the one who wanted a son and she swore she would keep trying until she got what she wanted. Johan just grinned. Fucker.

Ice was lost in thought when a hard smack on his back pulled him back to the present.

"I'm out of here, son. Try and make it to supper one night this week, your mum misses you." His dad gave him a hard hug.

"Tell her I'll be there on Thursday evening, and Dad, no fucking sneaky set ups this time or I'm not coming over for the next six months at least. You make sure you warn her. The last bitch she tried to set me up with was damned hard to get rid of. No more giving out my number either. It's not cool at all. I'll find my own damned woman I don't need my mother to find her for me."

Bulldog and his brothers were howling with laughter and Ice just shook his head as he watched his dad walk out the clubhouse with Sam following him. His parents had a house on club property so he didn't have far to go but Hawk had still put a prospect on him.

Better safe than sorry.

Ice had become a prospect on his eighteenth birthday and had moved into the prospect dorms when he joined the club. When he received his patch he was given a small room towards the back of the clubhouse. After he had been voted in as Hawk's VP he had moved upstairs into the VP's rooms. Unlike some of the other brothers he didn't have a place outside the clubhouse, he didn't need it. Everything he needed was right here.

When he found the woman he wanted as his old lady he would build them a house on Iron Dogz land. He knew the exact spot where he would build. Finishing his beer Ice set the bottle down on the bar and made his way outside. He needed fresh air, to feel the wind on his face and the road under his wheels.

Today had brought too many demons to the fore front of his mind and he needed them gone.

Riding out with Sin and Wolf he felt all the shit fall away as the peace of the road soaked into him.

CHAPTER TWO

River

Seb and I hung over the blanket covered fenders of the car guiding the engine in as Jannie slowly winched it down. We kept our hands on it making sure it aligned perfectly. My dad was crouched down at the front of the car and threw both thumbs up as with a creak of springs the engine settled in place.

"Perfect. Let's get to it guys. We've got to get this engine in and running like a dream before eleven tomorrow." My dad threw over his shoulder as he walked away with a wide grin.

"He says the same damn thing every time, it's just the timeline that changes." Seb grinned while I sighed and shook my head.

"I know. He's a pain in the ass at the best of times but when we're close to finishing a rebuild he gets worse." I complained.

Seb and Jannie laughed because they've heard this complaint many, many times before. I grinned as we started fitting the reconditioned engine. A few hours later we were ready to start her for the first time and as always we were jittery with nerves and excitement. The beast came alive with a whine and a cough. We listened intently nodding and grinning when I tapped the accelerator. There were a few things we would have to tweak, but nothing big. We would bring this one in on time, as promised.

Much later I lay in bed staring up at the ceiling in the dark. I was so damned tired. Sleep was once again evading me as my life ran like a movie through my head. Considering all the bad stuff in my past, this life I had built for myself and my son was a good one. I never thought I would ever get here, to this place. To contentment. It was a big one for me after the heartache I had put my parents through as a teen because of my stupid rebellion. I had been so full of shit. But then I met him and it all changed. He changed me, made me grow up and now I was older and wiser.

Some nights, like tonight, I missed him more than I could bear. I missed him so fiercely I physically ached. He wasn't given the chance to see his son born. His enemies took it from him, took it from his son. God, he would have been such a good dad. My pregnancy had not been planned but Dylan "Sparrow" Martins had stepped up and faced my dad's wrath, declaring he loved his daughter and even though he had already claimed her as his old lady he was going to marry her as soon as possible. But I wanted to wait until after the baby was born, I didn't want to look fat in photos. So young and so stupid. We moved into the small two bedroomed cottage on my parents' property and started our life together, looking forward to the day our son would be born.

If I had known then what I know now I would have married him the very same day. And I would have spent every single minute of every day showing and telling him how much I loved him.

Turning on my side I stared at the baby monitor on my bedside table and listened to my son breathe and the music playing softly in the background. Early on in my pregnancy Sparrow had started playing music for the baby. He had heard somewhere it was good for his development and had put together several playlists for his boy. The one playing in the background now was his bedtime playlist.

Like many, many times before I fell asleep with tears in my eyes and his name on my lips, while listening to the music he had chosen for our son.

Waking up slowly I stared at the beeping alarm blearily and groaned as I reached over to turn it off. Why the hell had I agreed to open up early today? I wasn't a fan of early mornings, but I was the one with the kid, an early bird kid at that, and had agreed after Seb and Jannie had pointed out I would be up anyway. The sneaky bastards. Through the baby monitor I heard Duncan waking and stretching and then the patter of his feet getting softer and softer.

Shit, I hope the kid aimed inside the toilet this morning and didn't hose the place down. Sliding out of bed I quickly went into my tiny bathroom, did my business, and washed my hands before heading to the kitchen.

Duncan was already there, on the step stool reaching into the cupboard to pull out the cereal.

Kissing him on the temple I held on to him as he wobbled. "Hey, boykie. Did you wash your hands?"

My boy gave me a look then grinned and waved barely dry little hands at me. "Hey, Mumma. I made a pee and washed. See?"

"Good boy. Can I help you?" At his smiling nod I reached into the cupboard but stopped before pulling anything out. "Which one do you want? Superman or Spiderman?"

An adamant headshake. "No, I want Batman food."

My boy is obsessed with Batman and trying to get him to eat healthy I decanted my mum's homemade muesli into containers I had stuck super hero stickers on. And anything in the Batman container became Batman food and he ate it, no problems.

"You get down and I'll get it for you."

Sipping on my coffee I watched my boy wolfing down his breakfast, milk dripping down his chin and onto his jammies. I didn't care, it was washable and this moment right here was one I might never have again. He was growing so fast, his fifth birthday was approaching and he was turning from my baby into a little boy. Before I knew it he was going to be old enough to go to big school and he would change again. I treasured these moments with him.

"When you've finished we must get ready, boykie. Nana is taking you to pre-school because I have to finish the yellow car today."

"'Kay. Can I come see later?" He asked between chews.

"Sorry, boykie, it will be gone by the time school comes out. But maybe if you ask nicely Nana will bring you to have a look at the bike that came in yesterday. The guy took a hard fall but we're going to fix his bike as good as new."

LOST AND FOUND IN BLUE

Duncan grinned as he shook his head, his dark blonde hair flopping over his forehead. "Better, Mumma, we fix it better."

I smiled as I looked into eyes the exact green of his father's and my heart warmed. "You're right, boykie, we fix it better."

After walking my boy over to my parents' house I drove to work and opened up the bay with the almost completed rebuild. The bright yellow classic Camaro had red flames licking down the sides and over the boot and bonnet. Not my favourite colour for a car but the owner's wife loved yellow, he liked red, so yellow with red flames was their compromise.

As eleven rolled around we had just pushed the car out onto the forecourt after the final polishing. She shone in the sunshine and Wouter and Annalie, the owners, were grinning as if Christmas had come early. And with it only being April, for them it had. I left my dad to do the handover and walked through the garage to my domain. I had several repairs and a rebuild waiting for me in my workshop at the back.

When my dad started out he had focused on rebuilding cars, mostly muscle cars and classic cars. But my passion had always been bikes and when I joined the business we added a large space on to the back of the garage for my babies. I broke the space up into several small bays with short walls delineating each space. I had five bays with small stands in each, a central hoist, a large storage space and a small reception area with a desk, a computer, chairs and two couches. A big old fashioned and reconditioned Fridgedaire was filled with water, cold drinks and beer. A fancy coffee machine sat on a table with cups, teaspoons and little packets of sugar.

The reception area hadn't always had couches but I had found bikers liked to hangout and talk shit as they watched us work on their rides. And they were the reason why we had beer in the fridge.

Ah, yes, that's the only reason. And not too much of a fib either.

The poor bike I had told Duncan about stood crookedly in bay five, the bay furthest from the door. Taking a clipboard from the wall I started listing the visible damage as I walked around the machine. Poor girl, she had taken a nasty beating but I would have her back to her previous glory as soon as I could. Taking the clipboard with me I sat at the desk and pulled up the owner's information on the computer and typed up a quick provisional quote. We wouldn't know the extent of the damage to the engine until we opened her up. I sent off the e-mail and went back to finish the work on the bike in bay one.

I glanced up when I heard the door between the two buildings bang shut and hid a grin as an obviously horribly hung over Kevin "Wrench" Clarkson walked into the workshop. He was white as a sheet as he slunk past and went straight to the coffee machine. I went back to work on the bike in front of me but kept an eye on Wrench.

Wrench was the only one working with me on the bikes and he was slowly but surely finding his feet as we both settled into working together. Wrench had recently done his trade test and was now a fully qualified mechanic and he wanted to specialise in bikes. When he came for the interview he didn't hide that he was a prospect with the Iron Dogz MC and it was because of his honesty that I decided to take him on despite my misgivings. He committed to work hard and give me enough advance warning if club business was going to keep him out of the workshop. So far I had been lucky, he was here almost every day, even hung over and obviously suffering as he was today. Plus he had called me last night to let me know he would be late because of club business.

I grinned as the whine of the air drill made him cringe. Taking pity on him I put it down and joined him at the coffee machine.

"Big party last night?" I asked.

"Yes, Boss, our president gave his old lady his ink and his patch yesterday and the party got out of hand. Had a massive clean-up this morning. Sorry I'm dragging today."

Chuckling softly I shook my head. "How long have you worked for me now, Wrench?"

"Seven months or so, Boss."

"Good, and have you ever not finished a job I've given you or gone home early or stayed away when you're hung over and sick as a dog?"

"No, Boss. This job is important to me and I don't want to fuck it up."

"So, there you have it. We're good. Take some paracetamol and drink a lot of water. Alcohol dehydrates the body, hence the headache, dry mouth and nausea. Next time you tie one on remember to drink water as you throw back those shots. Sit down, drink your coffee and start in bay three when you feel a bit better. Okay?"

"You are the best fucking boss in the world." Wrench mumbled as he took the bottle of headache tablets from the desk drawer.

Laughing softly I went back to work and not too long after I heard the sounds of Wrench getting stuck into the job I had assigned to him.

Time flew and it was only when I heard Duncan's high pitched giggle that I realised I had been working without a break for the last few hours. Wrench looked a whole lot better when he stepped out of bay three grinning as Duncan ran into the workshop.

"Hey, little brother, how was school today?" He asked as Duncan skidded to a halt close to him.

My boy pulled a face. "Okay, Sammy, Robby and I ran away from Kelly and her friends all day. They wanted to kiss us. And it's gross. And we never got to play 'cause they chased us."

Wrench and I gave each other big eyes before he sank down on one knee in front of my boy.

"So, little brother, you don't like Kelly?" Wrench asked carefully.

"No, she's nasty and her mummy's nasty and not nice. She hugged me and I didn't like it. And she said stuff 'bout my daddy and she said I was gor-jus jus' like him."

My mum-antennae were up immediately but before I could say a word Wrench continued talking to my boy so I just crouched down next to them and stayed silent.

"So, you don't like Kelly and you don't like Kelly's mummy hugging you. Why? Does she make you feel uncomfortable?"

"What's uncomf'able?"

"When she hugged you did it make you feel not good?"

Immediately he nodded. "Her tits are too big and I couldn't breathe."

My eyes nearly popped out of my head. What the hell? And who the hell told him breasts were called tits?

The mum part of me stepped up before I could pull it back.

"They're called breasts or boobs, Duncan, not tits, it's a rude word and only for grownups, okay?"

"Oh, okay. Boobs, I like boobs. Booooobs." He said with a tiny giggle.

Wrench snorted with laughter and I was hard pressed not to either.

"Her boobs are huuuuge." He said with wide eyes. "Really, really huge." His bright green eyes swivelled between me and Wrench and I sighed. Then he looked down at my chest and frowned. "Why don't you have big boobs, Mumma?"

Oh dear God.

"Uhm, not everyone is the same, boykie. Some people have bigger boobs than others."

"Oh, why?"

Sweet baby Jesus. Not the why. How do I explain this one?

Wrench tapped my arm. "I got this, Boss."

"You know how you and Sammy are the tallest boys in your class?" He asked and my boy nodded. "You guys are both tall because your daddies are tall, right?" Again the nod. "The other kids are all different too, aren't they?"

"Yes, they are short, not like me and Sammy." Duncan said with a very superior look in his green eyes. The little shit.

"Boobs are like that too, little brother. Some are big and some are small. It's just the way it is."

Duncan stood looking down at his shoes as he puzzled it out for himself then he looked up at Wrench and nodded.

"I don't like big boobs." He said with a disgusted face. "When I'm big my old lady is going to have boobs like my mumma so I don't suf'cate when she hugs me."

My mouth hung open as I stared at my boy. What the hell was going on at his school?

"Who said you will suffocate?"

Duncan drew in a deep breath before he started his story.

"I was waiting for Nana with Sammy and his daddy when Kelly's mummy came to fetch her. And she's very poor 'cause her clothes are too small and all the mummies and daddies were looking at her. And then she hugged me and I didn't like it and Sammy's daddy told her to get away from me. Then she said rude words to him and took

Kelly home. Then Sammy's daddy said the reeeaaally bad word and told Robby's daddy her tits almost suf'cate me. Than Nana fetched me." He shrugged and looked around the workshop.

"Can I help Wrenchie today, Mumma?" As far as my boy was concerned now he had explained he was moving on to the next most important thing in his life. Bikes.

All I could do was nod as I straightened up out of my crouch.

"Keep an eye on him please, Wrench. I'll be back."

I stormed out of the workshop and into the office where my mum and dad were sitting chatting.

"Did Sammy's dad talk to you about the woman who was all over Duncan at the nursery school today? Or did any of the teachers say anything to you?"

"No, sweetheart, I got there, signed him out and came straight here. What happened?"

I rubbed my hands over my thighs as I tried to cool the anger.

"It seems a woman connected to the club has put her kid in Duncan's nursery school and today she approached him, hugged him and told him he was just as gorgeous as his dad. Going by Duncan's description of what she was wearing she has to be a club whore." I blew out an angry breath as I reached for the phone on the desk. "If the bitch comes anywhere near my kid again I'm going to rip her fake tits off her chest and stuff them up her ass."

"Who are you calling, River?" My dad had a hand on my arm.

"Dagger, and he had better sort this shit out before I lose my mind."

I felt better after talking to Dagger, my brother-in-law and the president of the Sinner's Sons MC, the club Sparrow had been a part of. He told me not to worry, he would sort it out. By the sound of his voice I knew he was pissed and he would find out who the bitch was and end her shit.

My boy didn't need bitches like her around him sprouting shit about his dad.

Growing up without him was hard enough.

CHAPTER THREE

Ice

Riding down the long paved drive towards his parents' house Ice was looking forward to dinner until he spotted all the cars parked in the driveway. Too many cars plus Spider's bike. It meant the entire family was here for dinner. Then he clocked the fancy white Audi and anger surged.

After he had fucking asked his dad to get his mum to back off she had gone ahead and done it again. Invited some bitch to dinner to try and set him up. He was about to turn his bike around and leave when he saw his mum and dad waiting for him on the wide veranda.

That was odd. They never came out to meet any of them when they arrived. They only did it for guests.

Pulling up next to Johan's SUV he kicked the stand down, turned the bike off and swung his leg over the seat. Because his folks lived on the same property as the clubhouse he hadn't worn a helmet, just his beanie, sunglasses and a bandanna pulled up over his nose and mouth.

Slipping his sunglasses off he hooked them into the neck of his tee and pulled the bandanna down as he walked over to where his folks were waiting. His dad was pissed and his mum looked worried. What the fuck was going on?

His mum didn't give him a chance to ask.

"I'm so sorry, sweetheart. She arrived out of the blue and I didn't know if you or Genna had invited her so I asked her to stay for dinner. I only realised my mistake when your dad and Genna arrived and nearly bit my head off."

Ice frowned. "I didn't invite anyone. Who the hell is here?"

Bulldog stepped up and put a big hand on his shoulder. "It's Emmie, son. She ambushed your mother and got herself invited to dinner."

"What the fuck?" Ice growled.

"My sentiments exactly." Bulldog said softly. "We'll understand if you need to leave."

"Fuck that, Dad. This is my fucking home, not hers. She's the one who needs to leave and I'll personally fucking throw her out."

"Gray." A soft voice interrupted them and Ice felt his backbone go steel hard as he swivelled his head towards her. She looked fucking stunning in her tight red dress and heels. Her hair perfectly styled and her face made up. Glancing over her body he saw her tits were bigger and her hips had a curve it never had before. He tried fucking hard to ignore the rush of blood to his stupid cock.

It didn't work, after everything she had done her body still had the power to turn him on.

But it took only one look into her eyes for him to realise she had bargained on that exact reaction. Totally explained the tight as hell dress, the fuck-me heels and the hair and face.

And just like frost under the morning sun his almost hard on disappeared.

"What the hell are you doing here, Emmie?" Ice gritted through tightly clenched teeth.

"I'm Emma now, and I tried to get Hawk and Genna to give me your number, but they refused and Hawk warned me not to set foot near his club. So I came here. I'm sorry I had to drag your parents into this. But it was the only way I knew I would get to see you. I have to talk to you, Gray. I need to explain."

Ice saw tears glistening in her eyes but he didn't believe those tears, she had always found it very easy to produce tears when she wanted to have her own way. And fuck knows he used to give her anything she wanted when she started with the waterworks.

But not this time, he was done being her lapdog.

"After Hawk's warning you still came on to Iron Dogz property, defying him. Let me make something very clear to you. You aren't welcome here, not now, not ever. You think I don't know what happened after you accused me of fucking Jane? You think I don't know you knew it was all lies? You think I don't know about the guys you fucked after you left? I know fucking everything. And that shit you laid on Hawk about seeing me getting a blowjob from a club whore? We both know it's a load of bullshit. So why don't we get to the point of this fucked up little visit of yours? Say what you've got to say and then get the fuck off our property and out of our lives."

Emma's mouth had opened and shut several times while he laid it out for her, right in front of his parents and his avidly watching siblings. Spider stood at the far end of the veranda, watching with an angry frown, his phone in his hand. The little bastard was recording the entire conversation. Spider had never made a secret of his dislike of the bitch.

A look came into Emma's eyes, a look Ice remembered very well. It reminded him of her bitch of a mother, she used to get the very same look in her eyes when she was about to lie to manipulate her daughter. Seems like the apple hasn't fallen very far from that fucked up family tree.

"I...I'm so sorry, Gray. Sorry I never came back or called you but I was so confused and hurt. I...I...I found out I was pregnant after I left and I...I wanted to tell you but...but then...then...I lost the baby and I thought it would be better if I never told you. Now I know I should've come to you. I should have told you. But the longer I waited the more I couldn't make myself tell you, so I carried on as if it never happened."

"But it did happen. We did lose our child and I wanted to say I'm sorry and ask you to forgive me and give me another chance. We love each other, Gray. We will always love each other. We belong together. Everyone knows we were meant to be together. Please give me a chance to show you I can be the woman you need. Please, Gray."

What. The. Fuck.

She sniffled and Ice watched as tears glistened in her eyes but never rolled down her cheeks. The fake as fuck bitch.

Ice was stunned. Stunned, heartbroken and enraged at the same time. Not only had she believed or pretended to believe Jane's lies but she had taken his child from him. She had left him when she knew she was carrying his child and when she lost their child instead of coming to him she had kept on running from him.

Jesus. How was he supposed to deal with this shit?

"You need to leave, right the fuck now." Ice bit out through tight lips then swung around and stormed around the side of the house away from the bitch.

He sank down on a chair on the back deck and dropped his head into his hands. Everything surrounding the shit the bitch had laid out was so fucked up. He was fucked up. Somewhere deep inside he still felt something for her, but it was for the girl he once knew. And that was the biggest fucking problem as far as he was concerned. How the hell could he still feel something for someone who had lied to him? Someone who was trying to manipulate him by professing her so-called love for him while dropping the bomb of their lost child.

What the hell was he supposed to do now?

The chair next to his creaked as his dad lowered his bulk into it and dropped his elbows onto his thighs, clasping his hands between his knees. Ice tipped his head slightly to the side to look at his dad, but he was staring at the wooden planks of the deck.

"She's gone. Son, I know right now there are a million thoughts going through your head. But there is one thing you need to get straight. Everything she laid on you tonight happened seven years ago. There's nothing you can do to change what happened. It's done. Over."

Ice pulled his beanie off and ran his fingers roughly through his hair and dropped his elbows on his knees, mimicking his dad. Playing with the beanie clasped between his fingers.

"How, Dad, how do I let it go? I waited for her for years before I made my move. I paid her fucking fees at University because her fucking mother got her hands on her student loan. I bought her a car so she would be safe going to class and the hospital. I did fucking everything for her and she knew I never stepped out on her and then she runs off and loses my kid."

His dad put a hand over his knee and just held on to him.

"What you need to work out for yourself, son, is if you still love her. I'm not going to blow smoke up your ass and tell you we'll be happy if you decide to get back with her. She not only hurt you, she hurt this family, especially your mother. Your mother is my old lady and my job is to protect her, but if you choose to be with Emma then we will try to understand and deal with it."

Ice shook his head. "I don't know, Dad. I don't know what I feel right now. Mostly I just feel empty and used."

"Take your time, Ice. Take your time and think this through. And if you need to talk it through with anybody I'm here. I'll listen, no judgement."

Bulldog stood and drew him up out of the chair and into his arms for a hard hug, slapping his back hard, twice, before he let go.

"Let's get inside before your mother comes storming out because we're ruining her dinner." His dad joked as he closed a hand over his shoulder and squeezed.

Dinner was a subdued affair until Gail looked up from her plate, took Johan's hand and dropped the bomb.

"We're having twins. One boy, one girl. We were going to keep it a secret but this family needs some good news right now. So, get out the champers, Dad. And apple juice for me, ugh." She pulled a face making everyone laugh while his mum shouted with glee.

After Gail and Johan's news the dinner became a celebration of the new lives being added to their family. Gail was over the moon that one of the babies was a boy and judging by the grin Johan wore he was just as excited.

Ice stayed as long as he could but eventually it became too difficult to keep a smile on his face and he left. Spider was right by his side as they rode through the compound gates and parked their bikes.

He was about to walk inside when Spider stopped him with a hand on his biceps. "I'm sorry for your loss, brother." He said softly.

"Fuck, Spider, we don't know if she was telling the truth. Or if the baby was even mine. Jesus, that's a fucked up thought. I have to know, man. I can't go through life not knowing." Ice looked down at his dusty boots then up into his brother's eyes. Spider's face went hard and cold.

"I've got this, Ice. I swear I will get the truth, just promise me you won't do anything until I can give you the truth. Don't go to her because you're feeling guilty or some shit. Take some time and think this through, brother. And know I've got your back, no matter what."

Nodding Ice gave him what he wanted. "Okay, little brother, I'll wait until I hear from you. Now I'm done with acting like a fucking bitch, let's get inside and have a beer."

"I'm with you, big brother." Spider grinned but the grin didn't reach his eyes. They stayed cold.

Ice and Spider were leaning on the bar, drinking their beers when Hawk and DC appeared next to them. By the sated grins on their faces he knew they had been having sex until shortly before walking into the common room. It was glaringly obvious to everyone in the room.

Hawk slapping a hand down on the bar counter had silence falling over the chattering crowd around them.

"Spread it around, brothers, we'll be having a family *braai* (barbeque) on Saturday. Only family and invited guests will be allowed through the gate. Give the names of those you want to invite to Ziggy. Background checks on everyone will be mandatory. The *braai* is in celebration of DC taking my patch which is why it will be family and friends only."

The announcement turned a quiet evening of a few beers into a celebration with plenty of shots being downed.

Hours later Ice's head was spinning as he stumbled up the stairs to his room after waving off more than one club slut who tried to lock him down for the night. Not going to happen. He never took them to his room. He always fucked them in the back rooms or they sucked him off in a dark corner. He was drunk and not thinking straight so there wasn't going to be any screwing tonight. Not ever going to make that fucking mistake.

Locking his door behind him Ice shrugged out of his kutte, threw it onto the couch and stumbled over to his bed. He collapsed full length across it and between one blink and the next he was asleep.

Hawk

The next day

Hawk grinned when his old lady walked into his office after one sharp knock, not waiting for him to give her permission to enter. Glancing at Ice he frowned when he saw his VP hadn't reacted at all. That wasn't right. It wasn't like Ice to be so withdrawn and lost in his own head. It had to be the fucking bitch slithering back into their lives that was fucking with his concentration. Making a mental note to talk to his VP later he turned to his old lady as she sauntered towards him with what looked like a list in her hand.

"What do you have there, little bird?"

"You asked everyone to give the names of those they wanted to invite to Ziggy. I did, but he said because it's a list and not one or two invites I had to run it past you first. So, this is my list of guests I want to invite."

His woman grinned when his eyes widened when he saw the extent of her list.

"Jesus, baby. Who are all these people? I recognise some of these names but not all of them."

She sighed and rolled her eyes at him and Hawk grinned. His woman was damned entertaining.

"All of them are important to me. You know my Warriors family and everyone who works at my shop."

Hawk tapped on a name that he didn't know. "Who is River Anderson?"

His little bird grinned wide. "I met her before we got together. She owns ARR, Anderson Rebuilds & Repairs, with her dad. She's the one who fixed the damage to my lady after I had to lay her down. I got to know her and I really like her. You know I find it hard to connect with people but it was easy with her. I want her to come."

Hawk glanced at his VP but it was clear the fucker was in his head somewhere and hadn't paid any attention to what DC had said. Fuck. He would have to have a talk with the bastard. Looking back at his old lady he saw she was frowning at Ice. She had noticed his inattention as well.

"Okay, little bird, give the list to Ziggy." Pointing up at the blinking red light of a camera he grinned. "He's watching, so he already knows I'm okay with it."

His woman stuck her tongue out at the camera, gave him a quick kiss and zoomed out of his office. On her way to give Ziggy a hard time.

As the door closed behind her he turned his eyes back to his VP who was still locked inside his head.

"Ice." He had to call out twice before it registered with his brother.

Ice shook his head and blinked. "Sorry, Prez. What do you need?"

"I need you to oversee the security arrangements for the braai with Jagger. We are going to have a lot of vulnerable people here on Saturday, make sure they are safe while on our property." Hawk was relieved to see his cousin was back to being his VP.

"I've got it, Prez. Jagger and I already sat down and hammered out a plan for Saturday. All we need to do now is allocate duties to the prospects and brothers." Ice looked at his watch. "I actually have to meet with Jagger now." He said as he pushed up out of the chair.

Hawk just nodded as he watched Ice leave with narrowed eyes.

That fucking bitch from his past was going to cause problems for his cousin. He could feel it in his gut.

CHAPTER FOUR

River

I had to be freaking crazy. I was on my way to a club *braai*, and not at a club whose members I knew. Nope, I knew only two people at this club and that was a scary thought. While I had worked on DC Michaels's bike we had become friends. And our budding friendship was why I had been invited to help celebrate her taking a property of patch.

Following DC's directions I turned off from the main road through big open gates onto a private but tarred road and slowly drove towards my destination. A high white wall obstructed my view of anything on the right hand side of the road while high game fence ran along the left. And then the high white wall curved away from the road and gave me a view of what awaited me. Huge steel gates.

The Iron Dogz MC's compound.

My heart was beating really fast and my palms were sweating as I gave the armed guy at the gate my name. He checked it off on a list before I was directed to drive through the enormous steel gates with the snarling dog emblem and into the Iron Dogz MC's compound. I was on another club's property and that alone was enough to make me freaking shake in my boots. Then there was the fact that even though Sparrow has been dead for five years, technically I still belonged to the Sinner's Sons MC and because of Duncan always would.

I had a personal invite from the old lady of the president of the Iron Dogz MC, but what if it wasn't enough?

My nerves did not stop me from admiring the neat layout of the clubhouse and the separate parking for bikes and cages. I was about to head towards where the other cars and bakkies were parked when a wildly waving Wrench headed me off and pointed me in the opposite direction to where a few other cars were parked under large shady trees. And knowing the way clubs worked I knew they most probably belonged to the families of the officers of the club. I slowly drove to where he pointed and he was right next to me when I stopped and turned off the ignition.

I wasn't cold so I left my jacket but took my phone out of my small back pack. Drawing in a deep breath I smiled at Wrench and got out of the car, locking it behind me then slipping the keys into the front pocket of my jeans. I slid my phone into the opposite pocket.

"Hey, Boss, DC told me you were coming so I was looking out for you. I thought you would be in the SUV so I didn't immediately recognise you. Hell, you hardly ever take this monster out of the garage. Which is why I had you park over here where your ride wouldn't get scratched. Where's my little brother? I thought he would be coming with you."

I gave him a quick hug and grinned. "The monster needed a run to charge her battery. I was nervous about my boykie running wild around people I don't know, but it's not the reason why he isn't here. It's Dagger's weekend with him and they've gone fishing and off-roading with club friends."

"I was looking forward to introducing my little bro to my brothers. But I'll do it the next time you come for a visit."

I looked around at the rows of shining bikes, the men hanging out on the wide veranda and the women hanging around them and shrugged.

"I'm not sure I'll be invited again when they know who my old man was, Wrench. The Dogz and the Sons are allies but they aren't friends."

Wrench grinned. "No worries, Boss. My prez knows who you are. Ziggy did a background check when I got the job with you and there's no probs, we're totally fine."

I wasn't sure if I liked that they had looked into me but it was months too late to get pissed about it.

"Damn, I've forgotten the way this shit works. I haven't been around club business in years. The closest I get to a club is when I drop my boykie off with Dagger."

Again Wrench laughed. "Come on, Boss. Let's find DC so you can relax and start to enjoy yourself. I'm on duty so I'll keep your ride under my eyes until you're ready to leave. And if you want to have a few drinks I'll drive you home, so no worries. Okay?"

LOST AND FOUND IN BLUE

He was such a sweet boy. I allowed Wrench to lead me around the side of the large clubhouse building towards the back from where the sounds of music and laughter could be heard. As we rounded the corner I almost turned around and ran. There were men in kuttes everywhere along with women who were obviously old ladies or girlfriends and a few scantily clad club girls. They were sort of hard to miss. Weird that they invited their club sluts to a family event, but this wasn't the Sons, this was a different club with different rules. According to their kuttes most of the men were Iron Dogz but I noticed there were Road Warriors out there as well.

Along the entire back length of the clubhouse was a large paved area with several picnic tables and benches set out and still more tables were scattered on the lawn surrounding the paved area. Big trees were dotted around the lawn with blankets spread out on the grass beneath them where people were lazing around talking and drinking. The outside bar was in a big thatched lapa, open on three sides and was manned by two women in low cut club support t-shirts. On the far right was an enormous braai area with fires already going and attended by two prospects.

Before I could comment on anything Wrench waved at DC where she was sitting at one of the picnic tables with some other women. Their eyes, along with those of several others, were on me as we approached. DC grinned wide, stood and came striding towards us.

"I'm so glad you've decided to come. Now I'll have someone to talk to around here. These bitches talk about shit I know nothing about. It's all about freaking fashion and shoes and shit. With you I can at least talk about bikes and cars and stuff. I hope you're not into fashion and shit."

I waved a hand down my body indicating the way I was dressed. Minimal make-up, a spritz of my favourite perfume, faded jeans, biker boots, a white t-shirt with one of Sparrow's old flannel shirts over the top. The long sleeves were rolled twice and covered the memorial tattoo on my right forearm and if it didn't get too hot my arms would stay covered. My hair hung loose down my back, nothing special about it. I had let it air dry after washing it in the shower this morning. At least it was clean and shiny.

I burst out laughing when I realised she was dressed almost exactly the same and she laughed with me. Wrench just shook his head at us as he started to back away.

"You need anything, Boss, you come look for me, okay?"

"Okay, Wrench, no problems."

As he disappeared back to the front of the clubhouse DC looked at me with a frown. "Since when did he get a club name? Everyone here calls him Kev, not Wrench."

"We've got another Kev working for us and it became too confusing." I said with a grin. "So I started calling him Wrench and now everyone at work does."

"I have to tell Hawk, it suits him and because of his job it's a great road name for him."

LOST AND FOUND IN BLUE

I felt his energy approaching before I saw him. The president of the Iron Dogz was as intimidating as everyone said he was. He was big, not only tall but wide and the width had nothing to do with fat, it was all muscle. The man was intimidating but undeniably hot, a kind of mix between Thor and Ragnar. I fought hard not to fan myself because of the sex heat he threw off. DC was one very, very lucky bitch.

"What is a great road name for who?"

DC grinned up at the big man as he slung his heavy arm around her shoulders and pulled her into his side.

"Hawk, meet River Anderson, she's the genius who fixed my lady after I had to lay her down."

He held out a hand and I cautiously put my hand in his. His clasp was firm as he shook once and let go. The care he took not to crush my hand was hot as hell.

Jesus. I had to stop this shit.

"Welcome, River. I've heard about your skills and saw the results. We need to sit down and talk sometime. I have some old bikes in storage I want to restore when I have more time."

"I'll be happy to help. Set it up with Wrench when you're ready and we'll see what we can do to help."

Hawk frowned and DC grinned. "She means Kev. They call him Wrench because they have another Kev working with them and it was confusing. Hence, Kev's new name."

Hawk grinned and waved at someone behind me. "Hey brother, come over here and listen to this."

I didn't turn around but I should have so I could have run far, far away before he entered my life and totally turned it upside down. But I didn't know it then, so I stayed.

The man who walked up and joined us was as big as Hawk and going by their similar builds and features it was obvious they were family. Where Hawk was a blonde with yellow eyes this guy had dark hair with his own version of those yellow eyes. He had more green in his eyes where Hawk's had more of an amber-brown cast to it. Unlike Hawk his hair wasn't shaved at the sides but fell over his ears and neck. The top was longer and he wore it brushed back but it kept falling over his face in long strands that he shoved back with an impatient hand. His beard was dark and trimmed to follow the contours of his face. His black t-shirt strained over broad shoulders and a big chest, the sleeves tight around his biceps. His kutte told me that he was the club's vice president. Tattoos covered both arms and the back of one hand and I could see the edge of another at the neck of his tee. It looked like they were mostly club tattoos, the same as Hawk's.

Holy hotness batman.

"River, meet Ice, my VP. Ice this is River, Kev's boss. Guess what she has been calling our prospect?"

The big ice man shrugged as if he couldn't care less, his eyes totally disinterested. "No idea man."

"Wrench, she calls the little fucker, Wrench."

A roar of laughter erupted from both men and DC and I stared at them in confusion. We looked at each other then back at them.

Ice was the one who answered our unspoken question.

"We were thinking of naming him Rip but Wrench is so much better. Way better."

He turned those yellow-green eyes on me and I almost melted. They were filled with laughter and warmth, so much warmth. Shit, I had to be really careful around this man.

"So, is River your real name or a nick name?"

"My real name. My folks did the deed on a river bank and I'm the result, so they named me River. Thank goodness they didn't decide to name me after the river because that would have been a disaster. And they must really like the outdoors thing because my brothers' name is Lake."

We were laughing when some of the other men came walking up. All of them looking at me with hard faces and questions in their eyes. And when there were no comments about Lake I knew they didn't know who my brother was. Phew.

"Brothers, let me introduce you to River. She's the one who did the repairs to my old lady's bike."

"And her work is freaking amazing." DC threw in with a grin.

Hawk grinned down at her then turned back to me. "River, the big guy over here is Beast and next to him is Sin, Jagger and Kid."

Holy shit! Beast was tall and wide and huge and totally intimidating with his cold frowny face. The others were big but no one was as big as this guy.

I smiled and nodded but didn't say a word as they checked me over. In their eyes I could see they were weighing up what they knew about me against the reality of me. They gave me chin lifts as their eyes ran over me without saying a word. There was interest in some of those eyes but I didn't want that. Interest wasn't good, not at all.

"Let's leave this lot and their grumpy asses and I'll introduce you to some of the women, and as I said, be prepared for some girly talk." DC cut through the silence that had fallen around us.

I was only too glad to get away from the men because their intent stares really started to freak me out.

As we walked over to the table where several women were sitting DC spoke softly. "Ignore their stupid suspicious asses. We have some shit happening around here and right now they aren't the warmest of puppies."

I grinned. "I already came to the same conclusion. I'm no threat to your club and I'm not interested in hooking up with any of the brothers so there's nothing to worry about."

DC stopped dead and swung around and looked at me with wide eyes. "Really? Not even one of them gave you a tiny little tingle? A little smidge of attraction?"

I forced myself not to glance back at the ice man as I shook my head. "Nope." I lied. "I'm not looking for a man, DC. I had the best and I'm not ready to replace him."

A strange look flitted over her face. There and gone in an instant. "You had a man? What happened if you don't mind me asking?"

I looked at the trees with leaves that were starting to turn yellow and rustled in the light breeze. Autumn was slowly creeping in. Drawing in a deep breath I looked back at her. "My old man was gunned down in an ambush. He died on the scene. I was eight and a half months pregnant and the shock sent me into labour, our son was born the next day."

"Jesus." DC said softly. "Did they find the bastards who did it?"

"I don't know. I wasn't in a good place for a long time and by the time I asked I was told it was club business and to let it go."

We were both silent for several minutes as we stood there looking into each other's eyes. Then DC nodded as if she had made a decision.

"I'm not asking about your club affiliation because I know if they were our enemies Hawk would never have let you come. But if you ever need any information about what happened to your old man don't hesitate to call me. I'll get it for you, no questions asked. Okay?"

Her eyes were dark and hard before they flipped back to warm and concerned. So weird.

I smiled, took her hand and squeezed. "Thanks, DC. And just so you know, my old man rode with the Sinner's Sons MC."

Again that strange look slipped into her eyes and it felt as if a colder version of her were looking at me out of her dark eyes before it disappeared and the warmth was back. Weird, very weird.

"Cool, now let's move on because those bastards back there are getting too interested in what we're talking about. We old ladies need to stick together."

With that we continued on towards the picnic table where I was introduced to the women DC considered her friends and family. All of whom were staring at me, their eyes filled with curiosity.

"I'll start at this end of the table and go round so you can put faces to names. This is Aunt Suzy, she's Bulldog's old lady and Ice, Spider, Gail and Genna are her kids. Gail isn't here today because she's about to pop out twins and is resting. Then we have Aunt Beryl, she's Hawk's aunt and the single reason we're not dying of starvation around here."

Aunt Beryl shook a finger at her but was grinning at the same time, as giggles came from around the table.

"Moving on swiftly, next we have Nadja, who works with me at Mainline Ink and will pierce anything you can think of, she's Shaka's old lady and he's a Road Warrior, then we have Linda, my bestie, she's Rover's old lady and he's a Road Warrior as well. And this lady over here is my surrogate mum, Aunt Liddy. She's Tiny's old lady, the Road Warriors' VP. The angry looking one over here is Aunt

Zelda, my other surrogate mum and don't worry about the face, she likes giving me shit whenever she can." Laughter around the table, including from Aunt Zelda. "This one here is my baby sister, Deena and she's still at school, so no alcohol or hot bikers for her. And next to her we have Grace who also works at Mainline Ink with me, she's Tiny and Aunt Liddy's daughter and my other baby sister. And the beauty next to her is Genna, Bulldog and Suzy's daughter and Ice's baby sister."

Waving over the table DC grinned. "These are the only women here that I can safely introduce you to because they are the only ones I actually know. The rest of them I've seen around but I haven't made an effort to get to know them. Most of them are nasty bitches."

"Don't listen to her, River. Come sit down over here and tell us all about yourself." Aunt Liddy ordered, and I knew it was an order by the way she pointed to a seat at the end of the table.

"Aunt Liddy, give the girl a chance to at least get a drink before you start interrogating her." DC laughed as she quickly led me over to the bar.

As soon as we each a drink, a beer for DC and a cider for me we went back to the table filled with nosy interrogators.

"Right, you have your drink, now tell us all about yourself."

I shrugged. "There's not much to tell. I'm a mechanic and work with my dad. I repair and rebuild bikes, classic cars and muscle cars. I live in a cottage on my parents' property. And I have a four almost five year old son."

"Did you bring him along today?" One of the women asked. I think it was Linda.

"No, he isn't here today."

I kept my answer short, but it didn't deter the inquisitive and nosy women.

"Where's his daddy? Is he still in the picture?" Aunt Beryl asked ignoring DC frowning angrily at her.

"He, uhm, he died before our son was born."

Aunt Beryl reached across the table and clasped a hand over my clenched fist.

"I'm so sorry. Forgive me for being such a nosy old bat."

I shrugged and smiled. "It's okay."

After a short embarrassed silence talk around the table returned to general subjects, and DC was right, it was mostly about girly stuff I knew nothing about. I couldn't add anything to the conversation so I just listened and nodded as if I knew what the hell they were talking about.

I so didn't.

I sat scratching at the label on the bottle when I felt eyes on me, looking up I saw him. Ice. He was leaning against a tree and staring right at me. Just staring. No smile. Blank faced and staring.

What the hell?

He made me feel damned uncomfortable and I avoided his eyes and looked back at the women around the table.

Thank goodness no one had noticed the stare down.

LOST AND FOUND IN BLUE

Or if they had no one commented on it.

Again, thank goodness.

CHAPTER FIVE

Ice

He couldn't keep his eyes off the blonde who came walking around the side of the clubhouse with Kev. They were walking together like they knew each other very well. Kev was touching her arm as he pointed to DC and waved her over.

Who was this fucking gorgeous woman who talked to Kev and DC as if she knew them well? Especially Kev, the little shit.

She was dressed in faded jeans, a plain white v-neck tee with a man's big red and black plaid flannel shirt over it. The shirt wasn't new, and looked soft and worn in. Her biker boots were well worn and he could see scuff marks that let him know they weren't for show. This woman rode a bike.

It was her hair that had first caught his eye and that of several of the brothers. It fell down her back to her ass in a straight light golden blonde mass. It shone and glittered in the sun like pale gold. The breeze tugged at a few strands and lifted it as she stood talking to Kev and DC.

And then she laughed. It rang out, smokey and deep and hit him right in the gut. He felt a stirring in his blood as he watched her.

Closing his eyes he forced himself to shut it down. He couldn't let this happen until he cleared his head about Emmie or fucking Emma as she now liked to be called.

But he knew if it hadn't been for all the shit looming on his horizon tonight he would have had her in his bed with those long muscled legs of hers around his back as he fucked her long and deep.

Hawk calling him over drew him out of the daydream of her on her back on his bed with her pale blonde hair glittering against the dark sheets. He forced himself to cool it as he walked over.

And then his prez introduced them and it felt as if he had been hit by a two by four. He immediately knew who she was. River Anderson, old lady of Sparrow Martins, the SAA of the Sinner's Sons MC who had been gunned down almost five years ago.

Jesus. She was an untouchable. Royal game. And she was Sinner's Sons MC property.

He didn't care. He wanted her, badly. Threads of her scent swirled around him as the breeze lifted her hair and his gut clenched. It was faint, barely there just enough that he wanted to stuff his face in her neck and breathe her in.

Close up she was beautiful without even trying. The only make-up she wore was the black shit to make her eyelashes darker and those dark lashes rimmed the most amazing blue eyes he had ever seen. They were a strange sparkling icy pale blue with a darker blue rim around the outer edge. She was tall, about five eight he guessed and her body was trim and toned. She wasn't one of those bitches who walked around with a six pack because she worked out so much. No, she had the sweetest little tummy hidden behind her jeans. The kind of tummy that drove bitches wild when they couldn't get rid of it. But he liked it. It was something he wanted to nuzzle and bite before he went down on her.

He was in a total haze as he talked to his prez and let his eyes draw in every detail about the woman across from him. Despite the warm day she hadn't rolled up the sleeves of her shirt and he wondered why. What was she hiding behind those sleeves? He wanted to take it off her and explore.

He liked the sound of her voice. It was deep for a woman and had a rusty sort of purr to it.

And he wasn't the only one who liked her voice and her laugh. He immediately saw the interest in Sin's eyes as he walked over and was introduced. He gave the bastard one look but he just grinned and Ice knew the fucker was going to try and score this one.

It was not going to happen.

"So that's River Anderson." Beast growled as DC and River walked away. "I wondered what she would look like and I have to say it's nothing like I imagined."

"She's fucking stunning." Sin said with a grin. "I wouldn't mind a woman like her on the back of my bike."

Kid laughed. "Stop talking shit, Sin. You don't put bitches on the back of your bike and you won't have her there either."

"Why? She just might be the one who changes my mind." Sin grinned as he winked at Kid.

"Hands off this one, brothers." Hawk shot them all down. "She's not fresh meat to be fucked and chucked. DC invited her and if you mess with River my old lady is going to be pissed. So let's all take a step back and make sure she enjoys her day and goes home untouched tonight. Okay?"

There were grunts and nods all around and Ice was one of the grunts. No way was he going to nod in agreement.

"Ice, did you hear me?" Hawk asked with a frown.

Ice looked at his president and his brothers, winked and gave an evil grin.

"Dibs."

"No! You can't do that." Sin complained.

"I saw her first brother. I called dibs. She's mine." Ice shrugged.

"What about…" Hawk tried but Ice silenced him.

"Don't. Don't say that name. Not today."

Ice was done. He walked away making his way over to the bar where he got himself a beer then stood with his back against the big old oak and watched her as she talked and joked with the women around the table. She fit right in and there was some kind of a connection between her and DC. He wondered what that was about.

As night fell the lights came on around the big back patio, in the trees and on the tables, and the smell of the meat on the braai filled the air. Ice had moved around during the afternoon, talking to friends, but he always made sure he had her in sight. She drank sparingly and was only on her second cider, drinking water in between. A careful drinker. He liked that.

When Aunt Beryl rang the bell to tell them dinner was being served he made sure he was next to her. He nudged her aside as she was about to start dishing for herself and gave her his plate to hold.

"Hold mine and I'll dish for both of us. What would you like?"

Her blue eyes flew up and went wide. "Uhm, I can do it myself."

"I know, but I want to do it for you, so let me."

With a slight smile and a nod she let him and they shuffled companionably down the line as he loaded their plates. She didn't want a lot of meat, a small piece of steak, a pork sausage and a piece of *boerewors*, but the woman sure loaded up on the salads. After they got through the line she tried to hand him his plate but he just shook his head as he got them each a set of knives and forks wrapped in a serviette.

"Would you like water with your dinner or can I get you another cider?" Ice asked softly.

"Ah, water please. I don't want to drink more tonight because I have to drive home." She answered as softly.

"Baby, don't worry about it. Drink if you want to. We'll get you home, no worries." Ice said softly and ignored the confusion in her eyes.

Ice picked up two bottles of water before leading her towards the small table where Hawk and DC were sitting. He set the stuff in his hands down then took the plates from her and set them on the table. Pulling her chair out he settled her at the table, went to the bar and got her another cider and beers for himself, Hawk and DC. Back at the table he settled his chair close to her and started eating, not saying a word.

Across the way he could see his mum and dad watching him. His dad gave him a slight chin lift and Ice gave a slight nod. It was enough to let his dad know he was interested in this woman. More than he had been in anyone in a very long time.

He was still looking at his dad when the conversation at the table pulled his attention back. DC was talking to River and what she said froze his gut.

"Why didn't you bring your little boy today?"

River smiled such a sweet smile it unfroze the ice churning in his gut. She wasn't Emma, nothing like Emma. He reassured himself.

"It's his uncle's weekend to spend time with him and I didn't want to mess with it. He was so looking forward to it. They've gone fishing and off-roading with some friends and their kids."

"It sounds like a lot of fun." Hawk grinned. "Where did they go?"

"They went to a friends' farm near Rustenburg. He apparently has dams and off-roading trails on his farm and they've gone camping out there. And if I had to judge by all the stuff they loaded on to the back of the *bakkies* they are going to have a ball." River grinned. "I don't envy the guys, they took all the kids and they are going to drive them nuts."

"Are you saying they took little girls along on this weekend?" DC asked with an evil grin.

River laughed outright. "Oh yes they did. They've never taken the girls out for an entire weekend before. Poor bastards. You should have seen the grins on the faces of the women when they watched them driving away. They were about a mile wide and so very evil."

"Shame on you, River. You should have warned them." Ice teased.

"Nope, they brought this on themselves. I hope they take photos. Lots of photos." She said with a wide smile.

But her smile faltered as she looked at the man approaching the table. Doc Michaels came striding towards the table as if he owned the fucking place. A smile curved his mouth as he stopped next to DC and dropped a kiss on her head.

"You made it. I didn't think you were coming, Dad." DC said with a wide smile.

"Sorry, DC, club shit got in the way. But now I'm glad I came." He said as he turned to River.

"River-girl, I haven't seen you in ages, sweetheart. How are you?" He smiled as he pulled River up out of her chair and hugged her. And what do you know, she hugged him right back.

"Hi Doc. It's good to see you and I'm good." She was still smiling as she stepped back from him.

"Your dad and I had a beer last week and he told me how well your shop is doing. He was bragging about your boy and I couldn't brag because my daughter hasn't given me a grand baby yet. You need to bring your boy around these two so they'll get broody and get busy making me some grand babies." Doc teased.

River laughed at the shocked look on DC's face but Hawk just got a look in his eyes Ice knew very well. It said challenge accepted. Hawk was totally on board with knocking his old lady up. Ice felt like laughing on one hand but on the other he didn't like that Doc knew River and had obviously known her when her old man had still been alive. And he was friendly with her father, friendly enough to have a beer with the man.

It meant not only was she technically still a part of the Sinner's Sons, she was also a friend of the Road Warriors. If he made a play for her and it went south he could end up making enemies in both clubs. He had to cool this down until he had the Emma situation sorted out and then when he was free and clear he could go all out to see where this went with her.

Yes, that sounded like a good plan.

"I didn't know you knew my dad." DC said, obviously surprised.

"I met him a couple of times at the garage. He and my dad go out for a beer now again." River said with a shrug. DC nodded as if it made sense.

Hours and several whiskeys later he was leaning against the bar in the common room and laughing with Hawk as they watched the women dancing to some stupid song. Both of them were obviously no longer sober and were having a ton of fun as they hopped about like crazy chickens. When the song ended they came back giggling and Ice handed River a bottle of water she immediately opened and drank half down.

Hawk turned as he lifted a laughing DC up into his arms. "We're out. It was great meeting you River and we'll talk soon about those bikes. Have fun and don't worry about a ride home. Stay here, we've got plenty of space. Ice will take care of you, okay?"

"Yes, stay over then we can have breakfast together in the morning. Please, River, say you'll stay." DC begged.

"Stay, River. You'll be safe, I promise." Ice said as heat started curling in his gut.

She nodded slowly then faster. "Okay, yes, thanks, I'll stay over because I definitely can't drive home."

"Yay. See you for breakfast, *tjommie*." (Friend) DC giggled as Hawk carted her off.

Taking River's hand Ice started leading her towards the stairs when Wrench popped up in front of them.

"Hey Boss, if you're ready to go home I'll drive you." He said as he threw a frown Ice's way.

River smiled at him. "DC invited me to breakfast so I'm going to stay over. Thank you for looking out for me, Wrench."

"You're staying over?" He asked with a frown. "Where?"

Ice suspected the prospect was pissed off because he knew about all the shit swirling around him with the bitch that would not be named. As he frowned at him Ice knew he had to cut this shit short.

"I'm putting her in the guestroom upstairs, not going to let her sleep down here where I can't keep an eye on her."

That calmed the prospect down. "That's cool, VP." He said with a short nod. "Sleep well, Boss. I'll see you in the morning."

And then it was him and River. As he walked her up the stairs he felt the eyes on them but ignored it as he kept a hand on the small of her back. Her hair felt like silk between his fingers and he wanted to grab a fist full of the golden stuff and just hold on.

He didn't take her to the guestroom.

Walking her into his room his brain was screaming at him to turn the fuck around and deposit this woman in the other room. But he didn't. He closed and locked the door behind him, leant against it and watched her as she looked around his room.

"This isn't the guestroom." She said softly.

"No, no its not. It's my room. I don't want you in the guestroom. I want you here, with me." He said as he levered himself away from the door and slowly walked to her. She stood and watched as he came to her. Her eyes large pools of clear blue that he fell into as he came close.

"If you don't want this, say so now because I don't know if I can let you go once I get my hands on you." His voice came out low and rough as he reached out and clasped his hands around her hips and pulled her close.

"I want this." She whispered.

And those words were all it took for the want and lust to rage out of control.

Clothes flew as they kissed, devouring each other's mouths. Her moans spurred him on and Ice completely lost his head as he picked her up and threw her on his big bed. And the fantasy of her golden hair on his dark sheets came true.

She was beautiful, all long and lean with thigh muscles that said she ran. And a slight little tummy he now knew came from having her son. A little tummy he was going to bite and nuzzle the shit out of. Little tummies like hers had always been a turn on for him. And even though she'd had a baby her smallish tits were still high and tight. The nipples a pale rose, calling for his mouth to turn them bright red as he sucked on them.

Everything about her was pale and golden, even the strip of hair covering her pussy. The hair was the same pale gold as the hair spread out on his sheets and trimmed short. So short it was barely there. She was fucking beautiful, so damned beautiful. Everywhere.

Stroking his heavy cock Ice stood at the bottom of the bed and stared at the woman laid out before him. Every time his hand hit his piercing it shot streaks of pleasure/pain through him. Tonight she was going to be his, only his.

"Baby, spread for me. Show me what I want so fucking badly."

She smiled and slowly slid her legs apart and exposed herself to him. Ice sucked in a harsh breath and dived for her, his mouth slamming down on her glistening pussy. A pussy that glistened because she wanted him. Her smell and taste crashed into him as he licked and sucked and ate at the best pussy he had ever had.

When her hands curved into his hair he grinned against her lips and licked hard, shoving his tongue into her and his golden woman shuddered under his mouth. She was so fucking tight it was going to be heaven to be inside her.

"Oh, God, Ice, more, give me more of your beautiful tongue. Come on, baby, give it to me."

And he gave it to her, tongue fucking her until she was close to coming and he could no longer stand not being inside the writhing shuddering woman. Ripping his mouth away from her he lunged up over her and pushed inside.

She moaned long and loud and stiffened under him and he felt every single muscle in him freeze. Her tight heat surrounded him, squeezed him and had him on the verge of coming but he held still because he knew his size had caused her to feel pain. Something he didn't want for her.

"You okay, blue eyes?" Ice forced out between clenched teeth.

"Just, just hold still for a minute, baby. You're big and I haven't had sex in more than five years, so just give me a minute, okay?"

For whatever reason her words made Ice feel like a fucking caveman and he growled as he slowly slid out a few inches and then back in. And the minute she arched up against him he let go of the tight reign he had on himself.

He slid out and pushed back in faster and faster and she moaned and moved with him becoming wild underneath him. Her short nails felt so fucking good on his back as she held on to him. The warm, wet, slickness of her surrounded his cock and he felt himself start to leak inside her, his climax hurtling down on him like a runaway train.

Until she went solid beneath him and gasped out.

"Ice, Ice, baby, we need a condom."

Laughter shook him as he looked down in her laughing face, those amazing blue eyes sparkling up at him.

"You didn't just do that. You didn't just pull a Vanilla Ice on me in the middle of the most amazing sex of my life."

She rocked with laughter making her pussy clench around him and Ice groaned as he forced himself to withdraw. His climax was way too close and he knew for a fact he'd started leaking semen there at the end.

"You on birth control, Blue?"

"Yes, I have an IUD but I don't want to have unprotected sex, not yet anyway."

"No problems, angel."

Ice reached over to the bedside table drawer, pulled it open and started rummaging around for the box of condoms he knew he had in there somewhere. He groaned in relief when he found them and ripped the box open, extracted a condom, bit and tore it open then one handed rolled it onto his cock.

And then he was right back where he belonged, deep inside the most amazing pussy he had ever been in. Her internal muscles clenched as she climaxed and pulled him in as if they didn't want to let him go and he powered through them, slamming deep and coming like he had never done in his life.

It felt as if all of him was centered at the tip of his cock and flooding into the condom and he hated it. He wanted to paint the inside of her with his come. Mark her as his.

Ice froze at those thoughts and stared down at the woman beneath him. She was stunningly beautiful as the last of her climax flowed through her. Her pale skin was flushed a pale rose, her eyes closed and her bottom lip clenched between her teeth. Her pale golden hair surrounded her and was spread out over the dark blue sheets.

Holding on to the condom Ice slowly started to withdraw and her eyes snapped open as she moaned. Dropping his head Ice kissed her softly.

"I'll be back in a minute."

He got rid of the condom washed and dried himself then warmed a facecloth under the hot water, squeezed it out and walked back into his bedroom.

She lay exactly as he had left her. Her eyes closed and her legs open, displaying her wet and swollen red pussy and his cock jerked.

He ignored it as he crawled onto the bed next to her and gently cleaned her with the warm facecloth before throwing it back into the bathroom. She was asleep when he picked her up and slid her into his bed, sliding in behind her and drawing her into his arms. That's when he noticed the tattoo on her forearm. A cross with the name Sparrow across the arms and a sparrow flying overhead with dates underneath. A memorial to her old man.

She sighed as she settled against him and Ice lay there and wondered what the fuck he was doing. He had brought this beautiful woman to his room, something he never did and he had fucked her in his bed, another thing he never did.

What the hell did it mean?

And what about the shit with Emma? He still wasn't sure about what he felt or didn't feel for her. How could he draw this amazing woman into his shit? How could he expect her to understand that what had happened here between them could not happen again? At least not until his fucked up feelings for Emma had been sorted out.

He had fucked up. But before he let her go he had to have her again, and again, and again.

He spent the rest of the night fucking and making love to the most amazing woman he had ever met. And when he finally let her sleep she lay against his dark blue sheets like a golden well fucked goddess while he lay next to her, wide awake and burning with regret.

And shame, a hell of a lot of shame.

Regret had him kissing her softly against her temple as he gently moved her hair from her face. If he didn't leave now he never would.

Ice slowly slid out of the bed, pulled on his jeans and tee and silently walked out of the room and into the guestroom.

He lay on the bed not sleeping until he heard his bedroom door open then he slipped off the bed and quickly opened the door.

She stood there, dressed and when she saw him the warmth in her eyes disappeared and right in front of him she shut down. Turned into an ice queen.

"Ah, I see." She said with a small nod. "Tell DC thanks for the breakfast invite but something came up and I had to leave."

Then she walked away and disappeared down the stairs.

Ice stood there watching her walk away from him and he knew, he knew somewhere deep inside he had just watched the best thing that had ever happened to him walk out of his life.

And it was his fault.

"Please tell me there's a reason for the totally asshole move you just pulled. I need a very good reason not to hurt you right now." An ice cold voice snarled behind him and as he swung around DC or rather the Crow stood behind him staring up at him with cold dead black eyes.

"I fucked up, shouldn't have touched her." Ice muttered.

"You're right, you shouldn't have." She snarled.

Ice opened his mouth to try and explain but she didn't give him even a second to do so before she disappeared back into Hawk's room and closed the door softly but very fucking firmly.

He was fucked.

CHAPTER SIX

Hawk

Sunday Afternoon

His old lady was pissed and Hawk had no idea why but he had thought it wise to get himself out of the way until she calmed down.

He had called a meeting of his officers to get out of her way but it wasn't the only reason. After the party last night the men weren't at their best but Ice looked even worse. He wondered what the hell was up with him. Or was it just the shit with the bitch wanting to get back with him? Hawk didn't know because his cousin wasn't talking.

He wasn't going to let him get away with that crap. Ice needed to shake his fucking head because his eyes were stuck. Everyone but he could see the play the bitch was making. She was playing him, making him doubt what he was feeling. Before she reappeared Ice had been fine, and over the shit she had pulled seven years ago. Hawk even suspected he had been ready to start looking for an old lady. And after the way he had been with River Anderson last night he knew exactly who his cousin had in mind.

She would be good for him and the club. She had lived the life before, knew how things worked. And her ties to the Sinner's Sons would tie the two clubs closer together than the handshake he and Dagger had exchanged to become allies.

DC had brought the Road Warriors with her and if Ice took River as his old lady she would bring the Sinner's Sons. Between the three clubs they covered all of South Africa and that would make their enemies think twice about taking them on.

But by the look of Ice this morning it wasn't going to happen.

Okay, he could respect Ice's decision, what he couldn't handle was his cousin being taken for a ride once again by the bitch who had slithered back in to his life. That shit ends today, in this room.

Hawk smacked his palm down on the table and silence descended.

"Ziggy, I want you digging into Emma Coetzee and everyone connected to her. Go back as far as you have to. Don't leave anything untouched. I don't give a fuck who you have to hack, do it and get me the information. There's a reason why she's back besides wanting Ice to abandon the club and play house with her."

He ignored Ice trying to get a word in.

"Kid, Beast and Sin you're with me tomorrow. Ice, I want you and Jagger to check every single security measure and back up here and at our businesses. Make sure everything is in place and working as they should. Spider and Kahn, go over our books and accounts. Check everything. I have a burning in my gut telling me shit is coming and we've missed something. Meeting done. Get out of here and watch your backs."

Everyone left except Ice and he didn't have to wait long for before he let it all out.

"Back the fuck off Emma. She's my problem and I'll sort it out." He snapped his eyes dark with anger.

Hawk swallowed back his knee jerk reaction and coldly looked at his VP, right at this moment he was his VP, not his cousin and best friend.

"You have that one wrong, Ice. She's my problem because her shit has my VP tied in fucking knots and not thinking straight. And he's missing shit he never would have missed before."

"Bullshit. I have not missed a single thing."

Hawk raised his eyebrows. "So that surprised fucking look on your face when you realised who River Anderson was, that was done on purpose?"

Hawk shook his head as his cousin gritted his teeth and clamped his fucking mouth shut.

"You were there when DC brought me her list of invites before the party and I asked about River Anderson. The three of us were in my fucking office but you were off in your head and didn't hear a fucking thing we said. Hence the eyebrow twitching and surprise."

Hawk sat forward in his chair and stared right into his cousin's eyes. "I need you, Ice. I can't have your attention wandering because it could mean the lives of everyone in this club. I need you sharp. I need you at my back. Don't fight me on this shit with Emma. Let it go. Let it go and do your job."

Hawk watched as his cousin's head dropped and his chest expanded as he took a deep breath. His eyes were clear when he looked up.

"I'm sorry, Prez. I'm here and you can count on me. You're right. The shit with Emma needs to take a back seat to club business. But I have to tell you I'm fucking confused. I don't know if I ever really loved her, like my dad loves my mum. I wanted her, that's no secret, but love, deep like the love my folks have for each other? I'm not sure I ever felt it."

"Then let me do what I have to do, Ice. Let Ziggy look into her because I'm telling you something isn't right. Her story just doesn't feel right to me."

Hawk felt it deep in his chest when his cousin sighed heavily. "Okay. You and Ziggy do what you have to do. I only want one promise from you. If Ziggy finds shit I want to be let in on it. Whatever he finds let me deal with it."

"Not happening. If he finds shit we deal with it together, the way brothers do."

Ice reached a hand across the table and they clasped hands tight, and Hawk nodded. Relief coursed through him. He had expected this talk to end harshly, it didn't.

Thank fuck.

Ice

His cousin was right. He had to get his head on straight and concentrate on the club. They had a war coming and he was dropping the ball because he had women on his brain.

That stopped right now, right this minute.

He'd let Ziggy dig into Emma's shit and once it was sorted he would mend fences with River.

River was important to him, very fucking important and he had realised it almost too late. Once the shit with Emma was settled he would be making sure River knew exactly what he wanted from her. And he wanted everything. Every-fucking-thing.

Ziggy
Monday

Frowning Ziggy leant forward as he clicked and clicked again revealing more and more photos of the family *braai* in a bogus Iron Dogz MC Facebook page.

The club did have a facebook page but he was in control of it and he was very damned careful about what he posted plus their privacy settings kept people from snooping. The page he was looking at was wide open and had already been visited by a few hundred people. It did not take him long to flag it and have it closed down but he knew it was already too late.

What worried him was the majority of the photos were of DC and River and the women dancing with them. Not good, definitely not good.

Who had taken those photos and then posted them on facebook?

Laying the photos out on one monitor he pulled saved footage and started comparing angles. After two hours of comparing angles and pulling footage from several of the cameras he had three possible matches. Two of those he discarded immediately because it was DC and Hawk. It left the female he found holding her phone as if reading a message in most of the stills he had printed off. She looked faintly familiar. A better question was how did she get into the party? He had done background checks on every single invite and she definitely hadn't been on that list. He would have remembered her.

It was time to call in the boss.

Hawk

Hawk walked into Ziggy's office with Ice right behind him and looked at the photos on the monitors and immediately saw what had his brother so worried. Almost every single photo had DC and River and the other club women in it. Women belonging to the Iron Dogz and the Road Warriors. Not one of the club girls who had been at the braai were featured in those photos.

They were all of DC, River, the old ladies and the female family members of brothers in both of the clubs.

Then he looked at the photo of the woman taking the photos and frowned. He knew who she was but not personally. Shelly was a club girl popular with some of the brothers but there was something off about her appearance. Something he couldn't place just yet but he would eventually.

Pointing at the photo he lifted an eyebrow, waiting for Ziggy to fill them in.

"I'm looking into her, Boss. I think I've seen her here on open party nights but that's about all I know. I have no idea how she got in, she wasn't on the list. We need to ask the brothers if one of them maybe brought her in."

"That's Shelly, she's a hangaround. I've fucked her once or twice." Ice growled angrily. "What the fuck is she trying to do here? Get herself killed?"

Hawk shrugged. "Seems like it. Get me her address, Ziggy. It should be in the database."

Pulling his phone from his pocket he swiped and spoke as soon as someone answered. "Kid, take Beast and a prospect with a cage and bring the bitch called Shelly in. Bring any electronics you find at her place as well. Ziggy will text you her address."

Ice

Rubbing a hand over his chin Ice stared at the photos on the monitors and frowned. What the hell was going on here?

An hour and a half later they had a petrified bitch sitting in Hawk's office. His prez silently stared at the woman, not saying a word. Ice stood behind Hawk and coldly stared down at her as she fidgeted and bounced her leg with anxiety.

"You've been hanging around the club for almost two years now, am I right?" Hawk asked quietly.

"Yes, yes, Prez. Why am I here? Am I in trouble?"

"That depends on what you say next, Shelly." Ice growled before Hawk could answer.

"I swear I've done nothing. I wouldn't. I love it here, love the club and everything." She looked up at Ice and he saw tears in her eyes. "You know I wouldn't do anything to jeopardise the club, don't you, Ice? We've always been good together and I wouldn't do anything to hurt you."

Fuck. Not another one. Ice gritted his teeth as Kid softly snickered next to him.

"Fucking Ice has nothing to do with why you are here. Answer my questions and you might walk out of here. Who invited you to the family *braai*? Why did you take photos of the women at the party and post them online?" Hawk's voice was cold and hard.

In front of them Shelly deflated. She shrank into herself and tried to look as small as possible.

"What did you do, Shelly?" Ice was so angry his voice was a low rumble as it grated out of his throat.

If the bitch could have she would have dropped lower in her chair.

"They came to me two weeks before the *braai*. They had photos of my family and my little sister. They said if I didn't do what they wanted she would disappear never to be seen again. Sold to some pervert who likes to hurt little girls." Tears were now running down her cheeks. "I couldn't let them hurt her so I agreed to do anything they wanted."

She sniffed loudly before she continued and Hawk threw a box of tissues at her. Ice did not want to think about why his cousin had a fucking box of tissues in his office.

"At first they just asked questions about the brothers. They wanted to know how many of the brothers lived at the compound and who had families outside. I couldn't tell them everything they wanted to know because I didn't know. They told me to find out. I tried to drag it out while I got my family out and to safety." She blew her nose loudly before she continued.

"On the night before the *braai* a woman came to my flat. She said my name had been added to the guest list. She gave me a phone and told me she wanted photos of all the claimed women who attended and especially photos of anyone who spent time with Ice. The next day she came back for the phone and told me she would be in contact soon."

Her eyes scanned over all of them before she looked back at Hawk. "That's all I know. She hasn't been back and the men haven't been back either."

"Will you be able to recognise them if you saw them again?"

Shelly nodded her head.

Hawk motioned Ziggy closer and he smacked the laptop down in front of her angrily.

The bitch immediately nodded and pointed at one of the photos. "That's her. She gave me the phone. I've never seen any of the other people in the photos."

Fucking Emma.

Hawk rested his steepled hands against his mouth and stared at her before he sighed.

"You should have come to me, Shelly. You should have trusted that we would take care of you and your family but instead you chose to betray us. You will stay here but when this shit is over you are done with the club. As of today consider yourself banned. Any brother who fucks you after today will find out what it means to piss me off."

Waving a hand at Beast to take her away he waited until her snivelling ass was out of the office and the door closed behind her.

Ice and Kid sank down in the chairs in front of the desk.

"Fuck, Hawk, they're targeting the women in both clubs. We need to warn Doc and we'll have to warn Dagger. River is under his club's protection. Do you think this is the old woman's next play?" Ice battled to calm himself as he waited for his presidents' answer.

Hawk sat back in his chair with his hands over his face then slammed them back down on his desk. "Lock it down. Get every single fucking female back here and lock it down. We can defend from here but not if everybody is scattered all over the fucking place."

"Hang on a minute, Prez." Ice cautioned. "Just think about it. What if that's exactly what they want? All of us and the women in one place. What if we haven't found all the bastards working with the fucking old woman? What if they come at us like they did in Durban?"

Hawk looked as if he was about to explode but calmed slightly. "Okay, I'm listening."

"Let me set the shit up with Emma. We keep an eye on her and gather more information before we move on this. In the meantime we make damned sure the women are never without a guard. It will spread us thin but it seems like we're the only chapter being targeted at the moment. We could call in some of the brothers from the other chapters to help out."

Kid nodded. "Yeah, it's a damned good plan. We call a general meeting or something and call in specific brothers, some of the Nomads as well. They wouldn't know we're calling in an army as we wait for their next fucked up move."

Hawk was about to say something when his phone rang and when he glanced down and saw the caller ID he held up a hand.

"Hey, little bird, I'm in the middle of some shit here. Can I call you back in a few minutes?"

His expression went nuclear as he listened. Ice glanced at Kid with a frown before he looked back at his president. What the hell was going on now?

"Lock the doors. All of you in the office. No one leaves, DC. No one. Who's on duty today?"

He nodded and Ice could see him calm slightly.

"Good. Call Doc, he needs to send brothers to escort Nadja and Grace. We've got you and the others. We'll be there as soon as we can, little bird. Sit tight, okay?"

As soon as the dropped his phone he barked out orders.

"Ice, get the big cage ready to take DC and her people home. I want you behind the wheel. Kid, call in the brothers who are nearest, we're on our bikes. The bitch just made her next move." He stood as he spoke and moved around the desk. "An hour ago an official from the Department of Health arrived at DC's shop and told her they were investigating complaints about hygiene violations. He obviously didn't find anything but informed her it's standard practice to close down the shop until they've done their investigation. He wanted them to vacate the premises immediately and give him the keys, DC refused. She insisted on having her lawyer present. And the fucker became a tiny bit too antsy. My woman is concerned about his motivations. Gav and Sam escorted him and his sidekick out. Now they're all tucked away in the office waiting for us. Let's ride."

Ice didn't waste any time. He ran out to the garage and pulled the huge SUV out. He hit the road and called up the shortest route to Melville on the on-board computer. Plugging his phone into the phone dock he dialled Hawk. He knew his cousin would be wearing his full-face helmet with his phone plugged in.

"Hawk." His cousin snarled over the sound of his bike roaring.

"I'm on the road and taking the shortest route I can. I've got Boots and Wolf escorting me. You hit the road and ride hard, cuz. See you there."

Ice didn't expect an answer from Hawk and there wasn't any.

The threat to the club had now sharply escalated. No one made threats against the women and children of a biker club and lived to tell the tale. They could not allow this to stand.

Blood was going to be spilled and very soon.

Later that night after everyone had been taken care of Ice sat at the bar and stared down at his phone. As much as he hated it he was going to have to do it. Slamming a shot down he cracked his neck and started typing.

Emma, we need to talk. When can we meet?

The answer came back almost immediately.

I'm on a rotational shift this week but I'm free next week. How about Tuesday evening at my place?

Jesus. Fuck.

Okay. I'll be there at 7.30pm

The answer came back almost instantaneous.

Looking forward to it, Gray

Jesus. It made him want to vomit but he slammed down several more shots before he stumbled up to his room where he fell on his bed and passed out.

CHAPTER SEVEN

Ice

Tuesday night came way too soon and Ice swallowed down his anger as he and Kid pulled up in front of Emma's house. It was just as ostentatious as Hawk had described it. A fucking mac-mansion. Ice went over the floor plan in his head as he rang the bell.

He looked back at Kid, who sat on his bike, his legs stretched out, crossed at the ankles and feet resting on the curb. The asshole grinned as he crossed his arms over his chest and sat there like he owned the damned place.

Why the fuck did the bitch have a doorbell when she was the one giving her visitors access to the fucking estate? Fucking stupid.

The bitch opened the door and was dressed unlike anything he had expected. Ice almost laughed at her attempt to look like a biker chick. She stood smiling up at him in a tiny little denim skirt with a very low cut tank top and bare feet. With the conservative hairstyle and make up it just didn't work. Although it showcased her tits and ass to the max Ice's cock stayed completely uninterested. Her perfume hung like a heavy invasive cloud in the air and gave him an instant headache.

He avoided the hug she was planning to give him and stepped past her into the house. She frowned at Kid sitting at the curb before closing the door.

"This is some house you have here, Emma." He prodded and she reacted as planned.

"I love it. I designed it with the architect employed by the estate and everything is exactly as I want it."

How long has the bitch been back in the country? He needed Ziggy to find out.

Ice slipped his keys into his pocket but set his helmet down on the easy chair in the lounge as he nodded with feigned interest.

"Let me show you around, I know you'll love it as much as I do. It's exactly like the house we dreamed about years ago."

Where the fuck did this bitch come up with this shit? He had never in his life said he wanted to live in some fucked up Tuscan Mac-Mansion in some pussy estate. But he played along and nodded.

Ice followed her through the house, starting downstairs and ending upstairs where she had an office and the main bedroom. While she wandered around ahead of him pointing out the built in shelves he planted a tiny bug and camera in those very same shelves while pretending to look at books. When they reached the bedroom Emma obviously had plans to get him on the bed and he avoided her grabby fucking hands.

"I'm here to talk, Emma. Fucking you will just cloud the issues between us."

She was visibly pissed. "We never fucked, Gray. You always made love to me."

"Be that as it may, I'm not here for sex. We need to talk about the shit between us before anything else can happen."

Her face brightened as she nodded and Ice immediately left her room and made his way back to the lounge. He sat in the easy chair with his helmet on his lap as he waited for her. He didn't have to wait long.

"I'm having a glass of wine can I get you a beer? I bought the kind you always preferred when we were together."

Not happening. "No thanks, I'm on my bike and I don't drink and ride."

Something sly slid through her eyes and he wondered if he would have been able to leave if he had taken her up on the beer. Probably not. Thank fuck Kid was waiting for him outside.

He watched as she settled herself in what she most probably thought was a sexy pose across from him. It made him want to puke when he realised she wasn't wearing any panties and flashed him every time she crossed and uncrossed her legs. Which she did a lot.

He needed to get the fuck out of here before his head exploded.

"You said you used Jane's lies as an excuse to get away from me. Why?"

Emma rubbed a finger along the edge of her skirt trying to get him to focus there instead of on her eyes. He didn't.

"The club was turning you into someone I didn't know or liked and it scared me. I didn't want our children growing up in such a violent and debouched environment but you wouldn't listen to me. You insisted on following your dad into the club. You had so much potential to become one of the best lawyers in the country and you were throwing your life away on people who didn't have your best interests at heart. I had no option but to leave to force you to come after me. I was pregnant and I needed you to be a father to my child not to be some biker with no prospects."

Ice nodded, noting that she called the baby her child and not theirs. "So it was all a plan to get me to come after you. To leave the club for you and your baby."

She tried to look sad but he saw right through her pretence.

"When you say it like that it sounds so cold and calculating but it wasn't like that." She wiped underneath her eyes as if she was wiping away tears, but there were none there to wipe.

"If I scared you so much years ago why are you back? You have to know I'm much worse now than the man who scared you seven years ago. And the way you left pissed me off. I hated you for a long time but I got over it. I got over you and moved on with my life."

She smiled as if he was being a silly little boy and her voice when she spoke had the same inflection.

"Everyone can change if they really want to, you can be the man I always knew you could be. Gray, you will always love me. We are soul mates, meant to be. We both knew it when we first saw each other.

Even as a fifteen year old I knew you were going to be mine and I was going to be yours forever." She again slipped that leg over ever so slowly as she flashed him yet again and this time he looked and felt abso-fucking-lutely nothing.

Slowly lifting his eyes he looked at her with absolutely no expression on his face and in his eyes. He kept it dead.

"I have a lot I need to think about. I'll call you."

He was up and moving to the door before she could do anything but follow him out.

He felt her eyes boring into his back as they rode away. The entire encounter with the bitch had left him feeling dirty and invaded and he couldn't wait to get home.

He only started breathing normally when he rode through the gates of the compound.

Emma Coetzee was seriously fucked in the head. He now knew it for a fact. And he wasn't going back into her fucking house anytime soon.

Not if he didn't have to and not without back up.

He was fucking relieved he hadn't started anything with River. It would have put her right in the middle of this mess.

RENÉ VAN DALEN

River

Ten days. Ten days since I had made a big mistake that left me feeling empty and used, and the bastard was still on my mind. I wanted to kick my own ass at my stupidity.

It's not like I haven't been busy living my life. I have. But late at night when I lay in bed in the dark thoughts of the bastard flooded my mind. And spiked my damned libido.

But I was fighting the vivid memories, fighting my libido. The man was an asshole.

And not a little one either.

Ugh. Now I was thinking about another part of him that wasn't little.

Damn.

CHAPTER EIGHT

Hawk

Hawk was impatiently waiting for Ice to get back so his VP could listen to the recording of the call the bitch had made shortly after he had left her house. They needed to find out who she was calling and Ziggy was already following up on it.

The shit the bitch told Ice had made Hawk want to thank whatever deity had saved his cousin from making the biggest mistake of his life. He was no longer sure the kid she had apparently lost had been Ice's. Her choice of words had been very specific.

She needed him as a father to her child. Not their child. Her child.

Who the hell had she been fucking while she had been with Ice? Turning to Ziggy Hawk set him a new search. Find the fucker and find him fast. There had to be a trail somewhere, they just had to find it.

Ice

Ice walked into the clubhouse and straight to the bar. He needed a drink, badly. Sniffing at his clothes he swore he could smell her heavy perfume on him. He didn't waste time going up to his room to change. He took off his kutte, laid it on the bar then ripped his ruined tee off and threw it behind the bar.

"You can use that as a bar rag." He snarled at the prospect pouring his shot. "And wipe my kutte, it fucking stinks."

The prospect grabbed a clean rag, tipped a bit of Vodka on it and wiped his kutte down before handing it back. Sniffing it Ice grunted and pulled it on over his naked chest.

He was on his second shot when Hawk walked in and grinned. "Starting to strip a bit early aren't you, brother."

"Fuck you, Hawk. She ruined my fucking tee with her heavy perfume. Couldn't stand smelling it another second."

Hawk leant closer and sniffed loudly. "Hell, my brother, you smell like a hooker." He teased. "Finish your shot and come to my office."

Following Hawk into the office he sank down in a chair then sniffed his arm. Fuck, he could still smell her on him. It made his stomach turn and he swallowed hard. He needed a shower and very damned soon or he was going to hurl.

"Stop fucking smelling yourself, Ice." Hawk growled.

"Can't help it. I can smell her on me and it's making me want to hurl. I need a fucking shower." Ice growled right back.

"Fuck, go, but make it fucking quick."

Ice didn't hesitate, he was out of there and up the stairs to his bedroom. Minutes later he was in a hot shower scrubbing her stink off him and airing his kutte in the steam. Pulling on clean clothes he didn't linger and ten minutes later walked back into Hawk's office.

"Right, now that Ice no longer smells like a hooker let's get to it." Hawk said with an evil grin.

Ice knew he was never going to live it down.

"Ziggy, give us what you got."

Ziggy had his laptop plugged into the large television against the wall and immediately several different views of the inside of Emma's house appeared on the screen.

"These are the views of the cameras Ice was able to place around the house. We've got the front entry, the kitchen, the lounge, her office and her bedroom. The bugs were planted in the same rooms and we've got great visual and audio."

He clicked a couple of times and played a small clip of Ice talking to Emma, and don't you know, the camera he had placed next to the chair gave a perfect view of her fucking snatch.

"Fuck me." Kid swore. "You sat there while she flashed you her snatch and didn't take her up on her offer."

"I wouldn't fuck her with my worst enemy's dick." Ice snarled. "Get that shit off the screen, brother, it makes me want to vomit."

Ziggy nodded and clicked a few buttons on his laptop.

"This is what happened after you left." Ziggy said as he clicked on an icon on the side of the screen.

Ice listened as she reported their conversation almost word for word to whoever she had called. She promised she would get more usable information when she saw him because she knew his weaknesses and how to play on them. And if that didn't work they could always go with the drugs. Either way they would have the information they wanted as long as whoever she was talking to guaranteed Ice would be unharmed when the time came. She didn't care about anyone else as long as Ice made it through. She asked about the action taken against the soft targets they had identified. Unfortunately they didn't clarify who they were talking about. He supposed that one of those targets had been DC's shop.

As the screen went blank they all sat back and looked at each other.

"She's deep inside the organisation and by the sound of it has been for years. We need to dig deeper into her background, her mother's background, and we have to find out who her father was." Ice tapped his fingers against the arm of the chair as he stared at the black television screen. "She never spoke about him and neither did her mother. We need to find him and find their connection to the Maingarde Organisation."

"Ice is right." Hawk said. "We keep eyes on the bitch and in the meantime Ziggy gets us everything on her family. Let's proceed carefully with this shit." Hawk turned to Ice and he knew he wasn't going to like his presidents' next words.

"If she wants to meet up you go and play nice. But you don't go on your own, no matter what she fucking says. You'll have a brother with you at all times. We can't take the chance that she won't drug you and hand you over to whoever is pulling her strings."

"Jesus. Okay, Prez. But you fuckers are going to owe me a huge fucking party for this shit. This bitch is seriously not right in the head." Ice grimaced. "Plus she smells like she dumped an entire bottle of some horrible smelling perfume on herself."

Laughter rang through the office and it made Ice feel better. He was home and surrounded by his brothers who would always have his back.

Hawk grinned. "We can make that happen, Ice. You get us what we need and we throw you a blow-out party. And we'll send your kutte to be cleaned because I'm sure by the time this ends it is going to smell to high heaven."

Ice shook his head as his brothers laughed. The next few weeks were going to be hell.

Hell that smelt like a fucking hooker.

Ice couldn't sleep. He was sure he could still smell River on his sheets and that was total bullshit because they had been washed.

Rolling on his back he lay staring at the ceiling reliving their one night together. It had been the best sex of his life with a woman that stirred something inside him.

He wanted to see her again. No, if he had to be honest, the truth was he needed to see her again.

Coming to an instant decision he rolled out of bed and got dressed in the semi-dark. Shrugging on his kutte he grabbed his keys and left his room. As he quietly locked his door the door next to his opened and Kid stood in the open door, just looking at him.

"Anything you need, brother." Kid said quietly.

"I need to ride." Ice answered as quietly.

"Give me a minute." He disappeared into his room and Ice leant against the wall waiting.

He didn't have to wait long. Soon they were outside and riding out the gate. Ice breathed in the night air as they rode and without a conscious thought steered his bike to where a woman he wanted with everything inside of him lay sleeping.

They rode past the closed gates and Ice grunted in disappointment. Her cottage wasn't visible from the street. The main house, her parents' house, hid it from view. It was a quiet neighbourhood and the sound of their bikes started a dog barking and Ice gave the house one last look before he rode away.

On their way back Kid sped in front of him and took the off ramp to the all night petrol station and diner next to the highway. Minutes later they were sitting across from each other with cups of coffee.

"What did we just do, brother?" Kid asked as he blew on his coffee to cool it down.

Ice shook his head. "I don't fucking know what I'm doing. I just had to be near her. I know I can't go there, but fuck brother." Letting out a hard breath he looked up. "I think she's the one for me and I've already fucked it up. And now there's all this Emma shit I have to handle."

"One thing at a time, brother. Take it one thing at a time. While you deal with Emma I'll watch your back, no worries, Ice." He grinned. "And the next time you need to do a drive-by you call me. I've got your back, brother."

Ice grinned. "Thanks, brother. Let's get out of here, their coffee sucks."

He felt slightly more at peace when he slid back into bed and closed his eyes.

CHAPTER NINE

River

Four weeks ago I made a huge mistake. A mistake that left me once again feeling the emptiness I had felt after Dylan's death. I didn't go to the damned party to find some man and have sex. I went because I thought (and wrongly I now know) I would stay a little while, hang out with DC and then go home.

Unfortunately that's not what happened.

I allowed myself to be seduced by a man who had made me feel something for the first time since Duncan was born.

I stupidly allowed myself to be used and the next morning chucked to the side.

I'm not saying it wasn't one of the best nights of my life, because it was. For a few hours I forgot about the constant ache living in my heart and allowed myself to just feel.

And boy did I feel. I felt so much and I mistakenly thought he had as well.

The way he left me said it all. He didn't even stay in bed with me. I woke up alone and thought he had gone for coffee or some shit. But no, that was not it. He had left me after he'd had his fill and went to sleep in the guestroom, a clear sign that it was a one-and-done as far as he was concerned.

Now I was here, ignoring the little glances Wrench threw me as we worked and doing my best to get on with my life. But the big bastard had woken something up inside me and now I couldn't get it to shut the hell up.

I angrily banged at the broken exhaust I was removing from a Ducatti that refused to move.

"River." My dad's voice sounded over the banging and the music.

Looking up I saw him standing in the open door with a man in a grey suit and a woman dressed in a dark brown conservative dress with brown conservative hair and brown conservative shoes. What now?

I put the tools down and stood. "Yes, Dad?"

They came walking towards me and I saw Wrench moving to the side where he could keep an eye on them.

My dad was furious but hiding it really well.

"River, this is Mr du Plessis and Mrs Havenga from the Department of Child Welfare. According to them they've been notified by Duncan's pre-school that they received complaints from a Dr Coetzee accusing you of neglecting Duncan and exposing him to unsavoury characters."

"What?" I was shocked and stunned. "That's an absolute lie. Who is this Dr Coetzee? I've never heard of him."

"Ms Anderson, I'm sorry to just drop in on you like this." The woman said with a fake smile. "We just wanted to meet you and compare your situation to the information we've been given."

"Information you've been given about me? And what did your informant say about me?"

The man answered. "The informant said you didn't have any formal employment. Your father informed us our information was incorrect."

I shook my head as I frowned at the two government assholes. Okay, maybe not assholes, just people trying to do their jobs after receiving bogus information.

"Why don't we sit down and you can tell me why you're here because I have no idea what's going on here."

I led them over to the couches and waited for the two to sit down and the woman immediately opened her briefcase and pulled out a thin file. I sat on the other couch with my dad by my side and waited. And then the woman shook the foundations of my world.

"The principal of your son's pre-school contacted my department after she received a letter from Dr Coetzee, a paediatrician practising at the Midrand Hospital. Dr Coetzee's letter stated she had been made aware that the child, Duncan Anderson Martins, was being exposed to drugs and drunken and debouched behaviour by his mother and her choice of companions. She claimed you have used drugs on several occasions while Duncan was in your care, Ms Anderson. Dr Coetzee is highly respected in her field and we have her sworn statement about the information she received of you participating in a drunken orgy at the Iron Dogz biker gang's clubhouse four weeks ago. She supplied us with photographic evidence of the occurrence."

Anger unlike anything I had ever felt before rolled through me and I had to swallow hard to keep a hold on it.

"You have been misinformed. They're a club not a gang. I was invited to celebrate the engagement of DC Michaels to Hawk Walker at a family *braai* held at the Iron Dogz MC's compound. DC is a client of mine and I attended as a courtesy to my client. We ate, had a couple of drinks, danced and DC offered me a guestroom because I didn't want to drive after having a few drinks. I stayed the night, and left early the next morning. It was my first and only visit to the clubhouse. I have not been back nor have I had any other contact with them."

The man sat taking notes as I spoke but I ignored him. The old bag in front of me was the one who had it in for me.

"Thank you for you honesty. There is another complaint and this is the one that worries me the most." She said insincerely. "Did you leave your son at the Sinner's Sons biker gang's clubhouse with questionable supervision while you attended the party? Leaving him vulnerable and exposed to drugs, alcohol and depraved sexual practices."

What the hell was going on here? Who was targeting me? Someone wanted to take Duncan away from me and I won't allow it.

"Again, they're a club not a gang. And no, I did not. My son went on a camping trip with his uncle, Darren Martins. I didn't just drop him off and leave. I helped pack the vehicles along with the mothers of the other children who went on the camping trip. It was a bonding weekend between fathers and their children. My son lost his father before he was born and his uncle, Darren Martins, took him on the weekend.

"Darren loves Duncan and would never, ever expose him to the stuff you are accusing us of. I have no idea where this Dr Coetzee is getting her information from and I really don't care, she is lying. And I would just like to add, I have never taken my son to the Midrand Hospital to be examined by Dr Coetzee. His paediatrician is Dr Elaine Brummer and I can give you her contact details if you need them."

For the first time the guy spoke and I could see in his eyes he wasn't in agreement with the bitch by his side.

"Ms Anderson, we need to inspect Duncan's living conditions and your home to make an informed decision. And I would advise you to retain legal advice. Should we find it necessary Duncan will be removed from your care and placed with either a close family member or in a place of safety."

Horror curled through me at the thought of losing my boykie.

"Sure, you can come and inspect my home. I have nothing to hide. We can go right now if you want."

He shook his head when the bitch was about to answer. He answered instead.

"No, we are doing this by the book. We will do a home visit tomorrow morning at eleven. Please be available to show us around. We have all we need for now. Thanks for seeing us and we'll see ourselves out."

With that he got up, handed me a piece of paper and they left. I sat frozen on the couch and my dad took the paper from me. Who hated me enough to try and take my son from me? I turned and looked at my dad and the tears just started pouring. I leant against his chest and shuddered as the tears kept coming. I was being held tight in arms that had comforted me so many times before. But I needed to pull myself together. I had a fight on my hands and I wasn't going to go down, not now, not ever.

Whoever this Dr Coetzee bitch was she had not ever come across someone like me. Someone who had lost a part of herself and had come out the other side stronger than ever.

"I need to find a lawyer. And I need to speak to Annette at the pre-school to find out why she didn't contact me when she received the letter. She knows me, she knows Duncan. Why the hell did she go to the department without talking to me?"

But dad disagreed.

"No. You're not going to talk to anyone, our lawyer is going to be doing the talking. This sounds like an elaborate scheme to discredit you and have Duncan taken from us. We're not putting one foot out of line and running the risk of losing Duncan. Don't worry, sweetheart, we'll get this sorted out."

I shook my head and my dad's eyes narrowed. "Dad, I've never heard of this paediatrician. How the hell can she hand in a report on Duncan? He's never been sick enough or hurt enough to be taken to a hospital. And if he had been I wouldn't have taken him to a Midrand hospital. We would have taken him to Century Clinic were Dr Elaine would have taken care of him. She has been his paediatrician since the day he was born. When he stays with Dagger and complains about any damn thing he calls her. He calls her so damn much they're on a first name basis!"

Wrench suddenly spoke. "I don't like the sound of this, Boss. I think we need to let Dagger and Hawk know what's going on."

Before I could say a word my dad jumped in. "I can understand calling Dagger but what has Hawk Walker got to do with this?"

"They're accusing River of taking part in an orgy at our clubhouse and I know for a fact it's a lie. I was on duty the night of the party and there definitely wasn't any funny business. Yes, everyone was drinking and dancing but that was all. It was a family party, not an orgy like they are trying to make out." Wrench explained to my dad.

"I'm going to fetch Duncan from pre-school. I don't want him to be somewhere these people can get to him." I jumped up and ran for my keys.

"You fetch my little brother, Boss, I've got things here, no worries." Wrench called out.

"Dad, will you call the lawyer and send him the paperwork they gave me please?"

"You fetch our boy, sweetheart. I'll get on to the lawyer immediately."

My dad must have called the pre-school as well because Annette was waiting for me when I arrived. I could see she didn't know what to say to me so I didn't say anything, just asked for Duncan to be brought to me. It was while we were waiting that she spoke.

"Please understand that I did what I had to do. We have strict rules we adhere to when we receive complaints, however unsubstantiated they may be. We know your parents, we know you and we know Duncan. Please know that we know this is a pack of lies and I made sure that I stated it clearly in my e-mail to the Department. I feel sure Mr du Plessis will sort this out, he's a good man to have in your corner."

The sigh that rushed out of me was heavy. "He's not the one I'm worried about, Annette. There's a Mrs Havenga involved in this mess and she's the one I'm worried about."

Annette smiled. "Don't worry about it, River. It will all be over before you know it. I'll just go check Duncan has everything, one moment."

As she walked away I stood there and wondered why my life had taken this sudden awful turn. A soft tap on my elbow had me almost jumping out of my boots I was so deep in thought. The shy and soft spoken new receptionist stood behind me and she looked really worried and glanced around furtively as if she was scared someone might see her.

"I know you don't know me, and you have no reason to trust me, but if I didn't say anything I will never forgive myself if something happened to Duncan."

Cold dread curled through my body at her whispered words.

"What do you mean?"

The young woman looked at her feet drew in a deep breath and what she said made every single hair on my body stand straight up in horror.

"At my previous job I heard rumours about the children taken away by Havenga, they were never given back to their parents. They disappear into the system and are never seen again. Get help, quickly. And don't leave her alone when she does her home visit. She plants evidence so they can take your kid and put you in jail. Please, River, call someone, get some help. Tonight. Don't wait."

Oh sweet baby Jesus.

All I could do was nod and she scurried away, disappearing into the office as if we had never spoken.

Duncan came running towards me with a wide smile and I swallowed down my fear and smiled as I hugged him.

"You're early, Mumma."

"I know, but I missed you and decided to come fetch you so we can spend some time together."

He clapped his hands and danced in place. "I know, I know, we can have horrogs and chocolate milk and play with my army men."

I laughed. "It's hot dogs, not horrogs, boykie."

He wrinkled his little nose in disgust. "No, uh-uh, it's horrogs. Dogs are our friends, and we can't cook our friends and eat them. That's yucky."

Wasting no more time trying to explain I signed him out. Duncan was still talking nonstop as I strapped him into his car seat then got in and drove us to the workshop. I was going to take the receptionist's advice and get us some help. And while I did I wanted us to be surrounded by the people who cared about us. For the first time in years I was nervous about being home alone.

Later that night I sat in my small lounge filled with men in leather kuttes. Dagger and some of his brothers had arrived shortly after Duncan and I got home. My boykie had been over the moon to see his uncle and had been super excited when we ordered take aways for dinner. I let him run around quite late before getting him bathed and into bed. He would not be going to pre-school in the morning.

And he got his uncle Dagger to read him his bedtime story. Now he had his music softly playing and was fast asleep. The baby monitor sat on the side table next to my chair.

It was time for us to come up with a plan of action for tomorrow and for the following days until this mess was sorted out.

"We've got two of the prospects going through your garages right now and early tomorrow morning Jinx will bring Kaizer over, he's a retired drug sniffer dog and he's still on top of his game. We use him all the time. I've put two brothers on guard duty outside and we'll keep a presence here until this shit is sorted. I'll be here in the morning and stay with Jinx and the dog until the government bitch leaves. With Kaizer on her ass there's no way she'll be able to plant drugs in the house. So don't worry about it, Rivzie."

God, every time he called me Rivzie the ache in my heart was almost unbearable. It had been Dylan's pet name for me and to hear it was a bittersweet ache.

"Okay, Duncan is going to stay with mum at the house and dad will be here with me. They can just damned well deal with my family getting involved. Our lawyer called in a colleague who specialises in children's cases. She will be here at ten so we can go over everything. She called me earlier and after I told her what had happened she was confident the complaint would be thrown out as spurious."

I laughed when quite few confused huh's sounded. "I had to look it up as well. It means fake, false, forged or deceitful. Take your pick."

Dagger raised his eyebrows then asked questions I couldn't answer. "And the photos dad was telling me about? The so-called photographic evidence of you participating in an orgy. What the hell is that about?"

Before Dylan died my parents and Dagger had become very close and they insisted he call them mum and dad, like his brother did. As far as they were concerned he was their family because he was

Dylan's brother and Duncan's uncle. My dad treated him exactly the same way he did my brother Lake. Like his son.

My dad spoke up even as I opened my mouth to explain.

"I visited Hawk Walker this afternoon and he said he would provide us with photos and video evidence which will prove the department's evidence has been photoshopped. He assured me they are investigating Dr Emma Coetzee from their side. She's apparently the ex-fiancée of their VP, Ice Walker, and she recently returned from overseas."

Dagger frowned at me and I kept my horrified reaction from my face.

"Why the hell would Ice's woman have her claws out for you, Rivzie?"

Deny, deny, deny. That's all I could do.

"I have no idea. I ate dinner with Hawk, DC and Ice, and then had a few drinks at the bar with them. Danced with DC and her girlfriends and then went to bed because I didn't want to drive home after drinking. Ice gave me his room and he stayed in the guestroom. I left early the next morning and came home. That's it."

He stared at me with narrowed eyes as if he could see right into my head. I knew he knew something wasn't right. I could see it in his eyes and the look did not mean good things for me. At some time in the future he would be asking questions I would find very difficult to answer.

"Is that all that happened?" Dagger growled.

"Yes." I nodded but stopped myself before I turned into a lying nodding bubble headed doll.

"Okay. I suggest we all get some sleep then meet here again tomorrow morning at eight. It will give us enough time to do one more sweep of the garden and Duncan's play area before the fuckers get here."

And then I was alone with my fears. My prayer as I lay in bed staring at the ceiling was a short one.

Please God, keep us safe tomorrow.

CHAPTER TEN

River

Morning came too quickly and the coming day hung around my shoulders like the weight of a heavy coat. Even with everyone telling me not to worry I was worried. If anyone had seen Ice leaving his room in the early hours of the morning it would not look good for me. And what about the cameras the Dogz had around their clubhouse? Would they not prove he had spent part of the night with me? Or will Hawk make it disappear?

I turned to where Dylan's photo sat in a heavy silver frame on my bedside table. I missed him and with what was happening in my life right now I missed him even more.

"I did something crazy, Dylan, and now our son is in danger. I feel so damned stupid." I said softly.

But of course my smiling man gave me no answers. Not that I expected any. With a heavy sigh I got out of bed, did my business then peeked into Duncan's room. He lay on his back, spread out like a little starfish and still fast asleep. I left him sleeping and went to the kitchen, turning the alarm off on my way there. I was in dire need of some coffee, very strong coffee. Preparing the French press I waited for the kettle to boil then poured the boiling water over the ground coffee and let it steep while I set out the milk and sugar.

Slowly pushing the plunger down the delicious scent of my favourite brew filled the kitchen. My mug stood ready and I poured then added a drop of milk and one sugar. I was sitting at the four-seater kitchen table taking small sips of the hot coffee when my dad appeared at the glass slider that served as my back door.

To open the door I had to go through a huge rigmarole. First I unlocked three locks on the security gate and shoved it back on its track, took the dowel rod out of the track of the sliding door, then unlocked the three locks on that door and slid it open.

Every time I did this I saw Dylan's face. He wanted to ensure we would be safe when he wasn't home and with Dagger's help had made our little home as safe as possible. Dylan had built the wide covered wooden deck with the help of some of his brothers. The deck ran along the entire back of the house and we had used it often. Our house had been open to his club brothers and they visited often. Sometimes crashing on the loungers after too many beers.

Some of the brothers still visited but mostly only if Dagger was at the house. I missed those carefree days.

"Morning, Dad. Want some coffee?"

"Please. Your mother is going crazy in the kitchen making food for an army. I couldn't get near the damn coffee and when I tried she smacked my hand with a wooden spoon." He grinned. "She's so damned feisty."

My parents were so sweet.

But then the grin disappeared and he turned serious. "We don't want you to worry today. We've got this, sweetheart. The bitch isn't going to take your boy from you, believe me. She's going to be watched very carefully the entire time she's on our property."

"I'm just scared we miss something, Dad."

"We're not going to miss a thing, and our boy will be safe even if we have to keep him home until this shit has been cleared up. Your mum is home every day and I can leave Jannie in charge for a while and stay with them. And we'll have the Sinners keeping an eye out. You will both be safe, River. I promise."

Duncan came shuffling in and we stopped talking immediately. He came straight to me and crawled into my lap. Not his normal early morning routine.

"Hey sweetie pie, did you have a good sleep?" I hugged him to me and pressed a soft kiss to his hair.

He didn't say anything, just nodded. My boy had not woken up in a good mood.

"Morning, boykie. Nana is making a huge breakfast. Uncle Dagger and Uncle Jinx are coming over this morning. Would you like to have breakfast with everyone at our house?" Dad asked.

Duncan's head slowly turned to look at my dad. "Hey, Grampa, did Nana make bacons?"

My dad grinned. "Oh, yes she did, lots. We can't have a big breakfast without bacon."

I tipped his head up and kissed his forehead. "You're coming to work with me today, boykie. Dress in your workshop clothes and don't forget your overall, okay?"

The bad mood disappeared instantly. "Okay. I'm going to work with Mumma and Wrench 'cause I'm getting big." He informed his grampa.

"That's right my boy. You're going to need a big breakfast to get through the day. Brush teeth and get dressed then you and I will go to my house while your mumma gets ready. We can help Nana lay the table on the back veranda."

"Okay." With a big smile he jumped off my lap and ran to his room.

"Thanks, Dad."

"My pleasure, River. That boy means the world to us."

My boy meant the world to a lot of people and they would all be here today to take our backs.

Dagger and Jinx arrived promptly at eight with a beautiful dog Duncan promptly fell in love with. He chattered non-stop as he followed Jinx around while Kaizer sniffed for drugs. Obviously they found nothing. After a breakfast with quite a few of the Sinner's Sons, Duncan and Kaizer played on the lawn while the men watched.

The lawyer arrived promptly at ten and I immediately liked her. Dahlia Sawyer was a take-no-prisoners kind of woman and I trusted her to keep my son out of Mrs Havenga's clutches. I invited her into my house and gave her my entire history. My rebellious teens, meeting Dylan, falling pregnant, losing Dylan. I told her everything and left nothing out. Not even the night I spent with Ice. She needed to know everything to keep us safe.

"I find it very suspicious that the department is wasting their time on a report which has very obviously been fabricated. When they get here I'll have a short consultation with them and lay out our case. Then take them on an inspection tour. At no time will I leave either of them alone and there will be no photos taken outside or inside the premises. Until we can prove otherwise I think we go with the rather safe than sorry approach." She smiled at Kaizer where he lay watching us intently from the open front door. "If she's carrying any drugs in her bag or on her person he won't allow her in the house and we'll know the information we received was correct. I'm not sure how we'll proceed from there because Kaizer isn't employed as a SAPS sniffer dog so it will be difficult to present the evidence. But it might just be enough to scare whoever is behind this off."

"When they leave today do you think it's necessary to keep the guards in place?"

Dahlia narrowed her eyes as she thought about it. "I think we keep them in place. We wait for the report from the department before we take the next step."

"I just don't understand why this is happening."

She suddenly laughed. "This Ice you had the little fling with, is he hot?"

"Scorching." I widened my eyes and waved a hand in front of my face.

Dahlia gave me a wicked grin. "Maybe after seeing those photographs his ex, Dr Coetzee, is jealous of the time you spent with Ice at the *braai*. And this is her way of hurting you and getting you out of the way. It happens more often than you might think. Her vindictiveness is wasting the departments' time, your time and mine. Not that I mind being here, I'm glad I'm able to help."

"I don't mind losing a few hours if it means my son is safe. His safety is the most important thing to me."

A white sedan with government issued plates pulled into the drive about fifteen minutes later and I saw the way the Havenga bitch looked around. Her eyes skating over the security lights and cameras under the eaves of my parents' house and my cottage. What the hell was she looking for?

Her eyes widened when she saw the leather kutte wearing men guarding both houses. She hitched a large bag over her shoulder as she scuttled along in the wake of Mr Du Plessis towards where I waited on the patio at my front door. Next to me Dahlia made a deep hmm sound as she watched them approach.

We greeted them but when Havenga tried to walk past Kaizer he stood in her way and growled, then barked and Jinx came running. I smiled insincerely.

"Oh, I'm so sorry. He's a retired sniffer dog and something on you or in your bag has set him off. Just allow him to sniff you and your bag, he won't let you in otherwise."

She reluctantly dropped her bag from her shoulder and Kaizer sniffed it, barked then looked up at Jinx and barked again.

"He's not going to let you inside with the bag. Put it down on the bench then give it another try." Jinx growled.

Very reluctantly she dropped her big bag on the bench outside my front door and again tried to enter. This time Kaizer sniffed and growled but let her pass.

I waved them into the lounge and took a seat next to Dahlia who introduced herself as my lawyer and handed Du Plessis her card. Then she got down to business. An hour later we watched as the piece of shit government car reversed out of our drive and disappeared down the road.

"Well, that was interesting." Dahlia said softly.

"Why would it take them two weeks to enter their favourable report in the system and finalise the case? I don't buy the shit that they're short staffed."

"I don't either. I don't think Du Plessis is very happy with this case and I'll keep in touch with him. She's definitely a shady character and is worth watching. She took note of every single camera and security feature in the house and that worries me. If possible I want you to beef up your security. Re-site a few of the cameras and add others in unexpected positions. Talk to your brother-in-law, I'm sure he will know exactly what to do. If you need me don't hesitate to call, even if it's just to ask me a question or to chat. I'm here for you."

She made me feel as if everything was under control.

"Do you think Duncan should go back to pre-school or should I keep him with me for a while?"

Following her to her car I watched as she dropped her briefcase in the boot as she thought about my question.

"I wish I could say with total certainty that Duncan will be safe at school, but I can't. If you can persuade the owners of the school to have his bodyguards near then okay, but if you can't I think wait until we get a clean record from the department."

"Okay, I agree." I drew in a deep breath and let it out on a loud huff. "I'm going to keep him with me. He'll be safer here at home being watched over by the Sinner's Sons and at the workshop where I can watch him."

Sliding into her car she glanced over to where Dagger and Jinx stood watching us with their arms crossed over their wide chests. "You know, I had many pre-conceived ideas about bikers. But coming here today and watching them around you and your family was an eye-opener."

I had to laugh. "Those ideas you had about bikers, most of the time they are true. The Sinner's Sons are all about their club, brotherhood and family but believe me they can be wild."

"I can see it in their eyes." She smiled and started her car. "If you have any questions or just need to talk don't hesitate to call me."

"Thanks, I will. And if you ever run into another case involving a club, call me. I can give you the *skinner* (gossip) on most of the clubs around here."

Dahlia laughed. "I'll keep that in mind. Bye now."

I watched as she drove away then walked back to where Dagger and Jinx were waiting for me.

"I searched the old bitch's bag and she had baggies of meth and coke zipped into a side pocket." Jinx growled angrily. "If we didn't have Kaizer here today bad shit would have gone down."

"You and Duncan will have a man on you when you leave the property, no matter where you go. I don't like mum being here alone while you and dad go to work so I'll have a man here as well and at night there will be two here, one at the back and one at the front." Dagger looked at me as if I was going to argue with him but I just nodded my agreement. "And I'll be here as often as I can. Unfortunately the club has some shit going down that I have to see to but we'll keep you protected. If I can't be here Jinx will be here with you and our boykie."

"Dahlia said we must move the cameras around. She didn't like the way the bitch checked out the positions of the security lights and camera placements."

A shudder ran down my back as I thought about someone breaking into my home and taking my boy.

"What the hell is happening here, Dagger? It can't just be Ice's crazy ex having her claws out for me. It feels as if something else is going on but I've got no idea what it is."

Dagger threw a heavy arm around me and pulled me into his side. "Don't you worry about it, Rivzie. I'll do some digging and see what comes up. Now let's go find our boykie and get the two of you to work, okay?"

"Okay."

Dagger

Looking over River's head as he hugged her Dagger met Jinx's eyes and saw the same worry there. He was afraid he knew exactly who had targeted River and Duncan. If it was who he thought it was the fucking Dogz would have some explaining to do.

He was going to get his sister and her little man settled and then he and Hawk fucking Walker was going to have a long damned chat.

No way would he allow the dark shit engulfing the Dogz to take down his family. They have suffered enough.

CHAPTER ELEVEN

Ice

Ice sat next to Hawk and watched the men walking into Zeffers closely. Dagger, the Sinner's Sons MC's president, with two of his men came towards them, none of them smiling. The men were his Sergeant At Arms, Jinx, and his Enforcer, Bull. Big guns for a meeting on neutral ground.

Dagger had called Hawk last night to arrange a meeting on neutral ground. Hawk agreed to meet with him at Zeffers in Kosmos. Dagger hadn't said why he wanted the meet, but Ice had an idea it had to do with River.

Dagger reached their table and nodded a greeting as he sat down.

"Thanks for meeting with me, Hawk."

"No problem, man. I understand you're having family problems. How can I help?"

Dagger looked at Ice before he answered.

"You can help by telling me why Ice's bitch is targeting my sister and her son. On Friday she sent her little Welfare minion to plant enough drugs in River's house that she would have gone away for a very fucking long time and Duncan would have disappeared into the system. And according to some information which came to light shortly before the visit he would have been snatched never to be seen again."

Ice's gut turned to rock hard stone but he met Dagger's eyes unflinchingly when the man turned to him.

"You get this one warning to pass onto your bitch, Ice. Emma Coetzee's time on this fucking planet is ticking away rapidly. The Sinner's Sons MC worldwide has put their mark on her and it will stay on her until we're sure she has backed off my family. If she does not." Dagger shrugged. "Then what will be, will be."

Fucking hell. Emma was crazier than they had suspected. Glancing at his president before he answered he got the nod and then tried to explain. It didn't seem like Dagger or his men could care less what he said. Until he laid out why they hadn't taken her down yet.

"I had a relationship with the bitch seven years ago. She played me and left but a few weeks ago she came back and has been trying to get me to start it up with her again. I'm not interested but have been stringing her along to get as much information as we can. We've been investigating Emma Coetzee for a few weeks now. We have eyes and ears in her house but haven't been able to get into her car or phone yet. We suspect she has ties to the Maingarde Organisation and with Winifred Maingarde in particular. We need to confirm this before we make our move."

Ice could see the rage burning in Dagger's eyes as he battled to get it under control.

"So, my four year old nephew is now the target of those sick fucks because your fucking bitch saw a few photos of you and River at a party and got jealous." Jinx put his hand on his presidents' shoulder and Ice could see that hand squeeze hard. The man's eyes were on him though and they were empty. Just nothing.

"Which photos are you talking about, Dagger?" Hawk asked quietly. "I don't remember any photos of River and Ice among the ones we sent to James."

"The Welfare bitch had photos of the party at your clubhouse. Your VP looked pretty fucking cosy with River but she assured me the photos had been photoshopped. And that's the only reason why I'm not killing him right the fuck now for putting his hands on my brother's old lady." Dagger snarled through gritted teeth.

Before he could shut himself up the words tumbled out of Ice's mouth. "She's his widow, Dagger, and he's no longer with us to claim her as his."

Dagger lunged across the table and shoved his face into Ice's. "She will fucking always be Sparrow's old lady, always motherfucker. And don't you fucking forget it."

Jinx had his hand on his presidents' shoulder and pulled him back into his chair.

Hawk pushed against Ice's chest when he started to react to the challenge, and then he gave Dagger the information they had so far.

"Dagger, it's actually good news. We have the bitch who took the photos and a positive ID of the woman who ordered her to take those photos. And now we know who she passed them on to and why. We're getting close. We just need a week or two and we should have it shut down and your nephew and River will be safe."

Ice clenched his teeth to stop from blurting it out, yes they will be safe. Because he was going to personally ensure that they were safe.

He had been unable to get her out of his head and no matter how many times he met up with Emma it was River who appeared behind his eyelids when he closed his eyes at night. He had spent one night with her and he was fucked. It was River who starred in his erotic dreams and had him jerking off in the shower more times than he cared to think about. An image of her smiling face underneath him suddenly appeared in his head but it disappeared when he heard Dagger's next words.

"Why waste time investigating her, why haven't you snatched her and called Doc in to let his Crow get you what you need? He's family and surely he'll do you a favour. It will end this fucking shit in a few hours not a few weeks."

Hawk just shook his head but Ice could see his cousin was trying hard to stay calm. He would never allow his little bird to get involved.

"I can't, Dagger. The Crow has been sent on another mission and won't be back for a while. In the meantime we're getting as much as we can, anyway we can. It's slow going, I know, but we'll get this bitch. You have my word on it."

Dagger picked up his beer and downed it then very carefully put the empty bottle down.

"I've got men on my family, because that's what they are, they are my family. But I had no idea who we were protecting them from until now. I need to get out of here." He stood then leant over and tapped twice on the table in front of Ice.

"If I don't hear what I need to hear within the next twenty four hours then..." He shrugged.

Dagger and his men turned and walked out, not once looking back.

Ice was about to speak but Hawk got there first. "You stay out of this, Ice. That's an order. We'll handle this as a club. Do you understand?"

There were confused looks on his brothers' faces because obviously they didn't know about him and River. Hawk apparently did.

"You got it, Prez." Ice grated out and Hawk nodded.

Ice knew exactly what Dagger, the bastard, hadn't put into words. He had given them the twenty four hours to get what they needed from Emma. At the end of those twenty four hours she would die, maybe the victim of a high jacking gone wrong or a botched robbery but the end result would be the same. She would be dead. And their link to the old bitch would be gone.

"We need to get them to back off, Prez. Once she's in the ground there goes our only link to the Maingarde bitch." Kid voiced his thoughts out loud bringing the attention back to the Emma problem.

"I know. I need to think about this. Let's get out of here."

The rode away and as they did Ice saw Wimpie waving and he gave him a low salute as he followed his prez down the road. If Wimpie had anything of value to give them he would call.

Ziggy was waiting as they parked outside the clubhouse and by his face Ice could see he had some news.

They all gathered in Hawk's office waiting to hear what Ziggy had found.

"As ordered I have been digging deep and I had to ask for help with my search. I recruited Mad Dog to help me search for anything that might throw light onto what we're facing. Early this morning he found a site on the dark web with photos of kids who will be going up for auction soon. River's little boy was one of them. We sent the links to the task force and about two hours later the site went down. Hopefully they were able to track it."

"Fuck." Ice growled. "Dagger is going to go fucking ballistic."

Hawk tapped the fingers of his left hand on the desk as the right stroked over his beard. Ice knew his cousin was considering how to resolve their problem.

"Kid, arrange for additional protection at River's workshop. Wrench is a good man but he's alone out there. I'll call Dagger and let him know what we've found."

He turned to Ziggy. "Tell me you got more on the bitch."

Ziggy grinned. "I got more on the bitch."

Linking his laptop with the television he tapped and Emma's face filled the screen. But this was Emma from years ago when she had still been Emmie, the young woman Ice had been in love with.

"She never left South Africa when she said she did. She spent some time in Cape Town and only left about four months after her supposed departure date. Someone altered all her documents but there were footprints and we followed it and were able to recover some of the data."

Ziggy clicked more on his laptop then turned to Ice and sighed. "Ice, brother, I'm so fucking sorry. I found the following documents and photos hidden in a secret cloud account. The date corresponds with the time she spent in Durban during her residency. She had a little girl. The birth certificate doesn't list a father only the mother, Emmaline Coetzee."

The next picture was of a very pregnant Emmie standing next to an older man smiling brightly into the camera. And then his heart dropped in his shoes as Ziggy clicked and a photo of a little girl who was the spitting image of Emmie appeared. She had long light brown hair, brown eyes and a wide happy smile. And she looked to be about seven years old.

What? What the fuck?

She said she lost the kid. She fucking lied. Again.

Was this his kid or was he once again being played? And where was the kid? She wasn't living with Emma in her monstrosity of a house, he had been through all the rooms and none of them had kid stuff in them. It had all been cold and clinical and empty.

He had to know because if the kid was his he had to get her out of Emma's clutches and fucking very soon.

Another thought occurred to him.

Thank fuck he hadn't started anything with River because right now that little girl on the screen was his priority and if he was her father he was fucked. He was fucked because he would go back to Emma if it was the only way he could get access to his kid.

"Do we know where this kid is? There's no sign of her living with Emma." Ice whispered.

And again Ziggy came up with the answers.

"She's living with a couple in Bryanston. She was given to them when she was a few weeks old and they are good people. David and Anna Howard. He's a school principal and she's a grade two school teacher. I checked them out and there's nothing in their backgrounds or in their bank accounts that raises any suspicions. I tracked them all the way back to primary school and I assure you there's absolutely nothing. An amount of money is deposited in their joint bank account every month which they promptly transfer out into a savings account they set up for Evie. That's her name, Evie Howard."

Evie. Evie who might be his.

Ice dropped his head into his hands and groaned. "I fucking hate Emma. What the fuck do I do if this kid is mine? I can't fucking live with the bitch."

"Ice, brother, don't go off on the deep end here. Let's first find out if this kid is yours or not. If she is then we cross that bridge when we get to it." Hawk's voice intruded on what he had thought was his internal dialogue. He must have spoken his fears out loud.

"We need to get hold of her DNA." Ziggy said. "It should be easy enough."

"Jesus, Ziggy. We can't just walk up to the kid and say 'open wide' and take a swab of the inside of her mouth." Kid snarled sarcastically.

"I know we can't. But what stops us from sending a team in to get what we need from inside the house? We wait until they're out, go in and grab hair from her hair brush or even her toothbrush. That's all we need. I know someone who will do the testing for us and it won't take long either." Ziggy shrugged as everyone looked at him.

Hawk nodded slowly then grinned slyly. "I like this plan. Yes, I like it and we need some volunteers to send on this little errand. Now we just need to get them out of the house for a couple of hours. Any ideas?"

"Why can't we just go in while they're at work during the day? We'll have more than enough time to get in and out." Sin shrugged.

"Good idea, Sin, but unfortunately we can't. They live in a boomed area with access control." Ziggy warned. "We have to do it at night, sneak in and out before we're noticed. I can get us past the fence alarm and the house alarm no problems. We just need someone to pick the locks on the doors and we need them out of the house. How do we do that?"

Jagger suddenly laughed. "We send them a meal voucher from a restaurant for the night we want to get in the house. Something like, 'You've been randomly selected blah blah blah' and while they're having a nice dinner, we're in and out. No sweat."

"I volunteer to be on the team." Spider said quietly. "Ice can't go, he's too close to this but I'm not. I'll go."

"Can you pick a lock, Spider?" Hawk asked with raised eyebrows.

A very sly smile tipped Spider's lips up as he nodded. "Taught myself that shit so I could break in to Ice's room when I was fourteen. He had the outside room on the veranda and I got through the security gate and past the locks he had on his door. No problems."

"Little shit." Ice growled with a grin. "I knew someone had been through my stuff, just didn't know it was you. I thought it was one of the girls."

Hawk got right to business. "I want a three man team on this. Spider will be the lock man, so we need two more to go with him. This is on a voluntary basis, so let's see some hands."

Jagger and Sin had their hands up before anyone else and the team was set. Now it was just to finalise the details.

By Wednesday Spider had been threatened more than once as he practiced on the doors around the compound. And the little shit opened every single one, triple locked security doors included, without any problems what so ever.

On Thursday evening Ice had yet another 'date' with Emma and he was hard pressed not to shake her as she flirted and rubbed herself up against him. But he had made sure they were in a public place and nowhere near her house. He bought his own beer and drank from the bottle, never letting it leave his hand. He wasn't worried though because Kid was with him, making sure he was safe during the fucking 'date'.

Emma wanted him to come home with her. Promising to rock his world if he'd only let her. She tried everything from rubbing up against him to taking hold of his cock under the table and rubbing and squeezing it. And his stupid fucking cock reacted by going hard. It made the bitch smile so fucking wide but what she didn't know was his cock might be hard but it wasn't hard enough. And the minute he thought about the little girl he went as soft as a fucking marshmallow.

He couldn't wait to get away from the bitch and breathed easier when he rode away with Kid next to him. He wanted to get home and wash the feel of her lips from his mouth and her scent off his skin. Like every time after he had been with Emma he made straight for the bar the minute he got home. He was slamming down a shot when Kid sat down next to him and gave him news that made him feel like a total shit.

River had been at the restaurant, having dinner with friends. And she had seen him with Emma. Had seen her hands all over him and had seen him kissing the bitch. Down in his gut he knew it was a good thing because she now had proof that he was bad news.

But it still made him want to fucking puke. He drowned it in booze until he passed out.

His hangover was going to kill him. His head ached, his gut ached from puking all morning and his eyes were red and swollen. Ice sat at the kitchen table and groaned as Aunt Beryl slammed a mug down in front of him.

"Drink." She growled. "Now. You'll feel better once you get it down."

Ice didn't argue he just drank the foul smelling brew down and waited for his gut to settle.

"You have to stop this, Ice. Every time you see that woman you come back here and drown yourself in drink. It has to stop." She said quietly as she rubbed his back softly.

Ice frowned at her and she shook her head. "I'm not stupid, Ice. I know what's going on."

Ice sighed in resignation. It was useless to try and hide anything from their Aunt.

"It will be done soon, Aunt Beryl. I just have to get through a few more weeks then it will be done."

"It's taking too long, my boy. Your mother and I are worried about you. Actually, everyone is worried about you."

She put a bowl down in front of him and thankfully his gut stayed quiet.

"Eat. You haven't been eating well since this mess started. And don't try to tell me any different, Ice Walker. I changed your nappies and wiped your ass, I know you."

Ice gave up, lifted the fork she put in his hand and took a bite. And before he knew it the bowl was empty and he was feeling a hell of a lot better.

The day passed damned slowly but eventually it was time for their team of burglars to head out. Beast and Ziggy went with them. Ziggy to hack the alarms and Beast to keep a lookout and help if they needed it.

Like every other Friday night at the clubhouse there was a party but it was fairly tame because they still haven't opened the gates to all comers. Ice sat at the bar and drank water as he waited anxiously for his brothers to get back. Several of the club bitches had tried to get on his lap but he had waved them all away and eventually they left him alone and concentrated on the brothers who wanted their attentions.

It felt like hours later when they walked through the doors, Spider with a very, very wide smile on his face. Ice immediately got up and followed them down to Hawk's office. Beast knocked and tried the door but it was locked and they all looked at each other and grinned. The boss was getting busy in there with his old lady.

Leaning his shoulder against the wall Ice waited with his brothers until the locks clicked and a very satisfied looking Hawk opened the door. DC sat on the desk, her legs swinging as they walked in and sat down.

Spider stood at the desk and laid down a small plastic baggie with a twist of light brown hair in it. Then he added two more baggies to it.

"While I was in the house I thought 'why don't we test all of them?' so I collected hair from all the brushes. I was going to swop out the toothbrushes but none of the ones I bought matched, so I had to leave them behind. Howard has a thick beard and there were some hairs in a small brush I think he uses. So we have that as well."

Jagger grunted. "The little fucker wanted to use one of those sticky rollers to pick shit up from their sheets but that just freaked me the hell out, so I said enough is enough and got him out of there. We would still be there collecting 'samples' if he had his way. He's been watching too many fucking crime shows."

Spider sniggered and shrugged. "I was being thorough, brother."

Ziggy picked up the baggies and grinned. "Fuck, Spider, you even labelled them."

"Told you, too many fucking crime shows." Jagger growled.

"No, this is seriously cool." Ziggy grinned. "My guy is on his way. I'm meeting him at the Shell garage in Samrand, now all that's left to do is collecting the sample from Ice."

All eyes turned to Ice and he sighed then gave a fatalistic shrug. "Let's get it done."

Ice sat impassively and opened his mouth as Ziggy swiped the bud against his cheek then slipped it into the container and sealed it. He could clearly see his name on the side.

"How long before we know?"

"My guy will be rushing this for us. The results will be here by the end of next week, at the latest, brother." Ziggy reassured him.

Ice nodded as he sagged back in the chair and watched Ziggy, Jagger and Spider leave. DC had emotionlessly watched, never saying a word. She hopped off the desk and drew in a deep breath. For the first time since she had seen him with River her voice didn't freeze him where he sat.

"Don't take this the wrong way, Ice, but I'm hoping the test comes up negative. As a kid who was raised by a biker single father, I know how stressful and lonely a life it can be. This little girl is happy with these people. She's being raised with love and care and should have that for the rest of her life."

When she left the office Ice sat there not knowing what to say. He didn't know what to say because he didn't know how he felt about being a father. But then he looked at the photo of the little girl and his heart hurt like hell. If she was his then he at least wanted contact with her.

No fuck that. If she was his he wanted her. Wanted her to know he was her father.

More than that he didn't know. He just knew he would do whatever he had to for his little girl.

And didn't that say it all. Calling her his little girl when he didn't know if she was his or not.

Hawk didn't say a word when Ice got up and left.

He had to get out of there and ride. Beast and Kid followed him out and they rode until the road worked its magic and he felt more relaxed.

And he had done it again. Rode past River's house, going against the orders of his president.

It was totally fucked up. But the reason he felt more relaxed was the very obvious presence of the Sinner's Sons on the property.

He didn't sleep any better but at least he would have answers to his questions soon.

CHAPTER TWELVE

River

We'd been very busy at work and I hadn't had much time to obsess over the voluptuous and beautiful woman I had seen with Ice a week ago. The woman had been all over him, groping and kissing not caring who saw. The bastard sat back and allowed the groping and kissed her back.

They had ruined my night out. A night out my best friends since high school had insisted on. Krissie and Mari stayed my friends when I started a relationship with Sparrow, unlike my other so-called friends. They gave him the benefit of the doubt and were my rocks when he was killed. If not for the two of them I wouldn't have survived the deep depression after his death and Duncan's birth. Mum and Dad helped but it was those two who got me through. They virtually moved in with me and took care of us until I was able to cope on my own.

For that alone I will love them forever.

And of course they noticed every single thing about me. So I had to spill about the party, the amazing sex and the horrible morning after and now my besties were pissed as hell at Ice Walker. Not that he would care, he never even noticed me. His friend did though but I pretended I hadn't seen them.

And thank the pope they left long before us. I was saved from having to watch him getting all touchy feely with a woman who looked like a painted up doll, nothing like me.

And why the hell did that little nugget keep on popping in my head?

It had to be because I was a crazy damned bitch with the hots for a man who was very obviously unavailable and I was grabbing at straws to make me feel better.

Or the more obvious reason for my fascination with Ice Walker was the fact that he was only the second man I had ever had sex with. And like Dylan he was really good in bed.

So good in bed my long dormant libido had woken up with a roar. And said libido necessitated a visit to an adult store on Saturday morning with Krissie which still had me blushing. The woman had no *skaam*. (She wasn't shy)

My new vibrator was worth the blushes and every cent I had paid for it.

I was stretched out on one of the couches in the small reception area taking a break when the door opened and DC strolled in and fell onto the couch opposite me.

"Tell me you keep beer in the fridge over there." She growled angrily.

"We sure do. Help yourself." I said as I slowly sat up. "And then tell me why you're so pissed off."

Jumping up she pulled the fridge open and threw me a grin over her shoulder. "You just became my favourite mechanic. You have my favourite cider."

I grinned. "I'm honoured to be your favourite."

Once she had the cider open and sat back down opposite me I was sitting up and ready and waiting.

"You know men and their shit are at the root of all evil, right?" Taking a long drink she slid down on the couch in a slouch. "I'm so done with living in a fucking clubhouse filled with Hawk's ex fuck bunnies. And I'm so done with gritting my teeth and ignoring the shit they do to get his attention and piss me off." She sighed. "I'm going insane in that damned place. Can I sleep on your couch, just for tonight? He's on an overnight run and I just can't stay there tonight. I could go home but for some reason I don't want to be alone."

I totally understood. It must be excruciating to live surrounded by your man's cast offs.

"My door is open and my couch is yours. Anytime you need it. Have you told him you hate living at the clubhouse?"

"Thank you, Rivvie. You might not realise it but you saved some bitches from tasting my knife today." She smiled but evil lurked deep in her dark eyes. "And no, I haven't exactly told him, I just sort of hinted at it. But he's so caught up with club business right now I didn't want to make it worse."

River lifted an eyebrow and DC gave a tiny shrug. She realised her friend was in need of some unbiased advice from someone who cared about her.

"I've been where you are now. Sparrow was a total manwhore before he met and claimed me and those club bitches were freaking brutal. Remember, I was only eighteen and clueless about the life. But one thing he had said to me right from the start was to 'use your mouth, Rivzie. Tell me if you're not happy' so I did and it saved us. Those bitches are bargaining on you trying to sort this on your own, don't do it. Tell your man. Let him know you're unhappy, don't let it fester. And then let him deal with the shit his behaviour created. If you keep quiet and don't say anything he'll know something is wrong and most probably come to the wrong conclusion. Men are stupid like that."

DC laughed and shook her head. "You're such a surprise, River. You're like a biker-mama-guru or something."

My heart ached but I smiled through it. I missed Dylan today, so very much and talking about him made it worse.

"But there's something not right with you today." DC said with narrowed eyes and I shrugged.

"What is it?" She persisted.

Rubbing my hands on my thighs I drew in a deep breath and looked at her, blinking away the burning that would become tears if I let it.

"I miss him today, so freaking much. Every morning I look at Duncan and he's growing up so fast and looking more and more like his daddy every day. And he'll never know the amazing man his dad was, how his face came alive every time he felt Duncan kick inside me. He won't have Sparrow teaching him how to ride or fix his bike, about girls and sex and birth control. He won't have his dad teaching him how to be a good man and some days it hurts more than others. And today is one of those days."

Shaking my head I laughed. "Ignore me, DC. I'm a tad hormonal today. Must be my period letting me know it's on the way."

DC clapped her hands and rose. "The cure for period blues is easy, chocolate in all its shapes and forms, a hot pad for your back and movies. I'm going to get out of here to buy a truck load of chocolate and we can binge watch Netflix while we eat our weight in chocolate tonight. Does it sound like a plan?"

I smiled and nodded. The heavy weight in my chest lifted a bit and as I watched her stalk out of the workshop I realised I had just added another sister to my posse. I would have to make arrangements to introduce her to Krissie and Mari. It would happen, but on another day, not today.

There was a very scary reason why I wasn't my usual self. With everything that had been happening I hadn't realised that my period was late. And I was never late.

It was how Sparrow had known I was pregnant before I even knew. He had been so in tune with my body, when my period was a few days late he had informed me I was pregnant. And half scared me to death. Sparrow had been ecstatic from the first.

And now it was way more than a few days. It was more like weeks. By my calculations almost eight freaking weeks in fact.

It was most probably the stress of the last few weeks that had delayed my period. I prayed. And with the way I was feeling and the tears that was so near all the time it had to be on its way. It just had to.

Anything else was just too horrifying to contemplate. Ice Walker was the last man on earth I would pick to be a father to a child of mine. Plus he had a woman. And he had been with me while he was with that woman which meant he was a lying cheating scum-dog. A man like him would not be a good role model for an impressionable child.

Oh God. If I was pregnant Dagger was going to kill him.

Nope. Not going to think about it. I wasn't pregnant. It was stress, most probably.

I got back to work and ignored the huge freaking elephant in the room staring me in the face.

DC and I were stretched out on the couches in my living room eating chocolate and watching a really bad death and destruction movie. We had been giving blow by blow commentary and cackling with laughter right throughout the movie. DC wasn't a big drinker and she was happy drinking juice. My excuse for not drinking? I had to work in the morning.

Lame. So very lame.

The movie ended and I looked at DC and she looked at me and we both raised our eyebrows.

"That had to be the crappiest cops and robbers movie I have ever seen. It sucked so bad it became a comedy." DC said with a grin.

"Those chase scenes were hilarious. They were so obviously sped up to make it look like they were driving fast. They didn't even use a green screen. This one is going into my crappy movies file for when I need to laugh." I grinned. "Want to watch another one?"

But DC went from laughing to serious in the blink of an eye.

"No, I don't want to watch another one. I want to know why my friend is swinging from one extreme to the next. I might not have known you for years, River, but I can see something is burning you up inside. I swear you can tell me and I won't tell a soul, you have my word."

I so badly needed to confess my fears to someone but I didn't think it was a good thing to tell DC. She was too close to the cause of my troubles.

"I can see you thinking about telling me but you're not sure. I promise you, I'm like a vault, whatever you tell me stays here, between you and me."

Closing my eyes I drew in a deep breath then whispered my suspicions. "I think I might be pregnant. And I've only had sex with one man since Dylan."

She immediately sat up and reached for my hands. They shook as she held onto them, her thumbs stroking over my knuckles soothingly.

"First thing we need to do is get a test. Once we know if it's yes or no we can decide on a plan of action. By my calculations it's around eight weeks since the deed was done so let's get that test done, okay?"

Withdrawing my hands from hers I clasped them over my mouth staring at her then dropped them to my lap.

"If I'm pregnant this is going to cause so much shit, DC. Dagger is going to lose his mind. He's super protective of us and I have no idea what he might do when he finds out who the father is."

Grabbing my hand DC squeezed it tight. "We're not going to worry about it now, River. Let's approach this one step at a time, okay? We have to find a reason to get you to your gynaecologist without rousing any suspicions. Have you had your yearly check-up yet?"

"No, it's only due in August."

"Change it. Make an appointment so you'll have an answer. Then we take the next step."

"What will that be? The next step?"

DC growled angrily. "Cutting fucking Ice Walker's nuts off and stuffing them up his ass."

I couldn't help it, I started laughing and couldn't stop and soon we were rolling on the couches giggling and snorting. Every time we looked at each other it set us off again. The front door opening silenced us but only for the few seconds it took Jinx to walk inside, then we started off again.

"What the hell are you watching? It can't be that funny." He grumped as he walked through to the kitchen and turned on the kettle.

"We just watched the worst cops and robbers movie I've ever seen." I quickly explained through my laughter.

He leant against the short wall between the kitchen and lounge with his ankles crossed and his hands in his pockets as he watched us with narrowed eyes. Those narrowed eyes settled on me.

"You know I've had an old lady, right? So I know shit about bitches I wish I didn't but I know it anyway. Right now I know you're blowing smoke up my ass but I'm not going to push. You come to me when you need me, Rivzie, and I'll help. Okay?" He said softly before he turned and walked back into the kitchen.

Who knew the hard as nails SAA of the Sinner's Sons had it in him? Not me.

And just like that the damned tears were threatening to spill over again.

"Would you ladies like some tea?" Jinx called from the kitchen.

"I'd like some Rooibos tea, Jinx. It's in the green tin on the…"

"I've got it. And you, DC?"

"Not for me, thanks, Jinx."

She made big eyes at me and I blinked furiously then made eyes back at her and grinned. And thankfully the tears disappeared.

"Where are the cookies mum made, Rivzie? I can't have tea without cookies." Jinx mumbled in the kitchen as I heard him going through the cupboards.

"It's in the blue and white tin on top of the cupboards where my boykie can't reach."

"Got it."

There were sounds in the kitchen and then Jinx came walking through with a tray set up with a mug of tea, a plate of my mum's cookies and a glass of juice. Without a word he set it on the coffee table then walked out again. We silently watched as he came out of the kitchen with a mug and a plastic zip lock baggie filled with cookies and left without another word.

"He's a nice guy." DC said softly and I nodded.

"He was Sparrow's best friend. Those two together were trouble with a bit T. They got into so many scrapes pulling pranks on their brothers. They were always laughing, but Jinx hardly ever smiles now and only when he's around Duncan. He's one of the best men I know."

"The way he acts around you I can see he's a good one." DC agreed.

Yes he was, and so were the rest of Dagger's brothers. We were family and they made sure I knew it. No matter what.

This pregnancy thing was going to blow my comfortable life right out of the water.

Would they ever forgive me for disrespecting their dead brother? Or would they blame the entire fiasco on Ice?

What was I thinking? Of course they were going to blame Ice and then they were going to beat him to a pulp.

Laying a hand over my tummy I looked at DC with wide eyes. "This is going to cause so much trouble when it gets out."

DC shrugged. "Maybe at first but babies should always be good news, River. No matter how they were made. And anyone who disagrees will have an up close and personal meeting with my fists. This baby of yours is going to have a very big job on her little shoulders."

"Stop it. We don't know if I am or not. And if I am there's a very good chance it will be another boy. And what is this job you're talking about?"

"That teeny tiny little fishy swimming around in your tummy is going to be the bridge between two clubs, River."

She was being so very serious and River just had to stop this baby talk.

"No, not my fishy and we don't even know if there is a fishy. It might just be stress or there might be something wrong inside or I'm having very early menopause or…or…or"

DC burst out laughing and I couldn't help it I laughed with her.

"Now I've heard everything. Early freaking menopause? Are you crazy?"

"Yes! Yes I am and I'm scared. I am already raising one child on my own and now I'm most probably adding another one. It is so difficult already how will I cope with two?"

"Stop. Just stop, River." DC urged softly. "I do know how difficult it is because I helped to raise Deena. You have a lot of support, you know you do. Your mum and dad, your friends, me, and let's not forget, both clubs. You know and I know the brothers from both clubs will take care of you."

"Shit, okay, okay, I just need to get my mind off this. Let's watch another mindless movie."

DC gave in without another word and we watched another movie but if you asked me which it was I won't be able to give you an answer. It worked though. I fell asleep on the couch and only woke up when Jinx moved me to my bedroom and put me to bed clothes and all.

Hidden behind the cold rough exterior was a warm heart. His old lady had been a very lucky lady, it's a pity she hadn't treasured his heart and had left him for another man. Loving a biker wasn't easy but I would never regret loving Sparrow. He too had hidden a warm heart behind cold eyes.

On that thought I slipped deeper into sleep.

CHAPTER THIRTEEN

Ice

Laying his stinking kutte and t-shirt down on the bar Ice grabbed the waiting shot and downed it. The whiskey burned all the way down, chasing the taste of the bitch from his mouth. He fucking hated this. And after every single date with the bitch he had the headache from hell because of her fucking perfume.

"Sam." He called the prospect over. "Take my kutte and get the stink out of it."

"No problem, VP." He picked Ice's kutte up and wrinkled his nose as he sniffed. "Jesus, that's a horrible perfume. What does she do, bath in it?" He muttered as he walked away towards the kitchen.

Ice didn't say anything because he had nothing to say. And yes he'd had the same thoughts about the perfume. It was as if the bitch injected herself with the stuff and it leaked out of her pores to hang around her like a damned heavy cloud.

"Ice." A cold voice intruded on his thoughts and he glanced to the side only to look into DC's cold dark eyes. He had no idea when she had sat down next to him. "How close are you to finishing it with this bitch?"

Narrowing his eyes he stared at her, trying to see past the blank stare. Why did she want to know?

"It's club business, DC. You know this."

"Not when it threatens my friend and her little boy. I warned Hawk and now I'm warning you, get this done before I step in and finish it for you." She slid of the stool and started to walk away then stopped and spoke over her shoulder. "And please, do us all a favour and go shower, you freaking stink."

He glared at her and then saw the small pack on her back. "DC, where are you going? You know Hawk is on an overnight run to the Bloemfontein chapter, you need to stay here."

Swinging all the way towards him Ice saw absolute rage fill her face and eyes as she stalked back to him. Her voice came out in an ice cold rage filled hiss.

"I will only stay here over my very dead body. I'm sick and tired of being disrespected and treated like I don't have a right to be here by your whores and some of your brothers. When Hawk gets back tell him I've moved out. I gave him time to sort this shit out, he hasn't. I'll be staying with River. At least there I'm not being targeted by nasty whores informing me how my old man ate out their diseased twats the night before. And I'll be protected. Jinx has stepped up and he is an amazing man, he totally has control of the situation around River. And he'll protect me, so no worries."

Without another word she swung around and left.

Ice was stunned silent. His brothers and the fucking bitches had done what? And Jinx was doing what? What the fuck was Jinx doing at River's house?

But more importantly they had dropped the ball where DC was concerned. Hawk had given the whores a warning but that was all. There had been no consequences for their actions and they used it to cause more shit. Instead of the whores being kicked out the door it was DC who was walking out the door.

This was not right. And with his brother not home he had to fix it. He was so sick and tired of the games the whores played, they were not going to be happy with his decision. But he didn't give a shit. This should have happened a long time ago. Right when Hawk brought DC here he should have laid down the law. He did, to some extent when he kicked them out, and then he brought his ex bitches back into the clubhouse for their own protection. And now shit had once again escalated.

Fuck. He was going to have to call his cousin. But before he did, he had a little justice to dispense.

"Prospects! Gather up all the bitches. I want a list of their names on this bar in front on me, you have five minutes." He looked around at the stunned faces. "Fucking move! Get it done, right the fuck now!" He snapped angrily.

Fifteen minutes later the common room was filled with chattering bitches, most of them posturing and flirting with the brothers on the other side of the room. There were seventeen of them.

"Sam, turn on the main lights, all of them." Ice ordered as he read through the list Terror had put down in front of him. When he wanted to move away Ice ordered him behind to bar with a notepad and a pen. Bright lights came on and immediately the scuffed up and stained furniture and the barely dressed whores were glaringly laid bare. He was never going to put his ass on one of those couches ever again, they were disgusting. And why the fuck were they wasting their time with these worn out bitches? Surely they could find better out there than the bitches with the bleached and teased hair and overblown bodies in front of him.

"When I point at you, you will come forward and hand your ID to Terror, you will get it back once we're done here."

"I don't have it on me, Ice. I'll just go back to the room and fetch it." One of the women called out.

"No, you won't. Prospects, go through their shit and find their ID's and bring them and their phones to me."

There was shuffling feet and shocked expressions from the whores as well as some of the brothers. Only Rider was smiling wide, very, very wide. Of course the bastard would fucking smile, unlike the rest of them he never touched the whores.

"Rider, you take over from Terror over here. Terror, ask Ziggy to come out here then join your brothers in their search. Anything look suspicious you bring it to me."

Crossing his arms over his naked chest Ice stood before the whores and looked them over. Some were worried others not at all. It made him wonder. Why weren't they worried? Did they think someone was going to step in and stop what was about to happen?

"It has come to my attention you bitches think you can do and say as you please in my club. And as I stand here and look you over I'm wondering why the fuck we agreed to have you here in the first place, none of you are worth the aggravation. You cause trouble and piss off the old ladies and our female family members with your attitude and lies, we don't need this crap in our lives."

He looked around as feet shuffled and a few of them looked worried and guilty.

"This shit ends right here, right now. Today you will know exactly why we have tolerated your fucking presence. Today I will very bluntly tell you what you are worth to us."

He silently looked them over before he continued.

"You're a hole to fuck. That's it. Just that, nothing more. Not a potential old lady or girlfriend." Ice pointed at the brothers silently watching. "And if you think one of them are going to step up and save your ass, think again. None of them will go up against me. Not a single fucking one."

And as he had anticipated Laney stepped forward, her hand on her cocked hip. "That's bullshit. Hawk wants me here. His word is the only one that matters here. You've got no say in who stays and who goes."

There it was, the source he was looking for. "Bitch, pull you head out of your fucking ass. I'm the Vice President of this club. You're a whore, nothing else. When did Hawk supposedly tell you he wanted you here, specifically you, not any of the others, just you?"

She threw her bleached blonde hair back with a little head toss. "Yesterday when I sucked his cock before he left on the run."

"Are you sure he said that?" Ice asked just to give her an opportunity to retract her statement.

"Of course I'm sure. I've sucked him off and fucked him plenty of times when that bitch of his wasn't available to take care of him." She claimed with a toss of her fucked up hair.

Turning to the bar Ice caught Ziggy's eyes and nodded. "Get me the footage and put it on the big screen." He turned back to Laney.

"You tell DC your fucked up lies?"

"They aren't lies. She needed to know she wasn't important to him. He's just with her to get the Road Warriors on our side. He told me. It's like an arranged marriage for the good of the club." The whore smirked.

Ice nodded. "So the sneak attack on DC, was that one of your plans as well?"

Laney preened at all the attention. "It was a joint effort between me, Lizzy and the other women and Hawk told us to do it. You know he did, if he didn't we wouldn't be here."

Ice pointed at the corner of the common room. "Everyone who was with Laney move over there."

Laney, Lizzy and six other women moved to the corner. Then Laney pointed at the group still standing in front of Ice.

"You bitches can stop hiding and get over here, right now. You know you were there as well." Two more women hesitantly joined the group.

Nodding Ice turned back to the bar. "Rider, put their names on a separate list."

Then he turned to the remaining bitches, there were only five left.

"Why aren't you lot in their little group? You're excluded Shelly, I know why you're here. Sit down over there." Shelly quickly sidled to the side and sat down.

A brunette on the side lifted a hand and Ice pointed at her to speak.

"I don't have sex with the brothers with old ladies. I've never touched Hawk, and I never will. He honours his old lady. It's not my place to make her think otherwise."

"And you are?"

"Chris."

"Okay, Chris, move to the end of the bar." He looked over the remaining three. "And you three? Why aren't you in their group?"

The one in the middle stepped forward and looked at the girls on either side of her. They nodded.

"The three of us came here together. We are friends and we only came for a party and a good time. When we tried to leave they forcibly stopped us from leaving and now we can't leave because you have us on lock down."

"Who stopped you?"

"Laney and her girls. They said they needed us to clean the place and keep the brothers happy and distracted. I don't know why. All we want is to go home. We don't want to be here. We don't want to have sex with any of the guys anymore. Please, let us leave."

"Join Chris over there."

Rage unlike anything he had ever felt before had him breathing hard and his fists clenched by his sides. He counted silently to ten to get himself under control. It wasn't easy but he got there.

"Which of you fuckers took those girls without their consent?" He snarled at his shocked brothers. "You know the fucking rules. You do not touch a woman who says no and looking at those three I'm fucking sure they said no. Step the fuck up before I have them pointing you out one by fucking one."

Only one man stepped forward. Dizzy.

"Dizz, man, what the fuck were you thinking?"

"That Laney bitch said it was a sex game they were playing. And I was completely fucked up drunk. I'm so fucking sorry, Claire. How can I make it up to you, sweetheart? I would never have touched you if I knew you were being forced, not fucking ever."

The girl who had spoken up just stood there with tears running down her cheeks shaking her head and Dizzy's face lost all colour. Suddenly he swung around and with a wild roar stormed at a widely smirking Laney but his brothers grabbed him before he got to her. He fought against them screaming at her as four of them held him back.

"You fucking whore! You turned me into a fucking rapist! I'm going to fucking kill you for what you did to her! I'm going to fucking kill you!"

"Hawk won't let you touch me, asshole." Laney retorted with an evil smile.

Looking at the smirking bitches Ice made an instant decision.

"Prospects, take all their clothes. I want them naked, zip tie their hands behind their backs. Put them in the dungeon."

There were shocked gasps and cries of outrage but Ice ignored it all as he watched the footage Ziggy had running on the big screen and nowhere was Hawk seen anywhere near Laney and her bitches.

"Ziggy, take their phones, go through them and find me something I can use."

"I'm on it VP. Terror has given me eighteen phones and there are only sixteen bitches. I'll let you know what I find. The two extra phones were found in Laney and Lizzy's room."

"Dizzy, brother, you're in charge of ensuring these three get home without anything else happening to them. Please make sure they're safe, okay?"

His brother nodded but Ice could see he wasn't in a good place and he could not do this on his own. He needed his brothers around him now.

"Sin, Spider, go with Dizzy and when you get back we'll deal with the rest of them."

"Shelley, go back to your room and stay there." She nodded timidly and virtually ran out of the room.

"Chris, do you want to leave with the girls?" He asked the brunette.

"If it's okay with you I would like to stay. I've been happy here and I like Aunty Beryl, she's good people and she's been helping me with my studies."

Ice nodded. "Okay, you can stay but you will complete an application as soon as Ziggy has it ready. Have you worked behind a bar before?"

"Yes."

"Good, you are the new bartender. We'll talk more at a later stage."

She nodded and Ice watched as she moved in behind the bar and started cleaning.

Turning away he looked at his brothers who were now angrily watching the naked bitches being led away.

"There won't be another mistake like this one at this club. From now on any bitch who wants to be a club girl is going to go through an application process. No more bitches walking through the door and staying because you have a hard on for her. We've been burned more than once now and it fucking ends today.

"This club belongs to us, to the brothers who have been patched in and to those who are prospecting to join us. Not to a bunch of whores who think they can do or say as they want because once upon a time they fucked the boss. Hawk was very clear about where he stands on this shit. So, as of today there will be no more pussy in the clubhouse until further notice."

Looking at the shocked brothers, some of whom were muttering under their breath and throwing him dark looks, Ice's temper sparked even higher.

"You got something to say motherfuckers? You think it's okay for our president's old lady to walk out the door because whores are more important than she is? Have you fuckers forgotten we have an enemy out there who would love to get their hands on her?"

"She'll be okay, Ice. The Warriors compound is safe." Someone mumbled.

Ice snarled in frustration. "If that was where she was going but she's not. She's now being watched over by the fucking Sinner's Sons. Anyone still pissy like a little girl because I'm getting rid of your fucking sluts? Well, get over it. When Hawk walks back in here he's going to lose his shit and heads are going to roll. So let's see how long your fucking little hissy fit lasts once he starts on you."

No one said a word and Ice sat back down at the bar. He was fucking tired and he stank of Emma's perfume, all he wanted was a shower and to fall into his bed for an hour or two. But now he had this shit to sort out.

It felt as if the day would never end.

His phone binged and he sighed, pulled it out and looked at the text message. It was Ziggy.

My office. Now.

Getting up he gave his brothers one last furious look as he stalked out.

"What do you have for me?" He asked as he walked into Ziggy's office and closed the door behind him.

Ziggy spun around on his fancy chair. "First things first. We got the results back. My guy sent the results to your mail. Do you want me to open it?"

Long icy fingers clawed through his gut as he nodded. His throat had closed so tight he couldn't get a word past it. He watched as Ziggy clicked through some shit and then a document opened on the screen.

He ignored everything but his name and the result next to it. Negative.

She wasn't his. Then his eyes slid lower. What the hell?

David Howard, Negative.

Anna Howard, Negative.

David Howard wasn't the kid's biological father which meant Emma hadn't been fucking him. If not this guy then who the hell had she been fucking while she was still with him?

No wonder she never told him she was pregnant and ran after the shit with Jane. He now knew it had to have been staged. Emma and Jane were two peas in a pod. Sly manipulative bitches.

Staring at the screen a thought wormed its way to the forefront of his brain.

They were working together. Emma reappearing in his life had been planned. She was the red herring to get attention away from Jane. Or was it the other way around? The question was why? Why this elaborate scheme? What was their end game?

"Bingo!" Ziggy suddenly called out from where he had continued working on the phones in front of him while Ice had been lost in thought.

"What?"

Ziggy grinned wide. "We've got a lead on Jane. These two phones have texts between her, Laney and Lizzy. If she calls again I can track the call. She's been running the entire show from behind the scenes. Getting DC and Hawk separated was at the top of their agenda. They want DC back with the Road Warriors which would break our alliance with Doc. Is that where she went? Do I have to contact Hawk?"

Ice shook his head with a sigh. "No, brother, it's worse. She's gone to stay with River Anderson. So right now she's under the protection of the Sinner's Sons. Hawk is going to go fucking ballistic when he finds out."

Ziggy's eyes went wide. "Oh fuck." He whispered.

"*Ja*, we are, we are totally fucked. He left her here under my protection and I fucking dropped the ball."

"No." Ziggy said adamantly. "Not just you, we're all to blame, Hawk most of all. He should have cleared those two whores out a long time ago but he let his fucked up sense of fair play get in the way. And now we have to deal with this shit show."

Ice sighed as he sank into a chair. "And I just realised something important. Emma and Jane are in this shit together. We are being played, brother. This whole thing is a con to get us looking in the wrong direction while they fuck us in the ass. But now that we're aware of what's going on, this shit ends and we use it against them. We keep those whores locked up in the dungeon and you lock it down up here. From now on you answer those phones." Ice grinned. "I'm sure you won't have any problems pretending to be those bitches."

"Fuck you." Ziggy said with a wide smile. But the smile fell and he was totally serious when he put a hand on his shoulder. "I know to some extent you're disappointed she's not yours, brother. But keep it in mind that if she was, you would never have been free of Emma Coetzee and her games. And she would have used you to get what she wanted by holding that little girl's life over you like a bargaining chip."

"You're right, brother, you're right. It's just very difficult to deal with the fact that I never saw the real Emma. The minute I showed interest in her, plans must have been put in place to get her deep inside our club. And fuck, I would have been the one to put her there. When she fell pregnant she knew I would have been onto her.

I had been fucking anal about not getting her pregnant and fucking up her career. Why didn't she have an abortion? And why the fuck am I only remembering this shit now?"

"Maybe because you didn't want to acknowledge the fact the woman you loved betrayed you and your club?"

Ice sighed heavily. "There's one thing I do know, Zig. I didn't love her. It was like I was in love with the idea of her, not the real person. Thank fuck. Now all I have to do is get the bitch to give us her connection to the Maingardes and I can be rid of her once and for all. The sooner the better, I fucking hate her perfume."

"You're not the only one, brother. We all fucking hate her perfume." Ziggy grinned. "And talking about that stinky shit, please brother, do us all a favour and go have a shower."

Ice laughed and left.

He was feeling better than he had been feeling for the past few weeks. A weight had been lifted from his shoulders.

The DNA results meant that when this was all done he could concentrate on River. But unfortunately not just yet. The club and the Emma shit came first.

Getting River to give him a chance was going to be difficult but he looked forward to it.

He knew it wouldn't be easy but it was going to be so worth it in the end.

RENÉ VAN DALEN

CHAPTER FOURTEEN

River

I sat in the chair in the doctor's waiting room flicking through a magazine while my leg bounced rapidly. Next to me DC slouched in her chair playing a game on her phone. A phone that had been chiming almost constantly with incoming texts. She wasn't answering any of them.

When she arrived at my house last night she had been coldly furious and after I heard the reason I knew I would have been as well. How dare Hawk treat her so damned shabbily? What kind of man was he to keep his fuck buddies under the same roof as his old lady? That was monumentally stupid.

"River Anderson." My name being called stilled my bouncing leg and I got up to follow the sister down the passage. I looked back at DC and she smiled her encouragement and nodded.

She had my back.

I submitted to the preliminaries before seeing the doctor.

I undressed and put on the stupid gown, and then I was weighed, blood pressure taken, relieved of urine and blood, and left to await the doctor in the examination room next to her office.

I had gone through this once before but back then I had Dylan holding my hand. I remember his hand had been sweaty and his left leg had bounced uncontrollably. We had both been so nervous and I had been scared. Until we heard Duncan's heartbeat. After hearing that amazing sound we had both become calm, calm and ecstatically happy. We couldn't wait to share our news with our families.

But this time I was on my own. Alone and unsure about what I felt.

Doctor Strauss breezed in with a wide smile and I knew the test was positive.

"Well, River, congratulations are in order. The test came back positive, you are indeed pregnant. We should have the blood tests back by next week Monday and the sister will call you with the results. According to your dates you are almost eight weeks along which means you'll deliver in January. I would have loved to do a scan today to do measurements, check on the development of the baby and give us an exact delivery date but the machine is giving problems. Please hop up on the table for me and I'll have a quick look."

After the examination she pulled over the machine that would make it all real. I lay like a statue as she moved the wand around with a little frown and then it filled the room. The strong even beat of my baby's heart. And my heart filled with love as I listened.

"This is a strong one, just listen to that." She grinned at me as she took the printout, looked at it with a tiny frown then added it to my file. "There's a bit of a murmur in the background but it's nothing to be worried about. We'll check it out during the scan just to set both our minds at rest. You can get dressed and come into my office when you're done."

I was dressed and in her office within minutes. She was typing something into her computer and looked up with a smile.

"We have a dispensary attached to the practice now so you no longer have to go to the pharmacy for your medications. They'll have them ready for you when you leave. Are you experiencing any nausea?"

"No, not yet anyway."

"Okay, but don't hesitate to call in for something if it starts. I'll make a note on your chart so the pharmacist knows. Please feel free to call if you have any questions or if you're worried about something. It's been five years since your last child so we'll watch this one carefully, okay?"

"Okay. Thanks doctor."

"Unfortunately we're solidly booked for scans but I was able to squeeze you in two weeks from today." She scribbled the date and time on a card and pushed it across the desk. I picked it up and after a quick look dropped it into my bag sitting on the floor next to me.

Not much later I was back in the reception area, a small plastic packet of medications hidden deep inside my bag. I nodded as DC asked the question without a word.

Neither one of us spoke until we were back in my car. We were in my monster because I needed to be near Dylan today even though this child wasn't his. I felt him all around me as I drove back to the workshop.

"Are you going to tell your family?" DC asked quietly.

"Not yet. I'll do it after I've had the scan and can show them the pictures. It will make it more real for them and for me." My hands clenched around the steering wheel. "Dagger is going to be so pissed off with me, and when he finds out who the father is he's going to freaking explode."

DC nodded. "Then you should maybe use the two weeks until the scan to meet with Ice and tell him what's going on. It's only fair he finds out before anyone else."

"You're right. But I can't do it today. I have to talk myself into it and I really don't want to get between him and his woman, you know."

DC gave me a confused frown. "What woman? I'm not aware of him having a woman."

"My friends and I saw him with a woman a while back and they looked very together to me. They were all over each other."

The same weird look that I had seen on her face before flitted over it. She knew something but it was most probably club business and she couldn't share. Damn it.

"Freaking hell. Okay, take your time, but girlfriend, you need to do it before you let the cat out the bag to your family. He needs a chance to do damage control before the Sinner's Sons arrive at our clubhouse ready to cut his nuts off."

I had to laugh but it wasn't a good laugh. "I promise I'll call him. Just not today or tomorrow. But I will call him. Okay?"

"Okay, but do it soon, River."

I had no idea why she was so adamant about calling him. I would do it, like I said, just not today and not tomorrow either. I needed time to get my thoughts together and prepare what I was going say to him.

Hawk

Staring down at his phone Hawk growled angrily then sighed heavily. He was tired, so fucking tired of this shit. According to Ice the whores had ganged up on his old lady and she had walked out of the safety of their clubhouse and had gone to stay with River Anderson. She was now being protected by the fucking Sinner's Sons.

He was going to fucking kill every single fucking twat when he walked back into his club. Who the fuck did they think they were fucking with?

"Beast, get everyone ready to ride." He growled to the man sitting next to him.

Beast didn't say a word, just downed the last of his coffee and went to gather the men.

Turning to Klippies, the Bloemfontein Chapter President, he opened his mouth to speak when the man shook his head.

"No need to say anything, Prez. Whatever you need, whenever you need it. You call and we'll be there to take your back. *Ons is broers en broers staan saam.*" (We are brothers and brothers stand together.) Klippies said as he clapped Hawk on the back.

"Good. I'll keep you up to date on what's going down. Make sure your boys are careful and keep an eye on your women and children. These fuckers we're up against won't hesitate to use them." Hawk warned as he grabbed up his saddlebags and walked out the clubhouse to his bike.

The ride back seemed to take for fucking ever and then at last he rode through their gates. He was home, but his old lady wasn't. A state of affairs he would immediately set to rights.

Stalking into the clubhouse he walked right up to his room and slammed the door shut behind him. He had his phone out as he sat on the side of the bed and called his woman.

"You're back."

No hello, no hi baby, nothing. Just a cold statement of fact. Hawk closed his eyes and dropped his elbows onto his knees keeping the phone against his ear.

"I'm sorry, little bird. So fucking sorry. This shit is going to stop. I swear to you not one of those fucking bitches will ever have another opportunity to even look at you. They're going to fucking disappear."

His little bird sighed. "You can't make them disappear, Hawk. They have families who'll miss them and before you can blink you'll have the pigs knocking at your door." And as she continued to lay it out for him his gut told him he was going to lose her. "Those bitches are under the impression they're untouchable and you gave them that impression by giving them the club's protection. You should have left them out there to fend for themselves. They are whores, no one would have considered them important enough to target."

Fucking hell. She was right.

"Yes, I agree. I never should have brought them back in and given them the club's protection. They are no longer a problem, DC. Ice instituted the new rules he and I had discussed a while back. I got side tracked with everything else going on and never implemented them. Everything that's happened to you is my fault, little bird, and I'm so fucking sorry." Hawk acknowledged his guilt. "Can you ever forgive me and come home, baby?"

"Being with you is so damned hard, Hawk." His old lady said sadly.

"Not going to be that way anymore, I give you my word. Please, I'm begging here, little bird. Can we at least talk about this face to face? Where are you?" Hawk asked softly.

"Yes, I think we need to talk. I'm at the shop. Are you coming here?"

"I'm leaving now, baby. See you soon."

"I'll be waiting."

Hawk grabbed his keys and with Beast following rode to talk to his woman.

LOST AND FOUND IN BLUE

Walking through the doors of Mainline Ink II he didn't give his little bird time to say a word. He picked her up and sighed with relief when her arms and legs clasped around his body as he walked them into her office.

He didn't let her go as he sat down with her on his lap and looked into her eyes. Fuck, the shadows in those beautiful eyes had his heart aching in his chest.

"I'm a fucking dick, baby. I should have kicked those whores out the minute I found you. I swear to you I haven't touched another woman since we started and I never fucking will. There are so many things I should have done and didn't, little bird. Can you forgive me? Can you forgive my fucked up decisions and come back to me? I can't do this without you, baby. Just knowing you're mine and that you will be waiting for me when I get back from whatever shit I have to deal with makes it all worthwhile."

Hawk dropped his forehead against hers as her arms tightened around his neck. He had been thinking about the two of them ever since she had taken his patch and his ink. It wasn't enough. He wanted more, he wanted everything. Her in his big empty house. His ring on her finger. His babies in her belly.

"I'm tired of dealing with the club whores but not only them, I'm tired of dealing with the way some of the brothers openly disrespect me. I can't do it anymore and I've been fighting Crow daily to stop her from doing something we're all going to regret."

Jesus. Fuck.

"You won't ever have to deal with them again, baby. The brothers will be given an ultimatum, respect or their kuttes on my table. No transfers, no second chances."

"You can't do that, Hawk." She jerked her head back to give him a wide eyed stare.

"I can and I will. It is my fucking club, they follow my rules or they can fucking leave." Hawk growled angrily.

Swallowing down the anger he softly rubbed his lips against hers. When her lips softened and opened beneath his he deepened the kiss, drawing the scent and taste of his little bird deep inside. Slowly drawing back he placed a soft kiss between her closed eyes.

"I love you, little bird. Without you I'm only half a man. Please will you come home with me?"

Hawk waited almost without breathing.

"I love you too, my Viking. I'll come home with you but the first bastard who disrespects me is going to meet up with my fists. I don't care who he is."

Hawk growled. "I'll fucking kill him before you can hit him, baby. I want you on the back of my bike. We can finish this talk in our room. Okay?"

His woman didn't argue. With a nod she slipped off his lap and prepared to leave with him.

He rode away with his little bird on the back of his bike, tight against his back. He held on to her thigh all the way back to the compound. Feeling her warmth under his hand settled the churning hell in his gut.

There were going to be some changes at the clubhouse and the fuckers who had disrespected his old lady were going to meet him in the ring. He would have their blood for disrespecting his woman and treating her like shit.

Ice's arrangements for the whores would stand as is. They would take it to the table but he would make sure those sluts were history.

Once he was done everyone will know he was the fucking King of his club and DC was his Queen.

No one would ever again doubt her importance in his life.

He would make damned sure of it.

River

Time passed too damned quickly and before I knew it a week had passed and I hadn't called Ice.

But I was going to do it today. I had taken the morning off and sat in the lounge with my phone in my hand both legs bouncing as I punched in the number DC had given me. My hands were shaking when I lifted my phone to my ear.

He answered after three rings. His voice short and cold.

"Ice."

"Ice, hi. It's River Anderson."

There was a heavy silence before he said anything.

"River. Yes, I remember you. Why are you calling me? I thought I made it clear I was done."

Jesus. But I forged ahead.

"Uhm, I need to see you. Can we meet somewhere?"

Again the silence but this time I felt anger pulsing down the line. And then he spewed out his anger and disgust.

"Let me make it fucking crystal clear to you. We were drunk and I needed a fuck, you were there. If it hadn't been you it would have been some other pussy I would have sunk my dick into that night. We are done. I never go back. Once I've fucked a slut that's it, I'm done with her. I don't know how to make it any clearer for you. I don't want you. Don't fucking call me again, you won't like the results."

What a fucking pig!

"Fuck you. When hell comes calling remember this call."

I ended the call and slammed my phone down.

And of course the bastard called back. His number came up again and again. And every time I refused the call until he pissed me off to such an extent with the stupid threatening messages I blocked him.

I never wanted to hear from him or see him ever again. I would be raising this child on my own. I had the support of my family and friends. I would be okay.

The day of the scan arrived. The wintery sky was like my heart, overcast with intermittent drizzle and there was a chilly wind blowing. I again made excuses to go to the doctor and saw the worry in Wrench's eyes as I left. My assistant wasn't as blind as I had hoped. He knew something was going on.

This time I was on my own. DC had a client she could not put off and I hadn't told anyone else about my pregnancy.

I lay on the cold table in my crackling gown and breathed deep to keep calm. The technician smiled as she covered my belly with goop and started moving the wand around. My eyes were riveted on the screen and then I saw him or maybe her, my baby. Mine.

But what the hell was the other white blobby thingy? Was there something wrong?

"Oh, will you look at that." The technician grinned as the moved the wand again. "There are two of them, River."

"What? Two? I'm having twins?" I gasped in a shocked whisper.

"Yes you are. Let me get the measurements and then I'll print out some pictures for you."

Oh dear God. I'm having twins. What the hell am I going to do? Two, two babies. I could cope with one, but two?

I left the exam room with the pictures clasped in my hand and wide shocked eyes.

I had to tell my family. Tonight. I was going to need their help to get through this. But first I needed to call DC. She answered on the first ring.

"So?"

"Twins, I'm having fucking twins." I wheezed, still not over the shock.

"Holy shit." She whispered.

"Can you come to my house tonight? I'm going to tell everyone and I need you to hold my hand."

"No problems, Riv. I'll be there. I've got your back."

"Thanks, DC. See you around seven. Bye."

I drove back to the workshop and sat in my car staring at the scan pictures for a few minutes before I tucked them into a pocket in my bag and got out of the car. Wrench stood outside the open door waiting for me.

"Everything okay, River?"

"I'm fine, Wrench. Can you come for dinner tonight?"

"Sure, you know I'm there for you, anytime." His eyes skimmed over me before he turned and walked back inside. I felt sure he had his suspicions.

Sitting on the couch in the reception area I sent out a block text to everyone I wanted at the house to hear my news.

Please come over at seven. I have some news I need to share face to face.

Not long after my phone started chiming with the incoming confirmations. Great. Everyone I loved would be there. I just hoped I would still have their respect once this night was over.

They were all there, Mum, Dad, Dagger, Wrench, Krissie, Mari, DC and Jinx. Bull had come with Dagger and was waiting on the back deck with one of the prospects. Duncan was playing cars in his room with another of the prospects.

I dragged my chair around so I faced them all. I had the pictures of the scan tucked into the big pocket of my cargo pants.

"A little while ago I did something monumentally stupid and now there are consequences because of my stupidity. I don't want to drag this out so here we go. I had a scan today and it confirmed the tests. I'm pregnant."

Chaos erupted, only DC and Wrench sat quietly watching me.

"Please, let me finish." I waited until my parents and Dagger had sat back down.

"There's more. I'm having twins."

Dagger leant forward his eyes flinty as he stared at me. "We have no twins in our family. Who's the father?"

I shook my head.

"He's not in the picture anymore. I gave him the opportunity to be a part of their lives but he's not interested. So, these babies are mine and mine alone."

"I'm going to kill the fucker as soon as I have a name, and believe me, River, I will get a name."

Then my big badass brother-in-law swallowed his rage, got up and knelt in front of me and put his big rough hands over my belly.

"They will never be without a dad, River. These babies are mine, just like Duncan is mine. I've got your back, sweetheart."

I burst into tears and watered his broad shoulder as my mum and dad joined our little circle.

"Rivvie, you're my little girl and these little babies are my grandbabies and I love them already." My mum whispered. "Don't you worry about a single thing. We love you."

"We'll get through this, sweetheart." My dad hugged me hard as he spoke in my ear.

Suddenly Krissie's voice rang through the room. "Out of the way, out of the way. Give the friends a turn to hug the lady who is pregnant with not one but two prawns in her belly. We need to hug her while we still can. With twins inside that little belly pretty soon we're going to have to take her from behind." There was a sudden stunned silence. "Did I just say that? Shit, I meant hug her from behind. Eeuw! I just grossed myself out." Krissie pulled a disgusted face and just like that she broke the tension in the room as we all burst into hysterical laughter.

I bathed, fed and put Duncan to bed before I joined the others. We sat down to the dinner I had ordered and talked about what came next with the babies. Dagger was already making plans to add a room to the cottage for the babies. And mum was making plans to go shopping for cribs and stuff. Through it all DC had been very quiet and it was only after everyone had left that she asked the question that had been troubling her.

"Did you tell him?"

I nodded but I shrugged at the same time.

"I tried, but he told me in no uncertain terms he wasn't interested in anything I might have to say. Called me a slut and pussy. So we're done, so very, very freaking done."

Anger flashed through her eyes but she controlled it.

"Fine. It's maybe better for you. He's all over some bitch from his past right now anyway." She waved a hand as if he was a fly to shoo away. "I'm with you, River, make no mistake about it. Anything you need you call me and I'll be here. Those babies in your tummy are going to get to know their Aunty DC very, very well. And I'm putting in dibs right now before anyone else snatches my place. I'm going to be holding your hand when you push them out, okay?"

My eyes widened.

"Please don't make me think about that right now. I have months to go before I have to start worrying about that." I whined.

Suddenly DC snatched me into her arms and hugged me hard. "You won't ever have to worry about a thing, Riv. I've got your back and so does the rest of your family. I've got to go because Hawk has been texting continuously and I need to sort that shit out but I'll see you again soon. Okay?"

"Okay. And thanks for being my friend, DC. Please, don't say anything to Hawk if you don't have to. But if you have no other option then it's okay."

She grinned as she left and I watched as she rode away with Wrench and two men following her.

I walked back into my empty house and locked up behind me. I don't know how I ended up in Duncan's room. But as I stood looking down at him I knew that just like I had coped with Dylan's loss and being a single mum to Duncan I would cope with the two new babies.

Going back into the kitchen I had to grin when I saw what my mum had done with the scan pictures. They were stuck up on my fridge with pink and blue magnets.

Everyone was already debating the sex of the babies. I didn't care, as long as they were healthy I would be happy with either sex.

Drawing a finger over them I smiled. "Mumma loves you my little prawns."

Shit, now I'm calling them prawns like Krissie had done.

Bad Mumma.

CHAPTER FIFTEEN

Ice

The way he had spoken to River when she called haunted him and he couldn't get it out of his mind. It fucked with his concentration at the most inopportune times. Like right now when he had to play the ass with Emma once again. But they were close, so damned close, to getting what they needed.

She had asked him to take her to Zeffers on the back of his bike and he had refused. Not fucking happening. Instead she had followed him in her car to an out of the way pub and grill where he hoped no one he knew would see them. The place was filled with older people so it seemed he was lucky this time. And unlike before, this time he had two of his brothers watching over him. Kid and Sin sat at a table where they could keep a vigilant eye on him, and his fucking beer.

Ever since Hawk had returned from his overnight run to Bloem things had been quiet at the clubhouse. His president hadn't said one word about the new rules Ice had set in place while he had been on the run. He had just nodded and gone up to his room. Soon after he had left with Beast and when he came back he had had DC on the back of his bike. They had disappeared into their room and only reappeared the next day. Ice knew without a doubt that shit was going to hit the fan once Hawk had his old lady settled down. He only needed to look in his prez's eyes to see the rage swirling in them. Retribution was coming.

Chris continued to work behind the bar and so far it had worked out fine. Dizzy however, wasn't good at all. The brother was silently going through hell and Ice didn't know how to help him. But he had seen Chris talking to him and maybe she would get through to him when no one else could. The girl was one of the good ones and they were damned lucky she had decided to stay. The brothers liked her even though she had stopped sleeping with them. They all liked talking to her and he often saw her with a mug of coffee in front of her leaning over the bar chatting with his brothers. She was a perfect addition to the club.

Bringing his thoughts back to the bitch next to him Ice tried to concentrate on what she was saying. She had been going off about Hawk banning her from the clubhouse for the last twenty minutes. But her next words had his full attention and he knew Kid and Sin were listening as well. He was wearing a wire and he had more than one tracker on him just in case.

"I heard DC made friends with a Sinner's Sons old lady. River something or another."

Why the hell did she always bring up River? Did she know they had been together? But how could she? No one knew except DC and she wouldn't talk. Did they have another mole?

Ice shrugged. "Oh? I don't keep track of what the old ladies do. Not my problem."

Emma smiled and Ice saw the calculation in her eyes. She was throwing out bait.

"I thought the Sinner's Sons and the Iron Dogz weren't friends. How could Hawk allow his old lady to fraternise with one of the Sinner's Sons bitches?"

Ice frowned at her as if he was confused. "What are you on about? Why would it matter if they were friends? They're bitches, not important."

"And what if she's friends with DC to get information on your club? DC is the presidents' woman and surely she knows things."

Ice laughed. "I don't think so." He frowned as he pretended concern. "What are you trying to say, Emma?"

She leant closer as if she was about to share a huge secret with him. "I think DC is passing information about the Iron Dogz to River and she's passing it onto the Sinner's Sons. I've heard whispers that Dagger is about to take her as his old lady. Something about a promise he made to his brother."

What the hell was the bitch aiming for with this shit? And what the fuck did she know about Dagger and Sparrow?

She looked at him through her lashes. "What do you think DC might be telling her?"

"I don't give a fuck because there's nothing to pass on." Ice said harshly and at last he seemed to get under her skin. But she very quickly hid it and pretended to be hurt.

"When are you ever going to trust me again, Gray? We used to share everything with each other and now you're keeping me miles away from you. I can help. You know I can. I always helped you to get clarity when club stuff got your head all confused."

What the fuck was the bitch talking about? Never in his life had he discussed club business with a bitch. And certainly never with her. He had considered her too young and innocent.

"Don't know what the fuck you're talking about, Emma. I don't talk about club business. I never have and I never will."

She pulled a face and Ice waited for her next move. He didn't have to wait long. "I bet Dagger talks to River and I bet her and DC hear a lot of things you think they don't and I bet they share it with each other."

"What the fuck do I care if Dagger shares his club's shit with some bitch? It has nothing to do with me. Not my business." Ice pushed a little harder. It was obvious Emma was trying to make him suspicious of DC's friendship with River. Why?

Emma shrugged as if she didn't care one way or the other. "I just thought I should tell you what I had heard. The doctors where I work were talking about how River abuses her poor little boy and how the Welfare got involved. So sad. If she could do that to a child I was just wondering what else she would do."

It took everything he had to keep his face impassive as the bitch pushed and lied to get some type of reaction from him. Why? What was she looking for?

"Not interested, Emma. Sad for the kid but it's not my problem." Ice twisted his beer on the table in front of him glanced at Kid and when he got the okay took a sip.

Her eyes flashed with anger and then a sly look slid through them and Ice braced for the fucked up shit she was going to come up with next. Her voice when she spoke was soft and fearful. It was so damned fake it made his gut ache.

"I have something to confess and you are going to be so angry with me. I'm actually glad we're here and not at home. I was scared of telling you when we were alone." She glanced up through her lashes to gauge his reaction to her once again calling her monstrosity of a house their home, and to her having something to confess. He gave her nothing.

"Spit it out, Emma." Ice growled. He had a suspicion she was about to play what she thought was her trump card.

And then she did.

"I lied." She said softly. "I've been trying to tell you for some time but I was so scared you would hate me. I didn't lose our baby, Gray. I had her and gave her up to a good family to take care of her."

Jesus. Thank fuck for the DNA test. If not for the test he would have been a fucking wreck right now. He used the rage at her trying to manipulate him to fuel his reaction.

"What? You did what?" Ice grabbed her hand and squeezed it hard, enjoying her grimace of pain.

"You're hurting me, Gray. Please." She begged softly.

"Where is she? Where is my daughter, Emma? You better tell me right now or you are going to regret ever walking back into my life."

"Please just listen, Gray." Again the soft pleading voice. "I was alone and my mum called my dad and he knew people who could help. We had broken up and I didn't know what to do. He contacted people who wanted to have a baby and couldn't. She's happy with them. They take good care of her."

Did she let it slip on purpose or was it a crumb she threw out to pull him further into her net?

"How could your dad have helped you? He wasn't ever in your life, Emma. Who is he? How did he organise an adoption without my signature?"

Again she gave him the sad and guilty face.

"I…I didn't put your name on her birth certificate. I'm so sorry, Gray. My dad called people he knew, important people, and they fixed it. At the time I didn't know he was my dad. He was just a man who sometimes visited my mum."

This was information they hadn't had before and there must be a reason why she so freely gave it to him. He had to be careful but not about how he felt right now. She was expecting his reaction.

Ice didn't have to pretend as he glared down at the bitch. He hated her and it showed in his eyes. And he told her as much.

"I hate you right now, Emma. You stole my child from me and gave her away as if she was a bag of old clothes. You and your family, your dad, you owe me. I want their names. Everyone who had a hand in this fucking adoption. Give me their names. If you don't I will make you regret the day you decided to take what was mine."

She shook her head sadly but he saw right through it. It was fake.

"It won't help. It was a closed adoption. My dad and her new parents insisted on it. She's gone and it's my fault." Fake tears stood in her eyes as she gave him some names and strangely included the names of the Howards. He would bet his last cent most of the names were as fake as her tears. But maybe not, maybe he was being set up for something else. The kid's kidnapping maybe?

"I can't be around you right now." Ice said as he got up and walked away.

And the tiny bug he left on the table had no trouble picking up her phone conversation after he had left. And with luck Ziggy would be able to trace the call to its origin.

Emma Coetzee was evil, right down to the bottom of her filthy soul. Using her own child to further her dark agenda proved it beyond a shadow of doubt.

Ice stormed back into the clubhouse and straight to the bar where Chris was already pouring him a shot of whiskey and Sam stood ready to take his kutte to get the bitch's smell out of it.

"Stop throwing your tees across the bar." Chris griped as she threw his smelly tee at Sam. "Ask Aunt Beryl to show you how to soak it, and then put it in the machine. It will be good as new after it has been washed."

Kid and Sin joined him at the bar and both signalled for shots as well.

"The bitch is some piece of work." Sin snarled as he threw his shot back and set the glass slowly back on to the bar.

"You had a fucking lucky escape, brother." Kid shook his head. "Her soul is dark, very fucking dark."

Ice tapped his shot glass on the bar and Chris refilled it but as he lifted the glass to his mouth he stopped and turned to Kid. "I'm worried about the Howards. She's put that poor kid right in the middle of her fucking game. We have to get them to a safe place until this shit is over. Emma is going to use the kid to get what she wants and once she's done with her the kid will disappear. We can't let that happen."

Hawk sat down next to him and patted the bar and Chris poured him a shot. Ice waited as his prez threw it back. "Already on it, brother. Just had a call from Rick, the taskforce took care of the Howards this morning. They've gone on an extended vacation. I have his word they won't be found and they will stay gone until this shit has been sorted."

Ice nodded and threw back his shot, feeling the alcohol burn down into his gut. But it didn't burn as much as the knowledge he had been in love with a fucking lie for years. Years he wasted yearning for something that never existed.

"You should have seen her, Hawk. Crying all soft and ladylike while she slyly watched for his reaction. The bitch is seriously fucked up." Sin shuddered and motioned for another shot. "The sooner we get our brother shot of her the better."

"We're working on it, Sin. Ziggy is busy with it right now and he said if he has to call in Skel to help he would. And that alone should tell you how serious he is about finding what we need."

Hawk had his elbow on the bar, his hand stroking over his beard, his eyes were sharp as he looked at Ice.

"How the hell did we miss the craziness inside her, Ice? She and Genna grew up right in front of us and we never noticed there was something really wrong with her. Have you talked to your sister about her?"

Ice sighed and rubbed his hands over his tired eyes. He had not been sleeping well lately.

"I was too caught up in wanting to fuck her to notice there was something off about her, and no, I haven't spoken to Genna. She's pissed at me after the shit Emma pulled with my folks and then the news that I'm 'dating' the bitch again has her about ready to kick me in the nuts. So I've been avoiding her and Gail, both those bitches are fucking dangerous when they're pissed. We need to end this shit before they cut my nuts off in my sleep."

Hawk laughed and clapped a hand on his back and Ice had to laugh as well. They were still laughing when Hawk's phone chimed. He checked it then showed it to Ice and the brothers.

It was from Ziggy.

I've got a lead on Jane

They followed Hawk down the passage to Ziggy's office. He had several things going at the same time on the monitors in front of him but it was the grainy photo of Jane that drew their attention.

"I set up a programme to track Jane by facial recognition in all the big cities, which was a very long shot, and I just got a hit. I downloaded the photo from a traffic cam in Port Elizabeth. She's somewhere near the harbour. Unfortunately I haven't been able to track her because she's very good at avoiding cameras. This was the only image I got and it was a total fluke. The camera that caught her was moved during a traffic accident and it was pointing the wrong way."

Ziggy looked at Hawk. "Do you want me to contact Greyhound in PE? They could start looking, see if they find anything."

"No, I'll call him. Book four tickets on the first available flight to PE for Ice, Beast, Sin and Wolf. I'll arrange for them to be picked up at the airport." Hawk frowned as he turned to leave then turned back again. "Get me some answers, Ice. And if you can get your hands on her bring the bitch in."

"You got it, Boss."

Ziggy got them on the late night flight out of Lanseria Airport and the brothers from the PE chapter picked them up and took them to their clubhouse. After a short meeting they decided to start their search on the docks and work outwards from there. The PE brothers were already talking to their contacts to see what they could find. So far they had very little.

Early the next morning they each paired up with a brother from the local chapter and started to turn over rocks. Somewhere someone knew something. They just had to 'ask' the right questions. It was very slow going but they started to pick up crumbs of information by their second day in town.

By their third day they still had nothing concrete, and then one of the club's contacts reported hearing whispers of a tall blonde woman who was seen at a small outlaw club called Satan's Savages MC. The club was known to be part of a pipeline running drugs from the port. The PE chapter of the Iron Dogz had never had any problems with them because they weren't in the drug trade. They kept an eye on them but they hadn't had any trouble between the clubs, now it seemed things were about to change.

As a courtesy Greyhound called the president of the club. The call did not go as expected. The Satan's Savages wanted a meeting, but not with Greyhound, they demanded a meeting with Hawk. Ice told Greyhound to go ahead and arrange the meeting. He would be the one attending the meeting with this asshole. The Satan's Savages insisted the meeting had to take place in a very public place, on the beachfront. It meant safety for both of the clubs. But it was absolute bullshit.

Greyhound had reached out to his contact at the SAPS and he had advised against meeting with the Satan's Savages. The club was presently under surveillance by the drug squad and there were rumblings they were about to make several arrests. If the Iron Dogz were seen meeting with them they would be implicated by association.

Everything about this meeting pointed to a set up.

Ice changed the location and time of the meeting by turning up at the gates of the Satan's Savages clubhouse in the early hours of the morning. It was obvious they had had a huge party the night before and there were several bitches and hang arounds stumbling about in the yard. The meeting went down at the gates of the compound and went about as Ice had expected it would. The fucker had nothing to say, just a bunch of empty threats. But that was fine, they hadn't expected anything anyway.

As he walked to his bike Ice turned around and raised his voice so everyone in the filthy little yard could hear him.

"There's a reward of five thousand rand for anyone who comes forward with information about the tall blonde woman who has been visiting this club. Her name is Jane Warne. She's a child sex trafficker and we'll pay to get our hands on her. You give us what you know and we'll keep your name out of it. All we want is the bitch. She sells innocent little kids to perverts. If you have young children keep them close and trust no one. And when I say no one, I mean no one. Call us if you know or hear anything that will help us put her away."

There were shocked rumblings among the people standing around watching.

LOST AND FOUND IN BLUE

As he walked away the president of the Satan's Savages was shouting at his men and the people in the yard but Ice ignored him as he got in the SUV and drove away with his brothers.

If they were lucky one of those bastards would be greedy or scared enough to contact the Dogz. He hoped it was soon because he wanted to get back to follow up on what Ziggy might have uncovered about Emma. Not that he had anything yet. Ice had been calling him every day to get an update but so far Ziggy didn't have anything more to share.

On their fifth fucking day in the windy city one of the Satan's Savages called. The information was sparse but worrying.

Jane had been in Port Elizabeth to do the ground work to set up another pipeline for the export of their product. The Savages hadn't been aware the product was young girls and boys until Ice had made his little speech. When confronted by his officers the Satan's Savages president had admitted to negotiating with Jane to set up the pipeline. She had offered a huge amount of money to the club. And his greed had resulted in the bastard becoming shark food.

Unfortunately Jane was gone. She had moved on to lure her next target into their filthy business. But they now had a trail to follow. She was targeting smaller clubs, clubs who needed money. Clubs who might be greedy for a piece of the tightly controlled criminal pie.

The Iron Dogz would be targeting those same small clubs in the harbour cities. They would all receive only one warning. Deal with Jane Warne and become an enemy of the Iron Dogz MC.

RENÉ VAN DALEN

Relaxing back into his seat on their late night flight home Ice sipped on his whiskey and turned his mind to the job waiting for him in Jozi. He had to find a break in Emma's armour.

Something told him their time was fast running out.

CHAPTER SIXTEEN

Ice

They had been back several days and Ziggy still had nothing of significance. He was working on the problem with Mad Dog and Skel, and the three of them were using all their skills to find the connection between Jane Warne and Emma Coetzee. They were digging deep into both of their backgrounds, refusing to give up and swore they would find the common denominator between the two.

Someone or something linked the two women to each other and to the Maingarde bitch. They needed to find that link.

Another thing that had them baffled was Emma's fixation on DC, River Anderson and the Sinner's Sons MC. Why?

Was Sparrow's death somehow connected to all this shit? What did they know about his death? Had he seen or heard something? Was that the reason why he was gunned down?

And what the hell did DC have to do with any of it? Was it because of Jane?

He had way more questions than answers. And he needed answers.

They needed a face to face with Dagger because he was the only one who could answer the questions they had about Sparrow. But they couldn't meet at Zeffers like they had last time. There were too many eyes on them there. They needed a place no one would expect either of them to visit.

And he knew just the place. He would have to ask Gail to let him take his nieces out for a treat. And the way she felt about him right now meant he would get an earful before she agreed.

Ice sat in the too small chair next to Dagger watching as his nieces and Dagger's nephew bounced on the trampolines.

The boy was tall for his age and had super straight dark blonde hair that flopped over his green eyes as he jumped. There was a remarkable family resemblance between him and Dagger. And even at this age it was clear to see the kid was going to look just like his old man. Anyone who had known Sparrow or saw photos of the man would know this kid was his. Even the fucking smile was the same. He would be a constant reminder of his dad every time Dagger and River looked at him. That had to be fucking painful.

Looking away from the kid Ice forced himself to concentrate on business and not on trying to see something of his mother in the boy.

Arranging for their meeting to take place here had been a good idea and not wearing their kuttes had been another good idea. No one gave them a second glance.

"Why did you want to see me? And why here? I told Hawk we'll give you some more time to settle the shit with your bitch. So what do you want?" Dagger said as he watched his nephew.

"I have some questions and we're meeting here because there's less chance of us being seen together. And just so we're clear, the bitch is nothing of mine. She's a job, that's all." Ice did another sweep of the indoor area. They were still clear.

Dagger nodded but kept his eyes on the boy.

"Ask. Can't promise I'll answer."

"Do you know of any connection between Emma Coetzee and Sparrow? We can't find any reason why she's targeting River. So we thought maybe there was something between Sparrow and Emma."

Dagger went from relaxed to tense in less than a second.

"No fucking way. I admit, my brother had a lot of bitches but it all stopped the minute he met River. She was only seventeen so he waited and while he waited he didn't touch another bitch. He loved his old lady, fucking worshipped the ground she walked on. Your bitch wouldn't have made any impression on him at all, he was all about River. And when his Rivzie got pregnant he was the fucking happiest man on the planet. He was that asshole who buys every single pregnancy book he can find and reads them all. Don't know how many times he grossed us out in church discussing shit we didn't want to know anything about. At the time he and Jinx were the only ones with old ladies at our table and the bastards made sure to rub it in our faces."

Dagger went silent and Ice gave him time.

"The night he was murdered he was supposed to take River out to dinner. But that same afternoon Jinx had found his old lady fucking some civvie bastard in their bed and went on a bender. He went to a bar our club frequents and that evening the bar owner called Sparrow to collect his buddy. He dropped River off at home and went to fetch Jinx. Sparrow calmed him down and got some coffee down him to try and sober him up. They walked out of the bar into an ambush. A blacked out Beemer was waiting right outside, windows open and Sparrow took three to the chest and abdomen. Jinx took two to the upper chest."

Dagger sat forward and rubbed his hands over his face and pulled down hard on his beard.

"As they were leaving the bar Sparrow had called me to tell me he was taking Jinx to his place. And I heard it all. My brother and his best friend going down, and as he went down Sparrow kept giving me information. Make, model, number plate, how many in the car. At first I don't think he realised how bad he was hit. And then he did. And still he tried to tell me something, tried to warn me about something, he mentioned you. And then it was all about his girl and his son."

Dagger breathed in heavily.

"Jesus Christ. My brother should not be dead. He should be sitting here watching his boy jump around. He should be the one putting babies in his old lady's belly."

Sucking the emotion back in he sat up and his voice went hard and flat.

"Jinx was drunk off his ass and blacked out when he was shot. Still has a no recall of that night. I recorded it, that last call from my brother. I started recording by mistake but once I realised what was happening I recorded it all. I can't fucking listen to it but I'll forward it to you. If anything, and I mean any-fucking-thing comes from it I want to be the first to know. Vengeance belongs to me and the Sinner's Sons."

Ice didn't know what to say. Listening to your brother getting shot and dying and not being able to do anything about it had to be one of the most difficult things to live through.

"If we find anything I'll call you immediately. You have my word."

Ice hadn't known Jinx had been with Sparrow the night he had been killed or that he had been a target as well. It changed things. If they could get Jinx to remember what he saw. He didn't know how but felt sure they could find some way to do it.

Some way to jolt his brain

While they sat silently side by side watching the kids he sent Ziggy a text and he didn't hide it from Dagger.

Research memory black outs. Find me a way to get those memories back. Fast

Ice took his nieces home and loved the hugs and kisses he got from them. And then he silently allowed Gail to give him hell about Emma, again. He would have given anything to tell her the truth but there was no way he could. He knew his sister, knew she would call Genna and the two of them would immediately rain hell down on

Emma. It was something he could not allow to happen, he had to keep his sisters safe.

By the time he walked back into the clubhouse Dagger had forwarded the recording to him. Hawk was sitting at the bar with a bottle of water in his hand. Waiting. DC sat next to her man, her eyes on him as he walked up. Those dark eyes of hers were so damned mysterious they hardly ever showed what she was thinking or feeling.

"Dagger sent me the recording I texted you about. Do you want me to give it to Ziggy?"

Hawk nodded slowly then glanced at DC. "Yes, once he's done whatever needs doing we will meet in the chapel. I've called the officers in so we have more ears listening. Maybe Dagger missed something. His brother was dying and that's what he would have concentrated on."

Ice cleared his throat before he could speak. "He did say he can't listen to it and I think he meant he couldn't handle hearing it again. So it's possible he missed something." Glancing down at his dusty and scuffed up boots Ice shook his head. "Must have been fucking hard."

Shaking his head to dislodge those thoughts he concentrated on what else he had found.

"Did you know Jinx was with him and got shot as well?" He was watching Hawk but he saw DC's eyes narrow before she locked it down.

Hawk frowned. "No, I don't think it was ever mentioned. Do you think the Sinner's Sons scrubbed it out of the reports to keep him safe?"

Giving it some thought Ice nodded. "It could be. It's what I would've done if it had happened to two of our guys. Dagger said Jinx blacked out and has no memory of what happened. I asked Ziggy to do some research, see if we can somehow jog his memory."

DC spoke so softly it was difficult to hear her with the noise in the common room. "Maybe listening to the recording would do it. Jinx was Sparrow's best friend. I think he blames himself for what happened."

"How do you know this, little bird?" Hawk frowned at his old lady and typical of DC she frowned right back at him.

"I know because River told me. She said her man and Jinx had been best friends and always pulling pranks on their brothers. Now Jinx hardly ever smiles and most of the time only when he's with Duncan. And since that bitch targeted River and Duncan he has virtually moved in with them to keep them safe." She shrugged. "And she's right, he never smiles or laughs."

"Fine. Enough talking about Jinx not smiling. We listen to the recording and make decisions after." Hawk growled.

Ice hid a smile. His cousin did not like DC talking about another man. And that man living with River? He didn't feel all warm and fuzzy about it either.

Ziggy had brought speakers to the chapel and he had set up his laptop and some other shit. Ice had no idea what it was and wasn't interested in finding out either. As long as what he did gave them a clear recording to listen to he was happy.

He was surprised to see DC joining them but said nothing. All the officers were in the room, including Bulldog, his dad. Ice knew in his gut this recording was going to change things. How or why he didn't know. He just felt it.

And then Ziggy cleared his throat and it was time.

"I've run the recording through a programme and cleaned it of hisses and hums so what we're going to hear are as clear as I can get it right now. I can work on it more after we're done here and clarify the background voices."

He drew in a very deep breath and slowly released it, then he clicked a button and a dead man's voice filled the room.

"I've got him, Dagger. He's fucking *stukkend* (broken and drunk), brother. When I get my hands on the fucking bitch she's going to be sorry. I'm taking him home with me. My Rivzie and I will keep an eye on him and we'll see you in the morning."

The sounds of scuffling and murmurs and then Dagger's voice.

"Good, you keep him with you, Sparrow. I tried to stop him when he left here but he wasn't in a good place and didn't want to hear me."

Sounds of grunting and heavy breathing.

"Jesus, fuck, Jinx. Why is your ass so fucking heavy, brother? Been eating too much of mum's good food lately, have you?"

"Fuck you, Row. You been eating too, and your ass is getting fat."

Laughter and shuffling sounded.

"Hey, Tone, can you get the door for me, please my man. Got my hands full over here."

"Sure, Sparrow. You take care of him now. Our friend here is not in a good place right now."

An unknown voice said. Must have been Tone.

"Listen, Sparrow, I want the two of you here early. We've got some shit to do …"

"Hey!" A voice called out, sounding high and thin.

"What the fuck! Ambush! Ambush! Dagger, fuck, brother…"

Sounds of multiple shots and dull thuds and groans.

"Jinx, motherfucker! Get the fuck down! Get down!"

Sounds of heavy bodies falling, grunts, groans and breaths hissing out.

"Sparrow! Fuck! Dylan fucking talk to me! DYLAN!!!!"

Sounds of a car accelerating, wheels squealing and then heavy breathing.

"Darren, brother, we're both down. Black Beemer, not sure of the year, tinted windows, chrome hubs, HGT735GP…th….three…. in the car. Two…..shooters."

Then the sound of stuttered breathing and Dagger running and shouting at his brothers calling them to ride.

As he did he continued to talk to Sparrow.

"Where are you shot, Dylan? Talk to me little brother."

"Oh fuck, chest…and… ab…abdomen. Jinx got…two…chest."

"I'm on my bike, little brother. You fucking stay with me, I'm ten minutes out. I'm coming, you hear me, you fucking stay with me, Dylan!"

Screaming engines from several bikes can be heard but the sounds of Sparrow struggling to breathe and talk virtually drowns them out.

Then another voice shouting. "Call an ambulance! Bring me some fucking towels, right the fuck now! Stop fucking staring and help me you motherfuckers!"

Scuffling and grunts.

"Hold on, Sparrow. The girls are getting some towels to stop the bleeding. You just hold the fuck on, brother, okay?"

The voice soothed.

"Have to…have to tell…you. Saw……the…..car…..before. Ice……Ice. He….he….hotel."

A heavy sigh then he continues.

"Ice……warn…….bitches."

"Did the fucking Dogz do this? Sparrow! Did fucking Ice do this? I'm going to fucking kill them all!"

Heavy struggling breaths.

"Tone…..please…..hold…..phone. Not Ice…..she…..warn…..bit….bitches"

"Almost there, little brother. I'm almost with you. Hold on, please hold the fuck on."

"Pro…..protect……my….s…s...son. Promise…..me. Protect…..my…..fam…..family, please….brother. Be……be…..ware…..bit…..bitches."

"I've got you, Dylan. I promise but hold on for me, please, little brother."

"Fuck…..don't ….want…to….die…..Darren. Love….you…..bro. Tell my…..Rivzie…..tell her……love her….past…..death into…..forever. Love….you….all so…..fucking….much…..take care…..of…..my…..fam…"

A struggling gurgle and then silence and then the sounds of a woman crying as the man, most probably Tone spoke to Dagger.

"Dagger, brother, I'm so sorry. He's gone, my brother."

Dagger screamed, and then there were no more words, just the sound of the big man crying but still racing to his brother before the call cuts off.

DC's head was on her folded arms on the table and her shoulders jerked as she cried silently. Hawk was crouched next to her, his arm around her shoulders as he whispered to her. Then she sniffed and sat up. She didn't hide her tears, just brushed them away as she reached for the bottle of water in front of her and took deep gulps.

"Jesus. Fuck. I never want to listen to that shit ever fucking again. I can't." Kahn said softly as he cried openly and wiped the tears from his eyes. "Knew him. He teased me when I was a prospect and watching over the bikes at a rally. Said I looked like the fucking Aga Kahn the way I stood watch. Gave me my road name that day. Always laughing, always ready to help. He didn't care if you were in his club or not. Made friends where ever he went. I want to fucking gut whoever did this. He did not deserve to die like that."

The minute Sparrow had given Dagger the details of the car Ice had frozen in his seat. He knew the car. Knew it very fucking well because he had bought it for Emmie. The car she had told him had been stolen from the campus parking lot.

"The car was Emma's car" His voice sounded harsh and loud in the silence. "The car she told me had been stolen out of the campus parking lot a few days before she walked out on me. It was never recovered. Where the fuck was that car before it was used for the hit on Sparrow? And where is it now?"

Kid sat forward and tapped a finger on the table. "A better question. How did Sparrow know the car was linked to Ice? He clearly said he had seen the car before and he kept on saying bitches and she. He identified two shooters. I think they were female and he knew who they were but being mortally wounded and trying to get a message to his family he didn't think to name them. But the clues are there. We just have to listen very fucking carefully."

Spider shook his head. "He said he'd seen it before. That's the clue. He had seen the car with bitches in it somewhere before and those bitches got antsy and took him out before he could put it together."

"He repeated 'warn' twice." Bulldog said very quietly. "What if he meant Warne as in the surname? And why mention Ice and bitches? I think Sparrow saw something go down with Jane and Emma but he most probably shrugged it off as Iron Dogz bitches doing whatever. Emma wasn't supposed to be in South Africa at the time. So I have two questions. What was Emma doing here? And why was she with Jane, a woman she's supposed to hate?"

"He said 'hotel'. He was trying to say something about a hotel. It sounded like he said 'he' but what if he was trying to say the hotel's name?" Jagger pulled on his goatee. "There are a few hotels in the area starting with an H. Ziggy, would they keep records of guests going back five years?"

"If it was one of the fancy ones, yes, certainly. But if it was the smaller ones it's doubtful." Ziggy tapped on his laptop. "I can put a list together if you want."

"Yes, do that. I think Sparrow saw the car with the two bitches at a hotel with someone they did not want to be seen with. There's our connection." Jagger sighed. "And instead of waiting to see if he was going to rat them out, they hit him first. If we're lucky Jinx might have been with him the day he saw them and it's the reason why he was shot as well. Not remembering anything about that night most probably saved his life."

"I have photos of the fucking piece of shit car." Ice growled. "We can show them to him and see if he recognises it. Plus we need photos of Jane and Emma from five to seven years ago. Both of them changed their looks quite drastically."

A horribly cold voice with absolutely no inflection in it at all filled the room and everyone froze.

"I want Emma Coetzee in my dungeon. If you don't give her to me I will have her picked up and taken to a place where I can play without any interruptions. She will face the Crow and confess her sins."

Holy. Fucking. Shit.

DC was no longer DC. She had become the thing nightmares were made of. A nightmare he had watched at work and hoped he didn't have to ever again. The Crow.

"Baby, no." Hawk's voice was soft and he reached for DC's clenched fist. "Crow, we can't allow you to take care of Emma right now. We need the bitch without any marks on her. But maybe when we're done with her, maybe then there would be time for you to ask some questions. Okay?"

"Are you bargaining with me, Hawk?" That flat, cold and scary as fuck voice asked.

"Yes." He said without hesitation. "Yes I am."

A heavy sigh flew past DC's clenched lips, and it was as if she was battling herself and then she blinked and warmth flooded back into her dark eyes.

"Fuck." She whispered. "Sorry, that wasn't supposed to happen. I've got it under control now."

"Can I just say, you are one scary motherfucker, DC." Spider shook his head and then gave her a sly grin. "I'm fetching you the next time Genna threatens to cut my nuts off while I'm sleeping."

Laughter rang out and Ice could hear the sudden relief in their voices. Trust his little brother to break the tension in the room.

Hawk rapped his knuckles on the table and silence fell once again.

"Let's get back to work and solve this puzzle. Ice, you and Kid arrange with Dagger to have a meeting with Jinx. Ziggy will get the photos together and let's see if Jinx can help us out."

Drumming his fingers on the arm of his chair he sat back and looked around the table.

"We now know they won't hesitate to shoot if they think they've been compromised. We are going on alert until this is done. I've got a burning in my gut and it just won't go away. We are going to be careful. I don't want to lose anyone of you. We keep our eyes peeled for the black Beemer. I think they use it to hit their targets. You see the fucking car you duck and cover. Ice, no further meetings with the bitch, we're getting too close."

Ice didn't want to but he had to disagree with his president.

"Prez, she's going to call. You know she is, and I can only stall her for a short while. She thinks she's got me against the ropes with the kid thing. By now she's found out the Howards are gone and she's going to make another play. If I'm not in contact with her how are we going to prepare for their next move?"

But it wasn't Hawk who answered him. It was a very pissed off DC.

"And what if she makes another attempt on River and Duncan? What if that's her next play? You freaking dropped the ball with River once already, Ice. And now there is so much more at stake. You have no freaking idea. We cannot allow the bitch to get her dirty hands on River or Duncan. Dagger would lose his freaking mind and so would Jinx."

Everyone looked at DC with confused frowns.

"What are you talking about, little bird? What aren't you telling us."

"I can't say because I promised I would keep my mouth shut." She gave a disgruntled sigh. "I already said too much and even though she said I can tell you if you push I'm not going to. It's for her to tell." She growled at Hawk but her eyes slid to Ice and stayed on him.

What the hell?

Ziggy stared at DC with narrowed eyes, tilted his head as he did when he was thinking and then started typing furiously. Suddenly he froze, lifting his hands from the keyboard leaving them hanging in the air in front of him he looked at DC with wide shocked eyes.

"Oh shit. She really, really can't get her hands on River right now." He murmured.

"Why?" Hawk snarled. "What did you find, Ziggy?"

"Okay, okay, but I just want to make it clear. This doesn't feel right. I don't like doing this and when it gets out, and believe me after I tell you it will, I will fucking deny any involvement."

"For fuck's sake stop moaning and just tell us." Beast snarled.

"Don't, Ziggy. This is her business, not club business." DC warned.

"But it is club business, DC. If she told you then you know why it is." Ziggy said with an apology in his voice.

DC sighed then nodded. "I know. I just wanted to give her some more time."

"Enough with all this fucking back and forth shit. Ziggy, tell me what the fuck is going on. Right the fuck now." Hawk laid down the law.

Ziggy drew in a deep breath and Ice frowned when for some reason he looked right at him before he opened his mouth.

"River is pregnant. With twins."

Shock coursed through Ice as he clenched his teeth to stop words he didn't want to say from passing his lips. And then his cousin did it for him.

"Does the file tell us who the father is and how far along she is?"

Ziggy covered his face with his hands as if he was praying or something.

"Yes to both. And that's why it's club business."

"Stop fucking dragging it out, Zig. Just give it to us." Bulldog said. "It can't be that bad."

"Oh, but it is, it is that bad. According to her file she's about fourteen weeks pregnant. So please do the math motherfuckers. It happened around the same time as the family braai we had here and our esteemed VP is the fucking daddy." He hissed.

And then Ziggy exploded. "How the fuck could you do this to her? You dumped her to go after fucking Emma? Jesus. No wonder she doesn't want you to know."

"Oh fuck." Kid whispered. "She saw you with Emma. And the bitch was all over you."

Spider shoved his chair back and looked ready to launch himself at Ice. "Seriously? Are you fucking with me right now? You've been allowing the piece of shit whore to climb all over you while your woman is pregnant with my nieces or nephews? Shame on you, bro." Spider looked like he had smelt something really bad. "No wonder you need to hose yourself off every time you've been out with the evil slut."

Shock hurtled through him as he reared up and out of his chair, he heard it bang into the wall behind him but he only had eyes for his dad who had slowly pushed himself up from his chair. His dad was furious and disappointed at the same time. Ice saw it very clearly on his face and in his eyes.

Bulldog had both hands on the table as he leant forward, his eyes hard as they focused on Ice. "You will fix this. Those children are my grandbabies. As of right now you're off the Emma Coetzee shit. Your family comes first. Do you understand me, Ice?"

Ice nodded. Yes, he understood but at the same time he didn't understand. Why hadn't she come to him?

And then it hit him. The phone call. The fucking phone call. He reared back and slammed his hands on top of his head and roared at the ceiling. He fucking roared with rage at himself.

Slowly the rage left him and he looked back at his dad.

"Ah fuck, Dad. I fucked up, I really, really fucked up. I was trying to keep her safe. She hates me and after what I said to her I don't blame her. But I didn't mean it, I swear." Ice swung to face DC. "I swear, DC, I just said what I did to keep her safe. I didn't mean any of it. Not one fucking word."

DC sat down on Hawk's lap and crossed her arms as she stared at him and then she gave him an evil little smile.

"I'm not the one you should be telling this. You need to tell River and hope and pray she can forgive you for being the biggest asshat in the known universe."

And then it hit him. And it hit him so hard the world seemed to wobble on its axis.

"I'm going to be a dad." He whispered. "Holy shit, Dad. I'm going to be a dad and there are two of them. Holy fucking shit."

"Congratulations, you asshole." Spider grabbed him and hugged him hard. Ice held on to his little brother as the reality slowly sank into him.

Then the rest of his brothers surrounded him, teasing and hugging him. They congratulated him on his super sperm making two for the price of one. Jesus. Only his brothers would think of that shit right now.

Deep inside his chest a glow of satisfaction started to spread. And joy grew right along with it.

His woman was having his babies. His babies.

Now he just had to convince her she was his and he was hers. It wasn't going to be easy. Not after the fucking phone call and the Emma fuck up.

Hope. He had hope and this feeling inside. A feeling that grew and grew.

A feeling that was fast starting to take up all the space in his heart.

CHAPTER SEVENTEEN

River

For a couple of days now Dagger had been quiet and withdrawn and his eyes were filled with shadows. Exactly like they had been after Dylan had been murdered.

God. It still hurt every time I thought about or said that word. Murder.

Because that's what it was. Dylan had been murdered by a person or persons who had never been caught. The car had been reported stolen years earlier and there had been zero forensic evidence. The police said they had no leads and the case had gone cold.

Not that I had believed them. I had seen it in the investigating officers' eyes. They had just chalked it up to another gang shooting and moved on to what they considered to be more deserving cases. It had been as if Dylan's life hadn't mattered. And because of the way they had treated me at the time, I hated the police and would never call them for assistance under any circumstances.

With a sigh I rolled my neck to ease my aching muscles. I had been hunched over while working on the engine on the workbench for too long. I needed a break. When I turned around I caught

Wrench's eyes on me. The frown said it all. I was about to get a lecture.

"You need to sit down for a while and drink some fu...freaking milk or something. The prawns are getting bigger every day and you need to rest more."

And there it was. He had been around Krissie too much. Actually everyone was calling my babies 'the prawns' myself included. Wrench was being so sweet trying not to swear around them.

"And don't forget, you use the hand cleaner in the clear bottle. Not the other shit full of chemicals that might harm the prawns."

"Yes, yes. I'm going to get cleaned up and head home a bit early. Duncan has to take something for a cake sale at school tomorrow and he wants cupcakes. I wish I could just buy them and be done with it but he wants to bake them himself. So I'm getting one of those box cake mixes from the shop and hoping for the best."

Wrench was shaking with laughter and I pulled a face at him. He knew very well how bad I was at baking, he had seen the results.

"Call mum, ask her to come over and help out. You know she would love to."

Ever since I had revealed my pregnancy Wrench had been a big part of my family and like with the other men my parents had promptly adopted him. He too now called them mum and dad.

"Do you think my boykie would mind? I don't want to disappoint him. He's already so confused about the babies."

"No, he won't. He loves his Nana and you can hang out with them while they bake. It would do both of you good to spend some time with mum just hanging out."

"When did you become so wise and stuff?"

He tightened an imaginary tie and smirked. "I have always been wise, your prawness."

Dropping my head I shook it slowly from side to side, laughing as I walked out to go and clean up.

As I walked out of the workshop to where my *bakkie* was parked I sighed sadly. No more riding my bike for the next ten months at least. It sucked. Waving at the two prospects that would be shadowing me I slowly pulled out on to the road. Traffic wasn't too bad and I did a quick stop at the small supermarket near home and got a box cake mix just in case we needed it.

But I shouldn't have bothered. Wrench had obviously called mum and she and my boykie were already busy in the kitchen. Duncan smiled wide and waved the sieve in his hand and cake flour went everywhere. A white cloud flew up into the air and slowly sifted down on him. His eyes were wide as they skated between my mum and me.

"Oh shit." He muttered softly.

I know I should have reprimanded him, but damn, it was so funny I burst out laughing and so did mum. A wide happy grin settled on Duncan's face as he watched us.

"Sorry, Nana, sorry, Mumma. I made a beeeg mess and I said a bad word. Sorry." The little shit apologised but didn't stop grinning.

"As long as you know it's a bad word and you don't say it again, okay? And you are definitely going to help us clean this up."

"Uh-uh. Wrenchie said the prawns have to sit." He frowned heavily as he stared at my belly then pointed at it. "Sit prawns, sit." He ordered.

Mum and I looked at each other and burst out laughing again. I laughed so hard I had to cross my legs to stop from peeing all over the floor. Mum pulled out one of the kitchen chairs and pointed while she snorted with laughter.

"Sit prawns, sit." She gasped through the snorts and giggles.

When I stopped laughing, if ever, I was going to call Krissie and kill her, over the phone.

On the deck outside I heard the prospects laughing and knew, I just knew, this was going to spread like wildfire through the club.

Later when I was tucking Duncan in before reading him his nightly story he looked at my belly and then at me with a puzzled frown.

"Are they really prawns with ugly feelers? We eat prawns. I don't want to eat our babies."

"No, sweetheart, Aunty Krissie was just teasing. They aren't really prawns. They are tiny little babies and when they get here they will look just like you did when you were a baby."

He thought about it then nodded. "Okay. But they must be boys, I don't want girls."

"Why? What's wrong with girls? I'm a girl and Nana is a girl and you love us."

He sighed as if the weight of the world was on his shoulders. "If they be girls I have to take care of them. It's a big brother job. Sammy told me. An' I'm still too little."

Ah fuck. I felt the tears threatening and blinked them away. "You don't have to worry, my boykie. If the babies are girls we'll have a lot of help taking care of them. We have Nana and Grampa and Uncle Dagger and Uncle Jinx and Wrenchie who love us and they will love the babies too. And don't forget about Aunty Krissie and Aunty Mari, they helped me when you were a baby and they will help again because they love us."

Again he lay there thinking about something and I could see it puzzled and worried him. With his next words the tears could not be stopped.

"The prawns don't have a daddy, just like me. Did their daddy go be with the angels too?"

Sweet baby Jesus. What do I do? What do I do? Honesty, always honesty.

"No, my boykie, he didn't, he can't be here with us right now. Okay?"

"Where is he? My daddy's in heaven and he can't come back. Can the prawns' daddy come back?" His big green eyes looked earnestly into my watery eyes.

This little man of mine. He was so damned precious and sweet.

"Yes, yes he can, sweetheart. But right now he's busy somewhere else and can't be here. I'm sure he loves the prawns just as much as we do and he'll help to take care of them. Just not right now. Okay?"

He gave a big sigh then smiled. "Okay. Can we read Green Eggs and Ham?"

And so we read Green Eggs and Ham and I tucked my boykie in and kissed his forehead before starting his music, turning on the baby monitor and his night light.

It was only once I had walked into my room and softly closed the door behind me that I allowed myself to cry. Big gulping sobs that I smothered in my pillows.

Fucking Ice. Fucking, fucking, fucking, fucking Ice.

CHAPTER EIGHTEEN

Ice

Hawk was stretched out in his big assed chair in his office, and those hawkish eyes of his hadn't left Ice's face since he had walked in and sat down across from him.

"You're going to be the second of the Walker males to have a child. Do you have any idea of the shit the women in the family are going to pull? Fucking glad I'm not you."

For a fleeting moment something dark moved through Hawk's eyes and Ice knew he was thinking of his lost child. So he did what he always did, gave his cousin something else to think about.

Ice shook his head and forced a wide grin onto his face. "Brother, the day DC tells you she's having your baby you won't give a shit about the family. What they think, what they do, what they say. None of it will matter. All you'll think about is the life you put inside of her. A life that turns your two halves into a whole."

"Jesus, Ice. Since when have you become all sensitive and shit?" Hawk teased.

Ice laughed. "No fucking idea."

"Okay, let's get back to business." Hawk's relaxed posture was gone. "I called Dagger and he agreed to a meet. But because we don't know if either of our clubs are being watched I had to get creative."

He raised his eyebrows and grinned. "DC is going to visit Doc. She'll be taking a cage along with you and Rider. Wolf and Dizzy will be escorting you. Dagger and Jinx will sneak in through the back entrance at the Warriors compound. Doc will be overseeing the meet because he's a fairly neutral party."

Clenching his fingers around the arms of his chair Ice sighed and nodded in agreement.

"Hopefully we get some answers to a few questions tonight. Dagger is going to be pissed when he finds out I bought the fucking car. Even worse, I could have helped to find Sparrow's killers or pointed them in the right direction if I had paid attention back then."

"Ice, brother, stop. Stop with this shit. You bought a bitch a car. How does buying her a car make you or us fucking responsible? Get that shit out of your head or you will be staying here and I will take this meeting. Are we clear?"

There was no doubt in Ice's mind he had just been verbally smacked against the head by his president.

"Yes, we're clear, Prez. I'm out of here." Ice nodded as he stood. "I'll call if something new comes to light."

An hour later Ice was sitting in Doc's extremely dusty and disorganised office with Doc, Dagger, Jinx and Skelly. Doc included

Skelly to handle the information on the USB Ice had brought along with him.

"Okay, I'm only saying this once, don't make me fucking repeat myself. There will be no physical shit in my office or in my compound. You talk about your shit like the fucking gentlemen you aren't." Doc laid down the law according to Doc.

Ice sighed as he handed the USB over to Skelly who immediately got to work.

"After listening to the recording we did some digging and we found something. The car used for the hit…" Ice had to pause to settle the clawing in his gut before he continued. "I bought the car for Emma Coetzee and she reported it stolen two days before she left me. That was seven years ago, give or take a few weeks. It was never recovered. Then it suddenly reappears two years later during the hit on Sparrow only to disappear once again."

Taking a deep breath Ice continued as a heavy silence hung in the office.

"There's more. We think Sparrow saw the car somewhere before. Somewhere it shouldn't have been and we think he saw two bitches in the car meeting with someone. Someone they did not want anyone to know about. So before he could put it together and burn them they took him out."

Dagger and Jinx were staring at Ice, eyes intent as they listened.

"In the recording he tried to warn you and he kept saying 'bitches'. He said 'warn' more than once. We think it wasn't a warning but a name. Jane Warne. We think he saw Jane and Emma Coetzee at a hotel a couple of days before the hit. Ziggy is putting together a list of hotels starting with the letter H. We think he was trying to give you the hotel's name. But he knew he didn't have a lot of time and gave more personal messages before he died."

When no one said a word Ice continued.

"We know Emma Coetzee wasn't supposed to be in the country at the time of the hit. We are trying to find out why she was here and who they were meeting. If we're lucky the hotel they were spotted at keeps records of past patrons and we can go through a process of elimination to find who it was."

Dagger's voice was rough when he spoke.

"So, to summarise. You bought the car for Emma Coetzee. It was stolen. It was used during the hit on my brother. My brother saw something that got him killed. Jane Warne and Emma Coetzee are responsible. There is an unknown person involved. You might have a lead on the location where my brother saw these women. Anything else you have to add?"

Ice ran his fingers through his hair and drew in a deep breath. This was going to suck.

"I brought photos of the car and photos of the two women from about seven years ago and a few more recent ones. We would like Jinx to take a look."

Ice turned to Jinx who sat like a damn statue in his chair. "Jinx, I know this must be fucking torture for you. But maybe looking at these photos will jar a memory loose. Even just the smallest one might help us to pin these fuckers down."

Jinx shook his head. "It's a huge big blank spot in my memory. I've tried and the last thing I remember is Sparrow throwing his arm around me and telling me I was getting fat. After that it's all a blank."

Dagger clasped a hand on his shoulder. "Have a look, brother. What could it hurt?"

"It hurts every fucking day of my life, Dagger. I let him down and he died. If not for me he wouldn't have been there that night." Jinx ground out.

Ice got there before Dagger could say a word. "If he hadn't been with you he would have been with River. Weren't they supposed to go to dinner? These people don't give a shit about innocent bystanders. They would have killed her. Think of it this way, Jinx. Your bender saved River and Duncan's lives."

Both Dagger and Jinx let out heavy breaths. Jinx nodded more than once then sat forward in his chair.

"Show me the photos."

Skelly flipped his laptop around and pushed it across the desk towards Jinx. He pulled the laptop closer and frowned as he clicked through the photos, over and over. Then he stopped on one and stared at it for quite a few minutes. He clicked to another and did the same. And another.

"Jesus." He whispered his eyes locked on the screen. "You're right. We saw this car. We saw this fucking car. A bitch was driving and she had a passenger. Another bitch. She fucking cut right in front of us in heavy traffic, almost took us down. We were pissed and followed but they drove into the parking at the Hilton and we lost them. Sparrow was fucking livid and insisted on driving around the block. That's when we saw them again. They were parked in the open parking at the back of the hotel talking to an older woman and two men. They must have seen us. And they would have seen us in the traffic before they cut us off, would have seen our kuttes, maybe even our names."

Jinx turned to Ice. "Is that why they came after us? Why they killed Sparrow?"

Ice pushed the laptop back to Skelly. "Find me a photo of Winifred Maingarde."

The atmosphere in the room went electric as Doc shot forward in his chair. Skelly clicked then wordlessly turned the laptop towards Jinx.

"Is this the older woman you saw with the bitches?"

It didn't take him long. Jinx nodded angrily. "That's her, the old bitch we saw with them."

"Would you be able to identify the men if we got some photos together?" Ice pushed for more.

"I don't know, but I'll fucking try. At last it feels like I'm doing something to avenge my best friend. I'll do whatever I have to, to get these fuckers. They killed a good man just because he saw them talking to someone. We didn't even fucking know what we had seen was important."

Skelly pulled the laptop towards him and searched and clicked then pushed the laptop over again. A recent photo of Dominick Maingarde filled the screen.

"Was he one of the men you saw?"

Jinx immediately shook his head. "No, he's too young and his hair is the wrong colour. One of the men had thick salt and pepper hair, the other was a fucking ginger. The ginger looked like a bodyguard or something."

At least they now knew Dominick hadn't been involved. If he had been it would have sucked. Despite what he did for a living Ice liked the man. Would Dom help them to identify the man who had been with the old bitch? He didn't know but it was something to think about.

Skelly sat back in his chair with a frown and tapped his fingers against his lips.

"I think we've seen this guy, and it was recently. I can't swear to it but I think he was with the old bitch in Durban. I need to talk to Mad Dog and Ziggy and go through the footage. I'll let you know if I find something."

Ice nodded then looked back at Jinx. "Anything else seem familiar?"

Jinx was frowning as he slowly shook his head. Ice could see something was happening in his head but it wasn't enough. There was one more nudge they could try.

"There's one other thing we could try. But, Jinx, it won't be easy. It will be fucking hard, maybe even soul destroying but it's all we have left."

"You want me to listen to the recording."

Ice didn't say anything just nodded.

Clasping his hands behind his head Jinx leant back in his chair, he folded his bent arms around his head as he looked up at the ceiling. As if he was protecting what was in his head, or protecting himself from what he knew would most likely destroy his peace of mind. Or what little peace of mind he had been able to gather over the last five years.

"When?" He asked softly.

"We can do it now. Dagger doesn't want to hear it. He can wait for us at the bar. It's not very long but I must warn you, it's not easy to listen to."

"Let's do it."

Dagger immediately stood and after a hard pat on Jinx's back he walked out the door, closing it softly behind him. Doc and Skelly didn't leave.

And then the sound of Sparrow's voice filled the room and Jinx fell apart. At the end he sat bent over with his elbows on his thighs, his hands over his face as he cried unashamedly. For a while the only sound in the room was Jinx's sorrow, and then he sat up, wiped his eyes and sniffed. And by the look in his eyes Ice knew it had worked.

Jinx remembered.

"The car was there, waiting for us when we walked out. And the back end was dented and scratched to shit as if it had been in an accident. Windows were open and those bitches shot at us. I tried to get in front of Sparrow but it was already too late. We were both hit by the time we went down. I hit my head as I went down and that was it. Nothing, until I woke in the hospital and Dagger told me Sparrow was gone."

He steepled his hands in front of his face groaned. "Why the fuck didn't I remember this shit? We wasted five fucking years! Five fucking years!"

"Nothing has been wasted, Jinx. Five years ago none of what you remembered would have made any difference to the case. The pigs weren't interested in hearing about it. Wrote it off as a gang related shooting. Done. Closed the case." Ice continued explaining.

"The good thing about five years having passed is when we serve out justice none of it will blow back on River and Duncan. And what we uncovered tonight is part of a very big conspiracy to take down and take over the prominent clubs in the country. I need to talk to my prez and clear some shit with him but I think we need a formal meeting of all the clubs who are involved."

"Okay, let's do this." Jinx said.

Ice sighed and stood.

"And now I have something personal I have to talk to Dagger about. Would you mind if we use your office, Doc?"

"Nope. I'll send him in. When you're done come and have a beer before you take DC home." Doc said with a sly grin.

Jinx hadn't moved, he stood and waited until Dagger walked in then looked at Ice. "I'm not leaving him alone with you. Sorry, Ice, can't do it."

Ice shrugged and moved away from them to give him some space in case the bastards started throwing punches once he told them what he had to.

"What I'm going to say is going to piss you off so I'm just going to come right out and say it. So here goes nothing." Ice drew in a breath. "River's babies are mine. I'm the father. I fell for her, Dagger, fucking hard but I had to push her away for her own safety. She is mine, her children are mine."

Deathly silence as two sets of eyes stared at him. Nothing showed in their eyes and then Dagger nodded and looked at Jinx. He held his president's eyes for a few seconds then nodded as if in agreement. Those eyes turned back to him. Then Dagger gave Ice an ultimatum he had no problem agreeing to.

"You have twenty four hours then I want to hear River is yours. Under your protection and the protection of your club. If she agrees you will marry her as soon as fucking possible and you will make her your old lady. River, Duncan, those babies and any other babies she might have will always be Sinner's Sons family and will have our protection as well as yours."

"Fuck." Jinx muttered. "Never thought one of the Dogz would become our brother-in-law. Always thought our girl would fall for some civilian asshole when the time was right."

Ice frowned at Jinx. "She's been mine for months but I had to push her away to keep her safe. Now with her pregnant and vulnerable I can't leave her out there. I'll be bringing her and Duncan on to the Iron Dogz grounds to keep her and our family safe."

Dagger laughed while Jinx's lips lifted in a small smile and both shook their heads. Then Jinx explained.

"Not going to happen. River will fight you tooth and nail. She won't leave mum and dad or her house. Make peace with it, Ice. You're going to have to move in with her. We've secured both houses as much as we can and we have brothers on her and Duncan 24/7. The same with mum and dad. And when you move in it means we have more brothers available to protect them."

"She won't let me move in, man. You both know it." Ice said.

"Who said anything about giving her a choice, brother?" Dagger said slyly. "You pack a bag, and we ride there with you, get you through the gates and the rest is up to you."

"Okay, I can do that. As long as she doesn't shoot me before I've explained."

Jinx shook with laughter and Ice could see by the way Dagger looked at him that his friend hadn't laughed in a very long time.

"There is the distinct possibility. She is really fucking pissed at you. Especially after seeing you with that slut. I always wondered what had pissed her off that night at the restaurant, now I know. I hope you have a really good fucking explanation for the shit we all saw." Jinx wasn't laughing anymore.

Ice shrugged. "I'll tell her everything and hope for the best."

Dagger laughed. "Come on, brother, let's have a beer and make some plans to get you into the house tomorrow. I have a few ideas of how we can play it."

Ice followed a laughing Dagger and Jinx out of the office and joined DC and Doc at the bar.

He made plans with Dagger to get him into his woman's house before they all left. Maybe not her bed, but he would be in the house and that was a hell of a lot closer than where he was right now.

But first he had to report to his Prez. God, he had so much to tell him.

CHAPTER NINETEEN

River

I cried myself to sleep and woke up with a headache and puffy eyes. Staring in the mirror after my shower I thought about the talk with my beautiful boy and made a decision.

My prawns deserved another shot at having a dad.

I was going to try one more time. Not now. Tonight would be soon enough.

And if he blew me off again then so be it. I would know I had tried my best.

First thing though was taking care of the disaster that was my face. I could not go to work looking like I had cried all night. Regardless of the fact that I basically did.

I got a look from mum when I dropped Duncan off before heading to work. I knew the look. It said 'we'll be talking later girlie'. Later would be fine, right now I was still feeling way too fragile. Maybe it was all the hormones flooding my body or maybe it was the silent dread I felt about the call I would be making later. And after the way he had spoken to me the last time I had called him I wasn't holding my breath that it would go any better this time around.

The man was obviously a pig and a bastard, but he was the father of my prawns and he needed to know about them. I did not like the idea of his fashion plate of a girlfriend having anything to do with my babies. Her behaviour in public had been super skanky and I didn't want any child of mine around that kind of person. So I was going to offer him the deal of a lifetime.

Personally I wanted nothing from him. No money. No involvement in their birth. No relationship at all.

All I wanted was for him to give them his last name, the protection of his club and if possible to show up at important events as their father.

If he refused then he could just disappear, hopefully never to be seen again. As far as I was concerned that would be the ideal solution. The prawns would have his last name but that was all. And if it left a hollow feeling in my gut I was not going to acknowledge it. Not now and maybe not ever. They would be mine, like Duncan was mine.

But if I had to be totally honest, Duncan wasn't only mine. He was part of the Sinner's Sons family, they loved him and made sure he knew who his daddy was even though he was no longer with us. Duncan loved his uncles and looked forward to spending time with them. The club was helping me to raise my boy and they would be the ones teaching him how to be a man.

If the prawns were girls I would be okay. But what if they were boys?

Would Dagger and the guys step up for them as well? And what would the Iron Dogz do when they found out I had had Ice's boys? Would Hawk want to get involved in their lives?

Shit. I had to call DC and talk to her about this.

But first I had to call Dr Strauss's rooms. I wanted a scan to find out the sex of the prawns, as soon as possible. If they were boys I might have a problem and I wanted to face it now rather than after they were born.

As I made my way through the early morning traffic I frowned when I realised I now had two more men on bikes escorting me to work. It didn't seem to worry my usual escorts so I put it down to Dagger being over protective and went back to worrying about Ice and the sex of the prawns.

Wrench was waiting when I pulled in. Like he now did every single morning. According to him he was waiting on the inevitable hurling stage he was certain would appear when we least expected it. And he wanted to know in advance if his day was going to include holding my hair back while I vomited. So far I had been super lucky. No morning sickness, touch wood.

"You look like shit. What's wrong? Oh fuck, did the hurling start? No worries, Boss, I got your back. I stocked us up with several kinds of crackers and soda water and juices and all that crap. We have Wet Wipes to wipe your face. I called my mum and she said I had to get hard sweets for you to suck when you feel nauseous but aren't hurling. So I got several types and flavours. I'm happy to report we're all set up for the workshop to turn into a vomitarium."

I had to laugh at the slightly grossed out look on his face.

"No, the hurling didn't start. I just had a bad night, couldn't sleep for some reason."

As we walked into the workshop I looked around at the work we had to get done and sighed. I was going to have to hire another mechanic soon. We had more work than the two of us could comfortably cope with already and when my belly got too big I wouldn't be able to work. And to be honest it wasn't the safest environment for the prawns. There were always chemicals and exhaust fumes hanging around. And then there were the fumes from our tiny spray booth. Luckily none of them hung around too long because of the huge extractors mounted on the roof of the workshop.

And those fumes were the reason why Wrench handed me a facemask with a filter in it every single morning. He got quite pissed when I didn't wear it. To stop the continuous nagging I wore the damned uncomfortable thing. My dad and the guys jokingly started calling me Moto Doc. I was hoping like hell the name didn't stick.

By lunchtime I was feeling a lot better and wolfed down the sandwiches we had delivered from a nearby sandwich shop. I used the break to call and set up an appointment for the scan and was lucky. I got an early morning appointment for next week Wednesday.

LOST AND FOUND IN BLUE

All I had to do was get through the next five days. Actually only four and half days because the day was already half way done.

On my way home I again had four escorts instead of just two. Okay, this wasn't normal so I needed to call Dagger. Was there some threat I needed to be aware of? But first I was getting out of my work clothes and having a shower before I called him. Mum and Duncan were playing Legos on the carpet in the lounge and I smiled at their total concentration on the job in front of them.

"Hello, family, I'm home."

"Hello, sweetheart." Mum smiled as she handed Duncan a blue Lego piece.

"Hey, Mumma. I'm building a room for the prawns and Nana is helping."

"Wow, that's great, boykie. I'm going to have a quick shower then you can show me."

All I got was a nod as he concentrated on the building in front of him.

I was drying off when I heard bikes and recognised Dagger's but not the bike that came in with him. It meant I wouldn't have to call him. I slathered lotion on my skin to try and prevent too many stretch marks. I had been lucky with Duncan and only had a few low down on my belly. This time I didn't think I was going to be so lucky. These kids were already showing and they were only going to get bigger.

I slowed in the act of pulling on my panties and listened to the rumble of male voices.

"Uncle Dagger! Look! I'm building a room for the prawns." Duncan shouted excitedly.

And then my boy spoke to someone else.

"Mr Icey! Did you know my mumma has prawns in her belly? Two of them! I'm going to be a big brother. We don't know if they be boys or girls. They don't have a daddy just like me. Mumma said their daddy didn't go be with the angels like my daddy. Sammy says their daddy will come see them 'cause mumma is very pretty. And Sammy says his daddy says mumma is a fox. Why is he calling her a fox? Mumma isn't a fox, she's a mumma."

I heard deep male chuckles and could virtually hear my boy taking a deep breath before he carried on.

"Their daddy must come soon 'cause Wrenchie said mumma's belly is going to get really, really, reeeally big and we's going to need strong arms to help her get up. Her belly is getting big already. I been eating all my vege'bles 'cause they make my muscles big so I can help."

Jesus. This kid of mine. Why didn't mum or Dagger put a hand over his mouth to stop him sharing with a stranger? And who the hell is Mr Icey? A new prospect? I rushed through getting dressed and pulled my damp hair back in a ponytail.

I didn't pay attention to what I was wearing and had I known who was waiting for me in the lounge I would have. I was dressed in comfy yoga pants and a tee shirt that did not hide my bump or my bigger boobs.

When I walked into the lounge I froze.

Ice was sitting on the carpet with Duncan. He looked up and smiled but the smile slowly disappeared when his eyes swept over me and became riveted on my bump.

What the hell? What the bloody freaking hell!

I looked around and spotted mum and Dagger in the kitchen whispering together. There would be no help coming from that front. I glanced back at Ice. The next minute it became clear that the bastards had been conspiring against me.

"Boykie!" Dagger called. "Let's go check on where we're going to build the room for the prawns."

Duncan was up and on his way to the kitchen like lightning. "Can Mr Icey come?"

"No, Mr Icey is going to talk to mumma while we have a look outside."

I could hear the laughter in Dagger's voice and I wanted to strangle him. And where the hell was my mother? The sneaky woman must have slipped out the back door. Not cool. Not cool at all.

I stood staring at the open slider through which Dagger and my boykie had disappeared. When I looked back Ice was standing right in front of me. I looked up into eyes that were so damn soft it made my tummy ache.

"Blue." He said softly. "I was a stupid bastard. I pushed you away because I had to ensure you would be safe while I took care of club business. It was a mistake. A huge fucking mistake. I should have told you what was going on. I want you, no that's not right, the truth is I need you in my life."

God. He looked so good and sounded so believable. But there was the woman I had seen him with. His so-called ex-girlfriend. The woman he had kissed, and who knew what else he had done to and with her. Oh hell no, not going to fall for the soft eyes and shit.

"And the woman I saw you with? What about her? Didn't you want to keep her safe from your precious club business?" I bit out angrily.

He shook his head roughly, dislodging his hair and it fell over his forehead. Damn, it looked good and I had to clench my hands to stop from brushing it back.

"No, Blue, because she is the club business." His deep growly voice was still soft and it just about killed me to ignore the shivers it caused down my spine. "I've been investigating her and the only way to get close enough without raising her suspicions was to pretend to go out with her. Yes, I kissed her but I didn't hold her and I didn't fuck her. Not once."

The fucking asshole, the unmitigated fucking asshole. It wasn't just kissing.

My temper boiled. "Oh joy. I saw her, Ice. I saw, as did everyone in the restaurant, how she stroked and played with your dick and you just sat there smiling, enjoying it while sipping your drink. So do not try to blow smoke up my ass. I have seen that freaking look on your face up close and personal, so stop lying."

He growled at me. The ass growled at me and shoved his face into mine as he growled out his explanation.

"Not once, Blue, not fucking once did I get hard because I wanted her. My body had a reaction to direct stimulation for a few seconds then it disappeared. She tried. I won't deny it. But she did not fucking succeed because the only woman I get hard for is you. The only thing I did was kiss her but I did not take it any further. I can't fucking stand the bitch but I had to go out with her to get the information we needed. I'm done with her. Done with the job. If the club needs more they can send some other poor fucker after her. I swear to you, I won't ever do that kind of job for the club ever again."

His eyes were focused on me as he pulled me into his arms and leant his forehead against mine and my poor heart raced and other parts quivered. I did not want to hear him but with his next words and actions he captured my racing heart. Damn it.

"Baby, the first time I saw you, you came walking around the corner of the clubhouse at the family *braai*. You were with Wrench and I was instantly captivated and so damned jealous. You were laughing and the breeze lifted strands of your hair, turning them to gold in the sun. When I got close enough the scent of your perfume made my heart race. I looked at you and was stunned by the amazing sparkling icy pale blue of your eyes and your natural beauty. But the part I fell for that night was the beauty you carry inside of you. A beauty you shared with me and a beauty I foolishly pushed away."

He carefully tilted his head and softly swiped his lips over mine and I froze. Shit. Damn it. Where was my backbone when I needed it.

"Please, Blue, please give me a chance to be a part of your lives. Yours and Duncan's and our babies." He grinned. "Or as Duncan calls them 'the prawns'."

This man was my kryptonite, I was hard pressed not to smile. And he definitely didn't deserve a smile, not yet, maybe not ever if I decided not to believe his explanation.

"You're going to find he's not the only one who calls them 'the prawns'. Everyone does. Krissie started it and now no one calls them anything but 'the prawns'."

I drew in a deep breath and gave him the hurt he had caused during that awful phone call.

"You called me a slut and other nasty stuff, Ice. It is not something that's easy to forgive and forget. You say you had to push me away to keep me safe. If you had wanted me safe why not just say 'sorry babe, it was a one-and-done, I'm not interested in more.'? Why use those terrible hurtful words to push me away?"

Closing his eyes he shook his head, regret clearly visible on his face. "I wanted to ensure you stayed far away from me, baby. If these people knew we were together they would have stopped at nothing to hurt you or Duncan, and I couldn't allow that to happen." He sighed.

"That I could have been less of a bastard is a given, but I was fucking terrified that someone would realise what I felt for you and what I so desperately wanted from you."

I frowned up at him. "So what has changed? Why are you now willing to endanger our lives?"

The ass smiled as he glanced down my body. "Everything has changed, Blue. I'm not endangering your lives by being here, I am protecting my family. Like I should have done from the start. We both felt it, the very moment I slid inside you and made you mine, we both knew it was forever. And don't shake your head at me, baby. You know it's the truth."

Fine, I did. I will admit to that but I also knew it would be a mistake to jump into a relationship with Ice. We had some things to work through, mostly it was about how insecure I felt. I didn't know if I could trust him to take care of us, of me, and not break our hearts. Because it wasn't just me. Duncan was one of the most important parts of my life and if he bonded with Ice and at some stage he left, my boykie would be devastated. I had to make Ice understand that Duncan's wellbeing was a priority for me.

"You have to understand, if I let you in, and that's a big if, Duncan will bond with you and if you left us he would be devastated. My boykie gravitates to all the males in this family and they have a very tight bond. Dagger and Jinx have been there for him since he's been born and have done an amazing job filling in for Sparrow.

Duncan has been asking about the babies' daddy. I heard him talking to you about it. So you know how…"

Ice didn't give me a chance to finish.

"Blue, baby, he will be my son. How could I ever walk away from my son? I want the four of you to be my family." He rubbed his nose against mine. "And before you start worrying, Duncan will always be Sparrow's son. We will make sure he knows what an amazing man his dad was. But he will be my son as well. Our son."

God. He made me want to cry.

He cupped his big hands around my jaw and lifted my face to his. His eyes were intent and very serious. One of his hands stroked over my cheek, down my neck, down between my breasts, stroked over and then cupped my bump.

"Lying here under my hand is the most incredible gift life has ever given me. I'm thirty seven years old, Blue, and I had given up on there ever being a woman and children in my future. And then you walked around the corner of the clubhouse and everything changed. My life took a one hundred and eighty degree turn and went from bleak to filled with light."

"On that day I was given a woman unlike any other to love and a son to raise as my own. The best thing about that day, the very best thing, is the moment we made these two little lives under my hand. But, Blue, I want you to get this, I would have been standing here in front of you regardless of whether you had our babies in your belly or not. I fell for you that day, baby, and I fell hard."

He didn't give me a chance to say a word as his lips crashed down on mine and I lost my mind. I kissed him back. With everything in me and more. I was breathless when he lifted his head and ran his thumb over my wet bottom lip. A delicious shudder ran down my spine.

"I know I'm moving fast and I know you might not be where I am with this thing between us. But you need to accept we are happening. I'm moving in, Blue. With you and Duncan and the prawns. If you're not ready to share a bed with me I'll crash on the couch, but make no mistake, baby, I'm here to stay. We are going to be a family."

What? Has he lost his mind? We spent a day together, one day. Speechless, I was absolutely speechless. He had taken all of my fears and excuses and kicked them out the door. How the hell was I going to keep space between us when I knew he would not be allowing me any space? I could see it in his eyes, he was very determined. But I was determined too. Determined to make the right choice for my children and for myself.

Was Ice the right choice? I didn't have the answer to that question. Only time would tell.

And it was something I could give him. I could give him time. Time for us to get to know each other and time for Duncan to become comfortable with having a man around all the time.

The thing I had to decide right now was where was he going to sleep? In my bed or on the couch?

"Okay, you can stay, but…" I got no further because my boykie came storming back into the house, his little face like a thundercloud.

"We's got a problem!" He shouted.

I looked from him to Dagger who had come in behind him. He was frowning and shaking his head.

"What's the problem, boykie?" I asked as I walked into the kitchen, Ice right behind me.

He sighed heavily and slammed his hands down on his little hips and copied Dagger's usual stance. But there was a worried look in his eyes.

"No space."

"We have lots of space, boykie."

"No, we don't. All my stuff is having space." Suddenly there were tears in his eyes. "My daddy built my tree house before I was borned. It's mine. The prawns can't have it. They have to go away."

I was struck speechless but not Ice. He dropped to his haunches in front of Duncan. "We will never give your space to the prawns, Duncan. Your tree house will always be yours. We can make another plan for the prawns, okay?"

He looked at Ice for several minutes before he nodded. "Okay." He said softly.

"Your mumma and I have something we want to talk to you about." Ice said quietly and Duncan quickly glanced at me before his eyes swung back to Ice.

Ice rose and caught Duncan under his arms and lifted him to sit on the counter in front of us. Dagger made as if to leave but Ice motioned him closer and the two of them moved to one side making space for me in front of Duncan. Shit. How to explain this to my boy?

"Remember when you asked about the prawns' daddy the other night, boykie?" Again the nod. "You were worried about him being with the angels and not taking care of the babies. And I told you he wasn't but that he couldn't be with them right now. Do you remember?"

He gave a deep put upon sigh. "Yes. I have to be a big brother and take care of them."

I nodded. "Yes, you are their big brother but you don't have to take care of them on your own, boykie. Like I told you, we will all help. But that's not what I wanted to talk to you about."

Okay. Right. Big breath in. Here we go.

"Ice is here because he's the prawns' daddy."

Duncan's eyes went wide and his mouth fell open then he grinned. "Really? Mr Icey is their daddy?"

"Yes, Duncan." Ice answered. "I'm their daddy."

"You're not going to go be with the angels before they get borned?" His grin was instantly replaced with a frown.

My freaking heart dropped. What the hell was going on in my boy's head?

"No way, little man. I'm not going anywhere. I'm going to stay with you and your mumma. And after the babies come out of mumma's belly I'm still going to be here and I will take care of you and the babies and your mumma."

Duncan tilted his head as he thought about it. He nodded very slowly then bent over to try and see into the lounge. We all turned to look at where he was looking. It was Ice's big duffle bag sitting on the floor by the front door.

"You bringed your jammies." Duncan shuffled his little bum indicating he wanted to be let down. Ice picked him up and set him down.

Duncan barrelled past us and grabbed hold of the handles of the duffle and with grunts and groans started dragging it towards the passage. His little body almost bent double with effort.

"I got it!" He shouted. "Sammy says mummies and daddies share the bed. Mr Icey can sleep in mumma's bed. Her bed is bigger. Mine's too small. Sammy says babies cry all the time. And Sammy says two babies are going to make a lot of noise." He huffed out a sigh. "I's glad Mr Icey is here. Sammy's baby sister is very loud. I don't like it."

As he sighed out the last little gem of information he disappeared around the corner and we stood stunned silent as we heard him huffing and puffing and the sound of the big bag sliding across the wooden floor.

"Jesus." Dagger said softly. "That kid. Every day he reminds me more and more of Dylan at that age."

"As it should be." Ice said equally softly. "He's Dylan's legacy."

Dagger clapped his hands and grinned but his eyes were dark with sorrow. "Well, my work here is done. I'll leave you three to sort out the rest. And Ice, lets meet tomorrow. I'll text you a location."

He drew me into his arms for a hard hug then kissed my forehead.

"Don't think so damned hard about what's happening, Rivzie." He whispered in my ear. "Let it happen. He will be good for you and our little man."

With a last wave he was gone and Ice and I were alone again. He drew me into his arms and held me against him, his head against the top of my head. The heat of his body leached through my thin clothes and it felt so damned good. Too damned good for my peace of mind.

"Have you two had dinner yet, baby?" He asked against my hair.

"No, we haven't, but I think my mum might have left something for us. The way she snuck out of here I'm sure Dagger let her know you were coming."

Ice pulled away, smiled and winked at me. I knew it, they had all conspired against me.

"Okay, Blue. Let's get you and our boy fed then we'll see where the rest of the evening goes. Okay?"

I nodded. I needed a little bit of breathing space.

Ice had walked through my door and laid himself bare. He hid nothing and what he gave me was beyond precious. He had destroyed some of my fears. He was here, with me, one hundred percent. All I had to do was believe in him. Even though it was going to be difficult I was willing to try.

For the second time in my life I was blessed with a good man. A man with a hard exterior but with a very big heart.

And I was already half way in love with him because of the way he treated my son.

Oh, who was I kidding?

I fell for the man the very same day I met him. All it took was one look into his intense and so very warm eyes followed by great conversation, heart stopping kisses and earth shattering sex. And I was his.

Boom!

CHAPTER TWENTY

Ice

Ice was smiling when he walked into the clubhouse. Something he hadn't done for the last few months. Chris reached for the whiskey bottle but he shook his head, there was no need for it.

"Pour me a coffee please, Chris." He pulled out a stool and sat down as she set the mug down in front of him.

"Smiling and drinking coffee. What happened to you in the last twenty four hours?" She quizzed.

Ice shook his head and sipped his coffee. When he had called Hawk to let him know Dagger's plan had worked his prez had asked him to stay quiet about his new status.

Hawk had called all the brothers in for church and the common room was slowly filling up.

"Hallelujah, he's not drinking." Sin said sarcastically as he sat down next to him and pointed at Ice's mug. "I'll have the same, thanks, Chris."

Sin turned, stuck his nose on Ice's kutte and sniffed. "Thank fuck you don't stink today. Don't think I would have lasted through church if you were wearing your usual perfume." He teased, sat back frowned then leant over and sniffed again. "Hmmm, I like this one though. It's light and spicy with undertones of flowers. Perfect."

Shaking his head Ice laughed. "Jesus, you're a fucking nut."

Before Sin could answer Beast sat down on Ice's other side and groaned. "Fuck, I'm tired. Chris, sweetheart, hit me up with some of that coffee, please." Turning to Ice he sniffed. "Thank fuck you don't stink, it would have been the fucking cherry on the shit cake that is my life right now."

"What's wrong, brother?" Ice looked Beast over and noticed the dark rings under his eyes. The big man had obviously not been sleeping.

"My fucking ex-wife decided now was a really good time to lose her shit and dump my little girls on my doorstep last night. According to the bitch she's tired of taking care of my little beasts and having no life." Beast scratched at his wild looking beard. "My babies are confused and scared and I spent the night trying to settle them down. Thank fuck for Aunt Beryl. She came right over to help me out. Don't know what the fuck I would have done without her."

"The bitch just arrived out of the blue?" Sin frowned.

"*Ja.* She's been screaming for more money for a while now and I shut her down. I think that's why she dumped them on me. I've been paying the grasping bitch more than what the courts decided would be fair from day one. Now, hopefully, I won't have to pay her another fucking cent. Called my lawyer, told him to sue for sole custody and he said he's on it and will call when he has answers for me. Even put a fucking PI on her ass." Beast took a slug of coffee and sighed.

"Take my advice, brothers. Make damned sure the woman you tie yourself to is the real deal and not a choice your dick made for you. I've learned my lesson the fucking hard way. No more fancy painted up bitches for me. If I ever again lose my head and decide to take an old lady, which won't fucking happen, she's going to be someone like Gail or Genna. A good girl."

If he hadn't been watching her pour coffee Ice wouldn't have seen the sudden stillness that came over Chris at Beast's words. He knew Beast had been spending time with her but he didn't think his friend had realised that giving his attention solely to her had sent the wrong message. As VP he should have been aware of this shit but he had been so caught up in his own crap he had missed it. He would have to talk to Beast and get him to have a talk with Chris. He liked the girl but she had been a club girl. And unfortunately for her club girls rarely became old ladies, hardly ever in the Iron Dogz MC. He knew it happened more regularly in other clubs but for some reason very, very seldomly in theirs.

And it wasn't because they discriminated against the girls. That wasn't it at all. It just seemed that when the brothers were ready to settle down they chose the good girls, as Beast called them. Women like his sisters and his old lady. Unless, like Beast, they got some club bitch pregnant and married her thinking it was the right thing to do.

It still made him fucking smile every time he remembered he had an old lady now. She was his. His old lady. And very fucking soon she would be wearing his patch and once the prawns were born he would be taking her to DC to have his ink put on her. And he was going to put his ring on her finger, not because he had promised Dagger he would, but because he wanted her to be tied to him in every way possible.

Last night he had slept next to her for an entire night and he had slept deeply for the first time in months. He hadn't made love to her, it was too soon to go there, but he had held her in his arms and breathed in her scent. And this morning he had dropped Duncan with his nana and followed his old lady to work. He'd had a quiet word with Wrench and he knew the prospect and the brothers watching over her would keep their eyes peeled. He might have overstepped but he had showed the five of them photos of Emma, Jane and the black Beemer.

He would rather be safe than sorry.

A thump on his back pulled him back to the present and Ice turned. His dad stood behind him with a wide smile on his face.

"Damned good to see you without a glass in your hand, son."

"Don't need it anymore, Dad."

"That's good to hear. Will your mother and I be seeing you soon?"

"We're still settling in but I'm on it. As soon as I can swing it we will come over. Okay?"

"Good, good. Your mother and I are looking forward to it."

They had both kept their voices low but there had been no way Sin and Beast hadn't overheard their conversation. Both were now looking at Ice with eyes filled with speculation. Thankfully before they could start interrogating him Hawk called them into church.

The brothers were dropping their phones into the basket Sam was holding, but not Ice. He pushed his phone into Sam's hand then leant close.

"If my phone rings and it's Wrench or River you answer it. If it's not urgent tell them I'll call them back after the meeting. If it's urgent you come get me. Do you understand, Prospect?"

Sam took his phone and nodded. "I've got you, Ice."

Ice nodded. "Good. You stay at the bar. Anyone give you shit you tell them to speak to me. We clear?"

Sam nodded and Ice walked into church.

Hawk was already sprawled in his chair and Ice sank down in his chair on the right hand of his president. A president who was grinning at him. Ice just sighed and sat back in his chair and crossed his arms as the room quickly filled with all the brothers except for those watching over the women. Ice was pleased Hawk had put fully patched brothers on the women and not the prospects. Should anything happen the brothers had more experience and would be quicker to respond.

The hammer slamming down had the sound of steel on steel ringing through the room and the hum of voices dropped immediately.

Hawk smacked both hands down on the table as he leant forward and looked around the room.

"We have a few things to get through this morning so let's get to it." He glanced around the room and Ice could almost feel the change in the atmosphere in the room.

"As you all know our VP has been putting himself out there dating a bitch to get information on her connections to the Maingarde Organisation."

"And can I just say the bitch's fucking perfume stinks." Spider mumbled.

Snickers sounded around the room but they ended as Hawk glared at them.

"Our brother took a personal hit to get us the information we needed. All the officers have already been informed but it's my pleasure to give the rest of you the news."

Hawk grinned wide and threw his arm around Ice's shoulders and dragged him close. "Our brother here has found himself an old lady. Not only did he find himself an old lady he got her pregnant with twins. It gives me great pleasure to announce our brother has taken River Anderson as his old lady. We'll all have a drink on his very good fortune once we're done here."

Howls rang out through the room as his brothers let rip. Sharing in his joy and good fortune.

The hammer hitting the steel had the howls and whistles subsiding until silence once again reigned.

"That was the good news. Now let's get on to the not so good news. Ice, brother, let's hear what you have uncovered."

Ice sat forward, resting his forearms and hands on the table. The fingers of his left hand rubbed over the nicks and scratches on the table. Nicks and scratches put there by the rings of the brothers who came before him.

"As you all know we've been fighting a silent war. We all thought the attack on the clubhouse in Durban and on our reputations had been the most serious so far. But believe me they have been very fucking sneaky. We've been under siege for years without realising it."

Ice reached out and clasped a hand around Hawk's forearm on the table next to him. Giving him his support.

"Information surfaced yesterday that convinced me the first blow had been struck with the death of Bounty. None of us were ever satisfied with the police report. Bounty was a damned good driver. Didn't matter what he drove, be it a truck, a cage or his bike. He had taught most of us older patches how to drive under difficult situations. Took us all to the skidpan. Teaching us what to do when we hit water or oil or whatever might be on the road. How the hell would a man like that go through the guardrail and off the side of the mountain? He wouldn't unless he was forced off the road."

Ice let his right hand rub over the nicks and scratches again while his left kept a hold of Hawk's forearm.

"Yesterday a brother who rides with the Sinner's Sons MC regained his memories of the night he and his best friend were gunned down by unknown assailants and left for dead. Sparrow Martins, the SAA of the Sinner's Sons, died at the scene and Jinx, his best friend, hit his head as he was going down and lost all memory of what had happened. The pigs closed the case and labelled it a gang related shooting."

Ice shot a look at Hawk before he continued.

"As I said, yesterday those memories returned. And Sparrow and Jinx gave us a positive ID of the cage as well as the shooters." There were surprised mutters. "Yes, you heard me right. Sparrow gave us the information we needed. You need to brace, brothers."

Ice sighed as Hawk reached out and clasped his hand tight over Kid's forearm. Lending him support.

"Sparrow had been talking to Dagger on his phone as they walked out of the bar and into the ambush. And Dagger recorded it. Sparrow gave him colour, make, registration and a description of the shooters' car. It was a black Beemer, the very same car I had bought Emma Coetzee, a car she said had been stolen from the campus parking lot years before."

The mutters rose to a rumble but Ice held a hand up and it stopped.

"That's not all. Sparrow gave clues to the identities of the shooters but Dagger had been so fucked up listening to his brother dying he missed it. Until now. Yesterday Jinx listened to the recording for the first time and it shook those memories loose. He said the back end of the Beemer had been dented and scratched as if it had been side swiped. He identified the shooters as two women with an unknown male driving. He identified Jane Warne and Emma Coetzee."

Pandemonium broke loose.

"You met with the Sinner's Sons without me?" Beast growled incredulously across the table.

"We had to do it on the down low, Beast. There are indications we are all being watched and we had to take steps to ensure the meet took place without letting our enemies know." Hawk explained as he let go of Kid's arm.

After a second or two Ice pulled his hand from his cousin's arm and clasped his hands on the table in front of him.

"I suspect when my interest in Emma Coetzee was noted a plan had been hatched to insert her into the inner circle of the club. As my old lady she would have seen and heard things even though we take care to shield our women from club business. Emmie and I had started to have some problems, she wanted shit I didn't and it caused some friction but not enough for us to break up. Then Bounty died and you all know what happened next. Hawk was voted in as

President and Bulldog and the older officers announced they were stepping down." Ice pointed a hand at the doors. "Right out there, in front of all my brothers, she accused me of fucking around on her. She called me a blood thirsty animal when I accepted the VP nomination when Hawk offered it to me and I was voted in by my brothers. She left and we didn't see her again until recently. All remorseful and informing me and my family she had been pregnant when she left and had lost the baby. It was all bullshit. She was trying to fuck with my head. And she almost succeeded."

Spider snorted angrily. "She was such a bitch, the way she stood there and told him their baby was dead. I didn't fucking believe her for a damned minute. I recorded the whole thing, just in case we might need it, plus I forwarded it to Ziggy just to be safe."

All Ice could do was nod in agreement. "I have always been super fucking careful about wrapping my shit up. I didn't want to ruin her plans for her career with an unplanned baby."

There was a sudden burst of laughter and everyone looked at Wolf, the brother hardly ever cracked a smile and now he was laughing. He met Ice's eyes still grinning. "Not sure you were being very careful this time, brother. You didn't just make one baby you made two of the little fuckers."

And of course his fucking little brother would not let a chance to tease pass.

"Not only wasn't he very careful brothers, no, there's more to this story. Those babies were made right here the first and only time they banged. Like I've said before, the bastard must have super sperm."

Howls of laughter followed his statement. Ice shook his head at his brother.

Eventually after the laughter died down Hawk cleared his throat but laughter still shone in his eyes.

"Ziggy, I know you've been working with Ice. I want the two of you to put a timeline together. Starting with Bounty and ending with what we have so far."

He looked around the room and then at Ice.

"I've put Boots and Dizzy on River's protection detail along with the brothers from the Sinner's Sons plus she has Wrench in the workshop with her. Her boy has two Sinner's Sons on him and his grandparents at all times and I want Dollar and Spook to back them up. DC will have three Warriors on her ass at all times. Doc assigned Alien, Rico and Skinny to her. And she still has Law watching over her in the shop. It helps that we don't have to cut our selves too thin as we try to keep our families safe."

He turned to Beast and Ice saw the brother knew he wasn't going to like what came next.

"Beast, you have your little girls living with you now. I want you to move them here. If you don't want them in the clubhouse move into the house with Rider and his old lady. I don't want any children vulnerable to attack. We all know what those bastards do to kids."

He looked down the table at Bulldog. "Bring the girls and Johan in. I don't care if Gail and Genna scream blue murder I want all those girls under your roof, where they will be safe."

Ice was relieved when his dad nodded his agreement.

"The rest of us will keep up the surveillance on Emma Coetzee and I want all of you to start thinking about where they could successfully hide that fucking car. I want it found"

Hawk looked around the room. "Anything else we need to talk about or are we done here?"

Rider stood up and stepped forward. "As you know, Prez, I had to take my girl to the doctor yesterday because she wasn't feeling great. They admitted her last night because her blood pressure was dangerously high and this morning the doctor decided they would be taking the baby out today. Her surgery is scheduled for two this afternoon. I would like to stay with her today if it's okay, Prez."

Hawk pointed at Dollar. "You're with him. Both of you get out of here, and Rider, let me know if you need anything. Good luck, brother."

"Thanks, Prez." Rider barely got the words out as he walked to the doors with Dollar right behind him.

"Good luck, brother." Resounded as they watched him leave and Ice's stomach clenched.

Fuck, before long that would be him. Rushing to the hospital to be with his old lady as she gave birth to their babies.

"Uh-oh. Look at that, brothers. Our brother Ice suddenly realised his old lady popping those babies out wasn't going to be as much fun as making them was." Sin teased with a deep laugh that was echoed by the rest of the brothers.

"Fuck all of you." Ice said with a grin because to some extent it was true.

Hawk laughed as he smacked the hammer down, ending church.

"Let's get out of here and have a drink to celebrate Ice's good fortune. And brothers, no one rides alone, no matter what. I want all of you watching your backs and keeping your eyes open. And let's find that fucking car."

CHAPTER TWENTY ONE

Hawk

Trying to arrange a meeting between the presidents of three motorcycle clubs took longer than he had anticipated. He knew they all had shit they had to do but this was fucking important. It took the whole damned day before they could all agree to a time and place.

Finally it was set for eight that evening at Underground. Skelly had so many cameras set up around the area they would immediately be alerted if they had been followed and the meeting had been compromised.

The tricky bit was getting there without being followed. That was why they were riding in a big group to the hospital to see Rider's new baby. Their plan was simple. Earlier the prospects, Sam and Terror, had driven a cage into the hospital's parking garage. They had stayed out of sight but watched to make sure the vehicle wasn't tampered with.

On arrival at the hospital they would take the lift up to the waiting room outside the Maternity Ward. Once up there Hawk, Ice, Kid and Wolf would take the stairs back down to the parking garage where Sam would hand over the keys to the cage. They would then drive to the meet.

Hawk wasn't worried about the meet, he was worried about Kid.

His friend wasn't doing well and Hawk knew they needed to have a talk. And at some stage he'd have to arrange a meeting with Kid's parents. Something he wasn't looking forward to. He knew Kid's mum, Aunt Essie, had been pissed at him for the longest time. And to some extent he understood her anger because Jane was her daughter. But there was no way she hadn't known about her daughters' very bad reputation. And the bitch had that reputation long before he got involved with her.

He had no idea how Flash felt about the Jane situation. After Bounty's death when the older generation had stepped down Flash Warne had not been happy. Hawk knew Flash had not been ready to step down and had his eye on the president's chair, and if he couldn't have that chair then at least the VP's. He'd had no chance of ever sitting in either of those chairs. Everyone had been ready for the younger generation to take over, and that's exactly what happened.

Flash never voiced his ambitions and he had supported Hawk's appointment. But Hawk suspected there was unresolved resentment still there.

But right now he didn't have time to worry about shit that had happened in the past. It would have to wait.

RENÉ VAN DALEN

Ice

Pulling into the warehouse Ice breathed easier when the roller shutter doors clanked closed behind them. They parked alongside two other SUV's. Dagger and his officers had arrived before them.

Alien, the Road Warriors' Road Captain, was waiting for them and escorted them to the lower levels where the meeting was taking place. The fight club looked very different from the last time they had been here.

A long table had been set up in place of the fighting cage. The cage itself had been hoisted up and secured against the high roof. The stands were gone as well. All that remained was the bar and the seating around it.

Doc sat at the head of the table and Hawk and Dagger faced each other across the middle. Ice and the others settled in the empty seats around them.

Doc immediately started the meeting.

"We have a lot to get through so let's get started. We don't want the bastards to realise Hawk and Ice have been at the hospital too long. Dagger is having a great time in the back room of a strip club which means no one will bat an eye if he's busy for a while." Doc raised his eyebrows at Dagger who shrugged and smirked.

"Next time we have a meeting can we do it at a strip club, Boss?" Wolf asked with a grin.

There were snorts around the table.

"Not if he wants to keep breathing. His old lady will cut his nuts off or she will retaliate by taking the women to a male strip club." Ice grinned at his boss who was frowning at all of them.

"You better stop grinning, Ice. You do know the women are going to take your old lady to a strip club for her bachelorette party when you decide to tie the knot, don't you? There's no way Krissie or Mari will let her get away with less. Those bitches are fucking crazy." Dagger informed him with a wink.

"Nope, not happening." Ice disagreed.

"And brother, just saying, we'll be taking you to Moonlight for your bachelor party. You know it's a tradition with the club. How can you tell her no when you are going to have strippers giving you lap dances and a lot more if you're up for it." Kid teased.

Everyone laughed. But Ice didn't. No bitch was going to get into his lap and no thong wearing bastard was going to grind on his old lady either. But now wasn't the time to talk about it. He would deal with the fucking strip clubs when the time came.

"Let's cut out talking shit and get on with it." Ice ended the teasing.

Doc immediately looked at Skelly and gave him the nod to start.

"Ziggy, Mad Dog and I have been combing the dark net for any sign of Jane Warne. She was last spotted in PE where she tried to set up a new pipeline but the Iron Dogz shut it down. Mad Dog and I were looking for any signs that might lead us to her when we came across another auction site. I've passed it on to Ziggy and he's busy tracking them. This site is very different from the others we have uncovered. They are auctioning off pregnant women. Rider's woman was on the site but her photo was removed earlier tonight. We are assuming it means she's safe but I suggest an increased presence at the hospital until they are home."

Ice knew what was coming as he sat frozen in his chair.

"Ice, brother, your old lady is on the site and she's getting a lot of attention because she's expecting twins."

Ice's blood ran cold in his veins.

"How the fuck did they find out about the twins?" Ice ground out through tight lips. "Her doctor has been made aware of the threats to their lives and has agreed to remove River's details from the computer system."

"Brother, not everyone is trustworthy. The scan technician or one of the nurses or an assistant could have been bribed. It happens." Dagger said softly. "But it doesn't mean I'm not going to be breaking fucking heads tomorrow morning. River is my sister and she means a lot to me and my club. Any threat to her is a threat to the Sinner's Sons. We'll find the fucking rat, don't worry about it. You concentrate on keeping her safe."

Ice nodded. For now he would leave the breaking of heads to Dagger. Keeping River safe was his top priority. He looked at Hawk then glanced at Doc. "We have to pass this on to Rick, let him and the taskforce do what they did for Duncan."

There were nods of agreement around the table.

Skelly nodded but by the look in his eyes Ice knew more was coming. "Consider it done. But that's not all we found. We have found Emma Coetzee's connection to the Maingarde Organisation. Her father is Frederick James Harrison. Winifred Maingarde's nephew and her brother's son and right hand man in London. Freddy has been visiting SA for years, he still does. We suspect he comes over to check on Winifred and the business. He is married to the daughter of one of their Eastern European associates, has been for years. They have two sons, and both joined their dad in the business. It doesn't look like he had much to do with Emma until her friendship with Genna was discovered. That's when he and Winifred became a big part of her life. During her years at University she was drawn into the business and became one of their top operatives. We also uncovered that she never went to the US. She went to the UK and was living and working there before her return to SA."

"So, you're telling us they've had eyes on us for fucking years without us being aware of it?" Hawk was visibly pissed off.

"Yes, we still can't find why Emma turned her attention to another man but I'm sure there was a reason behind her pregnancy. We just have to find it, and find the poor kid's biological father."

Suddenly it was as if a light had come on in Ice's brain. He had a very good idea what their fucked up end goal was.

"Jesus. I can't believe I had been so fucking blind. I was going to give the bitch my patch. But all she wanted was to get inside the clubhouse." Ice looked over at Hawk. "Brother, I'm having a really fucked up thought. What if she used that fucking drug on a brother? What if the kid belongs to one of us? We know it's not me because I've had the DNA test. But what about everyone else? Did Bounty somehow find out about it? Is that the reason why he was killed?"

Stunned silence hung over the table.

"Holy fucking shit." Kid swore softly. "How are we going to test every single fucking brother without causing untold shit?"

Rubbing his hands over his visibly tired eyes Hawk sighed then laid down the way it was going to get done.

"I'm going to call everyone in, retired brothers as well. We will take the test during church, in front of our brothers. There's no shame in it, because however this turns out, the bitch raped whoever it is by taking away his ability to say no. Fuck, I know as men we don't want to hear this shit but we all know it happens."

"How will a guy know if it had happened to him?" Wolf asked with a growl.

Skelly shook his head. "I didn't know about the attempt to drug Ice so my investigation is a total coincidence. Mad and I found a dark website run by the Harrisons, they sell a drug called 'Tranquillity' to whoever has the money to buy it. And let me tell you it's fucking pricy. We obtained a sample through a source. We had it tested at a lab we trust and it was found that this shit is super fucking dangerous. It causes a heightened sexual response, an inability to say no and finally total memory loss. The subject wakes up with no memory of the assault. It's worse than the known date rape drugs as the subject is semi-aware during the rape and will respond to stimuli and then lapse into a coma like state. There is a high probability of heart attacks and seizures."

"Jesus." Wolf whispered.

"The fucking bitch was going to put that shit into Ice's drink. Can it be put into anything else, like food?" Kid asked.

"No, it is more efficient if it's put into a drink as it gets into the blood stream quicker. Food seems to dampen the effects."

"What about our women? Can they be given this shit?" Hawk snarled.

"Unfortunately, yes. Everyone is vulnerable." Skelly replied.

Doc tapped on the table and everyone's attention turned to him.

"What this means is we no longer accept drinks we haven't poured ourselves. Or better yet, we stick to beer and insist on unopened bottles or cans. This drug is a danger to all of us but now that we're aware of it we can protect ourselves. Skelly will send a list of symptoms to your Information Officers. I suggest we make every single female, patch and prospect aware of the danger and give them the tools to know when they've been drugged so they can seek help before it's too late. And we pass this on to Rick as well. The taskforce needs to know about this shit."

Hawk and Dagger nodded their agreement. Silence settled in the large room as everyone contemplated the shit they were facing.

Ice filled the heavy silence turning their attention to the other matter they needed to address. "I've forwarded photos of the Beemer we're looking for to both clubs. These bastards have it hidden somewhere and if we all reach out to our contacts maybe someone will remember seeing it. We need to find it before they use it again. We've warned all our brothers to be on the lookout and to get out of the way should they spot it. It has been used for more than one hit that we know about and I'm sure there are others we're unaware of."

"If we all work together we'll get through this shit relatively unscathed." Doc said. "Take note I said relatively unscathed. We all know when they hit us we're going to lose people. Tighten security as much as possible. I suggest we close our doors, no more parties, not even for club members only. Send all hangers on and club pussy home until further notice. We pull the vulnerable women and children in to keep them safe and we step up our efforts to finish this shit."

He looked at Ice. And Ice knew he wasn't going to like what came next.

"Our first step is telling Emma Coetzee to fuck off. Be brutal, we need her to react. If we're lucky she'll call Jane in to help her with whatever fucked up plan she cooks up. It's a given that when she hears about River she's going to lose her mind and go after her. River is already a target because of the babies she's carrying. The bitch will tell your old lady you have a kid with her and that you abandoned the child and her."

Doc's intense eyes met his as he continued laying out what had to happen.

"We make damn sure River is covered and knows exactly what's going on. You tell your old lady everything, Ice. Leave nothing to chance. Emma Coetzee is like Winifred Maingarde, an evil manipulative bitch. And they don't like competition, especially female competition. Don't ever fucking forget what happened to Freeze's old lady and take the necessary precautions."

There was no way Ice would ignore the advice. Freeze's old lady had been gunned down in a drive-by shooting. It was not going to happen to River. Not now, not ever.

While Ice had been listening to Doc, Skelly had rushed from the room but now he was back with some electronic gadgets which he proceeded to connect to his laptop. He was tapping away with intense concentration then sat back and winked at Ice.

"Right. I'm ready to rock and roll." He said with a wide grin.

Everyone, except Doc and his guys, frowned at him.

"You are ready for what?" Dagger asked.

Skelly gave an evil grin. "I've set it up so we can all listen when Ice calls the bitch, but she won't know she's on speaker plus I've set up some background sounds that will make it sound like Ice is at the hospital." He gave a quick grin as he glanced at Hawk. "DC and River arrived at the hospital a few minutes ago, which means this is the best and safest time to kick the bitch to the curb."

Ice felt everyone's eyes on him as he pulled his phone from his pocket and shot it across the desk at Skelly. He immediately slipped it into a strange dock like contraption and typed shit into his laptop.

"Okay, we're ready when you are Ice." He said as he pointed at the open seat next to him.

Taking a deep breath Ice pushed his chair back and went around the table and sat down next to Skelly.

"So, this is how it's going to happen. We're going to call her, you're going to kick her ass out of your life, and she's going to plead, beg or threaten. No matter what she says, brother, you tell her you're done. You've got an old lady and she's pregnant with your kids. They already know about the twins so don't try to hide it. Let her know you're giving your old lady your patch and you're getting married. She's going to come at you with the other kid. You tell her you doubt the kid is yours or whatever you want to say. Are you ready?"

Ice drew in a deep breath and nodded. Fuck yes. He was ready to be rid of this bitch. He listened to the phone ringing and then she answered.

"Gray?"

"Emma, I'm not going to waste your time or my own. I'm done with this shit between you and me. I don't want to see your fucking face ever again, are we clear?"

"What? What the hell are you talking about, Gray? I thought we were working through our problems. Working towards becoming a family. I know you still want me, I know it."

Ice snorted derisively. "I was done with you when you called me names in front of my brothers, Emma. I needed to close the book on that fucked up shit and that's the only reason why I continued to meet with you. I don't need or want you, you fucking disgust me. My old lady is pregnant with my babies and we're getting married."

There was an angry screech. "No! You lie! You don't have an old lady! You want me! You'll always want me! What about our child, Gray? What about her? Are you going to kick us aside to play house with some bitch you screwed at your clubhouse? I won't allow it. I'm warning you. You are mine, you've always been mine and no one will ever take you away from me."

Looking up at his prez Ice raised his eyebrows and Hawk nodded as he made a note on his phone.

"It's done. I'm gone. And that kid of yours? No way she's mine. Try that shit on someone who might give a shit."

A wild scream sounded as Ice sat back in the chair and Skelly tapped a key to end the call. He kept on tapping away then leant forward and stared narrowly at the screen. Ice leant over and saw a street map with a pulsing red dot.

"This is not good." Skelly muttered with a frown.

"I traced the call while Ice delivered his message. It looks like she's on her way to the Iron Dogz compound. Hawk, I think you need to warn the brothers you left behind to be prepared."

Hawk didn't hesitate, he called immediately. "Jagger, you've got incoming. Close the road." He was silent for a beat. "Yes, don't let anyone through. It looks like Emma fucking Coetzee is on her way to stir shit either at the club or with Bulldog and the family. Ice just told her he's done with her skank ass. And the slut is a teeny tiny bit pissed off."

Hawk laughed at whatever Jagger said before he shut it down. The laughter disappeared as he focussed on the next step.

"We need to get out of here and back to the hospital. I think they are going to make their play early and I'd like to get my woman safely inside the compound."

Doc nodded his agreement. "You know they are going to be waiting for you on the road, don't you?"

Hawk sneered. "The bastards will be waiting for a damned long time."

There was an alternative route back to the compound.

They would return via back roads and through the hidden access on the neighbouring property. It belonged to the club but was hidden behind a shell company and was rented out to a family who didn't exist. Only the officers knew about it but now they would be revealing the existence to a few more brothers.

The bitch was going to be enraged when she was unable to get to her targets. Maybe it will push her into making a mistake.

A phone conference was arranged for the following day instead of another face to face meeting. Their enemies had to be kept in the dark about the fact that the three clubs were now united against them. The meeting ended and then they were on their way back to the hospital.

His woman wasn't going to like what he had to tell her. Ice didn't know how he knew she was going to be pissed. He just knew it. He hoped like hell she understood that her safety and the safety of Duncan and the babies were most important to him right now.

On the drive home he would tell her about the drug and Emma. But there was no way he was going to tell her Emma and Jane murdered her man. If he had his way she would never know.

He would leave the discussion of the move to the compound for when they were in bed. He might get her to agree if he held her in his arms while he explained.

During the ride back to the hospital they planned the evasion of the ambush that had been set up on the road leading to the club. The ambush was on the eastern approach to the club. Some of the brothers would take the long way around and approach the compound from the west. Riding without lights they would be inside the walls of the compound before the bastards knew they had been tricked. Hawk and those riding with him would use the back road and hidden access onto the property.

From now on they would make sure they had eyes on the roads around the compound at all times. They had almost been caught unprepared.

If Ice hadn't made that call there was a very good chance they would have ridden into an ambush. They would definitely have lost some brothers or even Hawk and DC. It was not acceptable. Along with Jagger he would be seeing to it that they stepped up their already tight security.

Ice hated letting someone else ride his bike but he wanted to be the one driving his old lady home. Sam and Terror rode his and Hawk's bikes as they both had the same idea. Plus he was using the drive home to tell River as much as he could without endangering her or the club.

"Oh my word! Are you serious?"

River was turned sideways in her seat her eyes wide with shock. Ice had to smile at those wide blue eyes.

"Very serious, Blue. Between planning to drug me and telling me she lost my kid and then changing her story and telling me she had the kid she was definitely trying to play her fucked up games with my head."

"Wow, what a bitch. Did you tell her you have DNA proof the kid isn't yours?"

"No I didn't. We decided to not say anything. We've got the kid and her parents in a safe place until we can rid ourselves of this problem. We can't be sure she won't try to use the kid to manipulate the club."

"I can't believe somebody could be so callous with their own child. It blows my mind. I would never do something so horrible to Duncan or the prawns."

Ice glanced at her and smiled. "You have a heart and a conscience, she doesn't. Blue, I need you to be very, very careful. You stick with the brothers assigned to protect you. You don't drink anything you haven't opened yourself. The same goes for your mum, dad and Duncan. And if she calls you end the call. You don't listen to her or talk to her under any circumstances. She'll say things that will hurt you and I don't want that."

His Blue gave him a frowny face. "Like what? What can she say that will upset me?"

"Baby, you know she will tell you shit about her and I. Shit that's not true but is going to sound like it is. It's best not to talk to her at all."

The frowny face was gone and a full on pissed off look took its place.

"Is there something I should know? Don't hide anything from me, Ice."

Fuck. He didn't want to talk about how his dick had been hard around Emma at first. It had been a sort of knee jerk reaction to what they'd had in the past. It definitely wasn't how he felt about her now. And it definitely hadn't happened in a long damned time. Sucking in a breath he explained.

"Okay, but I want to assure you it was a reaction fuelled by what we used to be to each other. When she first appeared I was confused as to how I felt and I did get hard but I did not do anything about it and it disappeared very, very quickly."

"Was this before or after we met?"

Fuck. There had been that one instance and he knew it would hurt his girl. What the fuck was he supposed to say? He wanted to be totally honest with her but this was something that would hurt her needlessly. It had been a knee jerk reaction of his body to stimulation and it hadn't lasted longer than a few seconds. Then again, he told her about it when he had laid it all out for her.

So truth it is.

"Mostly before, Blue, you know about the only other time. And I explained that shit."

His woman sighed and slumped in her seat. "I hate the thought of you with her, especially after I saw you together at the restaurant. You didn't look like you didn't like what she was doing, and I think that's what bothers me the most. I know I sound like one of those women who goes on and on about something that's in the past and refuses to let it go. But I keep comparing you and her to us."

Jesus, this wasn't good. His old lady was so confident and self-assured and this Emma shit seemed to be undermining her confidence and her confidence in him specifically.

"Blue, what you saw was an act. What you and I have together is not an act. I'm so fucking into you I can't think straight. I can be sitting in a fucking meeting and remember your scent and I'm instantly hard. I think about your smile and I'm instantly hard. I think about going down on your perfect little pink pussy and I'm so fucking hard I can't fucking think straight. All my blood is in my cock instead of in the rest of my body. And I stay hard for you, always."

And then he decided to confide in her, to tell her the one thing that used to worry the shit out of him while he had been with Emmie all those years ago.

"I need to tell you something. But remember this happened in the past. It does not happen now, I swear on my life it doesn't." He glanced at her before looking back at the road. "While I was with Emma I got turned on by other women, not only her. Strippers, dancers, a nice ass on the street, great hair, fucking anything would set it off. It felt as if I had no control over my damned cock and was being unfaithful. I think my dad realised I was struggling and gave me a talk about how some men had a higher sex drive and that it was okay as long as I didn't act on it." Ice tapped his fingers on the steering wheel. "I hid it from the bitch, pretending it was her turning me on when sometimes it wasn't. She had this way of talking down to me when we were arguing and it turned me off for fucking days, sometimes weeks. But I still got turned on by other women, just not by her. Until she accused me of fucking Jane. The accusations killed my sex drive for a while."

He quickly glanced at her again before he looked back at the road. She was watching him.

"After she left I lived my life as a single man and I had some women. Nothing like Hawk and some of the other brothers at the club, but still quite a few. Years before I met you I realised it was visual stimulation that turned me on. I learned how to either use it or ignore it, until it no longer ruled me. It worked perfectly until the first time I saw you. Every bit of control I had flew right out the fucking window. Like I said, I only have to think about you and I'm so fucking turned on I need to jerk off over and over. You now rule my cock. It's yours, Blue, only yours. Never doubt that."

He glanced at her again and his woman smiled at him and his heart settled.

"Thanks for explaining it to me, Ice." She gave a little laugh. "And giving me your cock. I promise I'll take very good care of it."

He laughed. "I know you will, baby."

During the drive home Ice hadn't once stopped checking for a tail. He had Sam and four brothers escorting them and so far he hadn't noticed anyone following them. But he would not let up on his vigilance. His family was at risk.

Hell, he loved saying it, thinking it. His family. His woman. His children.

His family.

CHAPTER TWENTY TWO

River

Earlier the same day.

I was bent over an engine when DC stormed into the workshop. Her eyes were wide and my heart immediately started racing.

"What's wrong? Did someone get hurt? Is Ice okay?" I asked anxiously.

"Everyone is fine. They're all doing whatever the hell they're supposed to be doing. I freaking hate being the president's old lady. Especially today."

Now I was confused. What the hell was she talking about?

"Why? What's going on?"

She stalked around the workshop poking at the bikes being worked on not saying a word and I looked at Wrench and mouthed 'what's going on?' He lifted his shoulders and pulled an 'I don't know' face.

"DC, stop wandering around and tell me what's got you so wound up."

She sighed and plopped down on the couch. "Everyone in the club has a job. You know this, because this isn't your first stint at being an old lady. Hawk takes care of everyone and as his old lady

I'm supposed to take care of and support the old ladies. And control the club sluts, that's supposed to be my job as well. Not that I give a shit about them, they can damned well rot down in the dungeon for fucking ever as far as I'm concerned."

What? There were sluts in the dungeon? What dungeon?

She slid down into a slump. "And now I have to go do the supportive shit for one of the old ladies. She's in hospital and due to have her baby this afternoon. I'm supposed to go to the hospital and support her and her man until Hawk can get there later. I fucking hate hospitals. They smell funny. And the nurses wear squeaky shoes. Can't stand that chie-chie-chie noise they make."

I couldn't help it, I burst out laughing and so did Wrench. And shortly after so did DC.

"I'm being such a wimp." She wheezed through her laughter.

"Yes you are." I grinned. "But so what? I'll go with you and the first chie-chie footed nurse that comes close I'll trip. How's that?"

DC grinned and held her hand up for a high five, I didn't leave her hanging. Smacking our palms together with a wide grin.

Wrench clapped a hand over the side of his face as he kept one eye on us. "You two are a scary, scary combination." He said mock seriously.

We both grinned at him before I turned back to DC. "So who's in labour and who is her old man?"

DC made a face. "I don't think she's actually an old lady yet. She's Rider's girlfriend and no she's not in labour. There are some complications and they're doing a caesarean at two this afternoon."

That sounded serious. "What kind of complications?"

DC shrugged. "I don't know, and bad me, I didn't ask."

"Okay, that doesn't matter right now. Let me get cleaned up so we can get to the hospital. Wrench, will you tell the guys we'll be leaving soon please?"

And now here we were, sitting in the waiting room outside the Maternity Ward, reading really old magazines and drinking vending machine coffee. I hate vending machine coffee. Especially decaffeinated vending machine coffee.

The surgery which had been scheduled for two had to be pushed back because the doctor was caught up in an emergency surgery. So Rider's girl was only being operated on at six. The poor boy was about to lose his mind. He had been in and out of the waiting room keeping us updated throughout the afternoon. And the later it got the more anxious he became.

At about five the swing doors opened again and Rider strode through, a very determined look on his face.

"We've decided on an epidural, I'm going to be in the theatre with her. I'll be out as soon as I can to let you all know how it went."

He didn't give anyone a chance to say a word, just swung around and disappeared back through the doors.

Throughout the afternoon the waiting room had slowly started filling up with rough looking bikers as they came to support their brother. The civilians had quickly separated themselves from the dangerous looking men, to DC's amusement. Six came and went and by six thirty the men were starting to look anxious and I wanted to laugh.

What did they think? That the doctor zipped her open, took out the baby and that was it? These guys had so much to still learn about women and having kids. Poor bastards.

"What the fuck is an epi-whatever-the-fuck he called it?" One of the guys asked.

And everyone looked at me. The pregnant one in the room.

"They insert a needle in her spine and then they administer drugs so she can't feel a thing from the waist down. It means she's awake while they do the operation and can see her baby when it's born." I explained.

"Are you fucking with me?" He asked with shocked eyes.

"No, not at all. People do it all the time."

"That just creeped me the fuck out." He muttered. "She's awake while they cut her open and take out the kid. That's just not fucking right. Fuck, I don't think I could do what Rider's doing."

DC grinned at me and winked slyly.

"I didn't think you'd be a squeamish one, Dollar. But remember this day when you think of getting into my little sister's pants again.

She will definitely insist on an epidural, she can't stand pain." DC teased.

The young guy looked about ready to start running as he gave her a look and shook his head.

I looked around as a heavy hand settled on my shoulder. While we had been talking Ice, Hawk and Kid and a brother whose name I didn't know had come into the waiting room.

Ice bent over, kissed me softly as he dropped his hand to cover my bump. "Hey, Blue, how are you and my prawns doing?"

"Your what?" Hawk gave us a confused frown.

Ice, DC and I burst out laughing. "It's my friend Krissie's fault." I explained. "She started calling the babies 'the prawns' and now everyone does. Even Duncan, but only after I assured him they wouldn't have ugly feelers and we wouldn't eat them."

There were bursts of surprised laughter and DC shook her head. "That boy is so damned funny."

The laughter stopped when Hawk bent over and whispered something to DC. And her face changed. It became watchful as she looked up at him and nodded. I didn't have to wait long to find out what he had said to her because Ice did the same. He whispered instructions to me.

"Stay here until we get back, Blue. Do not leave under any circumstances. Promise me, baby."

I nodded. "I promise."

Then they were gone. And DC and I went back to waiting.

We were wolfing down pizzas when the swing doors burst open and Rider came storming through dressed in blue scrubs. His face alight and with the biggest smile on his face.

"It's a girl! I've got a baby girl. She great and Penny is great. There were some scary moments with her blood pressure but she's good. She's in recovery and soon they'll settle her in her room. I'm going to the nursery to bath my baby girl now. Sorry, brothers, they're very strict here. You can't come in to see Penny, only fathers and grandparents are allowed. But you can see my baby girl through the window of the nursery. I'll come back and let you know when she ready."

His brothers surrounded him, hugging and smacking him on the back and not once did the wide smile disappear. I nudged DC and motioned towards him with my head and she got up with a sigh and went over and gave the guy a hug. I followed, hugged him and wished him and his lady well with their new baby. He just grinned and nodded.

And then he was gone again.

One of the brothers across from us gave me a sneaky grin before he looked around the waiting room. The name on his kutte said he was Jagger.

"I hope Ice and his freaking super sperm made boys because every single fucking brother so far has had girls. It looks like the next generation is going to be made up of girls. At least River is bringing us a boy and I'm hoping the prawns turn out to be boys as well."

A sly smile slid over the guy at the end of the row's face. Glancing at his kutte I saw his name was Ziggy.

"The betting book is open. So far we've got 5 to 1 they're girls. You want in on the action?"

"Hell, yes. I'm putting R50 on them being boys."

I smiled as I watched the men debate how likely it was that we would have boys not girls and Ziggy jotted it all down in a little notebook he'd pulled from the inside pocket of his kutte.

We were laughing when Rider came back out.

"Okay, who wants to go see my baby girl?"

I immediately got up. I definitely wanted to see her and I grabbed a very reluctant DC and dragged her along with me.

Rider stood behind the glass holding his tiny little baby girl in his arms and showed her off to us. The look on his face was a mix of love and pride. She was so precious and cute. And because she hadn't been through the birth canal she looked perfect. I could only imagine what the guys would have said if she had been all squished after hours of battling to be born.

After a lot of oohing and aahing DC and I made our way back to the waiting room. She was strangely quiet.

"What's wrong?"

"I don't think I could ever do that. Have a kid. I didn't grow up like other kids and I think I'll just screw up any kids Hawk and I would have."

"Nonsense. You're great with Duncan and you said you helped raise your little sister and she's a perfectly nice girl. Stop worrying. None of us know what the hell we're doing when we have our first one. That's why we have family and friends. And you have a secret weapon, you have me. Hell, by the time you and Hawk decide to take the plunge I'll have three running around."

And then the number hit me. "Oh, shit, I'm going to have three little maniacs running around the house. And if the prawns are boys I'm going to have three dicks to worry about when they start chasing girls. Can you imagine how many condoms I'm going to have to buy?"

DC cackled with laughter. "What if they're girls? Imagine them at fifteen surrounded by hot bikers. Lots of hot problems, Mumma."

"Ugh, don't put that image in my brain." I gave a tiny grimace.

"What the fuck are you two talking about?" Ice suddenly asked behind us.

"Nothing really. Just the sex of the prawns." I quickly explained but I should have known DC wouldn't leave it alone.

"We were just trying to imagine how many condoms you will have to buy with three boys. But if they're girls you will have another problem. Two pretty girls surrounded by hot bikers." DC gave Ice an evil smile and I held my breath for the eruption I knew was coming.

I didn't have to wait long.

"The first fucker who lays a finger on one of my girls dies. Problem solved." Ice snapped.

"Nope, not solved. Teenage girls are hell on wheels. You were there when I dragged Deena off Dollars' cock. Prepare yourself, Pappa Ice." DC still had the evil smile on her face.

My man was about to explode so I stepped in like a good old lady should.

"This argument is pointless. We don't know the sex of the prawns yet, so there's no point in getting all hot and bothered about it."

"We are finding out the sex as soon as possible." Ice snarled while Hawk looked on with a wide grin.

"I have an appointment for Wednesday, but we can't tell anyone because it will upset Ziggy."

"Good on the appointment but what the fuck does Ziggy have to do with anyone knowing if they're boys or girls?" Thunder clouds gathered in those eyes of his, suddenly looking more yellow than green. Oops.

Hawk quickly explained and I sighed with relief that he knew about the damn betting going on.

"Brother, Ziggy has been running a betting book on the sex of the babies. When I put my money down it was at 4 to 1 on the babies being girls. I agree with River, you need to keep the sex quiet for a while so I can make some money."

Ice frowned at him. "What, you think I'm having girls? It might be like Gail's, one of each."

Hawk grinned and shook his head from side to side. "Nope, those are boys, have to be, I put money down on them."

"Jesus." Ice muttered.

Shaking his head Ice pulled me up and into his arms. "You look tired, Blue, we need to get you home."

After saying our goodbyes Ice led me down the stairs with a prospect and four brothers following us. He carefully helped me into the SUV, closed the door and then rounded the front of the vehicle and got in behind the wheel. As the bikes rumbled around us I realised one of the prospects was on his bike. My man was driving me home instead of having the prospect doing it.

Once we were on the way I saw something was worrying him but I stayed silent, giving him time to work through whatever it was. Then he started talking. What he told me was shocking on the one hand but on the other it made me so damned angry.

The slutty bitch needed to be dealt with. She tried to drug my man and who knew whatever the hell she would have done to him if she had succeeded.

But it wasn't all he explained to me. Ice laid it all out.

He finally settled the doubt that still troubled me. He explained his history with the bitch and then he made my heart fly.

My Iceman made my heart fly by giving me his cock. I know, it might not seem important to most women, but to a bikers' old lady it meant everything. Bikers loved their freedom, the freedom to ride, the freedom to be who they want to be, the freedom to fuck whoever the hell they wanted whenever they wanted even after taking an old lady.

My old man just assured me I would never have to worry about him being unfaithful.

His cock belonged to me and only me.

Something still worried him but I would wait until we were home. Once we were in bed all cuddled up together I would get it out of him. We were together now and his worries were my worries, we were a team.

As his old lady it was my job to help him carry the load of his responsibilities. And I would start tonight as I meant to go forward.

Supporting my man. Loving our children and loving his club.

CHAPTER TWENTY THREE

Ice

Holding his old lady against his chest Ice drew in a deep breath, filling his lungs and head with her scent. His cock was rock hard but he ignored it. His woman wasn't ready for him yet. There were still a few things to iron out before he could make love to her.

And when he did she would not be walking away from him again. She would be staying.

Her hand stroked over his naked chest and he couldn't stop the shiver of reaction at her touch.

"What's wrong?" She said softly, her lips against his pec.

Ice sighed. He knew he had to tell her but he was hesitant to break the peace he felt just holding her. But he wanted it over, behind them. So he drew in a deep breath and explained.

"Before I tell you I need you to know that you're safe, baby. I would never allow anything to touch you or our babies."

She nodded but her arm tightened around him. "Tell me." She whispered.

"We found an auction site on the dark net and they had photos of you and Rider's girl." He felt her go solid against his side and her breathing became rushed. "I don't want you to worry, baby. We've got it under control. We passed it on to a member of the trafficking taskforce and they will shut it down and investigate the origin and hopefully make some arrests."

He tightened his arms around her. "But in the meantime I want to be sure you are as safe as we can possibly make you. You will have a security detail with you at all times, so will Duncan and your parents. And if it becomes necessary it would mean us having to move to the compound until the threat to you and the prawns have been eliminated."

Her voice was small with a tiny vibration in it. "What about my workshop? Can I still go to work? Will I be safe there? I don't want anything to happen to our babies, Ice."

Ice pulled her on top of him and surrounded her with his arms and legs. "I won't allow anything or anyone to touch you or our babies, my love. I promise you'll be safe and so will our babies."

Pulling his one arm from around her he pushed her hair away from her face, hooking it behind her ear and looked into her beautiful blue eyes.

"You can still go to work, Blue, but there will be brothers around you at all times. No one we haven't vetted will be allowed near you at any time. Wrench will be with you as well, and I trust that boy, he's got a very good head on his shoulders. But I want you to promise me that if I decide it's too dangerous for you to continue working you won't fight me. I need you to listen to my concerns and allow me to keep you and our children safe. Okay?"

He stared into her eyes as he watched her consider his requests. Then she dropped her head and kissed him. Softly, so very softly.

"Okay. I'll do whatever you tell me to do because I know you're doing it because you want to keep us safe."

Ice pulled her head down to him and kissed her and very quickly got lost in the taste and feel of his woman. It took everything in him to end the kiss. His hand was behind her head, his fingers threaded through her hair as he pulled her head back.

"Easy, baby. I'm not starting anything with you right now. I want us to settle into who we are together before we take the next step."

His River moaned with frustration as she rubbed herself over his hard cock.

"Blue, stop, stop. We're not going there, not tonight. I fucking want you, you can feel how much, but we are going to sleep, just sleep."

He rolled her off him and back against his side. Pulling her into his chest he settled her head on his shoulder and curved his arm around her, settling his hand on her hip.

"Can't believe we're not having hot sex right now." She grumbled.

Ice laughed softly and kissed her forehead.

"The next time I take you, Blue, we will not be having sex. I will be making love to you and you had better be ready, baby. It's going to be an all-night affair."

"Promises, promises." She mumbled.

Ice shook with silent laughter, he felt her relax against him as she slowly slipped into sleep.

"I keep my promises, baby." He whispered against her hair.

Glancing over at the bedside table where the photo of a smiling Sparrow with his hands over River's big belly still stood, Ice smiled. And he silently spoke to the smiling man.

I love her, brother, and I love your son. I swear I will raise him as if he's my own. I will make sure he knows the good man his father was. And I will make sure he stays close to his Sinner's Sons family.

Ice lay staring at the smiling man until his eyelids started to feel heavy and slid closed.

He fell asleep holding his old lady knowing his brothers were watching over them, keeping them safe.

After the early morning craziness of getting his new family ready for the day he dropped his boy with his grandparents and followed Blue to work. Traffic was light and they got to the workshop without any incidents. He parked next to her bakkie and escorted her inside, had a quick word with Wrench then kissed his old lady and left.

But before he left he checked on the brothers outside and made sure they knew exactly what to be on the lookout for. A banged up black Beemer. Because of the church call out from Hawk his woman would be guarded by the Sinner's Sons and Wrench today.

While riding to the compound his mind was on the testing that was about to take place. Hawk had called in every single member who could possibly be the father of the kid. All the retired brothers would be taking the test along with those who had been patched brothers and prospects at the time the kid had been conceived.

It was going to cause a tremendous amount of shit. But he and the other officers had their president's back. They needed to find the biological father of the kid to try and uncover the reason why he had been targeted by Emma. Ice had a horrible suspicion he knew who it was but he was going to keep his mouth shut until the results came back.

It was the why that was giving him the most trouble.

Why had she done it? What did she have to gain?

He still hadn't come up with any answers when he pulled into the compound. Rows of gleaming bikes were parked in front of the clubhouse and brothers were standing around chatting as he rolled his bike back and parked next to Hawk's ride.

Setting his helmet on his seat he made his way inside, stopping to greet some of the brothers he hadn't seen in a while. If it wasn't for the shit they would be facing in church today it would have been a happy occasion. But he couldn't lose sight of the reason why their president had called everyone in today.

Ice walked through the common room and down to Hawk's office. He knocked once and walked in. Hawk was sitting in his big ass chair with DC on his lap. Kid was in the chair in front of the desk and Ice sank down in the chair next to his.

"Morning." Ice said and included all of them in the greeting.

The three all murmured their greetings while watching him intently.

"What?"

"We were just wondering if you talked to River about moving in here." DC said with a little smirk.

That little smirk said she thought his woman had given him shit. Little did she know. His woman was the perfect old lady.

"Yes, I did and she's okay with it. Not happy, but she'll do whatever is necessary to keep our kids safe. It helps that she had been with Sparrow for those few years. He made sure she felt comfortable with the life we live and taught her how to be the kind of old lady a biker needs." Ice smiled at DC. "My old lady has my back and will do what I ask of her."

Kid leant over and punched him on the shoulder. "Fucking happy for you, brother."

Rubbing his shoulder Ice grinned. "Thanks brother."

He turned back to Hawk and DC. "Did you have a look outside, Boss?" His question wasn't for his cousin, it was for his president.

"No, not yet. I wanted to have my coffee in peace before I started thinking about the shit that's going to go down today." Hawk picked up his mug and sipped while DC frowned at Ice.

He ignored the fact that she wasn't happy with his answer because what was about to happen in church was too important. They needed to discuss it before Hawk faced their brothers.

"I did a quick look around before I came in. As far as I could see everyone responded to the call in. Do we have enough tests for everyone?"

"Yes." Kid answered. "Ziggy and I made a run to his connection and got a box full of the shit. I hope like fuck the kid's not mine. Don't want that slut to be the mother of a child of mine."

"We all feel the same way, brother. But we also know it's going to be one of us. And that means we suck it up and deal with it. I'm going to suggest to whoever turns out to be the biological father that he leave her where she is." Hawk sighed heavily. "Feel fucking sorry for the kid."

Ice nodded then asked the question that had been bugging him. "Why did she do it? That's what's bugging me the most. Why? What did she have to gain? And why was the kid given to that specific couple? What if it had been a boy? Would she still have given the kid away?"

DC pointed at him and nodded. "I see where you're going with this. You're wondering if the goal of the pregnancy was to have a boy. Because in a club boys are the legacy every brother leaves behind. They love their little princesses but their boys are the next generation, their legacy. It would have been a hell of a long shot, Ice. The kid is around seven now, right? How would a seven year old boy influence the club or the future of the club?"

By the look in her eyes Ice knew she was starting to suspect what the reason might have been.

"I don't know, DC. I'm just as lost as everyone else. But I keep asking myself, why, what was her end game?"

Kid shrugged. "Why do crazy bitches do the shit they do? No one knows. She's crazy brother, maybe there's no reason behind this at all. Maybe she thought it was one more way she could fuck with you. I think we should focus on why she had someone else's kid and not yours. Why wasn't it your sperm in her snatch?"

"I know exactly why it wasn't my sperm." Ice said. "I was fucking anal about her taking the pill and using condoms. Checking the packaging and condoms before pulling them on every single time. It fucking freaked her out but I refused to back down. I didn't want to have a kid that would end her studies." Ice shrugged. "You can ask any of the bitches I fucked, I double wrapped with all of them. Wore condoms even for a blow job."

"Wow." DC said softly then she turned and gave Hawk an evil grin. "I am now so very jealous of River. She got a virtually pristine cock while I got this one." She gave a pretend grimace as she pointed down at Hawk's cock.

Ice and Kid burst out laughing when Hawk swung a laughing DC over his lap and delivered two sharp slaps to her ass. DC was laughing so hard she hung helplessly over Hawk's thighs while he shook his head and laughed as well. Eventually she struggled back up and their brother settled her back in his lap.

"Don't ever talk about my cock like that again, little bird, or next time expect more than just two little taps." Hawk threatened with a grin.

DC wriggled on his lap and winked. "Promises, promises."

"Jesus. Enough of sexing each other up in front of us." Kid grouched. "It's time, Prez."

DC immediately hopped off Hawk's lap and grabbed the empty coffee mugs on the desk.

"Good luck, baby." She leant over, kissed Hawk then walked out the office.

"Let's do this." Hawk said with a sigh.

Before going into the chapel Ice gave Sam the same instructions as before. Keep an eye on his phone and come get him if any urgent messages or calls came from River or Wrench.

They were sitting at the table as the chapel slowly filled up. The prospects had brought in extra chairs but a few of the younger patches still had to give up their places to the older men. The doors were closed and Hawk opened the meeting with iron on iron. He slid a typed page over to Kahn who did a quick roll call then put the page into the back of the notebook on the table in front of him. Even though every word would be recorded Kahn was still going to take notes and add his observations. It was those observations that would come in handy later.

Hawk sat in his big chair and looked around the room. "I want to thank all the retired brothers and nomads for coming in today. We haven't had the entire brotherhood in a meeting in a very long time. And we all know when we do it's hardly ever good news. Today it isn't good news either. But it's not all bad news. I have the great pleasure to congratulate Rider on the birth of his little girl yesterday. Brother, I said it yesterday and I'm saying it again today. You and your little family are a part of a bigger family, the Iron Dogz family, and the sooner you give your woman your patch the better. Congratulations, brother."

Loud howls erupted as Rider nodded and Hawk let it carry on for a few moments then he held up his hand. Silence fell again.

"And as some of you already know, our brother Ice has a new old lady and she is pregnant with his twins. What some of you don't know is that his old lady comes to us from the Sinner's Sons MC and along with her comes her little boy, the son of Sparrow Martins."

There was a heavy silence in the room and some nods.

"Now some of you will be wondering why I'm sharing this and I'll tell you why. Sparrow died because he saw something he wasn't supposed to see. He saw two women meeting with Winifred Maingarde and they killed him for it. Unfortunately for his killers he left behind clues. And on following those clues we, along with the Sinner's Sons and Road Warriors, were able to identify his killers. Sparrow died five years ago, our troubles go further back than that but it is all linked. And those links are Jane Warne and Emma Coetzee."

Ice listened as his brother laid out the troubles the club was having with the Maingarde Organisation and how they found out Emma Coetzee was deep inside that organisation. He even revealed who her father was. And then he dropped the bomb.

"About seven years ago someone in this room was drugged and raped by Emma Coetzee. The result was a little girl. We don't know the reason behind it we just know that it was done. Today all of us will be taking a DNA test to find out who the father of that little girl is. And there's no need to panic because your DNA will not be in any database the law or anyone else could access. I know some of you weren't part of the club back then but to stop fingers from being pointed we will all do the fucking test."

The silence in the room was overwhelming. Shock and disbelief on every single face.

Flash, Kid's father, was the first to respond. "Hang on a minute here, are you saying my daughter and the girl who grew up in front of most of us is responsible for all the shit going down with the club today? I say bullshit." He waggled a finger between the three of them sitting at the top of the table. "The three of you are blowing smoke up our asses and covering each other's backs, like you've always done. I remember the day Emma came in here and accused that bastard of fucking around on her. He didn't defend himself, just stood there when she ran out. Didn't even try to follow her. Obviously the kid is his. No one else touched the poor girl. Now he's trying to smear her reputation with these fucked up lies you three have cooked up. He should never have been voted into that fucking seat. He's not worthy of that seat or this club."

Ice thought his dad was going to explode but he shook his head, silently asking him to stay quiet.

"Are you done?" Hawk asked in a hard and ice cold voice. He didn't give Flash a chance to answer.

"Accusing your president of lying without proof is a punishable offence, Flash. Remember that. Ice has already submitted to a DNA test and he is not the father. We have proof your daughter, Jane Warne, and Emma Coetzee are working together. Would that be the reason you're trying to point fingers at Ice, Flash? Are you trying to protect your daughter by diverting the suspicion to someone else? And if you're doing it I have to wonder if you know more than what we do? I have to wonder if you have been in contact with Jane and against the bylaws of this club didn't bring what she told you to your president. But more importantly, we have to wonder if you are now working with them against your brothers, against your club."

Flash opened his mouth to answer but Hawk didn't give him a chance.

Hawk leant forward and his voice was like a fucking arctic winter. "Shut up. You had your chance now it's mine. Your daughter is a leech. Doesn't give a fuck who gets hurt as long as she gets what she wants. And what she wants is power, just like you. She is the son you always wanted. She is your legacy, not Kid. Kid was the one you and your friends beat up mercilessly. Supposedly to make him a man.

You're an abusive coward, Flash. You will take the DNA test along with everyone else. We'll know soon enough who the father of that child is. I'm putting my money on you, you fucking yellow bellied bastard. I fucking doubt she had to drug you at all. Bet it was all consensual. We all know how you like fucking the club sluts, the younger the better."

Flash stared at Hawk, his eyes filled with hatred, for once he didn't disguise his feelings. He let it out to be seen by every single brother in the room.

Ice could see Hawk was battling not to totally lose it. He was reliving the memories of carrying a broken and bleeding Kid to the club doctor time after time after time. Between him and Ice and the other prospects they looked after their brother as best they could. Shielding him when they could, but it hadn't been easy. After one especially vicious beating they had realised it was up to them to put a stop to the beatings before the bastards killed Kid. That's when they went to Bounty with the evidence and he made sure it would never happen again.

And maybe that's what had started the ball rolling. But this shit between Flash and Hawk was diverting them from the course they had set for this meeting. Ice knew that at some stage they would have to take care of the problem Flash presented to the club. But that time wasn't now.

"Ziggy will be setting up back here and we will all be tested. If you want me to do the test again I have no problem taking it again." Ice said quietly in the heavy silence hanging in the room.

It was clear not one of the brothers wanted an enraged Hawk's attention to fall on them as they held their hands up and shook their heads. None of them wanted to face him in the ring. And the way their president was feeling right now that's where it would end. Might still end.

Throughout Flash's outburst Kid hadn't batted an eyelid. He sat in his chair, his big arms crossed over his wide chest, his face and eyes hard and emotionless. Ice knew that behind the cold façade shit was going on but nothing showed. And when the man sat forward in his chair and set his hands on the table a ripple went through the brothers. Kid was feared by many in the club because unlike Hawk he hardly ever showed any real emotions. Like right now.

Kid's voice was soft but totally without any emotion. He was at his most dangerous when he spoke in that soft voice. "You heard your president. We will all take the test. Ziggy, get the shit set up so we can get it out of the way. Anyone who refuses to take the test I will personally deal with. Are we clear?"

No one said a word. They all knew Kid took his job as SAA very seriously. He would protect the club and his president with his life.

Ziggy was already up and setting up with the help of Dizzy. One by one they all took the test then retook their seats.

Only once it was done did Hawk speak again. "We will have the results soon. You will be informed when we do."

He looked directly at Flash when he spoke again. "I'm not sure of your loyalty to the club. You are done here. Get out and wait in the common room until we call you back in."

There was a shocked silence and then Bulldog and Taxi, one of the other elders, took him by the arms and lifted him out of his chair. Wolf unlocked the door, his eyes never leaving Flash as he followed them out the room. The brother definitely had the potential to follow in Kid or Beast's footsteps.

Everyone could hear him clearly as he called out.

"Prospects, he stays in that fucking chair. No phone, no conversations, if he wants a piss bring him a fucking empty bottle. His ass stays right there in that fucking chair until I come back for him. Understood?"

"Yes, Wolf." Came immediately from Sam and Terror.

Wolf walked back in and closed and locked the door while Bulldog and Taxi silently retook their seats.

Hawk's voice no longer contained any anger. It was quiet and everyone listened intently as he spoke.

"Our club, our women and children, everything we love is under attack. I will not allow another life to be taken from us. We have lost enough. It is time for us to take the fight to our enemies and root their supporters out of our club. Jane Warne and Emma Coetzee are a threat to every old lady, girlfriend and female family member we have. As you all know my old lady has been attacked more than once already. I was lucky I didn't lose her. Now Emma has her eyes set on Ice's old lady and we are not going to allow her or her babies to be hurt. We protect what belongs to us."

He pointed at Ice. "After very reluctantly leading the investigation on Emma Coetzee last night we came to the conclusion that our brother Ice had to tell her he was done. And he had to do it as brutally as possible to force a reaction from her. Which he did and was very happy to do."

Hawk grinned. "And those of us who had to suffer through the perfume hell he brought in with him every time they had a meet were damned grateful it was at an end."

Ice shook his head but laughed right along with his brothers.

"Her reaction to the phone call came quicker than we expected." Hawk continued. "We were lucky Skelly of the Road Warriors was monitoring the call. He was able to warn us that Emma was on her way here. Jagger immediately closed the road. Soon after they were seen on the cameras we have hidden along the main road. The bitch had set up an ambush. We were able to evade them and got home without any shots fired." He looked around the room. "This time. We might not be so lucky next time. And believe me brothers there will be a next time."

The brothers all had the same reactions. Swearing. A lot.

Bulldog slowly rose and silence fell in the room. Even after all these years he still had the respect of everyone in the room. His eyes swept the room.

"Brothers, today I am proud and saddened at the same time. So damned proud of the three men we put in those chairs up there. And when I say 'we' I mean all of us, because we voted them into those positions. They're not there because of who their fathers are or were. They are there because they are the best men for the job and we all know it."

His eyes settled on the three of them and Ice's fingers clenched around the arms of the chair.

"I see no reason not to believe the facts as Hawk laid them out for us. I've known our president since the day he was born and he has grown up to be an honourable man. A man I trust with our club implicitly. If I didn't I wouldn't have stepped down seven years ago. And this is where the saddened part comes in. After Bounty died we as his officers agreed it was time for the younger generation to lead the club. Unfortunately not everyone agreed with our plans. I, along with Taxi and Buffel, took action to force the officer in question to retire with us and we made an enemy that day. Flash always wanted to wield the gavel. He wanted the power it brings to the man who sits in that chair and has hundreds of men doing his bidding. He was the one, as a newly patched brother, who initially brought the Maingardes to the table. At the time Bounty wasn't the president yet and had very little say in the decisions made at the table. We ran their drugs and guns throughout Southern Africa because of the money. It was greed, pure and simple. We started losing men in bloody gun battles that had nothing to do with our club and the money was no longer worth it. We wanted out. Bounty started us on the road to getting clear of that shit."

He paused as he looked at Hawk.

"And then Bounty was killed and the next generation stepped in and did what Bounty and I had worked so hard for. They got us out from under the Maingardes. And how did they do it? Hawk sat down with the new generation at the Maingarde Organisation and made a deal we could all live with."

Bulldog walked to the table and leant over between Jagger and Beast to look around the brothers seated at the table.

"You men sitting here around this table are what stands between us and the Maingardes right now. You have the lives of our women and children in your hands as well as the lives of all your brothers countrywide. We cannot allow the Maingarde bitch to get her claws into our club again. As the elders of this club we give you our full support as we fight to keep our freedom. A freedom we paid for with the blood of our brothers."

He stepped back and sat down and the brothers started nodding in agreement. It became stronger as a few voiced their agreement. Then Spider knocked his knuckles on the table and all eyes went to him.

"I'm so fucking proud to be the son of Bulldog Walker today. I joined this club because of him and my brother, Ice. I live my life according to the advice they gave me when I started prospecting. Give your club your heart, your honour and your honesty. The three H's. You give those three things to your club and your brothers and it will be returned to you threefold. My brother has given this club his heart, his honour and his honesty even before he became a prospect. For an ex-officer to call him dishonourable is an insult of the highest order. I want it known that I will not allow the insult to stand."

Kid tapped his knuckles on the table and the atmosphere went electric. But his words set everyone at ease.

"I second. We cannot allow the insult to stand."

Ice knew he had to jump in and get them back on track. There would be enough time later to debate the insult delivered by Flash.

"Brothers, Flash is a problem for later, we need to concentrate on solving the problems we have with Jane and Emma. We started the ball rolling when we shut down the pipeline Jane tried to set up in PE and now we have shut Emma's access to the club down. They are going to retaliate and we have to be ready. I know some of you are thinking 'they're two women, how dangerous can they be?' But they aren't just two women. They are ruthless killers and they are working with one of the most dangerous crime families in the world today. They have access to unlimited manpower and unlimited funds. They also have access to the law as we found out in Durban when we almost lost DC to them. We have to be careful and aware at all times."

Hawk sat forward and tapped his rings on the table. "We've been in here for two hours already, let's take a break, have a smoke or whatever the hell you want to do and be back in here in thirty minutes. No one leaves the premises and no phones."

He shoved his chair back, stood and then walked out the room. Wolf had jumped to unlock the door the minute Hawk moved and followed him out.

Ice stayed in his chair and tipped his head back with a heavy sigh.

This fucking sucked.

He needed to check on his woman, make sure she was feeling good. For some unknown reason he felt unsettled. It felt as if something was about to come down on them and he didn't like it.

He didn't like it at all.

RENÉ VAN DALEN

CHAPTER TWENTY FOUR

River

Ice was worried. I saw it in his eyes when he kissed me goodbye and walked out the large roller shutter doors of the workshop and stopped to speak to the men watching over me. And because he was worried I was now worried. And I could see Wrench was worried as well.

I reached back and ran my fingers gently over the holster hidden at the small of my back. For the first time ever I had come to work armed. I hated that it was necessary because it felt as if it sullied my peaceful workspace. But it wasn't the gun that sullied my peace it was the woman who necessitated the carrying of the weapon.

I wasn't wearing my overalls like I usually did. I came in dressed in ratty jeans, a left over from when I had been pregnant with Duncan, a big faded t-shirt Lake had left behind on his last visit and my work boots. I wasn't really expecting anything to happen but I didn't want to be caught unawares either. My babies needed my protection and by heaven I would give them that.

Wrench and I were working on a bike that had to go out later in the afternoon when we both heard it. The click-click sound of high heels coming towards us down the passage linking the front workshop to mine. We looked at each other and somehow we both just knew. Shit was about to hit the fan. Wrench moved really fast and stationed himself so he was out of the woman's direct line of sight when she walked in.

The bitch I had seen with Ice in the restaurant strolled in as if she owned the damned place. She looked around and gave a disgusted sniff. I stayed behind the heavy bike in front of me. It gave my babies some protection should things start to go horribly wrong.

"Can I help you?" I asked with a frown. Acting as if I didn't know who she was.

"No, but I can help you." She gave a sly smile as she stroked a hand over her curved hip and thigh. She was dressed in a white expensive looking blouse and high-waisted black skinny jeans. Her make-up was heavy but expertly applied nonetheless. And of course she was wearing a pair of those red soled and stiletto heeled seriously expensive black pumps. She had lightened her blonde hair since I had seen her last, it was now an unnatural shade of pale blonde. Somewhere between platinum and light blonde and she had had extensions done. Was I wrong or was the hair an attempt to make hers look like mine?

"Oh, and how do you think you can help me?" I said as I waved a hand around the workshop then raised an eyebrow as I let my eyes slide over her.

Her lip curved in disgust. "You are nothing but a distraction. We've been together for seventeen years and you are hardly a blip on his sexual radar."

I pretended to be confused. "I have no idea what you're talking about. Are you sure you're in the right place?"

She snorted angrily. "You stupid little bitch. Gray is mine, he will always be mine. We have a little girl and I'm pregnant with our second child. You are nothing but a drunken mistake we will take care of very soon. He will not allow those bastards of yours to interfere with what we have planned for our future." She gave me a mocking smile. "And his future is me. It has always been me. And will always be me."

She stood there waiting for my reaction and I gave her nothing. She didn't deserve a reaction. Instead I needed to know how she got inside without being noticed by the brothers or my dad. Maybe no one realised who she was because of the long light blonde hair and the jeans. It was a mistake we could not afford and I would make sure it never happened again. First order of business would be a security door between the two workshops. We needed to control access more stringently.

"I don't give a freaking fig what your crazy ass wants. What I do want to know is how you got in here without a bike or an appointment? This workshop is for customers only and you definitely aren't one. So why don't you turn around and march your fat ass right out of here? I'm busy, I don't have time to listen to your crazy bullshit."

I thought the bitch was going to explode with rage but she swallowed it down and then the filthy psychopathic bitch who lived inside of her came crawling out and freaked me the-hell-out.

"I'm going to remember this when we cut you open and pull those little bastards out of you. I'm going to enjoy every moment as you beg us for their lives. My hand will be the one ripping them out of your disgusting womb and dropping them in the trash where you will join them, slowly bleeding out. And as you die you will watch Gray fuck me on the very same table where we cut those little bastards out of you. We will roll in your blood as we fuck, coating ourselves in the power of your death."

I was frozen in place as she spilled her foul venom at me.

"Jesus, you're one crazy screwed up fucking bitch." Wrench suddenly said from behind her, his gun trained on her as she jerked around. "Get your fucking crazy ass out of here before I do it for you."

She ignored him and the gun pointed at her, whirling around and pointing a finger at me. "Your blood and the blood of those little bastards belong to me. I will be back to collect."

"My blood and the blood of my children will never be yours. I see you again and we will not be chatting. Get the hell out of my workshop." I gritted out through clenched teeth, refusing to let her see how much she had scared and freaked me out.

Turning to Wrench she drew a finger across her throat while smiling at him and then leisurely clicked her way out of the workshop. Wrench didn't hesitate he rushed to the open workshop doors and gave a piercing whistle. He ran back to me with the gun still in his hand by his side. His eyes sweeping between the open doors and the passage.

"How the fuck did she get past everyone?" He bit out.

I was shaking like a leaf and shaking my head because I had no idea. Someone let her walk right through the garage and into the passage. One of the men came into the workshop from the passage carrying a long black wig and a pair of glasses and we knew. She had used the most basic of disguises and fooled everyone. If her intention had been to kill me she would have succeeded. All she would have had to do was slip off her shoes. We wouldn't have heard her until it was too late.

But it would not happen again. We were now aware of how far she would go to get to me. Even changing her basic look to try and fool people into thinking it was me. She got the shoes and makeup completely wrong. The crazy freaking psycho.

And those threats. Those scary extreme threats.

Sweet baby Jesus.

Her threats had me shaking and horribly nauseous. So nauseous I had to run to the bathroom where I hung over the toilet and emptied my stomach. I vomited until there was nothing left to expel and I was left dry heaving and crying. It was the cold facecloth settling on the back of my neck that made me aware there was someone with me in the bathroom.

Dad. A very worried dad.

Holding on to the cloth I slowly levered myself up, rinsed my mouth at the basin then reached for the toothbrush and toothpaste I had to thank Wrench for and brushed the awful taste from my mouth. I rinsed then splashed my face with cold water. Taking the time to slowly dry off, trying to get rid of my red teary eyes before facing my dad.

"I'm okay now, Dad. I promise."

He shook his head. "No, you're not. Wrench recorded the confrontation on his phone and it has been forwarded to Ice. Unfortunately they are locked in an important meeting right now but I know as soon as he gets the message he will be here."

I nodded because I knew he was right. Ice would be here as soon as he could. But he wasn't here right now and right now was when I needed him. Not later. I needed him now.

"That woman is seriously unstable, Dad. The things she said. It was horrifying and she smiled the entire time and her eyes were so, so crazy. How could Ice not have seen how unstable she was? How did no one in their club ever see her for who she really is? She threatened to kill my babies, to cut them out and throw them in the trash and roll in my blood." I looked around the bathroom and sniffed back the tears. I didn't want the visual of her and Ice together in my head. But it pushed itself in anyway and I remembered the way they had looked together in the restaurant.

I shook my head to dislodge the memory.

"She made me afraid to be in my own workshop, Dad. My workshop became my safe place after I lost Sparrow and now she's dirtied it with her sick threats. She'll make sure I won't see them coming next time. I need to feel safe, Dad. And right now I don't. I don't feel safe."

My dad pulled me into his arms and hugged me tight and I felt the kiss he dropped on top of my head. I felt like I could sob my heart out against his chest but I didn't. Because the next minute Dagger stormed into the bathroom and pulled me out of dad's arms, hugging me so hard against him my ribs ached a tiny little bit. His breathing was ragged as he rested his face against mine.

"Fuck, Rivzie, my men were watching but the sick bitch was fucking clever. With that black wig she looked like some biker bitch coming to chat about a bike or something. They looked her over carefully and there was nowhere she could have hidden a weapon so she was allowed to get back here. This is my fault and it won't fucking ever happen again. We'll be more careful from now on."

I nodded against his chest. "Did you watch the video Wrench made?"

He pulled away and frowned down at me. "No, what video?"

Wrench spoke from behind us and Dagger let me go but kept an arm around my shoulders. I walked between him and dad as they lead me back into the workshop.

"I recorded the entire conversation. I forwarded it to Ice but they've been called into church so I'm not expecting to hear from him until much later."

"Send it to me." Dagger said. "I'll be outside setting up a new perimeter. Jinx is bringing Kaiser over to stay with you and I've got one of the brothers coming in to help him install a security gate in the passage and some more cameras. We'll have a monitor set up in here. One of the brothers will be monitoring the situation from in here."

He turned to me and smiled. "I promise you, little sister, I'm going to make sure you are safe. I know how much you love what you do and no bitch is going to take it from you. Fuck her and fuck the crazy train she rolled in on."

I slid my arms around his waist and hugged him hard. "Thank you, Dagger. I don't tell you enough but I love you, big brother."

"Love you too, River. And I want you to stay here until I can take you home. Lie down on the couch and have a rest while I organise shit around here."

Watching him walk determinedly out the small door set into the big roller shutter doors that were now closed I knew he would make it as safe as possible for me to be at work.

The problem was me. Right now I was terrified of my own damned shadow.

Dad's arm came around me and he kissed my temple. I looked up at him when he drew in a deep breath. What now?

"Lake is on his way home."

Oh shit. That definitely wasn't good news.

My big brother hated motorcycle clubs. Really, really hated them. I don't know why and he hasn't ever given me an answer no matter how many times I've asked. He never approved of Sparrow and I knew for a fact he wouldn't like Ice. Strangely they were too much alike.

"It's the middle of the season. He has two races coming up. He can't miss either of them, he needs the points."

Dad shrugged. "You know your brother. He listens to nobody and always does exactly what he wants. He says he has enough time between now and the first race."

I dropped my head against dad's shoulder and groaned. "They are going to hate each other. Lake hates bikers and if he starts his shit with Ice I'll have to choose sides and I really don't want to."

"Don't worry about it, sweetheart. Your mother will handle him." Dad soothed.

So now not only do I have to worry about a psycho wanting to roll around in my blood while fucking my man. I had to worry about my brother losing his shit because once again I'm with a biker and this time I'm pregnant with not one but two biker babies.

I freaking hate my life.

No, not really. I just hated the shit impacting my life.

And to be totally honest it was my association with the Iron Dogz MC that had dumped me in the middle of the craziness that has become my life.

If I had never fixed DC's bike I would never have gone to the family braai.

I would never have been introduced to Ice.

I would never have spent the night with him.

And I would not be carrying his babies inside me.

And I would still have been lost and lonely, missing Sparrow and raising our son on my own. Now I had a man willing to love my son like he was his own. A man who was careful and protective of me.

And who was going to lose his mind the minute he saw that damned video.

Shit.

I grabbed my phone and sent a quick text.

I'm okay, baby. There were some threats but she never touched me. Dagger and Jinx are here with Dad and Wrench. I'm safe.

I stood with my phone in my hand for a few tense seconds but when he didn't answer I blew out a relieved breath and sank down on the couch. Maybe Dagger was right, I needed to lie down and have a little rest. Stretching out on the couch I sighed and closed my eyes.

I woke as I was lifted and held against a strong wide chest and his scent filled my head. My man had come for me. Opening my eyes I looked up at him and smiled.

He wasn't smiling. His eyes were completely yellow and filled with rage. His voice was the same as he walked out of the workshop with me held in his arms.

"Taking you home, Blue. Wrench and Seb are going to finish up the bike so it's ready when your client comes to collect it later. Dagger and Jinx have the security situation in hand. Kaiser will be coming home with us. He's on loan to us until we can get our own dog which will be happening very fucking soon. I've got Jagger on it already."

Dagger opened the passenger door of my bakkie and Ice put me inside and fastened the seatbelt around me then carefully closed the door. Kaiser was already on the back seat and wagged his tail when I reached over and scratched behind his ears. I watched as Ice stalked around the front of the vehicle while talking to Dagger, they nodded, slapped each other's backs and then Dagger went back inside and my man got in and drove us home.

Ice never said a word through the entire drive. His phone pinged constantly with calls he didn't answer, he declined them one after the other. The calls didn't stop, they continued the entire ride home. Eventually he shut his phone down.

When we got home he carried me inside and set me on my feet next to my bed. He wordlessly and carefully undressed me leaving me in my panties then pulled one of his black tees over my head and tucked me into bed. Only then did he speak.

"I'm going to get you something to drink, baby. I want you to try and sleep. We will have a talk once you've rested." He kissed me on my forehead before he left the room.

One instant I was lying there wide awake and the next I was asleep.

I dreamt a smiling Sparrow stood at the foot of our bed. He held two tiny little bundles wrapped in blue blankets against his chest and Duncan was leaning against his hip.

"Don't worry, Rivzie. Our boykie and the babies are safe. I won't let anything happen to our family."

I woke with a gasp and immediately looked at the bottom of the bed. Nothing. Then looked over at the bedside table where his photo stood in its silver frame. His smile was the same as the one in my dream.

But it wasn't real.

It was a dream. Just a dream.

CHAPTER TWENTY FIVE

Ice

They had been back in the meeting for maybe twenty minutes when there was a knock on the door and Ice's blood froze.

But it wasn't for him. Sam came in with a call for Hawk.

His president must have made the same arrangements he had. Any urgent calls was to be brought to them immediately.

Hawk looked at the caller ID before he answered.

"Wimpie, what do you have for me?"

His prez listened intently, nodding as he stroked over his beard.

"Okay, brother, I want you to repeat what you just told me to the brothers. I'm putting you on speaker."

Wimpie's disembodied voice sounded tinny as he spoke. And very strange for Wimpie, he spoke in his normal voice, none of the Game of Thrones shit.

"Someone I trust approached me this morning with invaluable information. He only gave me the information after I gave him my word he would remain anonymous. He assured me the information is legit. He said Jane Warne is back in the city. She came back to organise and lead several hits against club soft targets. All three clubs have been under surveillance and according to the informant they know exactly where each club will send those who are the most vulnerable. Your women and children. You have to warn the other clubs and protect your people, Hawk. I don't know if they plan to hit the compounds or the homes but I know this is real. My guy would not lie to me. Keep your people safe, brother. If I hear more I'll call immediately."

"You have our gratitude, Wimpie. Thank you, brother."

Hawk slowly set the phone down in front of him then swept his eyes over the men in the room.

He drew in a deep breath. "Now we know what's coming next. Sin, prepare several escape routes in case it becomes necessary to get the women and children into the Sanctuary. Jagger and Ziggy, I want security to be jacked up to the max. I want the perimeter patrols stepped up. Ziggy, dig deep brother and see what you can come up with. Beast, choose the brothers you want on your team and start securing our most vulnerable positions. Rider, I want you and your family back here today. You are sitting ducks in the hospital. Take a cage and go fetch them. Wolf, you're with him."

As he turned to speak to Ice the door slammed open and Sam came storming in with wide shocked eyes.

"Ice, brother, you have a video from Wrench. I opened it to see if it was urgent but didn't watch all of it. Fuck, brother."

Ice grabbed the phone but before he restarted the video he saw the text from his woman and his blood ran fucking cold.

I'm okay, baby. There were some threats but she never touched me. Dagger and Jinx are here with Dad and Wrench. I'm safe.

Jesus. Fuck.

Before he could watch the video Hawk took his phone from him and handed it to Ziggy. Within seconds the video was playing on the plasma screen against the wall. Around him he heard the shocked and angry reactions of his brothers. But he was cold, so very, very cold.

He couldn't look at the shit on the screen a minute longer but as he shoved out of his chair his dad and Spider were there on either side of him. It was his dad's voice that pulled him out of the killing madness.

"Easy, son, easy now. According to the message Wrench added at the end there Dagger and his men have the situation under control. Your old lady is safe." His dad's voice soothed but nothing could soothe the knowledge that his woman was in danger because of him. He had brought the bitch into Blue's life. And that meant he had to take her out of his woman's life. It was his responsibility.

"She's dead. If I lay eyes on her ever again, I don't give a fuck if it's in public, I will kill her. She won't lay a hand on Blue or my babies. I swear it."

Ice wasn't a very religious man but right now he was silently praying to whichever deity was in charge to keep his family safe. Not only River and their children, but his mother, sisters and nieces as well. Thank fuck Gail and the kids have already been moved into his parents' house.

Hawk's hand on his shoulder calmed him, but not much. "Brother, we aren't going to allow that psycho to get anywhere near your woman. We've got your back. Okay?"

Ice could only nod because if he opened his mouth he had no idea what would come out. Hawk's hand tightened as he continued.

"This video is exactly what we needed. She made threats against your woman and children and threatened to cut Wrench's throat. We have options on how we use it to our best interests. We can open a case against her with the local pigs, which won't mean much, or we can share it with the taskforce. My suggestion is we share it with the taskforce. They are already involved and we won't have to try and explain what the hell has been happening."

Before he could continue there was once again a loud knocking at the door and Ice and their eyes swivelled to the door as Wolf unlocked it.

Sam came through and it was clear he was pissed. "Prez, there are some commando types out here who are insisting they need to talk to you. They won't take no for an answer."

"Fuck. What else is going to happen today?" Hawk muttered as he left Ice's side and stalked to the door. He stood in the open door and started speaking to someone we couldn't see and we couldn't hear what he was saying either. Their voices were pitched really low.

"Dad." Ice said softly to his father who had dragged a chair close to the back of his own when he sat down again. "I need to get out of here. I can't leave River to handle this alone. I'm going to give you my seat and go to my woman. Okay?"

Bulldog clapped a hand down on his shoulder and nodded. "I've got your back, son. You go and take care of your family. I'll keep you up to date on what's decided. I need only one promise from you. Promise me you won't ride alone."

That one was easy. "I promise, Dad."

Hawk turned around and pointed at Rider. "You and Wolf ride now. Do not waste any time packing shit. Get in and get out as fast as you can. The club doc will be standing by in case your old lady needs him."

Then he turned to Ice.

"Ice, brother, I know you are burning to get out of here. Go. Boots, Spook, go with our brother and watch his back. For tonight you will be safe at River's house. We'll re-evaluate tomorrow. I'll call later to give you an update on decisions taken."

Ice didn't wait for more as he hugged his dad and brother and got out of there with Boots and Spook following him closely. On his way out his eyes caught the smirking fucking face of Flash. It seemed as if the bastard was enjoying the goings on.

He took the time to text Hawk and suggested that the fucker be locked down, right now.

They flew down the highway to the semi-industrial area where the Anderson's business was. He hated having to slow for the robots but didn't dare sneak through any of them. He didn't want the law on his ass today. He was carrying more than one weapon.

He breathed easier when they pulled into the yard in front of the workshops and saw the very visible presence of the Sinner's Sons. They were controlling access not only to the property but to the buildings themselves as well. Jinx and his guys were up on extension ladders setting up lights and cameras on the flat roof of the building while others were adding a second layer of razor wire to the top of the electrified perimeter fence. They were making the building as safe as they possibly could.

Dagger was waiting at the small door set into the roller shutter doors which were usually open but were now closed.

"She's okay, brother. The bitch never touched her but she did scare the fucking crap out of her. I convinced her to lie down on the couch and she fell asleep. I've got things in hand here. Why don't you take her home so mum can fuss over her before fucking Lake arrives and the third fucking world war breaks out."

Dagger shook his head when Ice frowned. "Know the man is her brother but he's a fucking prick. Hates the club, hates bikers. He refused to acknowledge Sparrow in all the time they were together. Hasn't been home for one of Duncan's birthdays. He sends fucking big presents for the kid so I suppose it's okay. Apparently he was involved with some biker bitch before he became a famous F1 driver. Don't know exactly what happened but I can guess. Sparrow didn't like him and avoided him as much as possible. River doesn't know much about it either."

Ice sighed. "I've got enough fucking problems without some fucking pussy getting in my face about my relationship with his sister. He had better stay the fuck out of my way. Not in the mood for anyone giving me shit right now."

Dagger grinned. "Got you, brother. I'm going to finish up here but I will make a turn at the house later. Oh, one other thing. You keep your eye on that prospect of yours, he's going to turn in to a real asset for your club. If I could I would steal him from you." He laughed as walked away.

"Fucker's not going to steal our fucking prospect." Boots growled as he stomped inside behind Ice.

He immediately saw her. His Blue. Curled up under a dark grey blanket on one of the wide couches in her small reception area. He immediately started to walk towards her.

"Boss." Wrench straightened from where he had been working on a bike. His gun on the seat within easy reach.

Ice changed his course, dragged him into a tight hug and clapped a hand on his back. "Thanks, brother, for having her back and keeping her safe."

"No worries, Boss. Not going to let anything happen to her on my watch. She's my family and I'll fucking die for her."

"Don't want you dying, little brother. You keep yourself alive and keep your eyes on our girl. Okay?"

Wrench nodded slowly. "You got it, Boss. She crashed after that shit went down. Vomited quite a bit so she might be hungry when she wakes up."

"I'll take care of it, brother. Come by the house later before you head over to the clubhouse, okay?"

"I'll be there, Boss."

Ice gave a slight chin lift as he walked over to where his old lady lay sleeping. She looked so fucking peaceful but she was far too pale.

Carefully picking her up he was walking out when she woke and he reassured her. Told her he was taking her home.

After another quick word with Dagger filling him in on the latest developments he drove his old lady home.

He dressed her in one of his tees because he wanted her surrounded by his scent, by him. Settling her in bed he leant over and kissed her forehead then glanced at Sparrow smiling from the photo next to the bed.

Look after them, brother. They are my world. He instructed silently.

Why he did it? No idea. It just felt like the right thing to do.

Leaving his old lady to sleep he made his way to the kitchen. His brothers were sitting at the small kitchen table with a beer each and their eyes were on him as he walked in, grabbed a beer from the fridge and sat down. Opening the beer he dropped the lid on the table and took a deep drink then set the cold bottle on the table in front of him.

"Your old lady has a very nice setup here, Ice. I can see why she wouldn't want to move to the clubhouse. Her kid has a fucking fantastic play area out there, she lives close to her folks and she doesn't have far to travel to get to work and those big garages out there are a mechanic's dream. You're going to have a problem, *boet*." (Brother) Spook took a sip of his beer.

Ice nodded. "I know. If things were different I would have done the same thing Sparrow did. Move in and build a life right here. But our women and children have become targets in this fucked up war with the old bitch. They are no longer safe when they're off club property."

Boots suddenly got up and started looking through drawers in the kitchen and then the lounge. He came back holding an exam pad, a pen and some colouring pencils. He must have raided Duncan's stash.

He sat down and immediately started writing.

"What the hell are you doing, Boots?" Ice asked, totally confused by how his brother was acting.

Pushing the exam pad to the middle of the table he pointed with the pen. "This is roughly what our property looks like." He pointed to a small rectangle at the top. "This is the offices and shit next to the main road." He tapped the much larger rectangle behind it. "This is the compound and the smaller circles over here are the houses already on the property. This one here is where Rider and Beast are staying, that one is Bulldog's and the large one is Hawk's place."

He drew a line from the top of the property that ended at the circle that represented Hawk's house.

"This is the access road onto the property." Then he drew a line around the perimeter. "This is the road we use to patrol the fence. And this here is our back door." He smiled at Ice's sudden frown. "Not everyone knows about it but I'm not stupid, brother. I keep my eyes open at all times, my life and those of my brothers depend on it. So, as I was trying to explain. We have a huge fucking piece of ground to patrol and our defences aren't strong enough to hold out a concerted effort to gain entry. Plus we're low on manpower as we try to protect our women and children as they go about their lives. We need to build a true compound, brothers. We have to put up walls around the houses. Relocate those businesses we can here, we have more than enough space. We're lucky, we're surrounded by friendly neighbours, but what if they are forced to sell to an enemy of ours?"

Ice and Spook looked at each other when they realised that their brother was pissed about something. They didn't have to wait long to find out why he was so pissed off.

"The property on the left of ours will be going on the market soon, old man Bekker's kids don't want the property and he's too old to take care of it by himself. His kids want him to sell and divide the money between them now instead of waiting until he dies. Their plan is to stick him in an old age home, fucking bastards. I've been renting a cottage on his property since I started prospecting with the club and he's a good friend. He promised to sell only to me or the club.

And I want to take care of the old man until he passes, in his own fucking house, surrounded by his own stuff. Not some clinical fucking space that makes it easier for his kids to ignore him and never visit."

Spook drew the exam pad to him and frowned down at it. "Are you serious, brother? Getting our hands on the Bekker property would be fucking fantastic but it will add at least another 15 acres to the area we will have to protect. We're sitting on 20 acres of wild veldt with minimal builds on it. It's in our bylaws, keeping the land as pristine as possible. I think we need to re-think moving the businesses here. Ice's old lady works on cars and bikes and that means oil and grease and chemicals, not something we want to have seeping into the water table. We need to keep the spring clear of that shit. What I do agree with is moving everyone onto the property. We can build totally green with very little impact on the environment. We've got *duikertjies* (small African antelope) and *steenbokkies* (small South African antelope) living in the *rantjies* (hills) already. I heard a jackal calling the other night, so we might have a pair living on the property. We build small, no big fucking spreads and we build clever. We build green and convert the other houses as we go along."

Ice sat back and looked between the two and then grinned. "I've just been played, haven't I? You two have been waiting to get one of us to sit still long enough to lay your plans out."

They both grinned. "With all the crap going down lately, Ice, we've been having heavy discussions during church. It wasn't the right time to bring this up." Spook smiled. "Jagger is on board and so are a few of the other brothers. We've only discussed this with a very small group of officers and lieutenants. Not with any of the other brothers. So it's totally on the DL."

Ice drew the pad towards him and drew in a circle and both men frowned at him. "This is my land, Bounty gave it to me when I earned my patch. Kid has a piece as well. He wanted the three of us living close together and back then we didn't get it. Now I do. He knew this shit was coming." Ice sighed. "And we were too full of our own self-importance to pay attention to what he was trying to prepare us for. But we sure are paying fucking attention now."

Tapping the rough sketch Ice made a decision. "I want this drawn out properly. I want everything on it. A proper topographical map would be great. We need to pinpoint every single weak point and all our strong points. I want the neighbouring properties included. We'll buy the Bekker property through one of our shell companies the same way we did the property on our north eastern border. And I know just how we're going to play this." Ice gave a sly smile.

"We're starting a private game reserve, at first we'll only have small animals indigenous to this area, but it might change. We'll see how it goes before we expand some more. I'll get onto the licences we need and get the ball rolling. Boots, speak to old man Bekker and tell him it's a go on the buy and he can stay on the property for his lifetime. Tell him it's going to be part of the Iron Dogz Game Lodge."

Spook and Boots grinned but they both shook their heads.

"Brother you need to take this to the table first. You can't just do this without the go ahead of the full table." Boots said.

Ice laughed. "You let me worry about that, Boots. You just make sure old man Bekker is on board. We need to move on this before the fucking Maingardes buy the property. If that happens we're fucked."

As he spoke he pulled his phone out and called Jagger. He answered almost immediately which meant the meeting had come to an end.

"Ice, brother, what can I do for you?"

"I've been talking to Boots and Spook about the property, brother. I'm in. I need you to pull in Spider and Ziggy and get on buying up all the property around us. Boots will talk to old man Bekker and set that buy in motion. I want all the properties around us, we're going to need it. We're starting a private game reserve, brother. It means no one will think twice about the security we set up. We're protecting the game."

There was a short silence and then Jagger laughed and Ice could hear voices in the background wanting to know what was going on.

"I'm in the office with Hawk and the other officers right now, brother. I'll explain and we'll get back to you."

"Make that quick, Jagger. If the Maingardes find out there are properties available on our borders they are going to move to buy them and then we are fucked."

"Fuck. I didn't think about that. Just thought the fuckers were in Cape Town and not up here. You're right. Let me get on this. Talk to you later."

Ice dropped his phone back on the table and pulled the exam pad towards him again. This could work, this could really work, he thought.

He smelt her before her arms came around him and hugged him from behind. Lifting his hands he clasped them over her crossed arms and hugged her to him.

"What are you guys doing?"

"You've only slept for about an hour, Blue. How are you feeling?" Ice twisted his head so he could look at her as she leant over his back.

"I'm fine. If I sleep any longer I'm never going to sleep tonight. Is Duncan still with my mum?"

"Yes he is. They're baking cupcakes." He would have loved to tell her he could wear her out so she could sleep, but now wasn't the time for teasing.

He felt her nod as she leant her head against his. "So, I'll ask again. What are you guys doing?"

Ice patted her hands. "We're planning the future, baby. We're thinking of starting a private game reserve."

"I didn't realise you had such a big property. I like this idea. I like it very much." Her chin was resting on his shoulder as she looked at the rough drawing. "Duncan would love living on a game reserve.

Imagine the hikes we could take him on and with all the security we would need he could even wander around on his own when he's older. Our kids would be safe. I like this idea."

Ice pulled her around and into his lap. "This is still in the planning stages, Blue. We still need Hawk and the other officers to sign off on our plan."

She frowned. "And if they don't?"

Spook answered her question. "If they say no then we form a consortium and we buy up the land anyway."

His woman nodded. "Cool, I'm in. I've got some money put away I can invest."

"Let's not get ahead of ourselves here, baby. I don't think Hawk will turn us down without researching the idea himself. It means this is going to take time." Ice warned.

"Okay, but he better not drag his feet or I'll put DC on his ass." His woman said with a grin.

Ice looked at his brothers and they both shrugged.

Not having old ladies in the inner circle of the club meant none of them knew how to react. Old ladies having a say in what happens to the club was new to all of them.

It wasn't a bad thing at all. What it meant was that a softer element had been brought into the inner circle. It made them all softer but at the same time it made them more aware and more protective of the women around them.

His Blue was a blessing he hadn't expected. He was thankful for her every single day.

And he would protect her and their children with his life.

CHAPTER TWENTY SIX

Hawk

Hawk lay on his back, his little bird draped across his chest fast asleep. He couldn't sleep, there were too many things running through his head. Too many decisions he had to make that could cost one of his brothers their lives. It fucking sucked.

And even worse, today he'd had to order a brother to be locked up because his loyalty was in question. How the fuck had that happened? No, actually, he knew how it had happened.

For some reason Flash hated his son and used every single opportunity to belittle and abuse him. Even when Kid started prospecting with the club Flash and his fucking cronies targeted him. Hawk, Ice and the other prospects forced Bounty to take action. Why had his dad allowed the abuse of a prospect? Why did he allow Flash to do whatever the hell he wanted with very little consequences?

When Hawk became the president of the Iron Dogz he had gone through their bylaws and rewrote some of them. With the support of his officers they changed the bylaws, made sure no prospect would ever again be subjected to the shit that had happened to Kid.

He was worried about Kid. His friend was having a hard time dealing with the Jane and Flash situation. He would have a talk with him, and assure him he had the full support of his brothers.

Right now though he was way more worried about River and Ice. Yes, they had tightened security around her but they all knew you could never be secure enough. And if things went wrong and Ice lost his Blue and their babies Hawk knew his cousin would go on a blind killing spree. Starting with Emma and ending with whoever got in his way.

His cousin's road name had nothing to do with who he was. It was a tease. As a prospect he slipped and fell while carrying too many bags of ice and nearly unmanned himself when all those bags crashed down on his dick. Hence his road name, Ice. But if anything happened to his Blue that name would become very appropriate.

The latest news Ziggy had brought him hadn't been good. After delivering her fucking threat Emma had disappeared. She hadn't gone back to her mac-mansion and hadn't gone to work either. Rick and his team had been unable to locate her as well. That wasn't good at all. It meant they had no idea of her next move and Hawk had a crawling feeling in his gut it wasn't going to be good at all.

His gut told him Emma's next move was going to be violent and River was going to be her target.

And they still haven't located Jane.

Sighing he closed his eyes and tried to force himself to sleep. Or if not actual sleep maybe he could just rest.

RENÉ VAN DALEN

River

I woke up wrapped around my man and just lay there, with my head on his shoulder, breathing him in and tracing his gorgeous face with my eyes. I was glad I had woken up before the alarm was set to go off and had this time to just lie here peacefully and look at him. Asleep none of the strain that lately permanently sat around his eyes was there. His freaking long eyelashes were dark curves against his golden skin, and I kid you not, they were so long they touched his cheeks. His eyebrows were dark slashes against his golden skin, he had a long blade of a nose with a bump in it and I knew it meant it had been broken before. His lips were light pink and slightly open as he breathed soft and even. Those lips were surrounded by his dark, almost black beard. His hair was getting long and was bedhead messy and after having had my fingers in it I knew it was as soft as Duncan's. My man had great hair, really great hair.

I knew when he opened his eyes they would be sleepy and a mix of yellow and green, the most amazing colour I have ever seen. I was about to trace a finger over his high cheekbones when those lashes fluttered and his eyes slowly opened. He turned his head and looked at me and my insides melted at the warmth in those eyes.

"I could feel you staring, Blue." He rasped in his just-woken-up voice.

I smiled. "I was just admiring my gorgeous man."

His arm tightened as he drew me closer then turned so that we were facing each other. His free hand reached over and dragged my hips into his then clasped my thigh and lifted my leg on top of his. His hard cock was suddenly right there, against my mound and I couldn't stop the moan from escaping. He felt so damned good I pushed my hips into his, trying to get closer.

Ice's groan rumbled deep in his chest as he dropped his head to mine and softly rubbed his bearded cheek against mine.

"Fuck. I want you so badly, Blue. But I promised myself I would give you time to get to know me before we take that step again. And, baby, you need to be sure if it's what you want, because the next time I'm inside you I'm never leaving that pussy ever again." Ice whispered in my ear. A whisper that caused a delighted shiver to run like lightning through my body.

"I know what I want, Ice. If you don't make love to me right now I'm going to be forced to take matters into my own hands. I want you and I want you now. Morning breath and all." I hissed as I rubbed myself against him.

He groaned as he grabbed my hip and ground his cock into my oh so needy pussy.

"Make love to me, baby. Before Duncan wakes up and I have to go through another day without you inside me." I begged softly. "And just think about this. No condom, I'm already pregnant, so no worries."

"Jesus, Blue. Don't know if I can make love to you, I want you too much. It's going to be fast and hard, baby." He growled as he made quick work of the tee I had worn to bed and pushed me on to my back.

Ice came up over me and stared down at my boobs then dropped his head and kissed them, first the one then the other. "Your tits are bigger and your nipples darker, baby. So fucking beautiful I want to kiss, lick and bite them until they are covered in my marks." He dropped his head again and this time he rubbed his beard over them, starting tingles that made me gasp. They were so sensitive the slightest touch had me arching my back.

"Sensitive, my boobs are very sensitive now." I gasped.

Lifting his head he grinned. "Good to know. I'll be careful. Going to suck on those beautiful nipples until you are ready to go out of your mind." His hand slipped down, cupped my growing baby bump then carried on into my sleep shorts and slid over my mound. His hand widened my legs and then his hard strong hand covered my pussy and clasped me hard.

"This wet little pussy is mine. Going to fuck it hard this morning but tonight I'm going to kiss it and lick it until my old lady writhes in pleasure. Then I'm going to slide inside and make love to her slowly, very slowly until she comes all over my cock." He licked a path up my neck then softly closed his teeth over the hinge of my jaw before sliding his lips down to my mouth. His beard scraped over my sensitive skin and then his mouth found mine and all thought disappeared.

All my senses were centered on the mouth and tongue and beard of the man who owned me. As he kissed me he yanked my sleep shorts down and I helped by kicking them off and opening my legs wide. Allowing him access to the weeping core of me. I needed him inside me so very badly.

With a gasp I drew my head back. "Baby, I need you. Right now, inside me. Please."

The bastard just smiled and started to slide down my body. Kissing and licking his way around my boobs, sucking on my nipples until I felt like screaming my frustration. I felt his smile against my skin as he slid down further. Was he going to go down on me?

He stopped when he reached my bump. And then I was stunned by what he did next.

"Morning boys, it's Daddy. Love you so very much. But right now I need you to close your ears, turn away and brace, boys. Daddy is about to fuck mummy and it is going to be a rough ride." He kissed my bump as I started laughing but one look at his face as he rose over me stopped the laughter instantly.

With one hand he spread me open and his cock found me unerringly. He slowly slid inside, his eyes on mine as he slowly filled me, stretched me with his girth. It was the most amazing feeling. And then he stopped moving, his pelvis tight against me, my legs open so wide, so very wide it felt uncomfortable. I lifted my legs and clasped them around his back and he slid in even deeper which had me gasping.

"Baby, I warned the boys, now I'm telling you. This is going to be fast and hard." He allowed me one nod and then he drew out slowly and slammed back in.

My back arched forcing my hips up and tight against his. And then my man started powering into me and somewhere in there I lost the rhythm, but it didn't matter because he took care of me. Shoving an arm under my lower back and holding me up as he laid waste to me in the best way imaginable.

His eyes never left mine. He stared down at me, his teeth clenched, the tendons in his neck tensed as after months of separation we came together once again. And it was so damned good.

I climbed up, up, up and then I felt it like a tsunami storming through me. I started shaking and clasped my arms around his shoulders as the orgasm took me and shook my body. My muscles clenching around his hard cock as it kept slamming into me, lengthening the orgasm and keeping it going. My eyes had closed as the pleasure started to take me but when I heard his deep groan I dragged them open and watched my man come. It was one of the most amazing things I've ever seen.

He arched back, his hips kept powering and then he snapped them down one last time and dragged me tight against him. His head was back, his mouth open. His cock jerked deep inside as he came and left his seed inside me. I moaned and he looked down, his eyes so very green the yellow almost completely gone.

"Fucking love you, Blue." He ground out, dropped his head and took over my mouth.

The kiss felt like it lasted forever, but it didn't. He was still inside me and hard, his cock kept pulsing with every little spasm from my pussy. I loved it. He gave me tiny little kisses along my jaw as we slowly came down from our joint high.

"Fucking love you too, Ice, Ice, baby." I said with a grin.

We both started laughing and he hugged me tight and I hugged him right back. He rolled to his side and held onto my hips, ensuring that he stayed inside me.

"Love that we can love and laugh at the same time, Blue. You and our children are my life, baby. Never forget that you are my one. The one person in the world made just for me."

"You are my one too, Ice. I have been blessed to have found it twice in my life. I am damned lucky to have found you and that you are willing to raise Sparrow's son with me. Not many men would be able to cope with the daily reminder that his woman had had a child with someone else." I said softly.

Ice shook his head and kissed my nose. "I'm honoured to help raise my brothers' son, baby. I know if fate had had other plans for him I would not be here right now. There's no way I'm going to fuck up this second chance I've been given."

I smiled at him, but it was a sad smile. "A part of me will always love him, not only because he's the father of my son, but because he taught me that life was to be lived. And that love was a gift to be savoured every single day. He would be happy for me and for Duncan."

Ice shook his head. "No, baby, he would be fucking pissed that he wasn't the one lying here with you. What I do know is that if I were in his place I would want my woman to be happy, to find love again. I love you, Blue. You are my gift from him, a gift I will treasure for the rest of my life."

I grinned, reached up and placed a kiss on his beard covered jaw. "You're a good man. I love you, Ice, so very much."

He opened his mouth to answer when the alarm went off and as he turned to slap a hand down over it he slipped out of me and we both groaned. Through the baby monitor I could hear Duncan starting to wake up and I knew that our time alone was at an end. Our day was about to start.

"You take the bathroom first, Blue. I've got Duncan." Ice leant over, kissed me softly then slid out of bed and pulled his sleep pants back on. I watched as he settled the band of the soft pants on his hips, grinned and then walked out. I heard him in the bathroom down the passage and typical male he didn't close the door. Just like Sparrow and just like Duncan.

I tapped my belly. "I hope you two are girls. I need more female hormones around here."

LOST AND FOUND IN BLUE

That was when I realised that it was Wednesday. Today was the day we would find out the sex of the babies. I had an appointment for the scan at ten. It propelled me out of bed and into the shower. I slathered my body with lotion before I dressed for comfort and easy access to my bump. I wore a pair of black leggings and a big tee with my usual work boots on my feet and my damp hair pulled back in a high pony tail.

My men were sitting at the kitchen table wolfing down cereal and I had to smile. I was tempted to ruffle their hair they looked so cute. But first order of business was to find the bottle of instant decaf coffee I knew I had bought and shoved onto a shelf in the pantry somewhere. I sighed with relief when I found it then made a quick note on the shopping list on the fridge, adding decaf ground coffee. As I turned Ice winked at me and my smile became even wider.

Today was a really good day.

I waited as the kettle took its own sweet time to boil. Watching milk run down Duncan's chin as he chewed and grinned at Ice.

"Mr Icey and me, we's eating Batman food." He said through his milky smile.

"I see that, boykie."

"I'm not a mr, little man. You can call me Ice. Okay?"

Duncan nodded vigorously. "Okay."

"You want some breakfast, baby?" Ice asked and made to get up.

"No, you finish yours. I've got it." I pulled the muesli down and Duncan immediately pulled a face.

"Mumma likes the yucky stuff." He warned Ice with a screwed up nose.

"It's healthy, boykie and the prawns need healthy food to grow strong."

"Okay, but I don't need it. I'm already big and strong." Duncan said as he flexed both his arms showing off his little muscles. So freaking cute.

I looked over at Ice as I poured my breakfast into a bowl.

"Talking about the prawns. The appointment is today at ten. Will you be able to make it?"

Ice nodded immediately. "Definitely. I'll pick you up and drive you to the appointment."

Duncan's head flew between the two of us as he tried to determine what we were talking about. Such a nosy little boykie.

"Can I come?" He asked hopefully.

"Not this time, little man. I'm going to pick mumma up, take her to the doctor and when we're done I'm going to come back and pick you, Kaizer and Nana up. You're coming with me to the clubhouse today. Okay?" Ice explained.

"Yay!" Duncan bounced in his seat and milk and cereal flew.

I was so glad my boykie liked spending time with my man. It was the first step in the relationship the two would be building with each other.

We had made the plans for today while chatting with Boots and Spook yesterday. Duncan needed to get used to the brothers at Ice's club and this would be the ideal opportunity. My mum was going along just in case he became uncomfortable. Plus she was looking forward to meeting Ice's aunt Beryl and maybe even his mother, Suzy.

That made me super nervous. My mother at Ice's club. It could turn out to be a disaster. But it was no use worrying about what could happen. I would be focusing on the good.

Today Ice did the same as he had done yesterday. He came with me as we dropped Duncan off with mum and then he followed me to work. He didn't stay long but left after a long kiss and a quick grope of my ass. Apparently he loved the leggings, said it made my ass look very fucking stunning. His words, not mine.

I was nervous and excited as I stripped down a bike while counting down the hours.

And then Ice was there and we were driving to the appointment where he would see our babies for the first time. And we would find out their sex if they were in the ideal position. Babies sometimes kept you guessing for weeks on end. Duncan had been one of those.

I was nervous and excited but Ice was even worse. This would be his first time hearing the babies' heart beats and seeing them move. Oh, he saw the pics on the fridge but it just wasn't the same.

He stood right next to me, holding my hand as the technician swept the wand over my belly. His eyes were fixed on the monitor and then the room was filled with a whooshing sound and their heart beats. So fast and so very precious. I looked up at Ice and had to blink back tears. My hard as nails Iceman was overcome. His eyes glistened and his hand tightened around mine.

"Fuck." He said softly, reverently even.

I squeezed his hand and he glanced down at me then dipped down and kissed me. So softly.

"This is everything, Blue. Absolutely everything." He whispered.

The technician gave us a little bit of time, turning her back to give us a semblance of privacy. When Ice straightened she continued.

"Okay, so let's have a look. Oh, they are in a good position today. We have a clear view here mum and dad. I'm just going to take some measurements for Dr Strauss before we get to the big reveal. The measurements look good, they are developing as they should." She said with a smile in her voice as she clicked and clicked and then it was time. "Are you ready?"

"Yes" We said at exactly the same time.

She smiled. "Your babies are identical twins, not fraternal. And if you look over here you'll see they are both flashing you, typical males."

Ice's grip tightened around my hand painfully before it eased. "We're having boys, baby. You're giving me two more beautiful boys." He leant over and kissed me softly. "Thank you, Blue."

Lordy this man of mine.

We walked out with huge smiles on our faces, the tears totally forgotten. I had the babies' photos safely in my backpack. Ice had taken one of the scan photos and put it in his wallet. He wanted to keep his boys close, he said as he carefully folded the picture to fit. On the drive back to my shop we kept looking at each other and smiling. Even though I was going to be surrounded by penises I was happy. Our babies were healthy, I was healthy.

Life was good.

Ice parked outside my workshop and we sat kissing like teenagers in the parking lot.

He couldn't stay too long because he had to pick mum and Duncan up on his way to the clubhouse. I knew they were busy tracking that skank ex of his but didn't want to spoil our excellent day by mentioning her.

"I'll see you after work, baby." I said as I kissed him one last time.

"The Sinners have brothers on you today. I'll be going into church as soon as I get back but a prospect will have my phone. You call me if you feel anything is even a little bit off or if you're not feeling well. Don't fucking hesitate, baby, call me." He waited for my soft okay before he continued. "Drive safe when you come to the clubhouse, Blue. Maybe you should tell Wrench to leave his bike here and drive with you. He can drive your bakkie back tomorrow."

I laughed and blew him a kiss. "I'll see what he says and let you know. He might have a hot date or something after work."

Ice just shook his head. "Prospects don't have hot dates, baby. I'll call you later, Blue." Then he smiled and drove away.

Two of the Sinner's Sons were staked out at the entrance to the showroom, watching me as I stepped through the small door in the big roller shutter doors and into the workshop. Ice's orders, no more wide open doors, it was too dangerous.

I hated it. The damned bitch was seriously getting on my last nerve.

I hoped they found her soon so this shit could be done.

CHAPTER TWENTY SEVEN

River

Wrench has been begging the entire afternoon. He just wouldn't give up. He wanted to know the sex of the babies. Apparently he had a lot riding on the outcome of the bet. But I had promised Ice I would tell no one, so he was totally out of luck.

By the time four thirty rolled around I had had enough of work. Come hell or high water we were going to close on time tonight and by five Wrench and I had the workshop cleaned up and tools packed away. Earlier Wrench and Jannie had cleaned out the small spray booth after spraying some parts for a job Jannie was working on, so there was no need to stay late. Dad had left at about three to fetch mum from the compound because Lake was arriving later tonight and she wanted to cook him his favourite dinner.

I was not looking forward to his arrival. I knew he was going to be horrid to Ice. He had always treated Dylan like he was lower class and beneath him. My brother was a dick. A very snobby dick. And despite his shitty attitude I still loved him.

Just not enough to expose my man to him on the day he had seen our babies for the first time.

Nope. Not going to do that. Lake can just suck it up and wait.

Wrench and I did a final check of the interior doors and as I set the alarm I heard Jannie and Seb's cars starting up and driving away. Both had muscle cars, so the deep throbbing growl was hard to miss.

We were joking about the sex of the babies as Wrench dragged the door closed behind us and he was about to lock it when we heard the sound of racing engines.

"Fuck." Wrench swore as he shoved against the door but the damn thing chose now of all times to get stuck.

A blacked out SUV with a big bulbar across the front was racing towards the closed gates and rammed into them. The gates buckled but didn't give and the driver reversed and rammed them again. A battered black BMW was idling to the side, waiting for the heavy vehicle to batter down the gates.

It all happened as if in slow motion but in actuality it was fast, so damned fast.

Wrench rammed his shoulder into the door with an angry grunt and finally the stupid thing swung open.

"Your keys, River. I need your keys. Quick!"

Wordlessly I held my hand out and he grabbed the keys from me.

"Push the panic button, get into the bathroom. Have your gun out and be ready. They're going to come for us. We're going to have to hold them off until the cavalry arrives. Okay?"

"Yes. Panic button, bathroom, gun, cavalry. I got it."

Guns were firing and bullets were smacking into the heavy metal doors and breaking the windows. I was so damned grateful I never had the huge big glass doors installed that I had wanted at first.

Wrench ran back outside as I ran for the alarm. I wasn't about to search for the damned remote that lay somewhere in the bottom of my backpack. As soon as I pushed the panic button alarms started screaming. Almost immediately the phone rang. Our security company calling to confirm it was an emergency. As it continued to ring I ran into the bathroom, threw my backpack on the vanity and drew out my phone, my gun and the clips Ice had insisted I take with me.

I checked my gun then I called for help.

"Blue, what's happening? What the fuck is that noise?" My man growled.

"Ice, we're under attack! A black SUV crashed through the gates and a black Beemer followed it inside. I'm hiding in the bathroom but Wrench ran back outside. I can hear a lot of guns. I don't know how many of them there are. We need help. Please come quick."

"Fuck! They're attacking my old lady! We're riding out now!" He shouted. "I'm coming, baby. Stay where you are and keep your head down. Wrench and the brothers will keep you safe until I get there."

I heard shouting and boots running and then the roar of bikes and through it Ice stayed on the line with me. I knew he had his phone plugged into his helmet as he raced to get to me.

I was so damned scared. Wrench and the brothers were out there, fighting whoever this was.

Suddenly I heard the thunder of boots running on the workshop roof. The roof was IBR, not solid cement which would have kept them out.

But maybe it was the brothers up there, shooting at the attackers. I really hoped it was.

"Someone's on the roof, Ice. What do I do? Wrench hasn't come back inside."

"Stay where you are, baby. Please, just stay where you are."

"I don't like it, Ice. If they get past the brothers I'll be a sitting duck."

The thunder of bike engines took up a beat of time before he answered.

"It's the Sinners on the roof, baby. Jinx is up there, keeping you safe. If you can safely get somewhere higher up to hide, do it now. Keep your backpack with you. Don't leave any clues for them to follow. I'm coming, Blue. We'll be there in ten minutes. You hold on for ten minutes and I'll fucking kill every single bastard trying to hurt you."

I sucked in a breath and was about to answer when I heard the scuff of a boot on the cement floor.

"Someone is in here with me." I whispered as I pulled my backpack on and tip toed to the door.

My hand clutched my gun tightly as I ducked down and slowly peeked around the corner. Wrench was crouched behind the short wall that separated the last bay from the rest. He had an AK47 in his hands and he was bleeding.

Oh sweet baby Jesus. He was bleeding. A lot.

"Wrench!" I whisper screamed. "Get in here."

His head turned and he held a finger to his lips then went back to watching the door.

"Wrench is back, but he's been shot and he's bleeding, a lot." I reported to Ice in a whisper.

"Almost there, Blue. A few minutes more, baby, just a few minutes." He shouted over the sound of the bikes, the hum of the road, cars hooting and the whistling wind.

Dear God, by the sound of it they were breaking every single law of the road. There was going to be so much shit to clean up if we survived the attack.

Suddenly the small door slammed open with a clang and two men dived inside. Wrench started shooting and I saw one of them jerk back and lie still. The other rolled behind a tool chest and fired at Wrench. Bullets were flying but Wrench didn't shoot back, he was starting to slowly sink down from a crouch to his knees and then he very slowly toppled over.

Oh God. Ohgodohgodogodohgod.

"Wrench is down. Oh sweet baby Jesus, Wrench is down."

I didn't hear what Ice said because in the next breath I was on the move. I ran out of the bathroom then slid along the painted cement floor to Wrench. I crashed into the wall then dragged Wrench to safety. I took his place, slipped the safety off my weapon and waited.

Dylan and Dagger's training kicked in as I slipped my backpack off, dug out my make-up mirror and carefully sneaked it around the wall to take a look. The bastard at the door was getting ready to move. I watched and waited for him to commit. As soon as he did I dropped the mirror, popped up and shot him twice in the chest then ducked back down again.

He was most probably wearing a vest but two bullets to the chest will take him down for a minute or two. I cautiously looked around the wall. He was down but starting to move. I didn't have long.

Turning I ripped my hoodie off and shoved it over the bleeding wounds to Wrench's abdomen, took his arm and folded over the hoodie. I was hoping the weight of his arm would keep it in place.

"Almost with you, Blue. I'm coming around the bottom corner right now. Hold on, baby. Fuck, just hold on for me."

"I'm here, Ice. I promise I'll hold on."

I heard the bastard out there scrabbling to get up and peaked around the corner.

"Lie still or so help me I'm going to put a bullet in your head." I barked at the bastard on the floor. He instantly stilled.

"Push your gun away from you, shove it as hard as you can, no sudden movements."

He did as I asked with a groan and it was then I saw the blood underneath him.

"Now just stay right where you are and don't fucking move." With a groan he pushed his hand over his side and lay back.

I was just about to move towards him when the two bitches the Iron Dogz had been searching for came strolling through the door as if they were at the mall.

I dropped down and groaned. I bent towards where I had wedged my phone against the wall.

"Your fucking ex and her best buddy just strolled into my workshop. If they so much as breathe on me I'm going to shoot them." I whispered to Ice.

He didn't answer. Shit.

"Hey, bitch, we know you're in here. I'm here to deliver the promise I made you. A pity Gray isn't here to watch, I'm sure he would have enjoyed it. But no matter. I'll do this one on my own. I'm going to slowly cut you open and pull those little bastards out of you."

The bitches laughed hysterically and then I heard it. The thunder of a lot of bikes shook the workshop. It didn't please the bitches and a huge sigh of relief burst out of me.

"I thought you said you arranged something to keep them occupied somewhere else. You fucked up, Jane. The bastards are here. Now I'll have to hurry and not take my time like I planned."

"Don't be fucking stupid, Emma. There's no time to play with the bitch now. We need to get out of here while we still can. We need to leave, now. If they capture us there's no way we'll ever see the light of day ever again. Leave her, she's not important. The organisation is all that's important." The one called Jane tried to reason with the crazy bitch.

"No! She has to die. Those little bastards have to die. Gray is mine. I'll never let him go. Never!"

"Jesus, Emma. It's too late. I'm going, and if you're not right behind me I'm leaving you here. Fuck your fucked up plans. I have plans for my life and it does not include dying today."

I was stunned. The bitches stood there and bitched at each other as if they weren't in the middle of an attack on me and my business. The quiet squeak of a boot on the painted floor came from behind me. I flipped around and he was right there behind me. A tall, slyly grinning man. As I lay on the floor I shot up at him at virtually the same time as he shot at me. My shots were low, hitting him below his vest and I think in his junk. He dropped like a stone. Curling into a moaning ball.

I hurt. So much. My chest hurt. My arm was numb and my gun lay useless next to me. Breathing in short pants I rolled and picked it up in my left hand and swallowed down a painful groan.

Thank you, Dylan, for teaching me how to survive.

Pushing with my legs I slowly slid backwards. I knew she was going to come for me and I would be ready. Pushing my back up against the wall I glanced down and groaned. I was bleeding but I had nothing to push against the damned hole just below my shoulder.

"Baby, I'm hit." I whispered. "Please hurry."

I waited and waited and then she came creeping around the wall. She was barefoot which was why I hadn't heard her. She grinned when she saw the blood on my chest. Stupidly she stood and slowly strolled towards me, her hand with her weapon hanging loose against her side.

Stupid, stupid, stupid. I smiled up at her. Holding my gun tight against my thigh, I waited for my opportunity. She was so close there was no way I was going to miss.

"Look at it. Lying at my feet, bleeding. I told you he was mine. You should have walked away while you could, bitch." She gloated.

"He was never going to be yours you stupid bitch. He will always belong to me. To me and our children." I tasted blood in my mouth, let it fill my mouth then spat it at her. My tongue ached where I had bitten it when the bastard shot me.

Blood and spit splattered over her white pants and she screamed with rage.

Who the hell wears white when they go out to kill someone? This bitch was truly off her damned rocker.

"Look what you did to my pants, you bitch! Do you have any idea how much they cost? They are Versace! Now they're ruined. I'm going to kill you for this."

"I dare you to try. I guarantee you're not going to succeed. Get out while you still can, Emma. The cops are coming and my man will be here any second. Run, run far, far away. But know that there's nowhere you can hide. They will find you and justice will be done."

She laughed, the bitch fucking laughed.

"You have no idea bitch. You thought Sparrow died because of a random drive-by, but he didn't. Jane and I killed him. It was so easy. He came walking out of the bar and it was like shooting fish in a barrel. Bam! Bam! Bam! And he was dead."

My heart stuttered in my chest. No! No! Please God no! Why?

She laughed at me. "Look at you, all weak and helpless, just like he was."

Unspeakable sorrow turned into red hot rage. "Sparrow was never weak and helpless you crazy bitch. If I have to come back from the dead I will avenge him. You are going to die, you useless piece of human waste." I hissed at her then pointed at the ceiling. "Everything you said and did is being recorded. Video and sound. So keep talking bitch. I love every single second of you incriminating yourself." I smiled up at her. "Don't you just love it when the bad guys fuck themselves up the ass?"

Her shocked eyes shot around the workshop before they came back to me. She slowly started to lift her arm, bringing her weapon up. "You are going to die, but first I'm going to shoot those little bastards inside you and then I'm going to watch as you bleed to death."

She was talking too much and the gun fight outside sounded like the third world war had broken out.

I heard the thud of boots hitting the floor and the bitch jerked upright, forgetting about raising her weapon. Her eyes were on whoever was coming towards us.

"You move one fucking inch and I am filling you up with lead, bitch." I heard Ice snarling at her and grinned. My man had arrived.

"Gray, I did this for you. For us. We can have the world at our feet. I have to kill her, she took what was mine. Those babies belong to me, not her." She said in a whining little voice. "I have to kill them so we can start over."

I watched that gun hand of hers. I didn't trust her at all.

"Never going to happen. River is the mother of my children, my old lady, and the love of my life. You are nothing to me. Nothing at all."

It was becoming harder and harder to hold on to my damned weapon. It was becoming too heavy.

Then I heard Hawk's cold voice and what he said and the way he said it made me shudder.

"You're not dying today, bitch. You have a come-to-Jesus talk scheduled with the Crow. You are going to give us the information we need before you die."

Two shots suddenly rang out. She fell with a high scream and lay writhing on the floor. Her gun lying forgotten next to her as she moaned and cried. Men came out of nowhere and had her cuffed and gagged in an instant. Her white pants were turning red and she was quickly patched up and carried away. Holy shit.

I felt very sure she wasn't going to enjoy what was going to happen to her next. No, not at all. And I didn't care. She killed my son's father and for that she had to suffer for a long damned time. My heart felt broken all over again, it felt as if I had lost him all over again. I didn't know how I was going to deal with it. So instead I looked around for my man.

I stayed aware long enough to smile at Ice as he thudded to his knees next to me.

"Is Wrench okay? He kept them away from me for as long as he could." I asked softly.

The entire right side of my chest ached horribly.

"The paramedics are here, baby. Don't talk, just stay still, okay?"

Slowly turning my head I watched as paramedics streamed towards us. My eyelids were becoming too heavy and my vision was starting to blink in and out. Shit.

"Love you, Ice, Ice, baby." I whispered.

Ice started shouting for help.

Then it all faded to black.

I woke up to beeping machines and light that was way too bright. Slowly turning my head I blinked at the people scattered around the room. Ice sat in a chair right next to my bed, holding my hand. Mum sat with her head on Dad's shoulder in chairs on my other side. Dagger, Jinx and Lake were sitting on the floor with their backs against the wall. All of them were fast asleep. It was strange to see Lake anywhere near a biker.

Judging by the light in the room it was late morning and I was so very thirsty. I tried to move but the ache in my chest became a stabbing pain and I moaned softly. I tightened my fingers around Ice's hand and he immediately jerked awake. His eyes were on my face. He looked terrible. I think the word for it is haggard. He looked haggard, troubled and sad. Why was he sad? Was Wrench okay?

"Baby." He whispered as he stood, leant over me and kissed my forehead. "How're you feeling?"

"Thirsty."

He reached for the button lying on the bed next to my hand and pushed it.

"Calling the sister to come check on you before I give you any. Okay?"

All I could do was give a faint nod.

"Wrench?"

My man hesitated and the sadness increased. "Not good, Blue. They had to take him back into surgery earlier. He started bleeding internally. Hawk, DC and some of the brothers are with his family in the surgical waiting room. Krissie and Mari left a few minutes ago to see if there's any news yet."

The door opened and the sister came in with a smile.

"It's good to see you awake. Let me have a quick look at you."

"She's thirsty. Can I give her some water?"

"Certainly. You came through the operation really well, Ms Anderson but don't overdo the water, just a few sips."

Ice reached for the clear plastic cup with a screw on top and a straw sticking out the top. He slipped the straw between my lips and I sucked the beautiful wet stuff into my mouth. But three sips were all I could manage.

Licking my lips I asked the question that had been hammering at my brain since the moment I woke up.

"My babies. Are they okay?"

The sister lay a hand on mine and smiled. "They are doing well. See this here?" She pointed at a graph on a machine next to the bed. "These are their heart beats. And they're perfect. We are monitoring them just as a precaution. The three of you came through the surgery with no problems." She patted my hand. "I'm going to go call Dr Strauss and Dr Henry to let them know you're awake." She said as she left.

My hand slid down over my bump and Ice's immediately covered mine.

"Our boys are fine, baby." His thumb stroked over my fingers. "You're a bit battered but with some physical therapy you will be as good as new."

"What happened to that murdering bitch?" I whispered.

"Club business, Blue. But you won't have to worry about her ever again. It's been taken care of."

Damn. That sounded ominous. I hope she suffered before they ended her.

"Did you get Jane? She was there with her."

Anger sparked in his eyes. "No, she got away. We have no idea how she managed it but she was gone when the fire fight was over. I think she used the general pandemonium as a cover to make her escape. We've got the brothers searching for her and we're close baby. Much closer than we've been before. And that's all I'm going to say about that shit."

He leant over and kissed me softly. "I'm more interested in how my woman is doing." He whispered against my lips.

The smile came without any effort. "I'm good, just worried about Wrench."

There was a groan from the region of the floor as Dagger pushed himself up off the floor and came towards the bed. Ice stepped to the side to allow him access to me, but not very far away. Dagger bent over me, kissed my cheek and ran a hand over the top of my head.

"Don't fucking scare me like that ever again, Rivzie. This shit has aged me about ten years."

He muttered as he moved around the bed to stand behind mum and dad who had woken up with all the whispering that had been going on. Mum immediately started crying as she stood and carefully hugged me. Dad blinked as he took his turn.

"We love you baby girl, so very much." Dad said softly.

Mum couldn't stop crying and Dagger threw an arm around her, pulling her into his side. Lake and Jinx had woken up as well and I got more hugs and cheek kisses.

And it didn't take Lake long to let his asshole side out. Not long at all.

"This would never have happened if you had stayed away from bikes and these damned bikers. This entire mess is their fault. I hope you've learned your lesson and you'll now distance yourself from the bastards." He snarled angrily.

Closing my eyes I sighed. "The only asshole here is you, Lake. None of what happened was their fault. It was that crazy murdering bitch's fault. She did it all. Not Ice or Dagger or their clubs."

But of course Lake wouldn't let it go. "Wrong. She was a part of their club and his ex. Therefore it was their fault. Years ago I warned you about the way these people operate. But of course you didn't listen and now we once again have to deal with biker bullshit. At least this time no one has died, not yet anyway."

I gasped at his insensitive comment.

"You say one more word to upset my woman and you and I are going to step outside and settle this shit." Ice threatened through clenched teeth.

"You can try, motherfucker." Lake swore viciously and I heard mum draw in a shocked breath.

"You will stop this right now, Lake. You're upsetting your sister. Not another damned word." Dad took his arm and drew him away from my bed.

"Dad, don't. You know bikers only bring death and heartache. Don't let her do this again. She's been hurt more than enough already." Lake pleaded softly.

"Son, we both know where this is coming from. Am I sad both of my children lost people they loved because of violence? Definitely. It nearly broke your mum and my hearts to see the two of you suffering. But what happened to you and what happened to River are two completely different situations. You need to deal with the past and stop blaming the biker community for what happened. You are letting the past rule your life. It's been years, Lake. It's time to see someone to help you deal with it. Because, son, you haven't dealt with it at all."

Lake didn't say a word. He just stared at the floor but I could see the muscles in his cheeks move as he clenched his teeth. His blue eyes were blazing when he looked up but they softened slightly when he looked at me.

"Sorry, River. I need to leave. I'll come back later." With that he was out the door.

"I'm so sorry, Ice." Mum whispered and then she dashed out after Lake.

Like she has always done. He was her boy and she would always try to fix things for him. I'm not sure she could fix things this time. It was very obvious my brother was still suffering from events in his past that had changed his life drastically.

"I'm going to take those two home. See you later, sweetheart." Dad kissed my forehead and then he was gone as well.

"What the fuck is his problem with bikers? He's been fucking strutting around here all night pissing everyone off. I ignored his shit but now he has pissed me off." Ice gritted out.

Dagger shook his head as Jinx fell into the chair mum had been sitting in. And for the first time I heard what had happened to make my brother hate bikers.

"It's ancient history. When he was seventeen he fell for the daughter of the VP of the Rebel Rogues MC. The VP and his wife were separated and she moved to Pretoria with their daughter. The Rebel Rogues are a small club. Just some brothers who formed a club for the love of riding and freedom. Unfortunately they came to the notice of a gang running drugs who wanted their turf. There were some threats exchanged and the Rebel Rogues told the gang to piss off. They took Millie, the VP's daughter, and when the club got her back she was barely alive. The fuckers gang raped her, stabbed her multiple times and dumped her outside the clubhouse gates. She died a day later. The bigger clubs joined the Rogues in dispensing justice after they heard what had happened. Not a single gang member survived to face the law." Dagger explained. "What happened to his girl is the reason why Lake hates bikers."

Ice drew in a deep breath. "I heard about that. If I'm not mistaken the club is in Welkom, isn't it?"

"Yeah. They never got over that shit. Turned to the dark side for a while to keep the rest of their women safe. Millie's brother is their president now and he's got the club back to the old ways. They run totally clean. No shit what so ever." Jinx slapped his hands down on his thighs after his explanation and pushed up out of the chair. "Rivzie, so glad you and the prawns are okay. I'm off to go shower and get some sleep. I'll be back later."

Dagger followed him out a few minutes later, leaving us alone at last.

Leaning over me Ice kissed me softly. "I love you, baby, so very fucking much. I thought I had lost you."

"Never going to leave you or our children, baby." I whispered.

He smiled and his teeth shone through his dark messy beard. He had obviously dragged his hands over it and through it during the long night. His hair was just as messy. He no longer looked as haggard as he had done when I first opened my eyes. Now he at least had some colour back in his cheeks.

Lying against the raised back of my bed I could see out the open door and had to smile. There were leather clad bikers sitting with their backs against the wall outside my door. I was amazed security hadn't removed them yet. Ice sat down next to me on the bed holding my hand. The warmth that came through the touch soothed me, kept me focused on him and our babies and not on the worry hovering at the back of my mind. Wrench.

Suddenly the bikers outside my room straightened almost as one man and their faces became like stone and I knew the shitty part of the day was about to happen.

The cops were on their way.

They did not disappoint.

Two plainclothes detectives walked unsmilingly into my room and stopped at the bottom of my bed.

"Ms Anderson. I'm detective Myburgh and this is detective Steyn. We are investigating the shooting at your place of business yesterday. We would like to ask you a few questions."

I was about to say okay, go ahead ask your questions when Ice snarled at them. Yes, it sounded like a genuine snarl.

"My woman and my boys were almost killed yesterday. She woke up not even an hour ago. Her best friend is in surgery, fighting for his life after saving hers. She's still in shock. You fuckers can come back tomorrow to ask your damned questions after she's had a proper rest."

Outside my door the rumble of pissed off male voices instantly stopped and a few seconds later was replaced by the sound of laughing and palms slapping together as those who had bet on them being boys congratulated each other. Ice and his temper had crashed Ziggy's betting book. Oops.

The two detectives stood silent as their eyes swung from one to the other of us as my biker family streamed into the room. Manly hugging and back slapping ensued.

While I lay there shaking my head not even getting one hug. What? Didn't I have any contribution in the making of my sons?

And then my man went even further. He whipped out his wallet and showed them the scan photo of the twins. And all the while the detectives stood there, hard eyes on the bikers in the room, and then the one called Steyn grinned. He looked at me and shook his head.

"I have twin boys as well. They are two years old and an absolute handful. Congratulations Ms Anderson, Mr Walker. We'll leave you to rest." He reached into his jacket pocket and pulled out a card and handed it to Ice. "Call me later and we'll set up a time to take Ms Anderson's statement. Once again, congratulations."

With that he turned to his frowning colleague. "Let's get out of here. Tomorrow is soon enough to get a statement."

They left without detective Myburgh ever saying another word. Strange man.

Ice got back on the bed next to me and I relaxed into his side listening to everyone talking when I fell asleep. I had terrible dreams every time I dropped off but Ice was there, holding me, every time I woke up shaking like a leaf. He made it all better.

I sort of woke up when Krissie and Mari came back in but was so woozy I'm not sure I made any sense to them. They left after promising to be back for visiting hours.

I was awake when DC and Hawk brought us the news that Wrench had made it through the second surgery but the next twenty four hours would be critical. He was in ICU and only his parents were allowed to see him. The doctors were keeping him sedated to aid with the healing process but at the end of the twenty four hours they would start lowering the dosage and bring him back slowly.

It sounded so scary and horrible but DC insisted it was good news. I hoped like hell it was because I didn't want to lose him. He was an important part of our lives.

Ice refused to leave and sat next to me as I slept most of the day and night. I only woke with the nightmares or when the nurses came into take my blood pressure and pump more medications into me.

The early morning hospital noises woke me and as I lay there looking at my man asleep in the uncomfortable hospital chair next to my bed I knew I would never take anything for granted ever again. Life was short and to not live every day with those you love around you was a waste of the life you had been given.

Only now did I understand what Dylan had tried to teach me. Life was to be lived the way you wanted to live it. To be enjoyed the way you wanted to enjoy it. To be shared with the ones you loved every minute of every day you were given. He had lived his life that way and even though he lost his life way too early I knew he had loved every minute he had been given.

I knew I had had the luckiest of lucky escapes because a good man had been willing to give his life for mine.

I would owe him for the rest of my life. Before this mess he was a colleague and a very good friend of my family. Now he was more.

His actions turned him from a friend of the family to a very important part of my family.

It turned him into my little brother.

RENÉ VAN DALEN

CHAPTER TWENTY EIGHT

Ice

I t fucking sucked. Being away from his woman hadn't been in his plans today. But when his president called and demanded his presence at church she had been the one who had urged him to go.

The last two days had been difficult for all of them. River was recovering but Wrench was battling. He had suffered huge blood loss, lost a kidney and the perforations to his intestines had necessitated the removal of the parts that couldn't be sown back together. Infection was what had the doctors worrying the most. He was still in ICU and it looked like he'd be there for a while. He was awake but in severe pain which meant that he was flying on pain medications almost all the time.

River's friend Mari had struck up a friendship with Wrench's family and she relayed the daily doctors' report to the club and to River and her family.

Hawk smacking the hammer down brought him back to the present. He wanted this shit done so he could get back to the hospital.

"I just spoke to Mari, and Wrench is still on the critical list but he's stable and the doctors are cautiously optimistic. So far there's been no sign of infection but the doctors aren't taking any chances. He's filled up to the eyeballs with antibiotics." While Hawk gave an update on Wrench's condition there were nods around the room. Everyone was worried about him.

"It brings me to the next piece of business." The silence in the room became watchful. "Our prospect is fighting for his life because he was willing to give his life in the protection of Ice's old lady. In doing so he proved that he is everything we want in a brother." Hawk looked at Ice and he nodded, giving his agreement because he knew where this was heading.

"Wrench has been with us for just over nine months, usually that's not long enough to consider patching him in. Spider, you were the one who sponsored him. What do you think?"

Spider drew in a deep breath then let it out. "I've known Kev, or Wrench, and his family for years. His older brother Jasper and I went to school together, played rugby together and we were good friends. Kev was quite a bit younger than us but a good kid. After matric I lost touch with the family until I ran into Kev about a year ago. I liked him, liked the straight look in his eyes. I asked Ziggy to do a deep dive on him and his family. Jasper is in the military, like his dad. Kev was in for almost four years before he resigned and took some time off to travel. Came back, got his mechanic's certification, started prospecting with us and went to work for River."

"Why did he leave the military? Anything we should be worried about?" Beast asked.

"No, not at all. Wrench served with the peacekeeping forces up in the Congo. He actually excelled and was up for promotion. While up there he lost his best friend in a rebel ambush. And everything changed for him. He came home, resigned, went travelling, came back and the rest you know."

There were nods around the table. Hawk tapped the table and everyone's attention returned to him.

"I want to patch him in early. I think he's ready and he's a good man. What do you say?"

The answer was easy, howls echoed as everyone agreed.

"Good. It will be done as soon as he comes home." Hawk decreed.

"Now, onto our next order of business." Hawk continued. "As you all know we are holding a brother below. Flash is a brother, yes, but he's a brother with split loyalties. We have to make a decision regarding his continued membership of the club. Take your time and think about it. We will vote on it at our next full church."

Rings tapping on the table signalled the agreement of all the officers gathered at the table. Hawk continued after a sharp nod.

"The following piece of business could change the way forward for the club. It is Dominick Maingarde. Do we continue our association with him and trust he has our best interests at heart? Or do we throw him in the trash along with the rest of his fucked up family? And when I say his family I'm excluding Pixie, she's clear of all the Maingarde shit."

Sin tapped three times and all eyes went to him.

"Dom has played us straight so far. I suggest we call a meet, or if he can't make a meet then a video call. He has to jump one way or the other."

Kahn tapped. "I agree with Sin. We set up a meet and see where it goes before we make the final decision."

Kid tapped. "I'm in agreement but I want a face to face. It's easy to fucking pretend in a video call."

Hawk rubbed his hand over his beard as he leant back in his chair. "I agree with Kid. We need a face to face. Ziggy get on it. Send a message through the usual channels. Tell him we want a face to face as soon as possible."

"I'm on it." Ziggy nodded his head once, a quick up and down.

"Do you have any leads on Jane, Zig?" Kid growled angrily.

Ever since the shit with Jane came to light Kid had changed from a big man who seldomly smiled into a morose unsmiling bastard who snapped angrily at everyone. To some extent Ice understood the immense disappointment and betrayal he felt. His blood family had betrayed his family of choice. It wasn't an easy thing to accept, not for anyone.

"Not a single fucking thing." Ziggy snarled. "It's like she just fucking vaporised after stepping out of River's workshop. She has help, very fucking good help."

"Keep on it. Sometime, somewhere she's going to make a mistake and we'll be there to take advantage of that fucking mistake." Hawk ordered.

"I've got my mum on it as well. She's been calling what she calls 'the old lady network'." Kid suddenly shared. "She's on the side of the club, moved out of the house and is living with me for the time being."

"Brother, I know this is fucking difficult for both of you. We're here for you if you need us. And I just want you to know, Aunt Beryl wants her to move into the guesthouse with her. So, let her know that when she gets tired of cleaning up after your ass she has a place to go. She's family and we take care of our family."

Hawk very clearly laid it out for Kid and Ice could see the warring emotions in Kid's eyes.

"I'll let her know. Right now she's happy staying with me but you know her, she's not someone who's happy without anything to keep her busy." Kid looked around the table. "Fair warning brothers, she's going to get into your shit the minute she steps through our doors. Expect some fucking matchmaking and nosy shit. She's fucking relentless but it comes from a good place. According to her she wants her boys settled and making her plenty of grandbabies to spoil." Kid gave a thin smile. "Last night I had to listen to how lucky Ice's mum was and how Beast had brought his girls home at last. And then she asked me if I was gay. What the fuck?"

There was a second of stunned silence before wild laughter rang out.

"She has obviously never seen you laying waste to the willing bitches. She wouldn't have a single worry if she saw how often you got your dick wet." Spider teased.

"Fuck you, Spider." Kid cursed without any force behind it.

"No thank you, brother. I'm happy sinking my cock into female ass. Yours is definitely not on the menu." Spider was quick to reply.

"Jesus. Am I now going to have to hear fucking ass jokes all the time? My mother is a fucking nut." Kid groused.

Hawk tapped his rings on the table trying to smother his laughter. "Okay, enough with giving our brother a hard time. We're an equal opportunity club when it comes to fucking. Whether you like cock or pussy is none of my fucking business. Never had a problem with it, and never will." He tapped the table again. "Now that we have that cleared up, let's get back to business. Crow asked to be given the opportunity to get answers for us."

He pointed at Ice. "What are your thoughts on interrogating Emma?"

Ice had been leaning back in his chair, his arms crossed over his chest but now he sat forward, uncrossed his arms and placed both hands flat on the table. He did nothing to disguise his rage.

"Whatever the Crow wants or needs to do is fine with me. Cut her to fucking ribbons for all I care. All I want from the slut is answers to the questions we have. I know the Crow always has two to four brothers in the room while the interrogation is taking place. I want to be one of those brothers."

"No!" Bulldog spoke for the first time since they sat down at the table. "I don't want you in that room, Ice. You hate her now, but you used to love her and I don't want you carrying this load."

Ice laughed and he saw the surprised looks on his father and brother's faces. "No, you're wrong. I liked fucking her, what I didn't like was the way she tried to control me and I sure as shit didn't love her the way you love mum. For years I thought she was the one that got away. And then River Anderson walked into our compound. From one second to the next everything changed." Ice smiled at his dad. "I get it now, what you tried to tell me all those years ago. I see it in Hawk's eyes when he looks at DC, the same way I see it in your eyes when you look at mum. And I know it's in my eyes when I look at River. We would lay our lives down for our women." Ice ran a finger over his bottom lip, frowning as he thought about his next words.

"I would have protected Emma and I most probably would've been hurt in the process but my first priority would've been to protect myself and my club. And my reasoning would have been that to protect her I had to be alive. With River there is no reasoning. She is everything. My life is hers."

"Okay, I don't know about you motherfuckers, but that just fucking freaked me the hell out." Spider leant forward to stare at Ice.

"Who the fuck are you and what have you done with my brother?" He teased.

His brothers laughed and Ice joined the laughter and shook his head. "Fuck off, Spider."

All the laughter disappeared from Spider's face and he was suddenly very serious. "I have waited years to hear my brother laughing the way he used to. She fucking stole that from us. Stole you from us. We will not allow her to steal one more second of time from you. That is why I agree with Bulldog. You are not going to be in that room. I will do it."

Everyone started arguing about who should and shouldn't be in the room with the Crow. Hawk's rings tapping on the table ended the argument.

"It's not up to anyone of us who will be in the room. The Crow chooses the brothers and there's always a reason behind those choices according to Skel. So let's leave it for now." He looked around the table. "If no one has any other business I suggest we head to the bar and have a beer."

When no one spoke up he slammed the hammer down and ended church.

Everyone started chatting as they streamed out through the doors, heading towards the bar where Chris was busy setting beers out for everyone. And immediately Ice realised that with all the shit going down he had once again forgotten to speak to Beast. Shit. Watching his brother heading to the bar and joking with Chris and his brothers he decided to leave it for now. There would be time enough later.

Right now he had to have a quick chat with his dad and maybe a drink before heading back to his woman. The chat was more important than the drink.

Catching his dad's eye he tipped his head towards the front door. Bulldog gave him a nod, picked up two beers and headed towards Ice. They silently walked outside and Ice headed around the building towards the back where they would have more privacy. After the family braai where he had met River, DC had benches and picnic tables set up under the trees for anyone who wanted to relax outside. A damned good idea. Ice headed towards one of those tables now. They sat down and Ice was just about to lay his plans out for his dad when he saw Spider and Kid come walking out the back door. They didn't even pretend to not have followed them outside as they made themselves comfortable at the table.

"Right, what are we talking about?" His nosy brother wanted to know.

"You're a pain in my ass, Spider." Ice said without really meaning it.

"Nope, I'm not. That's Kid's area of expertise. I'm all about the pussy." Spider teased until Kid's fist slammed into his shoulder.

"Ow! Motherfucker! That hurt, you asshole."

"Stop with the fucking ass jokes and I won't hit you, you little shit." Kid threatened.

"Boys, stop your shit, I want to find out what Ice wants so I can go home. Your mother is baking today and you know what that means."

The three of them spoke as one. "Death by chocolate cake."

Ice grinned. "Maybe we should go home with dad and have this discussion over chocolate cake."

"No." His dad snarled. "You little fuckers stay away. I already have to share my cake with the grandbabies, not sharing with you lot. Now, what is it you wanted to say to me that you couldn't say in the common room?"

Ice drew in a deep breath then laid out his plan.

"I'm going to build a house for my old lady on my section of our property and I'm going to need some help. I don't want a construction company to have access to our land so I need some ideas on how to get this done."

"What did River say about moving here?" His dad asked cautiously.

Ice smiled. "She agrees with me. She wants our children to live somewhere safe and she feels they would be safest here. There are some conditions though. The most important being the moving of Duncan's tree house. Sparrow built it for him before he was born and I want him to have it at our new home. It's going to be damned tricky but I'm sure we'll get it dismantled and rebuilt here with minimal problems."

"We can all help with that and we ca…"

Kid was still talking when the rumble of engines and slamming cage doors intruded. Ice frowned when he heard the raised voices. Pulling his weapon he jumped up and raced to the front of the clubhouse. He skidded to a stop with Kid and Spider on either side of him, their eyes widening as they took in the scene in front of them.

A very angry Rick Townsend was facing off with an equally enraged DC. They were shouting at each other and were so loud there was no missing the reason for the argument.

Rick was here to take Emma into custody.

DC wasn't about to let him walk away with her prisoner, at least not before she had had a chance to interrogate the damned slut.

As their argument carried on Ice looked at the two men were with Rick but were leaning with their backs against the front fender of their ride, arms crossed over their chests. A big indicator that they weren't about to fight the brothers for what Rick wanted. They were both grinning as they watched him arguing with his little sister. Ice knew those grins, had met the men during the shit that went down in Durban.

Tucking his gun back into its holster Ice slowly strolled over to the two men, avoiding getting anywhere near Rick and DC. Kid and Spider followed him but his dad who had followed them stayed at the corner of the clubhouse, watching.

"I thought you guys worked with a retrieval outfit. What are you guys doing here?" Ice asked quietly.

"Hi, Ice, we still do." Roodt grinned as he nodded towards Rick. "He hired us in his personal capacity to retrieve Emma Coetzee. We took the job before we knew she was your prisoner. When we reported back to him he lost his mind. Now we're here." Roodt waved a lazy hand towards where Rick and DC were still arguing. "Watching the show and wondering when her man is going to come and lay out Rick's ass."

Kid didn't even crack a smile. "Oh he's watching this shit, but he won't interfere though. His old lady will have his nuts if he gets between the two of them."

Roodt and Tinman looked at each other. "We weren't about to make the same mistake we did in Durban. Not going to snatch someone from the Iron Dogz without a chat with the top dog. But you've been busy, so we decided to wait until we had something to chat about." Roodt said very quietly.

Tinman leant forward slightly as he spoke very quietly to Ice. "We have eyes on something of yours that you have been looking for. Emma Coetzee wasn't the only target we were given to retrieve." He glanced at Kid before he continued. "The other is Jane Warne. We followed her as she made her escape after their attempt on the life of River Anderson."

Kid was about to lunge at the two but Bulldog was suddenly there and his arms came around Kid from the back as if he was hugging him, but he wasn't, he was holding him in place. "Easy now, son. Let's hear them out." He said softly.

"The taskforce operate strictly according to the law, they have to." Roodt explained softly. "They will deliver those two to the authorities and count it as a job well done. The SAPS and the Department of Justice have been compromised. There are so many corrupt officials in both we all know those bitches will walk away without a single charge being laid against either of them. Knowing the way the organisation operates they will turn the tables and level charges at you and your club. You will end up in prison and your women and children will pay the price. We can't allow that to happen. It will tip the scales in the favour of the Maingarde Organisation and they will become untouchable."

"Who the fuck are you really?" Ice questioned softly. "No fucking way are you only a retrieval outfit. Who the hell do you work for?"

"I can't give you much, Ice. All I'm authorised to say is we're not the bad guys but we don't play according to the rules either. We can't allow the bitches to walk free, and that's where your club comes into play." Roodt paused and looked around the compound at the brothers watching DC and Rick arguing. "Your club has been elected to be the judge, jury and executioner in this case. There will be no blow back whatsoever. If you take this on there might come a time you will be asked to do something for us, but it won't ever be something you couldn't live with."

Ice shook his head. "No. We don't do shit like that, especially not to women. We won't become some shadow organisations' executioners. That's not who we are as a club. If the people you work for thought we would they obviously haven't done their homework. I will take what you have said to the club and Hawk will contact you. I can't do more than that. Give me your number."

Roodt nodded as he slid his phone from his pocket, pressed his thumb to the face then typed. Ice's phone pinged in his pocket and he shook his head. Whoever these bastards were they had reach. Enough reach they were able to hack his pre-paid phone. Fuck.

"Get Rick the fuck out of here. We don't have the bitch you're looking for." Kid hissed as he shook off Bulldog's hold and stalked back into the clubhouse.

After a few seconds Ice, Bulldog and Spider followed him inside.

Shit was about to become really interesting.

CHAPTER TWENTY NINE

Ice

Instead of sitting next to his woman's bed at the hospital he was back in his seat at the table laying out what Roodt had told him not even an hour ago. A heavy silence hung in the air as he finished.

Bulldog was the first to speak.

"We don't kill women, not even when those women are killers. We have never had a decision like this to make. We have to think carefully about what it would mean for the club."

"They killed Sparrow and almost succeeded in killing Wrench and River. If we don't kill them not a single old lady will be safe from them, not ever. We might have to accept their offer." Jagger said very quietly.

"You all know we've already got one of the bitches locked down." Hawk glanced at Ice then back around the table and at the brothers against the wall. He had called for the entire club to attend church. "If we agree to become the executioners of some unknown organisation they will most probably apprehend and hand over Jane for interrogation and disposal. Everyone here knows we've done things to ensure the safety and wellbeing of everyone connected to the club." He was silent for a beat as he looked around the room again. "What I want to know is how my brothers feel about what has been put before us. Do we step over this line none of us have ever crossed? Or do we find another way to eliminate the very real threat to our families?"

Silence. A silence alive with the very real moral dilemma in front of them.

Beast was the one to break the heavy silence.

"Everyone here knows me. I am the club's enforcer. It is my job to take care of the hard jobs, to ensure the safety of every single person connected to us. I've killed for my club, for my brothers, and I will step over that line whenever the wellbeing and lives of my brothers and club are threatened. What I've never done is lifted a hand against a woman." He gave a deprecating little laugh. "We all know I had more than enough incentive to beat my fucking ex to a pulp, but I didn't. Kahn can correct me if I'm wrong, but I'm very sure our bylaws forbids violence against or the killing of women and children. That being said, after what those bitches did I'm fucking okay with torturing them for information but killing them is something else."

"I agree with Beast to some extent." Sin said softly. "But we aren't a bunch of pussies who have never had blood on their hands at one time or another. Those of us who were here during the war with the ED know what I'm talking about. During the entirety of that war neither club ever stepped over that line. And then some members of the ED became involved with the fucking Maingardes and things changed. Big Ed attacked our prez's old lady, she was almost raped and if not for the intervention of the very same fuckers now asking us to kill for them she would have been murdered. By the very woman they are asking us to kill. I find it very difficult to find any compassion for either of the bitches."

"I have a suggestion." Wolf suddenly spoke up from where he was leaning against the wall next to the double doors. "Why don't we table this discussion? Give all of us time to consider where we stand on the situation before we vote on it. We come back tomorrow or the day after and discuss the issue then vote yes or no."

"I second Wolf's suggestion." Kid said. "Right now we can't take a vote because it will take hours we don't have to discuss the pros and cons of whatever decision we make. Let's take a day or two to talk it over with our brothers, feel out how we all feel and then come back and vote."

Hawk's rings on the table stopped the mumbles and whispers immediately.

"We're not taking two fucking days to discuss this shit. Be here at nine tomorrow morning for the vote." He snapped the hammer down on the block of steel. "Church is done. Ice, Kid, Spider, Sin and Beast stay behind, the rest of you fuckers get out of here and go do what you have to do. Last one out close the fucking door behind you."

Ice frowned as he looked at his cousin. The man wasn't happy, not at all. The door had hardly been closed when his bad mood was explained.

"You have been selected by my woman to have her back during the interrogation. Everyone that is, except Ice. She wants you back at the hospital with your old lady."

Ice nodded. "I don't have a problem with her decision, Prez. I'll be more of a liability in the room than an asset. I almost lost my woman and my boys because of the whore, not sure I can contain myself if I'm confronted by her."

"Good." Hawk gave a resigned sigh. "The interrogation starts within the next fifteen minutes or so. Dizzy and Wolf will ride to the hospital with you. Let them know. I'll call you once it's done."

Ice nodded and Hawk sighed again.

"Let's get the fuck out of here and get this done."

Ice couldn't wait to get back to the hospital and therefore he was the first out of the chapel.

"Wolf, Dizzy, you're with me." He called out over the loud voices.

With his brothers following and covering his back Ice rode away from the compound. His woman was waiting. He didn't give the interrogation another single thought.

RENÉ VAN DALEN

DC

I felt her pushing against my mental shields and had to hold on tight to keep her under control. I spoke to her in my head, trying to reassure her. But she was too enraged about what had happened to River, our friend, to listen to me. She wanted to cut, slice, spill blood and disfigure the whore locked up down below. And the more I tried to tell her she would have her chance very soon the harder she tried to break free. She wanted vengeance and she wanted it now.

I braced myself for another round of arguments…with myself! How weird was that? The door opened and Hawk, Kid, Beast, Sin and Spider strode into his office. Not a smile in sight.

"Ice is on his way to the hospital." Hawk growled as he pulled me up out of the chair and hugged me to his side. "As much as I fucking hate what I'm asking you to do I know you are the only one who'll get what we want from the bitch. She's deep inside the Maingarde Organisation. We need to know their plans and how Jane fits in with those plans. And we need to know how the sluts we've got locked in the dungeon fit in with their overall plans."

My man wasn't happy about what I was about to do, not at all.

"I need the bag I put in the back of my cupboard and a place to get ready. The Crow is angry and wants to get started." I explained with a shrug. "If Wrench was here he would be my choice to help me get ready and destroy evidence once I'm done. Who did you select for the job?" I asked.

"I'll be the one helping, little bird. We're not letting anyone else in on what's going to happen today." Hawk reassured her. "And your bag is ready and waiting for you below."

"Okay." I breathed in deep and let it out in a hard gust. "Let's do this."

Hawk gave Kid a short nod. My eyes widened as he pushed on something to the side of the big screen TV and a section of the wall slid away revealing a steep set of steel stairs leading down. The stairs were bolted into the rock wall while on the other side there was nothing but dark emptiness. Lights were set into the rock wall at regular intervals but only turned on as we neared them and again turned off as the last person passed. They did nothing to light up the dark echoing emptiness on our left. Scary as hell. Our boots clanged as we climbed down, down, down. The Iron Dogz were so very sneaky. The dungeon in the basement wasn't their real dungeon. We were descending even further below the club. The parts of the compound that everyone knew about were nothing compared to this.

"Wow, this is amazing." I said softly.

"We found a cave system below the clubhouse when we were prospects." Kid explained from behind me. "We were given the order to dig out another room for storage and while digging we found the caves. Hawk insisted we had to keep it a secret and it was only after he became president that we explored it and expanded into the space. The only access is from the office and through a hidden outside entrance. Only the officers know about this place, and now you."

"We have a secure setup down here should the shit hit the fan above. Letting everyone know about our bolt hole would have pissed Jagger off." Hawk explained and I could hear the smile in his voice.

Knowing Jagger I could totally understand. The man lived to keep his family secure.

And then we reached the bottom. The stairs ended in a small room with a thick steel door which Hawk opened after entering a code and had his finger prints scanned. We walked down a short passage into a huge cavern with several passages or caves leading from it. An enormous wrought iron chandelier hung on chains hooked onto large hooks at the sides of the cavern lit up the vast area. A massive round wrought iron table sat below the chandelier with heavy wrought iron chairs around it. There were wrought iron sconces set around the sides of the cavern at regular intervals, providing extra light. A brushed steel cut out of a snarling dog was bolted to one of the cavern walls.

"Wow, this is like the biker version of King Arthur's round table." My eyes zoomed around the space, taking it all in. "How did you get all this stuff down here? It's huge."

"It was brought in piece by piece. Our man Beast is a black smith and he made the pieces separately and once he had it all here he put it together. He built the access to the cells as well. No one is getting out unless we let them out." Hawk said.

"Actually, Boss, she's right. We are knights and you're our king and this is our hidden kingdom. Our Camelot. A Camelot we will defend to the death." Spider wasn't teasing, he was very serious.

The guys all gave agreeing nods. All except Hawk, he got straight to the reason we were down here.

"You can explore to your heart's content after the unpleasant shit is out of the way. Let's get this interrogation started." Hawk took my hand and led me to a cave that was covered with a steel grate with an electronic lock set in to the rock wall. He keyed in a code, again had his finger prints scanned and the grate swung open.

I followed him and stopped when he opened a heavy steel door with another electronic lock.

"This is where you will get ready. I put your bag and some extras in here for you. From today forward this is your room, your code will be the only one that will open the door. We'll be outside waiting for you."

He left me in the room and closed the door behind him. Crow growled softly in my head. She wanted her freedom. I looked around the room, taking note of my bag on the table but it was the bag next to my usual bag that had me tilting my head. What was my travelling tattoo kit doing here? I didn't have time to puzzle it out. Crow shoved me to the back and took over.

RENÉ VAN DALEN

Crow

Crow loved the room. It was cold and almost entirely bare and she would be able to store so many of her toys here. She could already imagine the racks she was going to have installed against the walls to hold her knives and tools. Someone had laid out new clothes on the steel bunk bolted to the wall and she dressed quickly.

Braiding her hair she tucked it down the back of her shirt, out of the way. Slipping the solid black contacts into her eyes she blinked to set them comfortably in place then pulled the thin black hood and black gloves over the skin that had still been visible. The solid black contacts ensured that her eyes showed no emotion whatsoever to her subject. Crow was ready.

Slipping her two favourite knives into her boots she tapped the bag with the tattoo kit. Narrowing her eyes she smiled. Yes, this could turn out to be more fun than she had anticipated.

Crow followed Hawk down a passage wide enough for them to walk comfortably side by side. They passed several steel doors before they stopped before the one standing open. Spider and Beast stood on either side of the open door and Crow smiled behind her mask as she stepped into the room. Sin waited for them inside.

A narrow stainless steel table was bolted to the floor in the middle of the room. The table was at the perfect height for Crow to work at comfortably. A narrow stainless steel shelf was bolted to the wall on the right hand side of the open door and held an array of instruments under a protective clear plastic cover. The entire room had been covered in black plastic sheeting. It whispered a welcome as Crow slowly walked towards the woman cable tied to the table. There would be no need to cut her clothes from her body as she was dressed in a bra and panties only. A black bra and panty set. Matching the room. Pretty.

Spider brought in a chair and set it in place to the side of the wide-eyed but still silent woman.

Crow sat down, crossed her legs and stared at the woman.

"You should not be here. You belong to Doc Michaels." The bitch said through tight lips.

"You're wrong." Crow hissed. "I belong to no one. I go where I'm needed. And today I'm needed here."

"I'm not afraid of you. I've seen your work and I've been trained to withstand it. You won't break me." The stupid slut who had tried to kill Crow's friends boasted.

Crow leant forward and a creepy hissing laugh came from behind the black hood.

"Dear piece of flesh, I don't need to break you. You are already broken. I'm just going to open those wounds up, push my fingers inside then wriggle them about until you give me what I want." Crow continued speaking in a low hiss. "You will give me anything and everything I want by the time I decide you've had enough of my tender care."

Getting up Crow walked to the covered table, lifted the cover and stroked a gloved finger over the instruments that were laid out. A large ungainly looking pair of shears sat at the one end. Picking them up Crow slowly walked back to the bitch and waved the shears in front of her face.

"This little piece of equipment is usually used to sever fingers and toes, but not today. Today is a spa day. Your spa day. And I've decided you need a new hairstyle. Snip, snip, snip."

Shoving the slut's head to the side so she couldn't move Crow started cutting. Hair fell in clumps to the black plastic clad floor. The bitch screamed and moaned but Crow just gave another creepy laugh and kept snipping away until half her head was down to short stubble.

Crow stepped back, cocked a head to the side and hissed. "That wasn't so bad, now was it?"

"You bastard! You crazy fucking bastard! The Maingardes are going to kill all of you for what you're doing to me." She screeched. "I'm never to be touched. Never."

Crow gave a soft evil chuckle and the men around the room joined in. "Bitch, they have no idea where you are. We made sure you disappeared and please, don't take us for fools, your tracking device was removed long before you got here. You're mine now, and I don't relinquish what I've claimed as mine."

Handing the shears to Spider to put away Crow sat back down and just stared at her quarry as she lay panting with rage on the table.

"You think cutting my hair will make me give in to you? It won't. But you have to stop if you want my cooperation. Why are you doing this for them? They can't give you what you need. We can. We can give you as many toys as you want. Let me go and I will get it for you. Anything you want, anyone you want you can have, even DC Michaels. I give you my word."

Crow gave a hissing little laugh. "How ignorant she is. DC has always been mine. Now you are mine." Motioning to the men around the room Crow continued. "They are already mine."

Silence, absolute silence.

"Someone gave you bad information, Emma Coetzee. Someone told you I play with humans like toys. They were wrong. I don't like toys. And I don't play. I gather information. Sometimes it's easy, sometimes it's not. You, I know, will not be easy. And that fills me with anticipation for the time we are going to spend together."

"Jesus." Emma whispered.

"Oh he's nowhere near here, dearie. There's only Crow and the boys. And they aren't going to lift a hand to help you. Oh, by the way, River recovered fully and the babies are doing really well. Our boy Ice is very, very pleased." Crow informed her with another creepy hissing laugh.

That little gem of information got some reaction. Emma screamed in rage, jerking against her bonds but she wasn't going anywhere. Not for a very long time.

"Now, let's see what you can tell me about Jane Warne. Where is she?" Crow's voice was no longer light and so strangely friendly. It was a deep dark menacing growl.

Emma just shook her head in denial. Crow shrugged and pulled the knife from where it had been hidden in her boot.

"I'm not entirely sure what I want to play today. Noughts and crosses or maybe I can draw a snakes and ladders grid on her belly…hmmm." Crow tapped the knife against Emma's bare quivering belly and stared down at her with black inhuman eyes.

With a lightning fast move Crow leant forward and sliced a noughts and crosses grid on the thigh of the leg to the left below the gunshot wound. The bitch screamed. Crow ignored the screams.

"Come on, Spidey, come play with me. I'm crosses, I'm always the crosses, and you'll have to be the noughts." Crow ignored the screaming and looked at Spider where he was leaning against the wall next to the door. He nodded, came forward and held out a hand for the knife.

"Oh no, I can't give you my knife. You have to use your own." Crow drew the knife back and let the blood drip to the black plastic covered floor.

Spider slipped his knife out with a grin and cut a circle in one corner of the grid. They played, ignoring the screams and when Crow won Spider insisted on a rematch. Which they played on the other thigh. This time above the gunshot wound. And again Crow won.

"I'm bored." Crow complained. "Oh, wait, I have a good idea. Let's tattoo grids on her and we can all play. We've got lots of space."

"I'm in." Beast growled from his place to the side of the bitch. "Me too, I'm in too." Kid said from the other side. "Oh, yes, that should be fun." Sin laughed.

"Have you done tattoos before? If you don't do it right it will form thick scarring." Hawk said with a smile the bitch couldn't see because he was behind her.

Crow shrugged. "It can't be that difficult. I've watched DC do it and it looks easy. Come on, let's play with her skin. We can even use different colours. This is going to be so much fun."

"She's on her way to the UK!" The bitch screamed.

"Really? Why? What's in the UK?" Crow asked as if totally disinterested.

"The boss wants her to meet someone. I don't know anything else." The bitch said through clenched teeth.

"Not enough. I want more. Tell me more."

"Fuck you. Fuck all of you." Her screams rang through the room.

"No thank you. Not sticking anything of mine in that snatch of yours." Crow said with disgust.

The men laughed hard and it pissed the bitch off even more. Exactly what Crow wanted.

"Where's the tattoo machine thing?" Crow snarled.

Kid and Spider left the room and after a few minutes walked back in with a big black bag and a fold up stainless steel table. Spider set the table up at an angle to the one in the middle of the room and Kid laid the bag down on the far end. Without any hesitation he set up the tattoo machine as if he had done it thousands of times before. He carefully set out the small tubs of ink and set out the container of needles with the alcohol wipes right next to them. Spider had left while Kid was setting up and he came back with a small bowl of soapy water, a towel, and a razor and set it on the table as well.

"You know, I've been thinking. I don't think I want to play games on her skin. I think I want to draw my patterns on her skin. Patterns that will show the world she belongs to me." Crow said softly and the bitch moaned.

"Don't do this. Please don't do this." She begged.

"Oh stop being such a baby. My patterns are pretty. It will look good on you." Crow admonished as she wet the side of the bitch's head. Emma started jerking her head from side to side. "Hold her for me." Crow ordered.

Kid and Beast immediately grabbed her head, shoved her left cheek to the table and held her in place. Crow made quick work of shaving the stubble, leaving her head smooth. And ready for the next step.

Picking up the tattoo machine it hummed to life in Crow's hand. With no plan and no idea what the end result would look like Crow started drawing. The bitch's screams were ignored as a screaming half human half crow face started to take shape. The face started on her temple and forehead, the face's hair was a wild mess of strands as if a heavy wind was blowing. Several strands fell over her forehead and laced over her cheek to her jaw. As Crow drew and dabbed and drew and dabbed the screams became less and less and eventually it morphed into soft crying as the subject gave up fighting. Crow started shading, using reds and blacks and blues. Then stood back with a satisfied grunt.

The tattoo was beautiful and horrifying at the same time. It covered the entire right side of her head and face. From the middle of her head down her neck and onto her back and shoulder.

"You are mine now. No one will ever look at you and not know who you belong to." Crow snarled viciously then bent and hissed in her ear. "Tell me a story, slave."

"Anything, anything you want, just stop, please stop." The broken woman sobbed.

"Who gives you your orders?"

"Win…Winifred Maingarde."

"When did she recruit you?"

"She didn't, my dad…my dad convinced me to join their organisation when I was…when I was…thirteen."

"Hmm." Crow hissed softly. "Why would a father hand his daughter over to someone like Winifred Maingarde?"

Emma Coetzee's voice strengthened slightly as she explained.

"He wants more power. He said if I brought them the Iron Dogz he would have a bigger share of the power and so would I. But Bounty was difficult to convince. And the baby was a girl not a boy like they wanted. So Bounty had to die and we had to try again. Jane tried but failed to get pregnant. Now it's too late, all the officers have to die."

Her voice changed and became an obsessed whine.

"But not Gray, he is mine. Mine. Mine. Mine. Mine. River and her bastards will die soon and then he will be all mine. Always mine. Only mine"

Crow dragged the cup of her bra down and slapped her hard on her naked breast and she went back to the soft sobbing.

"How will she die?"

A gasp, more sobs and then it came pouring out.

"We have people everywhere. She was shot and bleeding a lot. If she's in a hospital she's as good as dead. My people will get to her, they will, I know they will. They have their orders if I fail. One little injection and it will all be over. No one will ever know. She will be dead and he'll be mine. Only mine, always mine."

Crow looked up and frowned at Hawk. He pointed up at the cameras and Crow nodded. Satisfied that Ziggy was watching and River would be protected the Crow returned to the interrogation.

"When did Jane join the organisation?"

The bitch's voice was small as she explained and she gave them a lot more than they were expecting. "She…she joined when she was eighteen. She wanted Hawk but he didn't want her, not then. Everything she has done has been for the organisation. Now it's time for her reward. A Harrison will marry her, and her children will be the next generation of the organisation."

"Has she left yet?"

"I don't know. She had some loose ends to tie up before she could leave." The bitch whispered.

"Loose ends? How many loose ends are we talking about?"

The woman whimpered. "She has to find her dad. He's going with her but no one has seen him for days. Her mother isn't at home either."

"Jesus. Fucking, fucking hell." Kid snarled.

Crow held a hand up as he was about to move. "So Flash is a part of the takeover plans for the Iron Dogz?"

"Yes. He's been elected as the next president by the organisation."

Hawk laughed and shook his head. "This is so fucked up." He growled.

"So, does that mean Jane can't leave until she finds Flash?" Crow asked in a soft hiss.

"Yessss." The answer came on a soft moan.

"Good little slave. Very good. Let's fix you up quick. It's going to hurt a little but you'll soon learn to live with the pain. Won't you?" Crow said and stroked and hand down her arm.

"Yes. Anything you want. Anything."

"When I'm not here Hawk Walker will be your handler. You will answer any and all questions he puts to you. Do you understand?" Crow said coldly.

"Yes. Yes I understand."

"Good. Very good, slave."

The cup of her bra was roughly dragged back over her breast. And with calm efficiency Crow wrapped her wounds and coated the new tattoo in healing jell and closed it up. Reaching back into the black bag Crow drew out a little baggie with a capped syringe. Before any of them could move the syringe was out of the baggie, uncapped and the needle slid into their prisoner's pulsing carotid artery.

Crow set the syringe down, and stuck a tiny plaster over the entrance wound. Emma Coetzee's eyelids started to flutter and then slid closed.

Her breaths evened out as she slipped into a drug induced sleep. She would be down for several hours. Crow had given her enough to keep her down for at least four hours.

The men silently watched as Crow meticulously cleaned her equipment and slid it back into the black bag. Only once it was done did Hawk speak up.

"Let's get out of here and get you cleaned up."

Crow didn't say a word, just gave a slight chin lift and walked out the door after a last look at the drugged bitch on the table. Hawk walked out behind her.

The four men left behind looked at each other and shrugged. With practised efficiency they snipped the cable ties, carried the bitch to her new accommodations and set her down on the bunk. The end of the long chain bolted to the wall was cuffed to her wrist, Beast shook out the blanket at the end of the bunk and covered her. They silently left the room, locking the heavy door behind them.

Emma Coetzee would stay alive a little bit longer.

There were more questions for her to answer.

None of them felt any pity for the drugged woman behind the steel door. She deserved everything that was going to happen to her.

Her actions bought her this outcome.

Fifteen minutes later they were back in the clubhouse and heading to the bar. They sat on the stools at the far end of the bar and Chris immediately came to them.

"What can I get you guys?" She asked with a smile, her eyes shifting to Beast and then away to Spider.

"Four brandy shots and four beers please sweetheart." Spider ordered without a reciprocating smile.

She nodded and set them up then returned to serve at the other end of the bar.

They silently drank. They were halfway through their beers when Beast spoke quietly.

"We are never going to talk about that shit to anyone. It stays with us, for fucking ever."

"Agreed." Sin muttered.

"I agree." Spider said with a sigh.

"Agreed." Kid growled. "Crow is ours to protect. From this day forward."

Nods and grunts of agreement followed his statement. Then Spider beckoned Chris over and set them up with more drinks.

They drank quietly, each lost in their thoughts.

CHAPTER THIRTY

Ice

Looking at his old lady as she lay against the cushions stacked behind her back in the high hospital bed Ice had to smile. She was definitely feeling better and wanted to go home. This morning her doctor said he wanted her to stay one more day just to be certain.

His Blue wasn't happy about that decision.

His phone started pinging insistently and Ice frowned as he slid it from the inside pocket of his kutte. Ziggy. What did he want? Ice quickly read the text.

Possible threat against River inside the hospital. Allow no injections. Get her out. Now.

What. The. Fuck.

It didn't take him long to arrange her discharge from the hospital. Nor did it take long to arrange for a safe place to stay until the threats against her were neutralised. They were moving into Hawk's pool house where his woman and their children would be protected and safe.

By the time they left the hospital several brothers had arrived to escort them to River's home. His old lady had been very quiet since he showed her the text. She had a slight frown between her brows and some of the sparkle was missing from her blue eyes. Ice hated it.

At her home he made her comfortable on the bed while he packed for both of them. River's mum was packing for Duncan while their boykie packed his toys. The toy bag ended up being bigger than his bag of clothes.

Packing took a while but at last they were on their way to the Iron Dogz property. The sparkle was still missing from his woman's eyes.

"Blue, sweetheart, it's going to be okay. I'm not going to let anything happen to you or to Duncan, I swear it."

She smiled at him, the first real smile of the day. "I know you will, I don't doubt it for a second. I just wish these people would go away and leave us alone."

Unfortunately Ice knew it wouldn't happen. Not until the Maingarde Organisation was destroyed or Dominic Maingarde took over. And right now that was not going to happen.

"Once we're on the Iron Dogz property they won't be able to get near you or Duncan. You will be safe, and our babies will be safe." Ice took her cold hand and placed it on top of his thigh as he drove. Covering her hand with his he shared his warmth with her.

"I know." She said softly, twisted her hand, knitted their fingers together and held onto his hand.

In that moment Ice knew he would maim, kill and die to ensure the safety of his family. Emma Coetzee held the secrets he needed to keep his family safe and she had better still be alive because he was going to extract those secrets from her.

As soon as he had his family settled he was going to deal with the bitch.

River

I could see darkness moving behind Ice's eyes as he held my hand. He drove one-handed, only letting go if he needed to change gears. Sometimes not even then.

He hadn't hidden that they had uncovered a threat against me inside the hospital. I had been only too happy to get out of there. I had hated not seeing Duncan but I didn't want him coming to the hospital and seeing me lying in a hospital bed.

Glancing into the back seat I smiled at my boykie. He was so excited about us moving in with Ice he could hardly sit still. Thankfully he was strapped into his carseat and couldn't move around. Something he would have done if we had allowed him to sit in the back without a carseat. He would have wriggled out of the seatbelt in seconds. His carseat enabled him to see out the window and all his attention was focused outside the vehicle on the bikers protecting us.

"Are we there yet?" His little voice piped up as we started slowing down.

"Almost, son, we're almost there. Just a few more minutes." Ice answered with a grin.

Where had these come from I thought to myself as we turned off from the main road and drove through gigantic wrought iron gates that slowly opened as we approached.

I frowned and turned to Ice. "Those weren't there when I came to the *braai*."

"They were, but they were open, Blue. We closed them to control access to our property." He explained as the gates swung closed behind us and we drove down the tarred road towards the clubhouse.

But we didn't turn into the clubhouse, we passed it. And like the wrought iron gates at the entrance to the property the heavy steel gates were closed and there were heavily armed men watching us from the top of the walls.

"They got beeeg gates." Duncan mumbled from the back.

On our left was the high game fence and on the right the high white wall that enclosed the Iron Dogz MC's compound. Armed men patrolled on the steel catwalk along the inside of the wall, watching as we drove past. The wall eventually swung away from us, continuing towards the back of the compound.

We passed the gated entrance to a big house set away from the road behind a tall steel palisade fence. There were cars and bikes parked out front and heavy bars covered all the windows and a steel cage and a security door protected the front door. The two upstairs balconies facing the road were completely enclosed by steel cages.

"Who lives there?" I asked as we drove past.

"Rider and his old lady with their baby girl and Beast recently moved in with his two little girls. At one time it had been the club's guesthouse for visitors, but for the last few years it became somewhere Hawk stashed his women. Now it's a family home."

I glanced back at Duncan but he was totally engrossed in watching the scenery rolling past the windows. Hawk had more than one woman? Did DC know about this?

"Are you telling me Hawk has more than one woman?" I asked with big eyes.

Ice grinned. "Used to, Blue, not anymore. That shit happened before he met DC. He knew almost from the start she was the one for him and he got rid of all the women. We both know DC would have kicked his ass to the curb if he had tried that sharing shit with her."

Ice slowed as we approached a walled property with a guarded gate on our left. I caught a glimpse of a paved road snaking away from the gate and disappearing between thick trees as we slowly drove past.

"That's my mom and dad's place. It's where I grew up."

I looked around at the unspoiled veldt around us and marvelled at the way he had grown up.

"You were very lucky. Not many kids get to be so lucky."

Ice grinned and squeezed my hand as we slowed to an almost crawl. The road ended in front of another heavy steel gate and as we approached it slowly started to slide open. This property was walled as well, the unplastered bricks blending into the surroundings. Inside the gate two of Ice's brothers stood with automatic weapons cradled in their arms. They nodded as we drove past. The tar road stopped at the gate and a paved driveway led us further into the property. I was fascinated as the winter dry veldt slowly morphed into a well-kept garden.

I stared wide-eyed when an imposing thatch roofed house came into view. But we didn't head towards the house. We drove past and kept following the driveway as it circled around towards the back of the house. Through the trees I caught fleeting glimpses of the house but not enough to satisfy my curiosity. It was an enormous house for only one man. DC had better start making plans to fill that house with some babies, soon. My boys were going to need some friends around here. I grinned internally as I thought about DC getting pregnant. She would totally freak out.

My mouth hung open when we stopped in front of a smaller version of the main house.

I sat forward painfully staring at the house then looked at Ice. "This is his pool house?" I questioned in disbelief.

Ice grinned. "It isn't really a pool house it's one of three guest houses. My aunt used to call it the pool house and it stuck." He pointed to the left where the big house was hidden from view because of thick plantings of trees and shrubs. "The pool is down a path through the trees over there."

"Why did they build such a huge house when they only had Hawk?" I asked.

"The house was built before they knew there would only be Hawk but the house was never empty. Someone was always staying over or visiting. My aunt loved kids and she was always having us over so our parents could hang out at the clubhouse. She was a homebody and I don't think Bounty liked her hanging out at the clubhouse. They had a very different relationship than most of the other couples. I loved staying here and so did Kid. He stayed over more than I did because his dad was and is an abusive asshole."

There was more to the story but now wasn't the time to probe. We had little ears in the back seat that soaked up whatever was said in his vicinity and then blurted it out at the most inopportune moments.

The house was stunning. A double volume entrance led into a large lounge with a huge fireplace. There was a proper dining room and the kitchen was a dream of glossy grey granite counters and cherry wood cupboards. All the appliances were brushed steel and looked very expensive.

The dining room furniture was dark glossy wood and in the lounge there were leather couches with Persian rugs on the wooden floors. It was definitely not decorated with children in mind.

I was only allowed a brief glimpse as Ice carried me through to the main bedroom. A dark wooden sleigh bed stood waiting for me, it was already turned down and pillows were stacked for my comfort.

The white linen with deep blue piping gleamed in the sunlight falling across the bed. A vase filled with a colourful assortment of roses was set on a table against the wall. Their lovely scent filled the air. A beautiful welcome arranged on very short notice.

Ice set me down against the pillows and tucked me in with a soft kiss on my forehead. I relaxed into the comfy bed and between one blink and the next I was fast asleep.

I woke when I was gently pulled into a hard body and enveloped in my man's scent. I tried to pull back but he tightened his arms around me.

"Go back to sleep, baby." He murmured.

"Where's Duncan?"

"My mum and Gail came over to check on you and he was having such fun playing with my nieces they invited him over. Johan or my dad will bring him home later."

I was amazed. "He's already having a play date? He usually takes forever to make friends."

Ice's chuckle vibrated through me and it warmed me from the inside out.

"When you meet the girls you'll see he didn't have a hope in hell against those two. Those girls are super friendly."

"I'm happy he's made some friends. He's going to miss Sammy and Robby. They're his best friends."

"We'll see what we can do about arranging something for them, baby. Just not right now. We need to keep everyone safe and we don't want to endanger his little friends and their parents."

I didn't like it. Not at all. And I felt my entire body tense up and dull pain streaked through my chest.

"Baby, relax, nothing is going to happen to anyone, I promise."

"You can't promise that, Ice. These people are crazy. They killed Sparrow. Look what they did to get to me. They almost killed Wrench."

Ice jerked. "Who told you they killed Sparrow?" He growled.

"That crazy bitch did. She was bragging about how easy it was." My voice broke a little as I explained.

"Jesus, baby. I'm sorry you had to find out like that. I was going to break it to you gently at a later date."

"It's okay, babe. As long as she pays and we are safe. That's all I want." I whispered. His arms tightened even more.

"Shhh, Blue, we are safe here. They can't get to you and they definitely can't get to Duncan. The brothers will die before they allow anyone to hurt our boy."

"And that's what I'm worried about. I don't want anyone else hurt."

"Until we force these people to back off the club our lives and lifestyle is in danger, baby. We are being careful, and no one is taking any chances. You saw the men on the walls around the compound but what you didn't see were the men patrolling the grounds. These bastards think we're ignorant bikers but they are wrong. They caught us unprepared before, it won't happen again. We had a rat in our midst, but he has been neutralised." I gasped. "No, baby, he's not dead, he's just locked up."

I could hear the amusement in his voice at my shocked gasp.

"And now I'm done talking about club shit." Ice said forcefully and slowly set me back on the pillows. Taking care not to hurt me. He leant over me, his hands on either side of my shoulders.

His face was so very serious as he stared down at me, and my stomach contracted as I prepared for whatever he was about to say.

"We're getting married, Blue. As soon as you are well enough to walk down the aisle we're doing it. And I'm not going to listen to any excuses. I want you to be my wife before our boys are born."

Shocked I could only stare up at him.

"Aren't you going to say anything, Blue?" His dark brows drew together as he frowned down at me.

I cleared my throat because it felt as if I had a huge lump stuck in it. "We're getting married?" I whispered. "Aren't you supposed to ask me to marry you, not tell me it's what's going to happen?"

A wide grin lit up his beautiful face. "Not only are you my old lady, you are carrying my boys in your belly, getting married is the next logical step, baby."

Bikers, they are all the same, not a romantic bone in their bodies.

"What about the romantic dinner where you go on one knee, show me the ring and ask me to be your wife? Don't I get that?" I didn't really want that, I was just teasing. It wasn't what I wanted at all.

Ice smiled and it softened the hard planes of his face. Dropping his face into the hollow between my neck and shoulder he drew in a deep breath and kissed up to my jaw before pulling away and looking deep into my eyes.

"No romantic dinner right now, Blue, but I promise, once this shit is done we will be going away for a romantic weekend where I'll give it all to you."

I smiled up at him and drew his head down for a quick kiss. His lips were soft and I sighed against them.

"Okay, we'll get married and then have the romantic weekend. Trust us to keep on doing things back to front."

Ice balanced himself on one hand as he reached down and pulled something from his jeans pocket. His hand came back and held between his thumb and forefinger was a ring. A beautiful ring. A platinum band held a light blue sapphire surrounded by sparkling diamonds. I stared open mouthed then looked up in his warm green and yellow eyes.

"Ice, it's the most gorgeous ring I've ever seen." I whispered.

Shaking his head he sat back on his knees, gently took my hand and slipped the ring on. It was a perfect fit. Bending over my hand he kissed my finger and then the back of my hand. Coming back up over me he dropped a soft kiss on my lips.

"This ring is my promise, Blue, my promise to always love you. I can't wait to make you my wife."

This amazing man, he came into my life unexpectedly, then totally shook up my comfortably boring life and in the process gave me a precious gift, our babies.

"I love you, Ice. I'll wear your ring as my promise to always love you and I'll marry as soon as I'm out of this bed."

Ice gave me a lascivious grin. "Not going to let you out of this bed once you're better, baby. We're going to be spending a lot of time right here."

I smiled. "I'm looking forward to it, Ice, Ice, baby."

He laughed and his eyes twinkled. "I want to introduce you to my brothers, Blue. What do you think about an engagement party for our families and friends at the clubhouse?"

My man was moving at the speed of light. "That sounds nice. I would love to celebrate our engagement with our families and friends."

"Then it's a date. I'll get my mum and Aunt Beryl on it, you don't worry about anything, baby. All you have to do is be there at my side, the rest will be taken care of."

"Are you sure? I know my mum will want to be involved as well." I knew for a fact my mum would want to be in the middle of organising the engagement party and the wedding.

"No worries, I'll tell my mum to call her and between the three of them they can organise all the shit that needs to be organised. I'll call Hawk later to let him know."

And just like that we were engaged and soon to be married.

"Blue?"

"Yes?"

"Can't wait to marry you, baby."

He kissed me and I smiled against his mouth.

"Me neither, baby."

Ice

His woman was looking incredibly beautiful as she lay sleeping in their big bed. Every night he held her in his arms and thanked God she and their boys had survived the attack. It's been almost two weeks since the attack and she wasn't in much pain anymore and moved around quite freely. She had a check-up later today and it was freaking him out. He had gone over the safety precautions with Jagger more than once and he still wasn't happy. He would have been happier if the doctor could have come out to the house to check her wound.

Tomorrow afternoon was their engagement party at the clubhouse. He couldn't fucking wait. What his old lady didn't know was that she would be getting his patch at the same time. He had had her 'property of' kutte made soon after he found out she was expecting his babies but had been waiting for the right time to give it to her.

Tomorrow she would be wearing his name on her back and his ring on her finger and very damned soon he would be adding a wedding band to that ring. He had been lost until he found his Blue. With her by his side he would never be lost again.

Unfortunately he had to get going, he had club business that had to be handled before taking his woman to the doctor. His brothers had carried the weight of all the decisions regarding Emma thus far but it was time for him to step up and do his part. Hawk had explained what had gone down with the interrogation and Ice could honestly say he felt nothing. Nothing at all.

They had decisions to make regarding the information the bitch had given the Crow. According to Hawk she hadn't stopped talking. The information had come pouring out in a steady stream. A final decision had to be made regarding the sluts in the dungeon rooms below the club. Ice knew not all of the bitches were as rotten as Lizzy and Laney but all of them had conspired with Jane to attack DC. Punishment had to be seen to be handed out.

If they didn't punish the bitches the club and Hawk would look weak. And it would weaken DC's already rocky position in the club. They could not allow that to happen.

Hawk was going to have to make his decision and fucking soon.

Ice knew Hawk didn't want to be as harsh as Bounty had been. Bounty had never hesitated to use force and he never let a bitch fuck with the old ladies. They disappeared never to be seen again. His uncle hadn't regretted a single decision he ever made. That was one of the last pieces of advice he had given Ice before he died. Stand by your decisions, no regrets.

Hawk had wanted to be a more approachable leader but after DC walked out of the clubhouse and stayed with Blue he had changed. He was colder and harder around the men. Something was going on behind those hawk-eyes of his and Ice knew his president was at his most dangerous right now. He wondered who else had noticed the change in him.

If Ice had to be truthful, and he always tried to be, the attitudes of a few of the brothers were the reason why DC wasn't settling in. She came down to the pool house every single day after work and had dinner with them most nights. Ice could see it pissed Hawk off when DC ignored the plans he made for them to have dinner with the brothers at the clubhouse. She didn't feel comfortable surrounded by people who still haven't accepted her fully. People she didn't trust.

Ice wanted the fucking bitches out of the dungeon and gone, and the brothers who had a problem with it had the option of transferring to another chapter. Ice was going to see to it that they did. He didn't need men around he couldn't trust to safeguard their women.

If it was up to Ice the bitches would be permanently eliminated because they couldn't afford to set them free. Not now and not any time soon either. They knew too much.

Kissing his old lady on the forehead he silently left the room.

He knew without any doubt at all that if he had been in Hawk's shoes the sluts would have disappeared never to be seen again. Just the way Emma was going to disappear. And when they found Jane she would be gone as well.

He didn't give a fuck about their family ties. They betrayed the club. They betrayed his brothers. They tried to kill his old lady and his babies.

They were going to die.

Ice leant back in his chair listening as Hawk laid the latest developments out for their brothers. There was a long silence and then Wolf stood up. It seemed that the brother was becoming someone they could count on during hot situations. Ice was glad Wolf had been voted in as a lieutenant. They needed men like him.

"When we voted not to become the mercenaries' executioners my 'no' vote was one of the first. We are brothers, and we share a bond that those men will never have. I knew that we eventually would have to make a decision on those traitorous sluts. Not only did they try to kill our president's old lady but they have been supplying our enemies with information on the daily business of the club. Unfortunately their absence has been noted by their families and their employers, so killing them out right isn't going to be a good idea. I suggest we fire the bitches that work at the strip club and drop the whole lot of them on the ED's doorstep. I'm sure Snake and his boys will have a use for them."

"Jesus. That's fucking cold, Wolf." Beast growled angrily. "The ED's aren't known for taking care of their women. And none of them last very long either."

Wolf glared at him. "No, it's not, it's justice. I've never fucked those sluts so I don't give a shit what happens to them. It's the rest of you pussies who has to get with the program. You were used. Every single one of you who stuck a dick in those filthy bitches were used. And sorry Prez, that includes you. We need to be more careful about who we invite to share our clubhouse with us. Yes, we need club girls, that's a given, but we don't need whores who will turn around and sell us out. We need more girls like Chris. She's loyal and a nice girl."

Having said what he wanted to say Wolf sat back down and crossed his arms over his chest.

"Wolf is right." Ziggy said softly. "We need to get rid of them. If we don't DC is never going to settle in here. She spends more time with Ice and River than she does here. She doesn't trust us to have her back and I don't blame her. We chose pussy over our president's old lady."

Spider tapped his rings on the table and the mumbles stopped instantly. "I second Wolf's suggestion. Give them to Snake."

Hawk looked around the room, drew in a deep breath and nodded. "Let's vote."

Ice was shocked. No one voted against the suggestion or abstained.

And just like that the sluts were gone. That left the brothers who hadn't protected DC during the attack.

"Wolf, as this is essentially your plan, you're in charge of the delivery. I'll call Snake and set it up. If we're lucky they will be gone by tonight." Hawk said and smiled with what seemed like relief.

Ice looked at Wolf and gave a small chin lift when he met his eyes. Thanking him silently.

Ice tapped his rings on the table and silence fell.

"We have one more issue to discuss. There are brothers in this room who let our president's old lady down. They stood back and allowed the whores to attack her and if that's not enough they continue their shit by disrespecting her at every turn. I, as the VP of this club, call a blood debt on all of them."

Stunned murmurs and rustling as everyone shifted in their seats.

"You will face your president or his proxy in the ring. Today. And you will pay your blood debt to your president. If you refuse you will be given the option to put your kutte on the table or transfer out." Ice coldly looked around the room. "If Beast calls out your name I want your decision, right the fuck now."

Ice crossed his arms over his chest and waited.

Next to him Hawk sat stoically, his face blank and cold. But his eyes were alive with rage.

CHAPTER THIRTY ONE

Hawk

Leaning back in his chair Hawk watched as his VP laid it out for the bastards. He watched them, saw the furtive looks they threw him. Murmurs continued as Beast called out the names, but now those murmurs were no longer shocked they were pissed off. Seems like some of the brothers hadn't been aware of what was going on right under their noses. Just like him.

If not for Ziggy's cameras the bastards would have walked free from punishment.

Hawk smacked the hand down. "There will be no excuses, no second chances. This is it. You climb in the ring or you walk. What will it be?"

Hawk looked at the five who now stood at the far end of the table. Two were transfers from the Bloemfontein chapter and there hadn't been a hint of scandal attached to them. It was why they had accepted their application to transfer in. The other three were fairly new patches who had been patched in around the same time the other two transferred in. It could be that they had stuck together as the new guys at the chapter or that the sluts had filled their heads with a load of crap.

"We accept our punishment, prez. We were stupid and blinded by pussy, and let a fucking whore influence us against our presidents' old lady. Won't ever happen again." Buzz, one of the new transfers stepped forward and spoke for all five of them.

"I'll see all of you in the ring. If one of you disrespect my old lady ever again I will fucking end you. Do you get me?" Hawk snarled angrily.

There were nods all around, even from the brothers watching this shit.

The fights were short and brutal. Hawk didn't pull his punches at all and none of the brothers who stepped into the ring with him lasted very long. He didn't tag Beast who was his proxy. He wanted their blood on his own hands. Now that their punishment had been meted out it was over and done with and time to move on.

"You five, I'll see you at the bar." Hawk ordered the five men and they nodded as they shuffled out. They were going to be hurting for a few days.

An hour later the five were laughing and drinking with Hawk as if nothing had happened and when DC walked in after work he greeted her along with five very remorseful brothers. They each apologised to her in front of their brothers.

And the way DC handled the men wasn't missed by anyone in the common room. She met the eyes of each of the men and they were the first to look away, none of them could hold her eyes.

He was so damned proud of his old lady. She was perfect for him and perfect for his club.

Hawk saw his cousin silently walk out the front door and let it go. They would have time to talk before the party tomorrow.

Saturday
River

Swallowing nervously I glanced up at Ice as we walked into the clubhouse. I had no idea why I was so nervous, I just was. The common room was filled with laughing and smiling people. And the minute we were spotted a loud cheer went up.

Hawk and DC came walking towards us, both smiling broadly. For the first time in all the time I've known her DC was wearing her property kutte, declaring her the property of Hawk, president of the Iron Dogz MC. That was a huge step for my friend.

Silence fell as they reached us and Hawk smiled down at me. Damn the man was hot. Hey, I might be engaged to be married but I wasn't blind.

"River, congratulations on your engagement to my VP. We're looking forward to the wedding which Ice tells me will be soon."

I smiled. "Thank you, Hawk."

Before I could say more DC enfolded me in a hard hug. "Congratulations and welcome to the crazy zone, Rivvie."

"Thanks, DC, glad to be here. Do I need to be scared of the crazies?" I joked.

There wasn't a shred of humour in DC's eyes when she answered. "You don't have to be scared of anyone or anything, Rivvie. I've got your back."

Wow. Then Ice's next words had the nerves back in full force.

"I know you were introduced to people at the braai but there are some people here you haven't met." Ice grinned. "Come meet my family, baby."

Ice had kept everyone away while I was recuperating and I had yet to meet his parents face to face. The hurried introduction at the braai did not count. And then it was too late to panic.

"Blue, I'd like you to meet my mum and dad, Bulldog and Suzy Walker." He smiled. "Mum, Dad, this is my woman and future wife, River Anderson."

His hand was warm on the small of my back and then it was gone as his mum pulled me into her arms and hugged me tight while rocking from side to side.

"I'm so very happy to meet you, River. I have waited years and years for this moment. Welcome to our family."

I was pulled from her arms and enfolded in big arms and held against a wide chest. "Welcome to our family, River. We love your boykie already and have been looking forward to meeting you. You did a fine job with that young man." Bulldog rumbled against my hair.

I was pulled back against Ice's chest and I smiled at his parents. "Thank you very much for the warm welcome and for being so wonderful to my boykie. Without you he would have been a little bit lost over the last week or so."

His sisters came next and I grinned at Genna when she winked and whispered. "Fucking glad you're part of the sisterhood here at the club. Welcome to our crazy family."

Gail and Johan were more subdued but sweet with their welcome hugs and wishes. And I finally relaxed only to hear Ice swear softly and threaten someone.

"You fucking behave or you're a dead man."

That someone was a tall, wide shouldered, gorgeous, long haired and bearded blonde with laughing green eyes and a wide naughty smile. He had his arms opened wide as he approached me.

"Little sister, I'm Spider, the long suffering brother of the asshole you so unwisely chose as your man. You should have held out for the sexier and way more fun brother." He introduced himself.

He gently enfolded me in his arms and the hug was equally gentle. Beside me I could hear Ice mumbling all sorts of threats and I started laughing and looked up at Spider.

"Hi, big brother. I think you and I are going to be best friends. I like the way you operate." I winked and he burst out laughing.

"At last, someone who gets me!" He shouted to the laughing crowd.

The music came back on and around us people went back to having a good time. Ice introduced me to so many people I lost count and the names started to blur together. As we made our way around the room I noticed there weren't any club girls at the party. That was out of the ordinary for a club and I would be asking DC about it later. Ice would just gloss it over, not wanting to get into the entertainment his brothers enjoyed.

I was sitting on Ice's lap chatting to Krissie, Mari and Genna when a bell was rung and the room fell silent. Twisting to see over Ice's shoulder I saw Hawk and DC standing in the middle of the room, everyone else had moved back to give them space. DC held a flat white box in her hands. The two of them were looking at us and smiling.

"Ice, my brother, bring your woman over here. We have some business to conclude." Hawk called out.

Howls broke out from the men and I looked around in confusion. All the men had formed a big circle around Hawk and DC. What the hell was going on?

Ice immediately stood, and carrying me in his arms he walked to his president. Whistles and cat calls sounded in the room along with laughter as his brothers opened the circle to let us through.

Hawk grinned. "You can put her down, brother. We can't do our business while you're holding her."

"I hear you, prez." Ice slowly set me on my feet and we faced Hawk and DC. She winked at me and smiled, her dark eyes twinkling.

Total silence fell as Hawk started speaking.

"We are here today to celebrate the engagement of our brother to the woman who stole his heart. This is a very happy occasion for our club but it is an especially happy occasion for the Walker family. Not only are we welcoming Ice's woman into our family but her boy Duncan as well, and as you can see our brother didn't let any grass grow under his feet before knocking his woman up. We will have two more Walkers joining the Iron Dogz family in January."

There were howls and whistles from the men and screams from the women until Hawk lifted a hand and it died down.

"But before our brother Ice marries his woman there is something he needs to do. Something very important." He turned to Ice. "Brother, come forward."

Ice joined them and I stood in front of them and suddenly I knew. I knew what was going to happen next and tears filled my eyes. We hadn't talked about this. I hadn't expected it to happen so soon. It had happened very quickly with Sparrow but I had thought Ice would need some time.

I watched as Ice took the box from DC and took a step towards me and gave me the box. I held it in front of me as I looked up at him and he held my eyes as he began to speak.

"Blue, you wear my ring and have my sons growing inside you and soon you and Duncan will be joining the Walker family. Today I want to make you a part of my other family, my Iron Dogz family. Open the box, baby."

I carefully lifted the lid and dropped it to the floor next to me. I could smell the leather the minute the lid came off. Beneath the white tissue paper part of my future lay waiting.

Ice didn't hesitate, he lifted the kutte out, pulled the box from my nerveless fingers and dropped it on the floor. Then he very gently slipped the kutte on me. I stood frozen as he bent and place a soft kiss on my lips. Turning me so my back was to his president and his old lady he lifted my hair out of the way. I glanced over my shoulder at them as Hawk threw his head back and howled like a wolf. Total silence fell around us.

"As President of the Iron Dogz it is my pleasure to welcome River, old lady of Ice, Vice President of the Iron Dogz, to our family. Welcome, River."

Ice turned me in a slow circle to show the brothers who surrounded us. Howls erupted as his brothers celebrated for him.

Drawing me into his chest Ice dropped his head and very thoroughly kissed me as the club went wild around us.

"I love you, Blue." He said as he lifted his head.

Sweet baby Jesus, this man of mine was something else.

"Love you too, Ice." I whispered with my arms clasped tight around his waist, while on my back my new status as property of Ice was displayed proudly.

Our families surrounded us and more hugging ensued. My parents left shortly after as they were picking up Duncan from Bulldogs' house and spending the night at the pool house. Lake wasn't at the party as he had to return to Europe for a race. He still wasn't too sure about my engagement but had accepted it and wished me well.

When night fell the party kicked off to a higher and wilder level. The later it became the more scantily clad women appeared. Entertainment for the brothers. Shit was going down in the dark corners of the room that I did not want to see and the dancing was becoming totally pornographic. Pretty soon clothes were going to start coming off.

DC and I were playing pool and she wasn't drinking in support of my dry status. She was the best. My other besties were partying hard with Genna and some of the brothers, they were definitely going to be hung over come morning. We were just about to start a new game when we noticed our men were no longer in the room. What the hell? And how long had they been gone?

"Where do you think they are?" I asked softly.

DC looked around the room and frowned. "All the officers are gone. I think something came up and they are having one of those damned meetings of theirs. And they won't tell us what's going on either, the asses. We'll give them ten minutes and if they aren't back then we'll go looking." DC said as she racked the balls.

But before we could finish the game they were back and Ice and Hawk came straight towards us. Whatever had happened they both weren't very happy about it. We had finished our game when I became aware of the live pornos going on around us. Ice pulled me close to his chest when he saw my wide eyes.

"Taking you to our room, little bird." Hawk growled as he dragged DC away from the table.

She winked at me and tipped her head towards something on the dance floor and when I looked over I found it hard to look away again.

"Baby, it's time for us to leave. I don't want you around this shit." Ice said in my ear as I stared at two of the brothers dancing with a topless woman. They had her sandwiched between the two of them and one had his hands on her boobs while the other had a hand up her skirt. They were totally oblivious to the world around them.

"Let's go up to my room. I want to fuck you in my bed, Blue. The same bed where we made our babies." He whispered in my ear and my hidden parts quivered.

I nodded, oh yes, I could totally get on board with that.

We left the party and followed Hawk and DC up the stairs. Hawk scooped DC up and ran with her to their room the door slamming closed behind them. I looked up at Ice and grinned when he just shook his head and unlocked his door.

Ice closed and locked the door behind him and shut out the noise of the party. I sighed with relief. I hadn't realised how loud it had become.

"I want to fuck you wearing only my kutte, baby. Get rid of the clothes. Now." Ice ordered as he untied his boots and kicked them off.

I quickly got rid of my clothes then pulled my kutte back on. The leather was warm from my body and the lining stroked across my hard, tight nipples. I breathed erratically as I watched my man slowly taking off his clothes.

I loved watching him undress. The slow tease as his body was revealed did it for me every time. From the top of his broad shoulders my eyes stroked down over his pecs and sculpted abs past his navel to those two indentations that pointed the way down to his heavy cock. I knew exactly how sensitive those two valleys were. One stroke of my tongue would have him straining and so very ready for me.

"Like what you see, baby?"

"Always. You are so very beautiful, Ice."

"No, baby, I'm not the beautiful one, you are. Looking at you standing there wearing only my kutte and with your belly swelling with my children I'm so fucking hard and leaking for you." His hand curled around his cock and he started stroking it slowly. My eyes were riveted on his hand.

"Sit on the side of the bed, baby, and spread your legs for me. Show me how wet you are."

I climbed up onto the bed, sat down and spread my legs wide, showing him the core of me.

"I'm so wet for you, baby. I want you inside me. I missed your cock."

My kutte hung open, framing my body and I brushed my hands over my breasts cupped them and ran my thumbs over my nipples. I licked my bottom lip as Ice's breathing and his hand sped up and he stepped between my wide open legs.

"And I missed my little pussy. Going to slide in nice and slow. Going to fuck you slow and make it last. Don't want this to be over too quick."

Letting go of his cock he pulled me closer to the edge of the bed. Taking his cock in his hand he slowly ran the head from the bottom to the top of my wet pussy while we both watched. It was the sexiest thing I had ever seen. His piercing glistened with my juices and had me shivering as it glided over my flesh. I couldn't wait to have him inside of me.

Resting his cock against my pussy his hands came to my shoulders and he gently urged me to lie down. He was so careful not to hurt my shoulder. "Play with those beautiful tits while I push inside. I want to watch as my cock disappears inside you and your fingers pluck on your nipples."

I was so turned on I could hardly breathe. He slowly started pushing inside and stretched me wide. I gently pinched my very sensitive nipples and felt it all the way to my inner core. My pussy tightened around his tunnelling cock and both of us groaned loudly.

"Fuck, Blue, this is the very best pussy in the world and it's all mine. Mine for fucking ever."

"And your cock is mine, all mine for ever and ever." I echoed him.

He slowly started fucking me, sliding his cock deep before pulling back. His big hands curled around my hips holding me as he stared down at where his glistening cock was appearing and disappearing. I watched him watching me and marvelled that he was mine. He was so beautiful lost in his lust for me.

"Oh, God, Ice, that's so good, so very good." I moaned.

Speeding up his thrusts his breathing became ragged and sweat glistened on his body as he came over me, opening my legs wider with his hips and started slamming into me. Every down stroke hit my clit and had me spiralling higher and higher. I felt the pulses starting deep inside and I gasped at the enormity of the orgasm rushing towards me. I looked up at him and was immediately caught up in his eyes staring down at me. He had his bottom lip caught between his teeth as he went wild between my legs.

"Going to fuck you right through the fucking bed, baby. This is my little pussy, my fucking wet pussy, sucking me in so deep. Take me, baby. Take all of me." He growled over me.

The eruption when it came was enormous and I felt myself clenching around his fiercely pounding cock, flooding him. The sounds of our wet flesh coming together increased and I shouted his name as the orgasm rushed through me. Throwing his head back, tendons straining in his neck he groaned out my name as his semen pulsed from the end of his cock and deep into me.

"Ah, fuck, this is so fucking good. Never in my life have I come like this, Blue. Not fucking ever." He lowered himself over me and kissed my neck, dragging his teeth slowly down the sensitive skin he bit softly and sucked before letting go and kissing the spot.

"I love you, Blue." He whispered in my ear making me shudder and clench around him.

"I love you, Ice." I answered drawing my hands through his hair as his head came to rest on my chest.

We lay quietly for a few moments before he slowly pushed up and started to slip from me. I felt the rush of wet following his cock as he pulled out.

"Don't move, baby. Going to clean you up."

He left the room and I heard the water running in the bathroom then he was back with a warm facecloth and gently cleaned me. Going back into the bathroom I heard the water running again but this time it didn't stop. He was running me a bath. I haven't been showering because of my wound and he got into the habit of getting into the bath with me, holding me and playing with me but not enough to get me off.

Tonight I wouldn't allow him to play those games with my body. I would be playing with his. I was ravenous for my man and even though we had just finished I was gearing up for the next round. I could already feel the water and bubbles sliding over my skin as a rubbed my wet silken skin up and over my man. I was looking forward to riding him to completion in the warm water.

Pregnancy hormones were the bomb.

It was going to be a long night. A long and very, very satisfying night.

We had so much time to make up for. And I was ready to start playing catch up right now.

Ice came walking back into the bedroom, his cock erect and ready.

"Been dreaming of fucking you in the bath for a while now, Blue. Tonight I'm making that dream come true." He said as he slid my kutte off, picked me up and carried me into the bathroom.

And he did. He made those dreams come true in the most delicious and decadent of ways.

Life had gifted me with the love of two incredibly good men.

I had been so sure my life was over when I had lost my first love and then the second appeared when I least expected him. With him I had gained a second chance at love and I was grabbing hold with both hands.

Life with Ice wouldn't be easy but I was never letting go.

RENÉ VAN DALEN

EPILOGUE

Hawk

His phone was pinging constantly and Hawk sighed and let his old lady go long enough to pull the damn thing from his pocket. Terror was texting him from the gate. What the hell now?

Boss, someone at the gate. He says it's urgent. Has to talk to you right now. Says his name is Dom.

What the fuck?

"Little bird, please stay with Blue. We've got some shit to take care of quickly."

His woman didn't argue, just nodded and walked over to where Blue was talking to her friends. With a quick chin lift he had Beast, Kid, Ice and Sin walking down to the gate with him. A totally blacked out SUV waited right outside the gates and Hawk nodded his permission to slide the gate open just enough for the damn thing to drive through.

Dominick Maingarde did not get out of the cage. He opened the window but not all the way and sat in the dark as he gave them information that might save their asses and then again might not.

"I've been informed of a planned attack on your compound. You are being watched and it hasn't escaped those who are watching that you have very vulnerable people under your protection. They are planning to strike at your vulnerabilities."

Hawk played with his beard as he stared into the dark interior of the SUV.

"How solid is your intel?"

"Came right from the damned horse's mouth. They are searching for the bitch. They want her back, she knows too much about their organisation. They suspect you snatched her. I'll take her off your hands and she will disappear never to be seen again. I give you my word of honour." He was quiet for a few seconds. "In exchange I need a favour from you. I have someone here I need you to keep safe. She's being hunted by the old bitch's men as we speak. If you take her in and keep her safe I will handle your problem for you."

Ice's hand suddenly clasped tight over Hawk's shoulder and he pulled him away from the brightly lit area around the cage and into the shadows.

"Let him take her, Prez. We've got what we need and she's a liability now. He takes her and our hands are clean. It gets the bitch out of our sanctuary. I don't want her anywhere near my woman and children, cuz. Let him take her."

Hawk looked in his cousin's eyes and saw his determination and nodded in agreement.

"I agree. But we're going to have to bring this to the table, Ice. We can't make this decision on our own."

"I'll get the brothers together." Kid said quietly. He had his phone out and soon a ping let them know the text had been sent.

"Who is it you want us to keep safe for you?" Beast asked with a growl.

Hawk frowned. Beast had been very short tempered lately. Actually the man had always had a short fuse but it has been worse since the arrival of his little girls.

"She's one of Pixie's friends. She overheard plans to kill a business associate of mine but unfortunately she was seen. They were waiting for her when she came home, luckily she was able to escape but not before being beaten severely. Pixie called me and I made arrangements for medical attention and a safe house. But the bastards found her again which means I have a rat in my organisation. Until I have exterminated my problem she isn't safe in Cape Town. I will be back for her once the problem has been resolved." Dom explained in an emotionless voice.

At the end of his explanation Beast moved away, apparently satisfied, and disappeared into the shadows while Hawk and Ice moved closer to the SUV.

"I need a name, Dom. Not going to allow some bitch through my gates without a name."

There was a beat of silence. Then a soft mumble from the back of the SUV.

"Victoria Keating." Dom's emotionless voice gave them the name.

Hawk looked at Ice and shrugged, the name meant nothing to him. He would get Ziggy to look into her as soon as possible.

Dominick Maingarde was a fucking machine. Everyone was under the impression he cared about nothing and nobody, and here he was saving someone close to his sister. Why? Regardless of the reason it looked like he did care about someone. Good to know.

Hawk turned when he heard boots hitting the paving. All his officers were here. Fuck it. He was going to do this right here. They moved away from the vehicle and formed a tight circle around him.

"Dom brought me information of a planned attack on club interests. Plus he is offering to take care of our bitch problem. In return he wants us to watch over a woman who is important to Pixie and him. What do you think?"

"Do we trust him, Prez?" Spider asked softly.

"As much as we can trust a crime boss, Spider."

"I want that bitch out of our Sanctuary. Let him take her and rid us of a problem." Ice said coldly.

There were nods around the circle agreeing with him.

"So what will it be? Yes or No?" Hawk asked.

It was yes all around and Hawk nodded in agreement.

"Beast, Spider and Sin, you get the bitch ready for transport. Kid, you and Ziggy settle our guest in upstairs. Use the secure guestroom. We need to know exactly who she is and we won't until Ziggy can do a deep dive into her tomorrow."

Hawk immediately walked back to the SUV.

"Pull into the open garage right at the end. Don't get out of the vehicle. My men will take her into the clubhouse and settle her in. The package will be brought to you. Ice and I have to get back before people notice we're not at the party. Thanks for this, Dom. I won't forget it and we'll keep your girl safe, you have my word."

Dom gave a short nod. "Thank you, I appreciate this, Hawk. I'll be in touch soon."

Hawk and Dom stared at each other unblinkingly, then Hawk nodded and with Ice at his side he went back to celebrate his VP's engagement.

This night belonged to Ice and Blue and nothing would be allowed to taint it for them.

Tomorrow was more than enough time to talk to the bitch Dom had brought to them.

Victoria Keating and her problems could wait.

She was Kid and Ziggy's problem for tonight.

LOST AND FOUND IN BLUE

The ride continues…
NEITHER BLACK NOR WHITE
Iron Dogz MC Book 3

THE IRON DOGZ MC
JOHANNESBURG CHAPTER

OFFICERS

President - Cole "Hawk" Walker - Old Lady - Jasmine "DC" Michaels/Crow

Vice President - Gray "Ice" Walker

Sergeant At Arms - Nathan "Kid" Warne

Enforcer - Joseph "Beast" Van Den Bergh

Road Captain - Carl "Sin" Smith

Security & Tech - Ryan "Jagger" Du Plessis

Information Officer - Nolan "Ziggy" Porter

Treasurer - Griffin "Spider" Walker

Secretary - Edwin "Kahn" Naidoo - Old Lady - Lavashni "Vash" Naidoo

Chaplain - Gabriel "Bulldog" Walker - Old Lady - Susan "Suzy" Walker

LIEUTENANTS

Lodewyk "Boots" Schoeman

Warren "Spook" Hoffmann

Shane "Wolf" Edwards

LOST AND FOUND IN BLUE

MEMBERS
Jason "Dizzy" Mitchell

Marnus "Rider" De Ridder - Girlfriend - Penny De Klerk

Clayton "Dollar" O'Donnell

Duma "Bullet" Baloyi

Steven "Army" Patel

Christoph "Buzz" Esterhuizen - new transfer

Chrisjan "Krappie" Meintjies - new transfer

PROSPECTS
Sam Du Plessis (Jagger's youngest brother)

Owen Maharaj

Kevin "Wrench" Clarkson (River gave him his road name)

William "Will" Randal

Terrance "Terror" Makhubela (Sam's best friend)

ELDERS
Gabriel "Bulldog" Walker - Serves as Chaplain

Fred "Flash" Warne - Old Lady - Esther "Essie" Warne

Ted "Taxi" Cox

Koos "Buffel" Bosman

Kobus "Krokodil" Schutte

RENÉ VAN DALEN

NOMADS

Stone

Cracker

Venom

FAMILY

Beryl Davids - Bounty and Bulldog Walker's widowed sister

Please note that some of the characters mentioned above haven't appeared in the books yet.

LOST AND FOUND IN BLUE

PLAYLIST

Allen - Lande - Bitter Sweet

Alter Bridge - In Loving Memory

Chris Cornell - Nearly Forgot My Broken Heart

The Cranberries - When You're Gone

Cream - Sunshine of Your Love

David Cook - Wicked Game (Chris Isaak cover)

Daughtry - There And Back Again

Foo Fighters - Something From Nothing

Thunder - In A Broken Dream

Three Doors Down - Here Without You

Simple Minds - She's A River

Ozzy Osbourne - I Just Want You

Muse - Endlessly

Myles Kennedy - Love Can Only Heal

Metallica - Nothing Else Matters

Live - I Walk The Line (Johnny Cash cover)

Robbie Williams - You Know Me

Fokofpolisiekar - FLVJ

Wonderboom - Never Ever

Vanilla Ice - Ice, Ice Baby

Allen - Lande - Come Dream With Me

RENÉ VAN DALEN

GLOSSARY

- Ag Shame - Oh shame or Oh poor you. (Can be used in a derogatory sense)
- Bakkie - Slang for a pickup van/LDV. But it is also a small bowl
- Berg - Mountain; Drakensberg mountain range, mostly referred to as 'the Berg'
- Bloody - Used along with hell instead of curse words, like damn, fuck
- Boet - Brother
- Boeta - Brother
- Broer - Brother
- Broers - Brothers
- Bro, Bra, Bru, - All slang for brother used in different parts of SA
- Boerewors - A type of sausage but no translation available, just known as boerewors
- Boykie - Slang for little boy. Sometimes used to show affection between male friends
- Braai - Barbeque
- Braaivleis - Barbequed meat
- Buffel - African Buffalo

- Bundu - South African slang for uninhabited wild regions far from towns and cities
- Bundu bashing - Slang for off roading in uninhabited areas
- Dankie - Thank you
- Duikertjies - Small African antelope
- Durbs - Slang for Durban
- Eina - Ouch, ow
- Eish - Used to convey amazement, similar to 'oh wow'
- Ek - I
- Foeitog - Poor you; shame
- Fok; my fok - Fuck
- Fokken - Fucking
- Ja right - As if
- Ja - Yes
- Joburg; Jozi - Slang for Johannesburg
- Kak - Shit
- Klippies - Gravel, small stones, or as used in the book, slang for Klipdrift Brandy
- Klub - Club
- Kosmos - Cosmos
- Krappie - Small fast moving crab
- Krokodil - Crocodile

- Lewe - Life
- Maklik - Easy
- Meerkat - Meercat; Suricate, South African Mongoose
- Nee - No
- No worries - Don't worry about it. Don't worry
- Ons - We
- Rantjies - Hills
- Saam - Together
- Skaam - Shame, or no shame
- Skapie - Slang for lamb. Can be used as an endearment
- Skinner - Gossip
- Sies - Yuck; Yucky; Yuk; Yukky
- Siestog - What a pity; Shame; Poor you
- Spook - Ghost
- Staan - Stand
- Steenbokkies - Small South African antelope
- Stukkend - Broken, but also slang for drunk
- Thank the Pope - Thank goodness
- Tjommie, Tjomma - Slang for friend, alternative spelling - Chommie, Chomma
- Veldt - South African elevated open grasslands

Some words haven't been used in the book but I added them as a kind of reference.

ACKNOWLEDGEMENTS

No writer stands alone. To those who have supported and encouraged me on this journey, you have my eternal gratitude.

As ever, standing in my corner and cheering me on are my three. You have been my biggest fans and supporters from the very start. Love you to the outer universe and back.

A huge hug and a very big thank you to Danielle Burrows, my daughter, for the teasers and cover design. I love it!

Thanks to my betas, Pieter, Mari, Jacquline and Robyn. You help to give my dreams the wings it needs to fly.

Thank you to Unsplash and all the photographers for allowing free use of their photos. Their generosity made the teasers and cover possible.

A huge thank you to my fellow South African authors for their support and encouragement and making this journey so much more fun.

To the readers, thank you for giving the Iron Dogz MC your support. The Iron Dogz love and appreciate those reviews and ratings and so do I!

ABOUT THE AUTHOR

René Van Dalen grew up in a small town in the Transkei region of the Eastern Cape Province in South Africa close to the ocean and the mountains. After high school she moved to the city to go to College. She never left and misses the ocean every single day.

Her parents gave her the love of books and music. Haunting the library when she should have been studying helped to satisfy her craving to read more and more books.

Doing what the majority of people do is not for her, she loves who she finally turned out to be.

René likes her music loud and heavy, her coffee with a touch of milk and slightly sweet, and chocolate in all its shapes and forms. She's a voracious reader and a huge fan of J R Ward's Black Dagger Brotherhood. Her three adult children are the loves of her life.

Music is her muse. Her house is never silent. Whether she's writing or reading or just chilling there is always music playing.

CONNECT WITH RENÉ VAN DALEN

Facebook:
facebook.com/renevandalenauthor
Iron Rosez Reader Group:
facebook.com/groups/2202698126475020/
Goodreads:
goodreads.com/author/show/14116196.Rene_Van_Dalen
BookBub:
bookbub.com/authors/rene-van-dalen
Instagram:
Rene Van Dalen Author @renevandalenauthor

Printed in Great Britain
by Amazon